Unforgettable
Sun

HALE BROTHERS SERIES
BOOK THREE

KATHRYN ANDREWS

Copyright © 2015 Kathryn Andrews
Published by Kathryn Andrews, LLC
www.kandrewsauthor.com
Cover design © Arijana Karčić, Cover It! Designs
Formatting by JT Formatting

First Edition: March 2015
Library of Congress Cataloging-in-Publication Data
Andrews, Kathryn
Unforgettable Sun (Hale Brothers Series, Book Three) – 1st ed
ISBN-13: 978-1-508-61001-4

To my dear friend Elle . . .

Although WE MAY BE AN *ocean* APART,

OUR FRIENDSHIP LIVES CLOSE IN MY *heart.*

I AM *thankful* FOR YOU EVERY *day,*

AND ALWAYS *looking* FORWARD

TO THE NEXT *time* WE CAN

DRINK PINK *Champagne*

Love YOU...

Sun

HEAT FIRE,
BRIGHT GLOW LIGHT,
ALWAYS FOLLOW THE SUN,
SUN.

DAVY Z

Prologue

STANDING IN THE middle of the street, I stare at a two-story Gulf waterfront home in front of me. I know this house, I know it well. It's where Beau spends his days, and most of his nights. I can't say I blame him, though. Even from the outside, this house always smells like fresh-baked cookies and laundry.

Beau recently gave me a pair of binoculars and, at the age of seven, I have become the best kid spy ever. Drew is always swimming or studying, and I've never really had any friends, so Beau became my mission. Daily, I watch him and report his activities to my headquarters, Aunt Ella's backyard shed. He and Leila play on the beach and hide in the sea oats to watch the stars. When they are at Leila's house, I watch them through the windows. He doesn't know I'm there but, by doing this, I feel like we are playing together and I'm not quite so alone.

Tilting my head to the side, I focus on those same windows, just hoping that through my tears I will see something—anything—on the inside.

The night is silent, except for the water crashing onto the shore. The world is asleep and completely oblivious to what is happening before me.

There's a halo of smoke surrounding the house. Against the dark night sky, it looks gray, almost white.

The house is on fire . . . and Beau is inside it.

Broken glass crunches as the heavy trod of my father's boots make their way toward me. "Matt, what are you doing out here?" he hisses, while grabbing me by the arm. I barely feel it.

Thinking about his question, I want to be anywhere but here. My eyes are locked on the horror in front of me, and only one word, one name keeps repeating itself over and over in my mind . . . Beau.

Never looking at him, the arm he's not squeezing slowly lifts, and I point to the house. His head swivels back and forth between me and the house.

"Beau," I whisper. Another tear falls and rolls down my cheek.

"What! He's in the house?" His fingers tighten even more on my arm, and I welcome the pain.

I nod my head.

He pulls out his phone and calls 911. As he's pacing around me, I hear him talking urgently to someone, but I can't decipher what he is saying.

An orange glow appears in the window, and my whole body starts shaking.

I don't understand what is taking so long!

Where is he? He should be out by now!

The glow gets brighter, and it's no longer just shining out the window. It's peeking through all of the boards of the house, looking for a way to escape.

The smoke suddenly gets thicker, and flames burst through the French doors of the upstairs bedroom, causing me to take a step backward. Heat wraps around me, and the flames are so bright I have to shield my eyes. They remind me of what it's like to try to look at the sun.

Firemen arrive right as Beau emerges through the front door. He's carrying Leila in front of him. He saved her. Relief washes over me, and I let out a breath I didn't know I was holding in.

I take a step toward them, just as an explosion inside the house pushes them over the threshold. Beau loses his balance and falls right on top of Leila. At the same time, a large piece of the porch ceiling breaks off and lands on top of them.

Beau's screams echo through the night, and total chaos breaks out all at once.

Firemen rush onto the porch, throwing the wood off to the side. Two of them drape a blanket over Beau and another pulls Leila out from underneath him.

A hose is pulled out, and I can see two of the firemen spraying Beau. The fire that was just on his back is immediately put out.

I remember my mother once saying that to stop a burn you have to cool the skin.

The hose shuts off and is thrown down. The paramedics move frantically around him. Two of them begin to cut away his clothes, making him naked. A third shoves something down his throat. And a fourth pulls an IV and hooks it up to his arm.

Please don't let him die.

Silent sobs are now pounding through my chest.

More rescue vehicles arrive, with their lights flashing. People are racing around in every direction, and I realize not one person has seen me or said anything to me.

A siren shrieks, and I jerk at the piercing noise as an ambulance speeds off down the street. They must have Leila.

"Matt, run," my dad snarls at me through gritted teeth. Has he been standing next to me this entire time?

I blink up at him. I still can't move, and that's when he shoves me. Stumbling backward, I catch my balance and look back at the scene before me once more.

Beau is being lifted and placed on a gurney as they continue to hover over him. The hoses are back out and, from multiple directions, the house is being sprayed.

"Matt, I said to run!" He shoves me again, and that's when it clicks; I really do have to get out of here.

Turning, and never looking back, I head for the beach.

Putting one foot in front of the other, I start running. Over the dunes and into the sand, I push as hard as I can. With tears streaming down my cheeks, visions of the fire play out before me. Gasping for air, the smell of smoke fills my senses. I didn't notice it before, but now it is so strong I almost gag. Wiping my nose with the back of my hand, I desperately try to find some fresh air. But no, there it is again, that smell. It's on my skin. It's like it isn't just following me, but now permanently a part of me. Charging into the water, I dive under, into the silence. My hands run over my arms, my face, and through my hair. I'm frantic, and I have to get rid of the smell.

Washing up onto the shore, I curl up into a ball on the wet sand. My heart is broken for Beau and I'm so afraid; so very afraid. He's the one and only person who has ever shown me love, and the thought of losing him paralyzes me with fear. My sobs are still silent. I've been taught not to make a sound. But they hurt so much. Without a voice, I mouth his name over and over again. I just want Beau. I need Beau. He's the only one who can make this all better, and make everything about this dreadful night disappear.

But he isn't here, and he can't be.

With my eyes pinched shut, the smell of smoke in my nose, and the feel of a nonexistent heat against my skin, I know. I know it with a certainty that has robbed me of my voice and permeated itself into my pores that, no matter what, everything about this night will be . . . unforgettable.

Chapter One

ELLE

Fourteen years later . . .

I USED TO love being a fashion model. I thrived off of the attention, the lights, camera, and praise. But it's funny how over the years, what you once enjoyed becomes tainted and different truths become glaringly obvious. The brightest of those truths would be my mother.

My mother's sister, my Aunt Ella, has a niece, Leila. We aren't related. She comes from Uncle Ben's side of the family. She is the daughter of one of his brothers. Leila is five years older than I am, and when she left for college, she moved to New York City and followed her dream of being a fashion designer. As the demand for her designs became more sought after, so did her name and picture in all of the current fashion magazines. My mother subscribed to every magazine to watch her career grow, and, with that, her desire to one day make me rich and famous, too. Or should I say, make her rich and famous.

I've always been tall and lanky for my age. When I was sixteen, she enrolled me in my first modeling school. I was so excited. Over the next two years, the school taught me how to develop my personal image, self-confidence and techniques to work the catwalk, apply makeup, hair and skin care, nutrition, and most importantly, how to professionally work with a photographer. Slowly, my portfolio began to build. I started to go on go-sees and, before I knew it, I was being offered jobs.

Three months before I turned eighteen, my mother—who, by then, had declared herself my manager—sent my portfolio to Leila. Of course, she threw down the distant-family card and, next thing I knew, we were on a plane to meet with her design producers.

My mother and I have been living in New York City for the last five years.

Everything about my life is hers. None of it is mine. I used to think she was doing this all for me and I believed her but, looking back, I can see that all I have ever been is her puppet. She pulls the strings, forcing me to follow and, for some unknown reason, I do.

Although lately, these glaring truths have been shining so brightly that I don't know how much longer I can go on lying to myself without making a change.

Looking across the museum, I see her with her latest boy toy. A frown creeps on to my face and I'm filled with disgust. She's leaning into him in a dress that is clearly not appropriate for someone her age, and she's laughing like he has just said the funniest thing in the world. She's causing a scene and people are noticing. She doesn't even realize that people are shying away from her, completely uncomfortable with her blatant cougar behavior. He must be ten years younger than her, and half of the time, I feel like he is leering at me. I don't know what he is doing with her, not that I would ever in a million years give that guy a second glance. It's just so gross.

Tearing my eyes away from her, I proceed to weave through the people and walk around the room on the designated path.

Tonight's event is a charity event to support breast cancer awareness. All month long, thirty percent of the designer's proceeds from the online store are going to support the cause. Since tomorrow is Halloween, they decided to host the wrap party tonight. Fifteen new designs were made and, of course, they are all pink. Instead of walking a catwalk, the designer has us walking on a carpeted pathway, winding around the museum and the patrons of the party.

The lights have been adjusted to highlight the show more than the art, and I feel like they are burning right through the clothes and into my skin. The combined effect of the lights, the path I'm walking around the room, and the closeness of the people all makes me feel claustrophobic.

I understand that having me here is a big deal for the designer, but I'm really not liking how accessible, and up close, I am to the people.

Everyone I walk by smiles at me as if they know me, but they don't. My face and body have been on magazine covers around the world, but no one really knows me; except for Olivia, that is.

The summer after we moved, when I was eighteen, my mother married husband number two. Although they were never going to last, Olivia came with him, and our friendship did.

Raising my hand, I wipe the perspiration off of my forehead. The dresses that we are wearing are beautiful, I have to give the designer that, but the signature auction pieces of the evening are the vicuña shawls that the other models are wearing, and the vicuña top coat that I am wearing. This coat steals the show, and its bidding price starts at twenty-one thousand dollars. I can't help but wonder what the highest bid will be. This coat is also very warm, and I am burning up.

All night long people have been touching me; well, the coat that is. Gentle caresses to feel the softest and most expensive fabric in the world. Only, I don't like to have strange hands all over me.

People really aren't supposed to touch the coat. Oils from fingertips and hands can change the look of it, but that doesn't stop people or their curiosity. The women are kind and gentle, but the men continue to run their hands all over me; down my arms, across my back, over the lapels. They even dip their fingers in between the buttons to "feel the inner lining". I'm appalled that I have been put into this situation.

"Elle, look this way," a photographer calls to me. I stop, strike a pose that highlights the coat, and smile. After all, that's what I am being paid to do. The people around me hum with satisfaction. A few cell phones are brought out and raised for the photo as well.

"Darling, you look just fabulous," my mother says as she slinks up next to me, smiling at the patrons closest to us.

Stepping away from her, I'm back on the carpeted pathway and I resume walking through the gallery. She quickly walks up beside me and easily keeps pace. Admiring the coat, she also runs her hand down the sleeve.

"What do you want, Mother?" I say in aggravation.

"You know, it wouldn't hurt you to smile a little more. You never know who might be in the room."

There it is—jab jab jab, pick pick pick—I grit my teeth

together. Most mothers tell their daughters how beautiful they are. But not mine. It's all about being perfect and how I am never perfect enough. Her tone is always pleasant, in case someone overhears us, but the condescension seeps through.

I shoot her a look, letting her know she needs to back off, and I see that the boyfriend has sidled up next to her, too. He smirks and winks at me. *Gross.*

"Leave me alone, Mother. I'm working." Focusing on the carpeted pathway, she can feel through my irritated tone that I'm trying to brush her off.

"Fine. But after this is over, how about the three of us go out for some dinner?" she says this like it is a done deal that I'm going to have dinner with her and her skeevy boyfriend. What she really wants is for me to pick up the check for them.

"I have plans."

"Not with that Olivia, I'm hoping," she says distastefully. The scowl on her face shows her age. Wrinkles appear in her forehead and around her mouth. She needs another round of Botox.

"Yes, with Olivia. Always with Olivia. Not that your opinion of my friends matters."

"My opinion most definitely should matter. I am your mother and your manager," she says disapprovingly.

"Then you should understand that talking to me right now is inappropriate," I snap back.

She pauses and looks around to see if anyone is paying any attention to us. "Fine, but you will wait for me after the show." And, with that, she and the boyfriend blend into the crowd.

Rounding the back turn of the farthest room, uneasiness settles into my stomach. Looking around the room, I don't see anything that should make me feel this way but, then again, this room isn't open like the others. It is filled with tall statues and sculptures that block the view throughout, and around the perimeter there are columns wide enough that a couple could stand behind them and not be seen. I've felt like someone was watching me for most of the evening. I could never pinpoint who or where, but the hair on the back of my neck stood up more than once.

I begin to weave between the statues when a hand grabs me from behind, jerking me to a stop. A body, a much larger body, presses up behind me and warm air begins to seep into my hair. Fear slices through me and a cold sweat breaks out underneath this coat.

After the latest round of harassment letters, I just brushed the feeling off as nerves. Suddenly, I'm wishing I had paid more attention. My hands ball into fists.

The familiar scent of a man's cologne drifts up to my nose and I try to place it. I've smelled it before, but on whom?

The hands wrapped around my upper arms begin to squeeze, and I stop breathing.

Pain shoots down to my fingertips and an automatic whimper escapes. The man behind me chuckles. More hot air blows through my hair.

"Anytime . . . anywhere," he whispers, and then releases me.

I'm frozen and can't move. I should turn around to see who it was, but I can't. My vision has darkened and there are spots floating in front of me. My heart is slamming into my chest and I start to shake. Who would do this to me, and why?

The model who is spaced ninety seconds behind me closes the gap between us, passes, and gives me a curious look.

Did she see what just happened?

What *did* just happen?

Walking very quickly, I catch up to her, slipping out of the coat and handing it to her. Her curious look changes to one of confusion and shock. The night isn't over, but I just can't stay here any longer. Most likely I will lose the commission tonight, but I just don't care. Discreetly, I leave the show and head straight for the dressing rooms to change out of this dress. I have to get out of here.

Somehow, over the last two weeks, I have lost the sense of feeling safe. The overwhelming feeling that I am being watched everywhere I go, combined with the strange letters, has me feeling like I don't know where to go or who to talk to. I've avoided all social engagements and, other than work, I've stayed in my condo, locked up tight.

The heels from my Louboutins are clicking down the employee hallway, and the echoing sound reminds me that I'm the only one here. My nerves are on high alert. I rub my stomach, trying to calm them. "Five minutes and I'm out of here," I mumble to myself.

Pushing through the door to the storage room, I head straight for the portable lockers that were brought in for us to use, and swing open the door. I freeze at the sight. Earlier this morning, I bought some orange gladiolas at a street market and, one by one, there they are, chopped up, along with my clothes, and thrown into the bottom of the locker.

Tears prick my eyes, because that only means one thing; whoever has been sending the letters has now been in my home. *My home.*

I find a note lying in the locker. With shaking hands, I grab it, snatch it out of the envelope and scan the words. My heart clutches, freezes, and sinks at the same time. It's the same handwriting. It's the same person.

Do you see how easy it is for me to get to you?
Then again, you've always been easy.
Anytime, anywhere...and you are mine!

Looking around the room, I see that nothing is out of place. Frantically, I throw open all of the other lockers and see that no one else's belongings have been touched. Just mine.

A lump forms in my throat and I feel like I can't breathe.

What do I do now?

Slipping out of the dress as quickly as I can, I hang it up and empty out the contents of my locker onto the floor. Jerkily, I pull on my jeans and heels and stare down at the pile. My shirt and coat are not salvageable. Standing in this tiny room in my bra, shaking in fear, I know I have to get as far away from here as I can.

Panic sets in. No one can see this mess. No one can know what is happening to me. I find a plastic bag and shove everything inside it.

After the first letter came and I showed it to my mother, she laughed and told me to get used it. She called it a perk of being famous and beautiful. Nothing about this feels like a perk.

I'm afraid, and I feel isolated.

Think, Elle! Think!

I grab my bag and there inside it is a camisole. As a model, I always carry a large bag filled with all kinds of essentials. I just never know what I might need in a moment's notice. I realize a camisole is not appropriate for this weather, but really can't bring myself to care right now. With trembling fingers, I slip it on, throw my purse strap over my shoulder, and head for the exit of the museum.

I should have trusted my instincts earlier. I knew someone

was watching me.
But who?

MATT

BRUNO NUDGES MY arm, waking me. His nose is cold and wet, and he slips it under my hand. He wants to be petted. My fingers ruffle through his fur, and my eyes open and lock onto the ceiling fan overhead. Around and around it spins. It's still dark out, but the light of the moon shines in and casts shadows on the wall.

Today is November first. It's the day that I dread more than any of the other 364 days of the year. Squeezing my eyes shut, I run my other hand through my hair and suck in a deep breath as the empty hole inside my chest begins to ache more than usual. I should be over this by now. It's all in the past. But for whatever reason, on this day, I'm not over it.

To most, today is a day just like any other day, but to me it is so much more. It's the one day the ghosts of the memories slip in and remind me that things aren't always as they seem. Why I can shut out the ghosts the rest of the year and not today, I'll never know. For years, bad shit has littered my life, scarring different days and events, but it's this day that the voices return. I hear them, as loud and clear as they ever were back then.

November first also marks the changing of the seasons here on the island. It isn't even gradual; it's sudden.

Anna Maria Island is a barrier island off the west coast of Florida, and lies just north of Sarasota Bay. The winds that sweep up off of the water and onto the shore cool down and pick up at the same time. They are constantly blowing, which mutes the stifling heat that is present during so much of the year. The sunlight becomes more golden, less glaring, and the leaves on the trees don't change to shades of red, orange and yellow, but instead darken to a deep green as if to say, "it's time to rest for a bit".

I was born on the island, and I'll probably die on the island. I am the youngest of three brothers. I am the mistake; the unwanted one.

Drew is my oldest brother. He's eight years older than me, which is just enough to really not give us anything in common. Most of my memories of him are in passing. He kept himself very busy between swimming and school and, during his last few years at home, he stayed away from the house as much as possible. He moved away when I was twelve, and very rarely does he come back.

Beau is the middle brother. He is seven years older than me, and he is the one that I've always looked up to as a role model. When I was little, he used to slip into my room to sleep with me and, as the years passed, I found myself slipping into his. It didn't matter if it was day or night, Beau would hear me open the door, see me peek in, and would lift up his covers, inviting me in. Given our situation, he did his best for me and, looking back now, I am awed by him. He was a kid, just like me.

Most kids have a father who is loving and kind, but not us. The three of us, along with my mother, lived in constant fear of him. We never knew when he was going to strike again, and the anticipation of it was almost just as bad . . . almost.

Drew was the recipient of his emotional abuse. He used Drew's love for us as his angle to break him down and taunt him, by telling him that every horrific thing that happened to us was his fault. His words were harsh, brutal, demeaning, and heartbreaking. Drew has always been a swimmer, so he takes his shirt off for his sport. That left Beau as the one he used as a physical target for his rage. Day after day, in one way or another, he would put his hands on Beau. His skin was always littered with hidden bruises and marks. Daily, I would beg God that someone would see them and save him. As for me, I was taught at a very young age to stay hidden, keep my mouth shut, and never e*ver* say a word. He expected me to be invisible, as if I didn't even exist.

They tell me that he didn't used to be like this, that he only started acting this way over the last couple of years, but I can read between the lines and all that did was make me feel responsible. I'm the reason he was so vicious to everyone. It's my fault.

When I was twelve, my father crossed the line in his abuse and ended up in prison. Although I wasn't there to witness any of it, and had been told to stay at Aunt Ella's, I did steal a copy of the newspaper from the neighbor's driveway the next morning. There, on display for the whole world to see, was my family and all of our very ugliest truths.

On top of the front page, the headline read, *"Tragic Hale Storm Strikes the Island"*. There were *happy* pictures of us as a family: my parents' wedding, on the family business float for the 4th of July parade, Drew and Beau both smiling as they are winning some sports award, and even one of me sitting in Aunt Ella's café. But then, on the bottom of the front page, there were pictures of the horror that was our reality: my mother being taken out to an ambulance, Drew being removed in handcuffs, and a shot of Beau standing on the porch, with his face beaten, bloodied, and bruised, crying.

I knew the darkness and the horror that we lived with at home, but seeing it summarized and splattered all over the paper looked so much worse. Maybe it was this bad all along and I just didn't know it because they kept it from me, but seeing Beau looking this way made me cry harder than I ever had. I should have listened to the adults. Even now, years later, I can close my eyes and see those pictures perfectly.

The kids at school already thought I was a loner. I used to get made fun of for being quiet and not wanting to play with anyone but, over the years, they've just all learned to ignore me. I knew that having my family ugliness featured in the paper was going to make me an open target, and I felt ashamed. I knew that I shouldn't have cared what others thought. I should have been more concerned about my family, but never in my twelve years had I wished as much as I did then that I belonged to someone else. With these thoughts came guilt, as well as anger.

Just thinking about my father, his image looms in my mind and I shudder. He always had an ability to convey an entire threat by giving me just one glance, one glare. No words needed to be said, but I heard him loud and clear.

"You are unwanted, you little piece of shit."

"No one will ever love you."

"Open your mouth and just see what happens."

"Learn your place and don't show your face."

"You're not even my son."

After he went to prison, Mom took Beau and me to therapy and, in these sessions, I did learn that he spoke to all of us this way. But there was one gem, one line of venomous hate, which he saved just for me, and that was that I was no son of his.

I was fourteen years old when I finally learned the truth.

Beau was living in New York City at the time, and he had flown home to get some face-to-face answers from my mother in regards to Leila. Leila. How to describe her? Well, she is Beau's everything. They have been together for the better part of twenty years, and I don't ever remember a time when she hasn't been a part of my life. It wasn't always easy for them. There were some communication problems at times, and they were also lied to.

Eavesdropping on that conversation, and hearing my mother slip up to Beau, forever changed me.

Being fourteen years old, and not having a lot of friends, I often found myself sitting in a tree, watching people, pretending to be a spy. Beau gave me a pair of binoculars, and they are by far my most treasured possession. I've never taken them into the house. I am always afraid that he will see them and destroy them for his sick pleasure.

While the shed out back behind Aunt Ella's house is my home base, Ali's house across the street has an upstairs deck that makes the perfect lookout spot.

It's Saturday, and I'm sitting on a lounge chair that I found by the side of the road and dragged up to the deck. Ali keeps all of her patio furniture inside the garage and out of the weather, but I needed somewhere to sit.

A taxi pulls up to our house and I see Beau get out. I didn't know he was coming, and I'm so overexcited with joy that my heart leaps. He looks right at Ali's house, and I could have sworn that he looked right at me, but whatever is going on in his head, he isn't really seeing the house, which is why he never sees me, even when I wave.

The taxi pulls away, and Beau turns around and faces our house.

There's something odd about the way he is standing and the way he is taking everything in that causes me to stay hidden and not run out to see him. It dawns on me that there's a reason he is here and there's a reason he didn't tell us he was coming.

He walks up the front porch, throws his bag down, and slips inside the house.

With my heart pounding, I race down the deck steps and run across the street. I see my mom's head in the kitchen window, and I sneak up the back steps and crouch down. I don't really need to see them; I can hear them just fine. The weather has been cooler lately, so Mom keeps the windows open.

"I know you have answers. Why won't you give them to me? Why, Mom? Why did you go along with him? Why did you let him do this to us for years? Why didn't you ever tell me the truth? I need to know!" Beau yells at her.

"Why do you need to know? Can't we all just move on?" Her voice is exasperated and she sounds nervous.

"Because I need to know! And, no, I can't just move on! Don't you get it? He chose me to be his punching bag. He chose me to degrade the loudest, not only with his voice but his fists, too. He chose me to hate the most. Yes! I have to know why. What did I ever do that was so wrong? Why didn't you love me enough to protect me? To protect all of us? All of this has made me the person that I am today. And to top it all off, you managed to take the one good thing that was mine, and have it ripped away. Why? Why did you force her away?"

"Because...because Matt isn't your father's!" she gasps.

Silence stretches between them, and I realize that I don't need to hear any more. Suddenly, so many things that he has said to me make sense. I am crushed to know that everything was for nothing. I already lived with regret, but this just mag-

nifies everything. With my heart aching, I head to the one place that feels safest to me. The shed.

My phone beeps and shakes me out of the past. Blinking the room back into focus, I look over at the clock on the nightstand as I pick up my phone and see that it's five in the morning.

Leila – Breakfast at our house at 8.
Me – Thanks, I'll see you then.

It's ironic, really. Every year, on this day, they celebrate finally finding out the truth and starting their life together. Whereas, on this day, I'm condemned by the truth and my life stopped.

Letting out a long sigh, I toss the phone onto the bed and run my hand through my hair again. It's that moment, that conversation, that day so many years ago that changed me. November first.

Reluctantly, I push away the idea of staying in bed for the day, and force my body to stretch. Needing to work my way through some of the stress and memories that come with today, I climb out of bed and slip on my running shoes.

Bruno jumps down from the bed, lets out a happy whine, and starts jumping around.

I started running when I was seven, and since then it has always been my thing. Drew is great at swimming, Beau is great at tennis and, for me, running is the thing.

Stepping out the front door, the air is cool and I breathe it in. If only it could cleanse me in a permanent way.

"Come on, Bruno."

He runs in a circle around me, and then together we take

off for the beach.

Pushing the ghosts to the back of my mind, I focus on my steps and zone out the surroundings. *Nineteen hours to go until this dreadful day is over*!

Chapter Two

ELLE

DRIVING SOUTH ON Interstate 75, the sun has risen and just reaches the top of the tree line. It's shining directly into my driver's side window and it's warm, too warm. I throw on a pair of sunglasses and try to block the light as it glares off of just about everything around me. My head is pounding, and I'm cloaked in a tiredness that is bone deep.

After leaving the show, I went home and locked every door and window. On the way up, I asked the doorman if anyone had asked to be let up into the building under my name, but he said no. I don't understand how my apartment was accessed to get to the flowers. As I walked around and looked at everything, nothing seemed to have been touched except for the vase of flowers. The vase was still sitting in the middle of the table, but it was empty and there was a trail of water across the table that must have dripped off the stems as they were taken.

I spent the next two hours lying in bed and listening to every creak and sound that echoed off of the walls and floor. I'd never noticed how much noise drifts in from the windows and the hallway outside my condo door. With my blanket pulled over my head, I suffered through one of the worst panic attacks I have ever had. I decided right then and there that it was time to get away. I couldn't stay in that condo one more minute.

I threw a bunch of random things into one of my over-sized bags, grabbed Otis, my big gray tabby, and my guitar, and just started driving. Eighteen hours and a few rest stops later, I pulled into a place that I said I would never come back to again. The reasons then seemed to make so much sense but, right now, I can't remember what any of them were.

Dust kicks up around the tires as I drive down the little side road made up of a mix of dirt, sand, and crushed oyster shells. Up ahead of me, I stare at the house that still looks as picturesque as the first time I saw it.

A mixture of unwelcome feelings courses through me. On one hand, this place feels like home, although it never was, and on the other, it's the home she—my mother—always wanted and couldn't have.

The house is a large light blue Key West-style home with white columns, a huge wraparound porch, and what seems like an endless number of windows to let the light in. It faces west, and I remember every night at dusk the golden light poured in through the windows, warming the home, making it feel all buttery and perfect.

Parking the car on the circular drive, I get out and take a deep breath. I made it. The air is crisper than I expected, and smells clean. Looking around, I see that not much has changed here, and the familiarity this brings me is comforting.

Slowly, I walk up the porch steps to approach the front door. Assuming that she might just be waking up, I knock softly over ringing the doorbell. My heart is pounding in my chest and my palms are sweaty. Wiping them on my pants, I just stand there and wait for the door to open. A moment of regret sweeps through me. *Maybe I shouldn't have come here. Maybe I should have gone to a hotel.*

It suddenly hits me; why *did* I come here? Out of all the places I could have gone, the car steered itself here. Maybe it's because, deep down, I know I have nowhere else to go, or maybe it's the thought that the last time I truly felt happy and content was here.

The soft thud of footsteps gets louder as they quickly near the door. I stop breathing.

The front door opens and behind the closed screen door stands a woman in her mid-forties, who doesn't look at day over thirty-five. Her sandy blonde hair is pulled back into a ponytail, and she is wearing a yellow apron that says, "Be your own kind of beautiful". I want to laugh at this because, in my world, there are only two kinds of beautiful: those who are and those who aren't.

She looks surprised, but masks it quickly. Her eyes travel the length of me before she looks behind me. I wait for a greeting from her, but it never comes.

"I didn't want to ring the bell in case you were sleeping," I say quietly. Her eyes snap back to mine.

"I appreciate that but I'm up; have been for a while." Her hands start wringing her apron, and her curious expression changes to one of sadness.

Silence hangs in the air, and it seems to take on a thickness that feels like it is pushing me away from her. I glance at the ground while shifting to my left hip, and push my hands into my back pockets. My hands have begun to ache and the joints in my fingers have started to swell. I inwardly sigh. Of all the bad timing. Again, I think maybe I shouldn't have come.

Shaking off her train of thought, she looks at me again and gives me a small, very small, smile. "Well, my, my; just look at you. This is definitely a surprise." I can't tell if her tone is sarcastic or welcoming.

She's always been one of those people who are genuinely so kind and honest that she can see right through the layers and straight into the heart. Maybe that's why she never got along with my mother. Yes, she loves her, but they are complete polar opposites.

Right this moment, I feel like my layers are being pulled apart, and I find myself concerned by what she might find.

"Is it just you this morning?" she asks. A breeze blows by. I shudder at the coolness of it, and am then met with the unmistakable smell of baked goods.

"Yes." My eyes drop back to the ground. Understanding my mother better now, I feel guilty for how things were left between us. This woman standing in front of me was always so nice to me.

"How long do you plan on staying?" She props her hand on her hip.

"I don't know; that depends on you." My eyes prick and burn. I feel completely vulnerable and alone. I wonder if she sees this in my layers.

She takes a deep breath, runs her hands down her apron, and walks back into the house. I watch as she walks away from me toward what looks like toward the kitchen. She didn't invite me in, and my heart sinks. She doesn't want me here.

Not knowing what to do, I turn and sit down on the rocking chair closest to the door. The sound of the water breaking on the shore nearby hits my ears. I'm so used to the noise in the city that the quietness here instantly calms me. I take another deep breath of the salt-infused air, and decide that, no matter if she wants me here or not, I'm staying. I can do this and I'll find a place.

My skin warms from the rays of the sun and, as it soaks in, I feel like it's welcoming me.

It occurs to me that the sun is different here than it is in the city. In the city, the light peeks in and around the buildings, the shadows are constantly changing, and the heat is more stagnate. It just sits there, bouncing off of the streets and sidewalks, filling the air, leaving you hot and uncomfortable. Here, at the beach, the water sparkles, the plants bloom beautifully, and the rays wrap around me, giving me a sense of comfort and relaxation. Maybe people vacation here, not so much for the beach, but for how the sun makes them feel.

A few minutes later, she returns and opens the screen door. I stand and face her. Her lips are pressed into firm line, but her eyes are filled with concern. *Concern.* The calmness that I was just feeling leaves me, and a sense of security replaces it. Maybe she does want me here.

"I'm thinking it's best if you have your own space. Head back out to Gulf Drive, turn right, and about a quarter mile down you'll see a sign for The Cottages. They are on Oak Street. You can stay in cottage number two. We are putting new floors in, so I hope you don't mind a little construction and mess. Two weeks are on me, but after that you'll have to pay. We're approaching tourist season here, and those cottages bring in a lot of revenue for us. No noise and no visitors, those are my rules. I packed you some breakfast. You look like you could use some food." Her eyes drift over me again she hands me a large brown paper bag. "There's fruit, homemade muffins, coffee, o.j. After you've rested up, drop by the café later. I'll tell you how to find the grocery store and we can talk."

Hugging the bag to my chest, I take the key from her hand. Unintentionally, my eyes fill with tears. "Thank you," I choke out, past the large lump in my throat.

Aunt Ella takes her hand and places it on my cheek. "Darlin', no matter what, it's always good to see you." She gives me a faint smile, and turns around and walks back inside. The screen door shuts, ending our conversation.

Following the directions to the cottages, I realize that I don't remember them from the last time I was here, but it's been seven, almost eight years. As I drive down Oak Street, I find that there are five beach cottages on the right-hand side. They start at number five and end at one, which is closest to the beach. The cottages aren't spaced too far apart for privacy but, in a way, that's comforting. This is going to be the perfect place.

On the outside of the door, there is a weathered-looking wooden sign that says, "Welcome", with a large number two underneath. I smile to myself because I do feel welcomed, and I feel like I've found a sanctuary. I unlock the door, take a step inside, and feel free. Otis immediately makes himself at home.

The air inside the cottage smells like a Florida vacation home. The salt-filled humidity has saturated the interior over time. Add in the cold air from the air conditioner and, at this moment, it is the best smell in the world.

The cottage is small, and I peek everywhere to make sure I miss nothing. It has one bedroom and one bathroom, a small kitchen and living area, and loft over the bedroom. On the west side of the cottage, there are windows in the loft, and sliding glass doors underneath that lead out to a screened-in porch.

Although cottage number one blocks a little of the beach, the overall view is spectacular and calms me instantly. The screened-in porch wraps around to the back of the house, and there is a picnic table, a free-standing hammock, and a hot tub.

I am so excited by this little cottage that, regardless of my exhaustion, I feel giddy. I can't remember the last time I took a vacation, and am so proud of myself for coming here. I've escaped my life and, while I'm here, I'm going to do some living just for me.

The décor of the cottage is definitely what I would call tropical. The colors vary from coral to yellow, and remind me of a sunset. The furniture looks new, the kitchen has been redone, and I can see why the floors are being replaced next. There are abstract paintings of fish on the walls, a large picture of a fishing dock and a boat and, in the kitchen, a large hand-painted sign that says, "For whatever we lose, like a you or a me, it's always ourselves we find in the sea," E.E. Cummings. And over the door there is a sign that says, "If you are not barefoot, then you are overdressed."

Smiling to myself, I think I could live here indefinitely, pretty happily. Aunt Ella was right; it is best that I have my own space.

My hands begin to ache again, so I head back outside to grab my bag, Otis's food, and my blanket. The rest can wait.

The adrenaline from hopping in the car and driving here has started to recede. It's like my subconscious knows I have reached my destination, and now it wants sleep. I close all the blinds to block out the light, lock the door, and curl up on the bed in the little bedroom, with my blanket. Of all the craziness in my life, the one thing that I always have to have is my blanket. No matter where I am or what I'm doing, when I pull it over me, I don't feel so alone.

MATT

I PUSHED HARD on my run this morning, hoping it would leave me feeling too drained to think about my life today but, unfortunately, that didn't really happen. Walking through the front door to Beau's home, I rub that spot on my chest that always aches. The door lets off a beep beep sound, letting them know that I am here.

The smell of bacon floods my senses, and my stomach growls. Leila is good at many things, but cooking breakfast is right up there at the very top.

"Unca Matt!" Quinn says as she runs down the hall, straight for me. Her arms are held wide and she's grinning from ear to ear. Just seeing her big blue eyes makes my heart squeeze, and the storm that's brewing inside of me calms. The love that pours out of them, which is just for me, leaves me speechless. I've never done anything to earn this love from her, but yet she gives it to me so freely. Then again, all it took was for Beau to lay her in my arms after she was born, and this fierce protectiveness that I didn't know I possessed took over.

Scooping her up in my arms, she squeals and throws her arms around my neck. I just saw her two days ago, but the happiness shining out of her would make one think it'd been weeks.

"How's my girl this morning?" I ask her.

"Good," she says, smiling at me with her chubby little cheeks and mouth full of little baby teeth. My heart squeezes for her. She is so perfect.

It was right after my nineteenth birthday when Beau

called to tell me that he and Leila were moving back to the island. I always thought they'd buy a rental property here and just visit, but nope, the next thing I knew, they were closing on their forever home.

It wasn't until he told me they were having a baby that I finally understood.

At nineteen, the thought of having a baby was terrifying, and pretty much a full-time nightmare, but Beau was ready.

I'd never known a baby. In fact, I had never even held one. Sure, I have seen them on the beach and shopping and stuff, but when it comes to taking care of them . . . no idea.

All through Leila's pregnancy, Beau would joke around and say things like he hoped the baby turned out just like me; that I was the best baby, so quiet and sweet. I must've known, even then that, if I wanted to survive, I had to play my part and keep quiet.

Quinn is two and a half now, and pretty much the light of my life.

Holding her, I walk into the kitchen and give Leila a kiss on the cheek.

"What's up, fat head?" Beau says to me, while taking a sip of his coffee. His eyes are full of humor.

"What?" I chuckle, raising my eyebrows at him. Quinn starts patting my head.

"Oh, don't listen to him. You know he's just jealous because I think you're more handsome than he is." Leila says, giving Beau a sly smile.

I can't help but smirk at him, and he frowns.

Drew and Beau have always been good-looking. I heard this over and over again from girls, women, and even other guys for years. Eventually, I did catch up to them in height. I'm even slightly taller than Beau which, in a way, feels strange. He is my big brother, and I've always looked up to him, only now I actually look down. It was at about that same time that I noticed people starting to stare a little more and girls beginning to flirt with me.

If you lined the three of us up, it would definitely be noticeable that we are brothers, until you took a closer look. We are all pretty close in height, with the same skin coloring, and hair that is different shades of brown. We all share the same facial features, too. Drew has brown eyes, Beau has hazel, and mine are slate gray. It's like that children's game, find the object that doesn't match the others. When I look in the mirror, the eyes staring back at me are just another reminder that I'm not fully their brother.

"No, I'm serious. Did you know that your brain is made up of sixteen percent fat?" Beau says.

I grin at him. A long time ago, I gave up wondering where he came up with these facts, because he sure knows a lot of them.

Leila rolls her eyes at him. "So, how are you today?" she asks while glancing over at me, and then goes back to chopping vegetables.

"I'm fine."

Both Beau and Leila look at me this time. They know that today is not my favorite day, but they don't know why.

"Unca Matt hungry?" Quinn shoves her hand into my mouth, and all of us laugh. Her eyes sparkle with amusement.

"We told her you were coming over for breakfast this morning because you were hungry, and she had to put on her princess dress for you."

"That's because she is my princess; and the most beautiful one, too," I say, smiling at her. She pats my head again and then wiggles to get down.

26

"Breakfast will be ready in a few minutes. Do you want some coffee?" Leila asks me.

"Sure, that sounds great. Thanks," I say as she hands me a cup.

"Unca Matt, come with me." Quinn pulls me by the hand, and leads me over to the doll house that I built for her. As we sit down in front of it, I'm amazed at how much her vocabulary has grown over the last couple of weeks. She is always talking, telling stories, asking questions, and laughing. Her little voice has created a soundtrack in my life that is constantly playing, and I love it.

About six months after she was born, Beau retracted his statement of hoping that she turned out like me. She is completely different from me in every way, and he said that he hopes she turns out to be exactly who she is and who she wants to be. Even then, she was making noises, babbling, and laughing. I don't ever remember laughing as a child.

When we were growing up, our home was a quiet one. We always stuck to ourselves, and the only noise that ever filtered through the house was the nightly news. The old man didn't want to hear us, and we only had to be told once.

Being quiet just became who I was. I didn't mind, nor did I really know any differently. In a way, I found a sense of comfort in the quietness. However, things always change, and little did I know, at seven years old, that change was on the horizon for me.

For as long as I can remember, I have been going to the same hidden spot in the dunes, amongst the sea oats, and under the canopy of the sea pines. It's my favorite place. The freedom that I've always felt to kind of have a place of my own, where no one can find me, and I can just be . . . it's inde-

scribable. That is, it was.

The sun was setting, and I recall it being so beautiful. I'm standing in the lull of the dune, watching as it slips into the water of the horizon, when the peacefulness of the moment is suddenly broken. The birds that had been nestled down along the beach start squawking in warning. They shoot off up into the sky. Immediately, I'm on alert. The hairs stand up on the back of my neck, and my breathing increases. The only word that comes to mind is 'danger'.

Slowly, I begin to turn my head to the left, when a large hand reaches around from behind me and clamps down on my face and mouth. A body, larger than mine, smothers up against my back and heat radiates off it and onto me. A head drops down next to my ear and hoarsely whispers . . .

"Don't say a word."

"Don't say a word."

"Don't say a word."

The world starts to spin. Blue sky, white clouds, and the squawking seagulls swirl overhead, around and around. My heart is hammering in my chest and my stomach bottoms out.

He found me.

"Did you think this was your little secret hiding place? I know everything. It will serve you right to remember that. Your time is coming, Matt, and I'm going to collect. Remember . . . don't say a word . . . not even a whisper."

Questions fired through my mind.

Don't say a word about what? My time is coming? What is he going to collect? Wracking my brain, I try my hardest to think if I have done anything wrong.

Then he laughs. His laugh has such an evil cadence to it, that I always wondered how others didn't pick up on it. It slips beneath the skin and purposely tries to stab all happiness with its thorns.

"Remember . . . don't say a word." He shoves me forward, and a cool breeze replaces where he was at my back. He's gone. I can feel it and, along with him, so is the joy that I had always known here in the dunes.

Fear shoots through my veins like ice water. What does he want with me? My time is coming. Is he going to kill me? Don't say a word—I never talk now—how can I possibly be any more quiet?

Running away from a place that I loved so much, tears begin to drip down my face. Heartbreak and disappointment consume me as I realize, at seven, that, no matter what I do or how quiet I am, it is never going to be enough for him. Aimlessly, and as fast as I can, I run through yards, weaving in and out, trying to be lost and not found. I don't know where I'm going, except I end up in Aunt Ella's back yard. Looking around, I notice the bushes next to the stairs, and dive into them.

It's here that she found me sometime later, and it's here that she wrapped her arms around me . . . and I let her.

Beau is the only one who has ever really hugged me. My teachers occasionally throw an arm over my shoulders, but it's as if they could tell that affection wasn't my thing. Not that I didn't want it to be, it just never was.

I've always been drawn to Aunt Ella. Lately, I've found myself in her café after school more and more. She always smiles at me and gives me a snack. She makes me feel wanted, even though I know I'm not.

As the tears slow down, she pushes the hair off of my forehead, and her eyes lovingly sweep over my face. "Come on, little man, let's go over here." With her warmth surrounding me, she walks us over to the little shed in the corner of her yard and opens it up for us. That's when I knew that here, close to her, is where I wanted to be, and that this shed just became my refuge.

"Breakfast is ready," Leila yells through the house, shaking me from my thoughts. Quinn bolts back into the kitchen.

"So, are you going to talk to us today, or just sit there?" Beau asks me as he takes a seat next to Quinn at the table.

I can tell that he is trying to assess my mood, but this is not the way to do it. I sit down across from him and take my first bite. I've mastered how to shut off the emotions, even though anger burns through me. My expression is blank until I look up at him, and he smirks. He's trying to challenge me, and I don't know why. He knows me better than that.

My eyes narrow and my jaw tightens as I chew. I'm appreciative for the invite to breakfast, but I'm not going to sit here and listen to him. Today is not the day. Breaking eye contact, I look back at my plate and take another bite.

"Would you leave him alone?" Leila glares at him. "I'm sorry, Matt; don't listen to him. Tell me, how is the house coming along?"

I don't even have to ask which one. I know she's talking about the North Shore house.

Shoving my annoyance down, I suck in a breath. "Pretty well; the windows are finally in, so we're good to go with starting the inside." I glance at her in between bites. Beau is still watching me closely, and suddenly I've lost my appetite. As much as I love them, I want to leave.

"Well, I can't wait to see it once it's finished," Leila says.

"Yeah, you and me both." A chuckle breaks free.

For the rest of the breakfast, we talk about everyday things. Knowing Beau doesn't really mean any harm, I stamp down the darkness that lives in me and put on my best social face. I'm certain they are trying to distract my thoughts, and I love them for this, but I can't help but think breakfast was a bad idea.

I thought Beau understood me a little better. He's never questioned why I choose to stay quiet, or why I am so introverted. He has never asked me to be anything other than happy. If he only knew the truth, he would understand how hard this is for me. I try for him. I've always tried. I do so because he's my family and he deserves it, but if I had my way, I'd let them all go on without me.

I've just pulled in back at the cottage when I spot a girl unloading luggage from a car in front of cottage number two.

"Ugh!" she lets out an exasperated sigh and hoists a large bag over her shoulder, while getting a few more things out of the back seat.

I'm surprised to see her there, and I quickly run through the upcoming reservation calendar in my mind. I don't remember anyone scheduled to come in late last night or early this morning.

I also can't help but wonder why Aunt Ella put her next to me and not at the other end of the cottages, which are also empty. I'm supposed to begin working on the floors this week and I'm just waiting for the tile to come in. There's a wedding scheduled over the weekend, but it's only Monday, and not likely that someone would show up this early in advance.

I try to get a good look at her but, with all of her stuff filling her arms, all I can really see is dark blonde hair. I watch as she kicks the car door shut and walks back to the cottage. Right before she enters, the sun hits her hair and I would swear it glows, giving off the illusion of a faint halo. Thinking about the sun, I scowl, sigh, and run my hand through my hair.

She disappears inside.

Frustrated, I climb out of the Jeep and slam the door. As if today doesn't have my mind running enough, I now have a neighbor.

Chapter Three

ELLE

THE VIBRATING SOUND of my cell phone in my bag jerks me awake. How could I have been so stupid to leave it on? I was in such a rush to get out of the city that I completely forgot to turn it off. The phone has been sitting in my bag in the backseat, and I instantly wonder if coming here now was all for nothing. I didn't disable all of the location and tracking capabilities.

Throwing the blanket off of me, I rush over to my bag. Digging around, I find it on the bottom and pull it out to see Olivia's name flash on the screen. I decide to make it quick and take the call. I can't have her worrying about me. That's not a nice thing to do to my best friend.

"Hey, Livy," I mumble into the phone as I sit down on the floor. Otis walks over and rubs his body against mine, flicking his tail.

"Elle! I've been calling you since yesterday! Are you

okay? What happened to you the other night? I thought you were going to meet Jase and me at Connor's party," the worry in her voice evident.

"Yeah, I'm okay and I was going to, but at some point during the show I got a migraine and by the time I got home, I couldn't keep my eyes open. I needed sleep." Speaking of sleep reminds me of how exhausted I am as I run my hand over my face and push my hair back.

"Are you okay now?" she asks.

Looking out the bedroom door, I can see almost all of the living room. The blinds are drawn, and the quietness of the little cottage wraps around me. Livy's concern for me causes tears to fill my eyes. I should tell her everything, but I just can't. I don't want anyone to know about this.

"Not quite, but I will be. Was Connor mad that I didn't show?"

"You know he was. He told everyone that you were going to be there, and by not showing, he looked like a liar. People started leaving early. Just goes to show they were there for you and not him. I'm so glad you're ending it with him; he leeches off of your name, and that's so not cool."

This is the story of my life. Right after that first season where Leila spotlighted me, I felt like I had instant fame. People recognized me, designers requested me, and my career just took off. Everywhere I went, people seemed excited to have me there, and I loved the attention. It was new and overwhelming, but in a good way. Soon enough, though, I learned that motives weren't genuine and people weren't my friends. Oh, they all said they were, but it was never about me and all about them.

I do have a couple of industry friends, but mostly it's always just been Livy and me.

"Tell me about it. He's way more into the spotlight and fame than I am. Just wish he'd take the hint that I just want to be friends."

"Didn't you tell him?"

Connor and I met a little over two months ago at Fashion Week. He is also a model, which should have been my first big red flag. Models can be very vain. The first couple of dates that we went on, he seemed shy, almost passive, and I found this to be refreshing. However, the more we were together, the more his true colors came out. He loved to take selfies of us together. He would post them on Instagram and Facebook, always tagging me to get more exposure for himself. His plan did work, only, while he was soaking up the attention from all his new-found fans, he somehow missed the lack of attention from me.

"Yeah, last week. He just patted me on the back and said that I was overworked and tired, and after I got some sleep, I would see things more clearly. He was right; things are crystal clear now." A shiver runs through me now at the mere thought of him. Connor had these annoying habits that I hated like, whenever we were out in public, he would stand next to me, wrap his arm around me and place his hand on my stomach. He was always rubbing my stomach, or trying to push it in or something. He also ate these cinnamon breath mints nonstop. I despise the smell of cinnamon now. "Oh, my God; what a total tool! Yeah, he really doesn't know women. Once we are done, we are done," Livy laughed.

It was right after that conversation with Connor that I received my first letter. I'd had a few of them before over the years, but mostly they'd just made me uncomfortable. This one, however, caused fear to run through my veins.

Livy laughs. "Let's go get a late lunch."

A pang of sadness hits me. I would love to go to lunch with her. "Can't."

"Why not? We should be celebrating, now that you're freeing yourself of that leech."

"I *am* celebrating, and it involves a little rest and relaxation, hidden from the world." I get up off the floor and walk over to look out the window toward the beach. It's late afternoon and the sun is starting to drop. The sand is white, and it looks so inviting.

There's silence on the other end of the line.

"Wait, where are you?" she asks.

I can't help but giggle. "Don't you wish you knew . . ."

"Elle, that's so not funny. So, no migraine then?" she asks me curiously.

"Oh, I had a killer migraine, and that's when I decided it was time to get away. Don't worry, though. I'm not far." But far enough I think.

"You're not going to tell me, are you?"

"Nope. Kind of like being off the grid, which also means that, after we hang up, I'm going to shut off my phone." I smile to myself. It's such an amazing feeling to not have to think about anything but myself. No mother, no calendar, no work . . . no stalkers.

"No fair! I would have gone with you! What am I supposed to do without you?"

I laugh again as her pout comes through the line. "I'm sure there are some appointments of mine that you'll need to reschedule," I giggle. "You'll be fine, and I'll be back before you know it."

Livy is also my assistant. Together, she and I have been a team for a long time. My mother doesn't approve of her. I'm sure that has more to do with her father than her, but I know she trusts her enough to manage my calendar and all the little details.

"Okay, fine. But promise me you'll call me if you need anything or get bored."

"I will," I say, although I know I won't.

"Wait! What happens if I need to reach you?"

"I'm hoping you won't," I say pointedly.

"Speaking of reaching you, Mommy dearest has called me twice and texted me once. She's on the prowl looking for you."

An exasperated breath rushes out. Why can't she just leave me alone? I am twenty-three years old, an adult, and it's time she learns that.

"Hearing you say that just confirms my motives for disappearing for a bit. I think it's time for me to move on in more ways than one." I flex my hand and feel the ache between the joints of my fingers.

"I'm not so sure I like this plan but, then again, maybe both of them will take a hint. If you aren't around, hopefully Connor will move on."

"I should be so lucky." We both laugh.

"Don't worry about your mother. I can handle her until you get back," she says with confidence, and I know that she will. Her reassurance comforts me more than she knows.

"Thanks, Livy. I don't know what I would do without you," I say, letting out a deep breath.

"Call me soon?" she asks.

"I will."

"I'll miss you," she says.

"You too, Livy," and we both hang up.

Powering down the phone, I look at the clock and see that it's almost four. Now is probably as good a time as any to head over to the café. Between lunch and before dinner shouldn't be so bad.

Standing in the bathroom, I go about my daily ritual of 'putting on my face'. My hair is smoothed back, sprayed, and placed into a low bun. My foundation is evenly applied with powder brushed over it, eyebrows, eye shadow, eye liner, mascara, bronzer, lip liner, and lip gloss. Everything always has to be just perfect. *You never know who might be in the room.* I recall one of my mother's famous rants. Covering my head in a big straw hat, I grab the largest pair of sunglass that I brought. I don't think that people will recognize me and, although this really isn't a disguise, it's the best I can do without dyeing and cutting my hair.

The café is just a couple blocks up the beach so, instead of driving over, I wander down the footpath and onto the sand. Glancing back toward the cottage, I look at the one closest to the beach. It really does have a spectacular view. I can't help but wonder if anyone is staying there right now. There isn't a car in the driveway, and I wasn't paying attention when I pulled in earlier this morning, but that doesn't mean anything.

There aren't a lot of people on the beach today, which I'm thankful for. The sun is warm, even if the air is brisk and cool. It's beautiful outside. I swing my flip-flops while I head in the direction of the café. I'm completely lost in thought, when, all of a sudden I hear laughing—male laughing. The hair on my arms stands up, and my heart begins to race.

Looking behind me, I see that there are three guys quickly approaching me. All of them are wearing old-looking swim trunks and two have on tank tops with really large armpit holes. I don't think that they are too much older than I am, but their hygiene looks less than stellar. All three of them have on sunglasses, shielding the leer in their eyes, but the expression on their faces can't be missed. I've seen it before . . . many times before.

Turning forward, I pick up my pace. The café is maybe thirty yards ahead of me, and my eyes are singularly focused on the entrance door.

"Where are you going, sweetheart?" one of the guys says. They are closer than they were a few seconds ago.

Uneasiness creeps its way up my spine, and I clutch the flip flops to my chest. I've always had this stupid irrational fear about people walking behind me. I don't know where it comes from or why I have it, but when I hear people behind me, I feel like I am being followed or chased. Living in New York City makes this especially tricky and, oftentimes, I find myself stepping to the side and slowing down just so the person will pass. Relief always floods through me once they do.

"We want to talk to you. Don't you want to stick around and keep us company for a while?" The sickening way these words hiss out and find their way to my ears has my stomach aching and tears pricking my eyes. I hate that I can't control these emotions and, after all that I've been through over the last couple of weeks, panic sets in. I know I'm overreacting and that these guys aren't the ones who broke into my condo and sent me the mail, but my mind and heart aren't communicating with each other.

Running through the last part of the sand and over the sidewalk, I focus on the door. My feet hit the wood deck at the edge of the café at the exact moment a guy walks out and turns in my direction. He has a cup of coffee in one hand and he's looking at his keys that he just pulled from his pocket in the other. He reminds me of a J Crew summer catalog model, with his sleeves rolled up on his button-down shirt, and navy blue shorts.

From behind me, I can hear the men's flip flops hitting the sidewalk next to the parking lot, and the murmurs and chuckles being shared between them. These sounds push me faster and straight toward the guy with the coffee. Just a couple more steps and, without even thinking, I walk right into his personal space.

"Please, play along," I whisper. With that, I reach up and grab him gently by the neck, pull his head down, and place my lips on his.

He freezes.

My heart is pounding and all I can think about at this moment is, please don't be mad, please play along, and please *please* kiss me back.

MATT

LEAVING MY HOUSE, I glance over to see if there is any movement coming from cottage number two. The car in the driveway has a New York license plate. Assuming that this person has been driving nonstop, that explains why she checked in so early this morning. For her sake, she's lucky the floors aren't already here or I would be starting on them today.

Walking through the back door and into the café's kitchen, in so many ways I want to pretend that today is like any other day, but I can't. There are a lot of days that I don't stop into the café at all, that's just normal life, but today I know that Aunt Ella will probably be better off if she sees me, and vice versa.

After I heard my mom confess to Beau, I took off for the

40

shed. I needed to be there, in a place where I felt safe. Turns out, Aunt Ella had seen me tear through the yard, and found me curled up on my bean bag chair in the corner, sobbing. Everything about my life had always been so vacant. No friends, no parents, no brothers, no real interactions with people . . . definitely no love. So when she wrapped her arms around me, I leaned into her and let her hold me. No one ever touched me to show affection, and having her there at that moment made me feel more comfort than I had in a long time. Over and over again, I wished that she and Uncle Ben were my parents.

Thoughts of Uncle Ben make this day even sadder and more unbearable than it already is.

Aunt Ella is in her usual place between the kitchen island and the stove, so I walk over and give her a giant, but gentle, hug.

"How are you today?" I ask her. I can't help but notice that her eyes, which are usually a rich caramel color, are a little bit duller, darker, and more guarded. Another reason to hate November first; two years ago on this day, Uncle Ben had a heart attack and died.

People who saw us on a daily basis knew that I was close to Uncle Ben, but no one ever knew how much he meant to me. In every way possible, he stepped in and filled the role of the adult father figure that I needed. He was honorable and honest with everyone, and I don't remember him ever raising his voice.

One of my favorite memories is of him putting his hand on my shoulder and squeezing. He would do this whenever he saw me, and in moments when I knew he was proud of me. He was tall and thin, too, like Aunt Ella, and I loved looking up at him. He was always smiling, and it was so genuine that it would shine out of his clear blue eyes. Every day, I tried to do something that would make him proud of me. I craved that look, and I so desperately needed affirmation that I was worth something to someone.

Uncle Ben had this motto that he would always tell people: "Follow the sun." It pretty much became his coined phrase. In return, his friends all started to call him 'Sunshine'.

I asked him once what it meant and he just looked at me, smiled, and said, "Young Matthew, don't you know?"

He could tell that I had no idea what he was talking about, and his crooked smile got a little bigger. With his hand on my shoulder, he said, "Well now, I can't tell you all the sun's secrets. You'll have to figure them out on your own. But as long as the sun keeps rising, you just remember to follow it and you'll be alright."

I think about that phrase almost daily when I'm out for my morning run. I watch the sun rise over the trees and I chase after it. Time stops and I know there will only be a few precious seconds, but it's in these seconds that I feel the closest to him ever since he died. I'm grateful for the love he had for me. The seconds pass and the golden rays reach me. As the heat strikes my skin, the moment is gone and the hope he instilled disintegrates.

The heat from the sun. The constant reminder. The things I've seen and done that can never be erased. This is God's way of punishing me, I'm convinced. He'll never let me forget.

Uncle Ben always loved the sun and I thought I would, too. I wanted to be just like him. But over the years, things changed. The sun was no longer a friend but, instead, my tormentor. There is no point in my trying to *follow* the sun. The eternal ball of flames followed me. I couldn't escape it.

Why is it that significant events always seem to happen

on the same day? People die, babies are born, jobs are lost . . . confessions are made. Maybe we are all cursed and destined to have one day belong to us. Or maybe I should say we are all cursed and destined to belong to one day. We don't choose the day, the day chooses us.

"It's been a long day already and we've only just gotten through lunch." There's fatigue wrapped around her shoulders and in the way she stands. Something is wrong with her and, as I study her, my eyebrows pull together.

"What's wrong?" I ask her, and she goes back to scooping batter out of the bowl and pouring it into the muffin tin, not making eye contact with me.

"Nothing, sweetheart. I didn't expect today to be easy; it's just harder than I thought." She glances at me and gives me a small reassuring smile.

"I'm sorry I didn't stop by earlier. I should have. Can I stay and help you with the dinner crowd?" Some days I worry about her. She works really long hours, especially since Uncle Ben died, and this job isn't an easy one. She's on her feet all day.

"Bless your heart, no. You are young and so handsome. You need to be out there trying to meet someone. Besides, this is therapeutic for me. You know that."

I huff at this. She's always pushing for me to find someone. I'm not sure why, though. I've never had a girlfriend, nor do I want one. "We've had this conversation before. I'm not looking to meet anyone and certainly not right as we roll into the winter season."

"You worry too much. All of the renovations are mostly complete. Everything will be fine, and I think you'll be surprised how much you get done on the North Shore house."

"Easy for you to say, even though I know you've seen the

books." She doesn't comment after this statement. I knew that she wouldn't, but her eyes twinkle.

Every year during the week of Thanksgiving, the Heller sisters show up and stay through the end of the year. Repeatedly over the last year, I've tried to have Aunt Ella cancel their reservation, but she won't; judging by the hidden smirk on her face, she knows I'm not happy about this. Never in the past five years have I had more demanding guests than them. I think they purposely break things just to interrupt my day and have me work at their cottage.

"You could always pitch a tent up over at the North Shore house and we could tell them you're on vacation." A small smile escapes her.

"You do realize that you're running me out of my own home. Speaking of, I saw someone new showed up this morning. Were they scheduled?"

She drops her gaze and goes back to scooping the batter. "Nope, just knocked on the door, wanting to know if I had a place they could stay."

Knocked on the door? What door? We don't have an office and all of our guests go through the café to pick up and drop off keys. Something isn't adding up here, but I'm not going to push her. She'd tell me if she wanted to.

"Oh, okay. Why did you put them next to me?"

"Well, she's by herself and I have a feeling she might stay a while." Aunt Ella eyes me cautiously as she says this. She's acting strangely.

Watching her closely, I just nod. Since buying the cottages, occasionally we'll have a woman show up who is just looking for some quiet time. They never stay long, but just enough to catch up on some much-needed rest.

"Does she know that I'm going to be working on the

floors?"

"Yep, and considering how the other cottages are booked for the wedding coming up, she really didn't have a choice." There's a slight edge to her tone, but I let go.

"Alright, I'll keep my eyes and ears out for her."

"Thanks. I don't think that she will be much trouble, but you never know. Are you coming back for dinner?"

"No, I'm meeting Davy here in a little bit. He wants to talk about one of his client's houses. Apparently, it needs some basic maintenance and repairs."

"Well, that sounds like fun for you boys."

"I don't know if I would call it fun. He actually seems a little angry over this. Home repairs aren't really his thing."

"Stop back in soon, okay?" She looks right at me and her eyes are sad. I wish I could help with this sadness, but it's one that I live with, too. Daily.

Leaning over, I give her another hug. She holds on and I let her. I understand.

Walking out into the café, I find that Davy is already here. He's sitting by the window and people-watching. Davy is the closest thing that I've ever had to a best friend. He moved to the island almost a year ago after Old Man Littman retired and sold him his law practice. He's several years older than me, but that doesn't seem to matter.

I'm glad that he asked me to help him; he usually doesn't. He's like me in the sense that he'd rather just do things himself. I don't want to ask other people for help; it never ends up being as good as it would have been if I had done it myself. Luckily, I'm good with my hands. It's another thing I am grateful to Uncle Ben for.

The shed that Uncle Ben had in the backyard was one of those pre-assembled wood sheds, but it was painted the same color as their house, complete with two windows. To my seven-year-old eyes, it looked like a small house and, the first time I walked into with Aunt Ella, all I felt was sanctuary.

Every day after school, I would run straight to the shed. In there, I would do my homework and reorganize Uncle Ben's tools. Little by little, I noticed that the totes and other things that they were storing in the shed disappeared and, in their place, things like a bean bag chair, a lantern, and a radio were found. I understood that they knew I played in the shed, but no one ever said anything to me. In a way, I preferred it like this. It kept the shed my secret hideout and, after losing my place in the dunes, I finally felt like I belonged somewhere.

After a while, instead of organizing the tools, I began to work with them. They were fascinating to me, and I loved the idea that they could build and repair. My father always made it known that I wasn't wanted and, even as a child, I felt like I was living with a hole in my chest. I felt broken, and the idea of being able to fix things made me feel better. I checked out a few books at the library, and so began my love of construction.

Just thinking about the possibility of Davy's project has me antsy with excitement.

The chair scrapes against the floor as I pull it out. He looks at me and frowns.

"So, tell me about this house." I smirk at him.

"It's the one across the street from you."

"On Oak Street? The old vacant one?"

"Yep. I received a letter that the new owner will be coming to pick up the keys and the deed sometime soon. I need to get it show-ready."

The Oak Street house is a really nice home. For as long as I can remember, it has been empty and no one ever visits it. It crossed my mind several times to try to find the owner to buy it, but I asked Aunt Ella about it and she brushed me off, telling me to not even bother. So I never did.

"Why do you have to get it ready?" I'm confused by this.

"Long story. Will you help me?" he lets out a sigh.

"Of course I will. Why didn't we just meet at my house?"

"Because I was craving a Cuban and needed it immediately." He smiles at me.

I couldn't help but laugh. Aunt Ella makes the best Cubans.

"Alright, well let's go." Together we stand up and head for the door.

"Hey, I'm gonna say good-bye to Aunt Ella one more time and grab a cup of coffee. I'll meet you in the parking lot."

"Sounds good."

I am barely through the door when the blur of a girl rushes before me, almost knocking the wind out me, and starts kissing me. I didn't even get a good look at her, and from this angle all I can see is the brim of her hat and large sunglasses. I can't help but wonder if I even know her.

"Please, play along" she said to me, right before she slammed into me. Her hand wrapped around the back of my head and she pulled my mouth to hers. Both of my arms stretched out in shock, one holding the coffee in hopes to not spill it, and the other with my keys.

Her warm lips froze against mine, and a tremble ran through her body. I don't remember her other hand landing on my waist but, as her fingers tightened into my shirt, it snapped me out of my frozen state. The smell of peaches wrapped around me, and instantly I was lost.

Yes, I'll play along.

Hesitantly, I press my hand with the keys into her lower back. She leans into me a little more, her chest now flush with mine. She's taller than most girls and very thin. Her body pressed up next to mine feels amazing. Heat starts radiating off of me.

I'm not exactly sure when this fake kiss turned into a real one but, as she lets out a sigh and her sweet breath fans across my face, I am completely spellbound by whoever this is. In this moment, I would do whatever she asked of me. I part her lips with mine and deepen the kiss. At the first brush of our tongues, her fingers move from my neck and tighten in my hair. I can't help the small moan that escapes me. This kiss is unlike any I have ever experienced before. Maybe it's the mystery of the unknown but, whatever it is, I know I want more.

Without even seeing her face, the chemistry between us begins to spark. I know that we are standing on the sidewalk in plain sight, but I can't bring myself to care. The way she smells and tastes, the way she feels up next to me, it all feels perfect. Right this second, she is perfect.

This thought startles me a little. I've never thought anyone or anything was perfect and my heart slams into my chest.

Is it possible to never speak to someone, never actually see them, yet feel a connection that is so incredibly deep your soul feels alive and content at the same time? The pounding of my heart matches hers, and I realize my body is falling into sync with hers. It's like they are reacting to each other and becoming one. The hole in my chest begins to shrink, just a little bit. A couple of guys walk by and one whistles. "Hey man, way to go; can't say I blame you, a fine ass like that." They keep walking but, the second she hears them, her entire body tenses and she drops her head onto my shoulder and buries her face in my neck. She's squeezing me tight and, from head to toe, she starts shaking. Her heart loses its cadence, and pounds through her chest and into mine. Instinctively, my arms pull her tighter.

"Hey, it's alright. I've got you. They're gone."

She lets out a sigh and settles against me. Her lips press against my neck and the sensation permanently brands me.

I need to know who this girl is.

Chapter Four

ELLE

I COULDN'T STOP the shaking. I know this reaction is irrational and bordering on an anxiety attack, but I just can't help it. Tears are desperately trying to drop from my eyes and I focus on my breathing to calm down. Standing here in this guy's arms feels so good, and I feel so safe.

Blocking out the laughter from those guys, I replay the last two minutes in my mind. I can't believe that I just kissed a complete stranger, and that it had felt like that. For just a split second, I had forgotten where I was and what was happening, but with complete certainty I know that I will never forget that kiss.

Inhaling him one more time, I know I should let go, but he is just so warm and he smells so good. It's a mixture of a man's sporty body wash and some kind of fresh laundry detergent.

Letting out a deep breath, slowly I release him, but never

look up into his face. Part of me likes not knowing what he looks like. It'll keep this memory more magical, but the other part of me is just embarrassed. I adjust my sunglasses and look at how our feet are so close to each other.

"I'm so sorry to have done that to you, but I can't thank you enough," I say to him.

The guy doesn't answer me and silence hangs between us. Then it hits me.

"Oh, my God, I am so sorry. You have a girlfriend . . . or a wife! I am so sorry to ask you to do that. I wasn't thinking; I just reacted."

He chuckles just a little. "No girlfriend . . . no wife."

Relief rushes through me. I would have felt horrible for putting him in this position. And then I register the sound of his voice. His voice vibrates through me like I just struck the perfect chord on my guitar. The expression, 'music to my ears', comes to mind.

He shifts his keys to his other hand and then reaches up to cup my face. The unexpectedness of this calms the nerves flying around my stomach. He rubs his thumb across my cheekbone, and I can't help but to tilt my head slightly into his hand.

"Are you ok? Can I take you somewhere?" The genuine concern that comes through puts a lump in my throat, and tears return to my eyes. People never offer to do anything for me without wanting something in return.

"No, I'm fine thanks. I was just on my way to the café, and then I'm heading back home." He drops his hand, runs it down my arm, and links his fingers with mine.

"I'll walk you in," he says quietly.

I know that I really should decline, but I'm not ready to let go of him yet. He turns around, walks back to the café door, and opens it. He squeezes my hand and pulls me behind him.

Physical contact isn't something that I have a lot of. I really don't need it but, every now and then, it's nice. I briefly look at the back of him and see a head full of dark hair. A pang of regret slips in that I didn't get a good look at him when I approached him. Shaking away the thought, I pull my hat down to shield my face.

"So, you said you were going home. You live around here?" His question is a simple one, but I don't know how I should answer it. I glance up at him as he leads me to a table in the back, and my heart skips a beat. *Oh my.* He is even more beautiful than I thought. His face is covered with stubble, and I'm instantly surprised that I didn't notice it earlier. Looking at his profile, I can't see his eyes, but what I can see are full, long eyelashes that brush his cheek when he blinks. His hair is cut short, but not too short, and his lips are the perfect fullness. The thought of J Crew model pops back into mind, and then I think, no, more like Calvin Klein. This guy could make a fortune and he probably doesn't even know it.

"Ah, no not really. I'm just here visiting someone." He drops my hand and pulls a chair out for me. When I pass by him, his delicious smell hits me again. My body is in complete awareness of him, and I have no idea why. Keeping my head down, I never look him directly in the face.

"Anyone I might know?" he asks.

"Not sure, just my Aunt—" The door to the kitchen swings open and Aunt Ella steps into the dining room. She spots me right away, looks from the guy to me, and then down to his hands on the back of my chair. Her eyebrows furrow a little bit. She looks over to the guy and acknowledges him, "Matt."

His name is Matt.

Then she looks back over to me and cracks a smile. "So, I

was wondering when you were going to show up."

I don't know what to say to her, and silence floats around us. I'm flustered and she picks up on it.

She looks from me to the guy named Matt again, and says, "Okay."

The guy, Matt, must pick up on the strange vibe between us, because he squeezes my shoulders. He turns to face me, but I keep the rim of the hat down and don't look up at him.

"Thanks again. I really appreciate your help."

He reluctantly lets me go and steps away from me. "Sure, no problem. Enjoy your stay." With that, he turns around and walks out of the café.

"Well, it didn't take you long to run into Matt." Her tone throws me off. She's protective of him and I don't know why. "Are you and he all reacquainted?"

"Reacquainted? I just met him. I know it looked strange, but he was helping me." I say while pulling off the sunglasses.

"I see." She tilts her head to the side and looks at me questioningly. I know she is wondering why I am here on the island; I'm just not ready to tell her yet.

"You see what?" I ask her.

"Nothing, apparently nothing at all. I was just about to sit down for dinner. Can I make you something, too?"

My stomach growls. She hears it and we both smile. "Yes, please. Do you have salad?"

Her eyebrows quirk and she looks me over from head to toe.

"Yep, I have some butternut bisque soup, too. I'll be right back. Trish will be over in a sec to get you a drink."

I glance behind Aunt Ella and see a girl standing behind the counter, watching us.

After Aunt Ella walks away, the girl shuffles over to my

table and grins from ear to ear. I find myself grinning back, but that might be because of her caterpillar apron.

"I cannot believe that Matt was holding your hand." She's so excited by this and I'm confused.

"What do you mean?" Here I had been thinking he had really nice southern manners and charm.

"Matt is . . . well, he's different," she says quietly.

He didn't seem that different to me. She sees the confusion on my face.

"I'm trying to think of how to explain him. He's very quiet and keeps to himself. You'll never hear more than a few words from him. The only people I have ever seen him talk to are Aunt Ella, his brothers and their wives, and Davy; although Davy is new around here and he's just as quiet. Maybe that's why they get along so well."

I don't understand why being quiet and keeping to yourself makes someone so different.

"How long have you known him?" I ask her.

"Oh, I don't know him. No one really does. But I've known *of* him all my life. He was born and raised on the island, just like me."

Someone must know him, because he sure kissed me like he was an expert. Once that kiss started, he took over without hesitancy.

"I'm Elle, by the way," I say, introducing myself to her.

"Trish. Nice to meet you. How do you know Ella?" She pops her hand on her hip.

"Oh, she's my aunt." I can see the gossip wheel turning in her head, and I haven't even left the café yet. She's trying to decide who she's going to tell about this first.

"Wow! So, are you cousins with Leila?"

And there it is again. How many times have I heard this

over the years? Not that I'm complaining. Anonymity is what I need here. Then again, everyone around here would know her, not so much me. After that last summer I spent here, my mother moved us to Atlanta, and we stayed there until our big move to New York.

"No, my mother is Aunt Ella's sister. Leila's from the Starling side of the family, Uncle Ben."

"Gotcha," she says, nodding slowly in understanding. "So, what can I get you to drink?"

"Some water would be great."

She smiles at me, gets the water, and brings it back just as Aunt Ella emerges from the kitchen with our dinner.

"Well, it was really nice to meet you. Make sure you stop in and see me while you're here. I'll be around until next month. I'm getting married." She flashes her engagement ring at me and, just for a split second, I'm jealous. It must be nice to have someone to love, and to be loved in return.

"Congratulations and, you know, I'm not real sure if I will be here a month from now."

She cracks a grin, winks at me and says, "You will be," while walking off.

MATT

I COULDN'T GET out of the café fast enough. All it took was one look from Aunt Ella and I knew it was time to go. Pretty sure she has never seen me with a girl before. She's never even seen me take interest in anyone, so I can understand why she was looking at me that way. It was then that I realized it wasn't just her, everyone in the café was staring. Uneasiness shot through me; and instantly I placed my hands on her shoulders. I didn't mean to touch her again as I said good-bye, but the minute I let go and walked away, the contentment that had taken over slowly disappeared, and the hole in my chest stretched back to its original size. Part of me wonders, if that feeling would return, if I went back to her. Would the hole constrict again?

Pushing through the door, I turn to head back to the Jeep. I stretch out the hand that I had held tight to hers. It's tingling and it feels weird. I can't believe I held her hand, a virtual stranger. I've never held a girl's hand before, not that I can remember anyway. When my hand was wrapped around hers, an overwhelming protectiveness surged through me. It's like I needed the whole world to know that she was with me.

What the hell happened back there? That's all I can think.

Clearly she was freaked out by Rob and his friends, but they are essentially harmless. Maybe she just didn't know that. And why did she react that way? The muscles all through my shoulders and back tighten at the possibility that she has been hurt before.

And that kiss . . . I groan to myself. Just thinking about the way she felt pressed up against me, I think I would sell my soul just to feel it again. The only word I can come up with is 'perfect'. I know I haven't been out with a girl in a while . . . okay, a long while, but that can't be the reason that kiss was so spectacular. It was just . . . it was the way it made me feel. And that's just the thing; usually I feel nothing. But that was . . . thinking of her lips makes me wonder what her skin would taste like, too.

Groaning to myself, I'm instantly angry. I need to stop this train of thought immediately. I don't know who she is, where she's staying, or if I would even ever see her again. And speaking of seeing, I didn't even see what she looks like. I would have no idea if I ran into her somewhere else again or not. In the end, it doesn't matter anyway; she said she was here visiting, so she'll be leaving. Not that I would want her to stay. Being with someone has never been in the cards for me.

Approaching the Jeep, I look up to see Davy leaning against the side, smiling at me from ear to ear. I had forgotten about him.

"Dude, who was that?" I can't blame him for the curiosity. I want to know who she is, too.

A grin splits my face as I unlock the door. As confused as I am by the situation, I'm also flying high. Adrenaline is coursing through me, and his look of wonder and amusement is infectious.

"I don't know," I tell him.

"What do you mean, you don't know? It sure looked like you knew her." He smirks at me from across the hood of the Jeep, thinking I'm lying.

"Uh, I don't know, man. That just happened, and I don't know how to explain it at all. Wish I did."

"Really, you don't know that girl?" His eyebrows shoot up.

"Nope," I say, climbing into the Jeep.

"Did you at least get her name?" He gets into the passenger side.

"Forgot to ask." I didn't even get her name. I frown at the thought. She probably has a really pretty name, too.

"Sucks for you. Did you see the way she looked in those shorts?" Jealousy strikes and burns through my cheeks.

Was he looking at her? Did he see her face? Wait, why do I care? Ugh, I'm angry again. It doesn't matter if he looked at her or what she looks like; she's never going to be mine. It's over.

"Actually, no, I didn't really see much of anything. She had the hat on and the sunglasses. Her face was…blocked."

"Blocked is a good description. I guess you wouldn't have seen her with yours plastered to hers," he laughs.

Flustered by my reaction to her and to him, I start the Jeep and turn to head out of the parking lot.

"Doesn't matter, it's over. I don't know who she is, nor do I want to, so let's drop it. Let's just get to the house. I want to see what we're dealing with." Knowing how small towns work, and that I've always been a bit of a mystery to people here on the island, I wonder how quickly this little bit of gossip will spread. I try to stay off the radar as much as possible.

He laughs again, but continues to watch me. "Whatever you say, but you have to admit that was weird."

Instantly, I need to defend her and her actions. "Why was it so weird?"

"Seeing you with a girl, I've known you for a year and I have never seen you with a girl."

"What?" I scowl at him. I don't know what to say to him. He's right. He's never seen me with a girl, because there hasn't been one. Then it occurs to me that in the last year I haven't seen him with a girl either. He sees this realization flash across my face and he pales a bit. As good of friends that we have become, it's moments like these that remind me that I don't really know very much about him. He never talks about his past, but neither do I, so I've always let it go. But seeing his reaction just now, I wonder if he does need to talk about it.

"Whatever, Don Juan." He breaks eye contact with me and laughs again, dropping the subject.

The vacant house on Oak Street, directly across from my

cottage, is beautiful inside. I had always wondered what it looked like and now I know. Part of me is regretful that I didn't try to seek out and buy the home. The bones of it are strong, and the intricate details on the inside have a story that is just waiting to be told.

We ended up spending a good two hours looking it over. General maintenance is all that it really needs, and a good scrubbing on the inside. I have a few guys who can get started on it with him and, in between replacing cottage number two's floors and the North Shore house, I should be able to drop in and help.

Projects are always good for me. I do best when I am moving and not thinking. Time passes more quickly. Most probably wouldn't understand why I would want the time to pass; after all, nothing is happening and nothing is changing. But to me it is. Time separates the then from the now, and I want the then to be as far away from the now as possible. No, I don't want it . . . I need it.

After confirming our plans, Davy and I part ways in the driveway. He heads down Oak Street to get to his house, and I walk the thirty steps to mine. I'm about to step inside when I hear music start up from the cottage next to mine. My first instinct is to be angry. There is no way I am going to allow loud music to blare out from next door, especially when the cottages are so close, but then the music stops. About five seconds later, the same string of chords that I had just heard plays again, guitar chords. Huh, the girl plays the guitar. Well, as long as it's not some blaring radio music, I won't bother her.

Bruno jumps as I walk in the door, and then he circles my legs and rams his head into my hand. Bending over to pet him, I think about how much I love this dog.

I found Bruno four years ago, after just moving into this house. I was seventeen at the time, and probably shouldn't have been living by myself, but after my mother's confession, nothing was ever the same. It was almost as if by her saying it out loud to Beau, it became real to her, and slowly she became more and more withdrawn from me. I didn't mind; I was used to her ignoring me, so it didn't seem that different. She was different, though. I imagine that after being free from your abusive husband, and two of your three children leaving for college, you would find yourself at a crossroad.

Only, it would have been nice if she had finally told me. To this day, she thinks she's keeping this secret, and lying to me. For seven years now, I've wondered who my real father is. I try not to think about it, but today is that one day of the year when I can't shake it.

Mom ended up selling her family's business and split the money four ways: Drew, Beau, Mom, and I each walked away with twenty-five percent. She sold our house that we lived in with him, bought a new one, a smaller one, on the other side of the island, and I began looking into buying rental properties.

Yes, I was younger than most when I bought these cottages, but being a native to the island, I understand how lucrative rental properties can be. I'd grown up around it, never intended on going to college, and knew enough about this as a business that this was the direction I was headed with the money that was given to me. I have never planned on living an extravagant life, so the income from the houses plus a trust inheritance from my grandfather, is plenty to cover my cost of living.

Uncle Ben was a realtor so, when the cottages came up for sale, he helped me with the paperwork and co-signed as a joint owner, since I was still a minor. My mother didn't discourage this, not that I would have let her influence me one way or another. The cottages were horribly out of date, and Uncle Ben knew that I was the person for them and they were the properties for me. I vigorously began construction and repairs on them, and I've never looked back.

When he passed away, Aunt Ella signed them all over to be solely mine. They were anyway; I'd paid for them, but this cleared up any legal confusion as to who owned the homes. Aunt Ella helps me with the reservation calendar, and we use the café as the meeting point for payment and keys.

I found Bruno as a puppy, in the backyard of cottage number three, under a tree, shivering and bone-thin. He looked at me, I looked at him, and in that second I found a little purpose. He didn't hesitate when I picked him up and took him to the vet. He's been mine ever since.

Wandering through the house, I grab a beer from the refrigerator and head out to my porch. Bruno follows me and curls up next to my feet.

The music from the guitar picks up and floats through the air. The woman next door is definitely not an amateur guitar player and, judging by the way the music is stopping and starting, it sounds like she is writing a song. After a few moments of listening to her work on the same chords, she moves on to a melody that she already knows. It sounds like country music to me, which I don't particularly care for, but what I do love anytime anywhere is listening to an acoustic guitar.

About an hour later, she stops playing and I hear her door close. If she keeps this up, I'll have to remember to thank Aunt Ella. It's like going to a live concert from home.

Thinking about Aunt Ella, I'll have to ask her if she knows anything about the girl staying in the cottage. Her posture shifted uncomfortably this morning, making me think that she does; now I've just got to get her to tell me. Or maybe I don't. It's not like I plan on being friends with the girl anyway.

Thinking back over my day, as far as November firsts go, it really wasn't that bad. I finish off the beer and stare out across the water. The sun has just crossed the horizon line and the heat from the rays diminishes as they disappear. The burnt orange of the sky is fading, and lavender takes over. I watch the water as it rolls on the shore; the tide is out. I find this symbolic after the way today went, and think maybe the tide in my life is out, too. When the tide is out, it takes everything with it and wipes the slate clean. As morning comes, the tide will be back in, bringing new shells and changing the shore-line, but just a little. Maybe tomorrow I will wake up and find that I'm changed, too, but just a little.

Chapter Five

ELLE

FOR TWO DAYS, I haven't left the beach rental. Aunt Ella checked on me once late yesterday afternoon, but that was it. After the incident on the beach, I'm afraid to go outside. I'm afraid that someone will recognize me. I'm afraid those guys will return. I'm afraid that whoever is after me is going to find me. I have peeked out of the blinds to look at the beach a couple of times, but that's it.

In a way I'm disappointed. I was so excited when I first got here. The freedom that I felt being on my own in this beautiful place next to the beach took just eight hours to all be washed away.

I really don't know what my problem is; I've been to more places than most people will travel to in their lifetime, and I shouldn't be afraid. I've walked in front of all types of people, in all types of places, in all types of designs—even the revealing ones. Lately, it seems like I have to tell myself to just suck it up and do it, which is what I'm doing today.

My stomach growls as I gently and precisely fix my hair into a braid. I know I need to get some food, and I really can't put off going to the doctor anymore. Aunt Ella will be able to recommend someone, and right now those two things—food and a phone number—trump the fear. My hands have hurt so badly the last couple of days. I'm so tired and just generally feel sick.

As I finish 'putting on my face', I look in the mirror and give myself a small smile. Today, I am skipping the bronzer. Mother would be horrified, but I just don't care. That tiny bit of defiance, or crack in what is supposed to be my perfect image, has me feeling like a rebel. It gives me back a little bit of the feeling of freedom that I so desperately want to have.

Bending my fingers, I glance over to the corner of the room as I walk out of the bathroom, and look at my guitar. Playing the guitar is one of the very few things that I do that I enjoy, and lately it has become almost impossible. I've played the last two nights that I've been here, because I've got these chords and lyrics floating in my head that need to come out. The only two people who have ever heard me play are my mother and Livy.

Being on the road for photo shoots and going to go-sees, I've spent a lot of time over the years listening to music. When I turned twenty, I bought myself a guitar. My mother always hated me strumming on it. Playing the guitar, getting lost in the sound, is just about the only thing that makes me feel like me. It's the only thing that I have ever done for myself.

Not too long after I started to play, I felt the pain. The pain wasn't in just one finger. It was in them all, both hands. Of course, my mother blamed it on the guitar, but after a few secret trips to the doctor I found out otherwise.

Grabbing my beach hat, I shove it onto my head, pick up my keys and sunglasses, and head to the door.

Staring at the knob, my heart begins to race. I know I have to do this; no, I need to do this. I can't just stay here and starve to death. Taking in a deep breath, the words *just suck it up and do it* float through my mind and push me out the door.

The sun hits me and I squint at the brightness. Anxiety creeps in as I look at my surroundings. I think maybe I should call Aunt Ella to find out the doctor's number, but that doesn't help me with the food situation. Why is it so hard for me to leave the cottage? It's not like I am agoraphobic. I used to love being outside, around people. It's the fear of celebrity that has made me like this; the fear of who might be watching and what they might want to do to me. The letters have instilled this fear in me, and I hate it.

Quickly climbing into my car, I think about driving back over to Aunt Ella's house, but instead I opt for the café. I figure she's probably working, and it'll be the best place for me to get some food quickly. I can go to the grocery store tomorrow.

Pulling up to the back of the café, I decide to park here instead of next to the beach. It's more private this way, and I don't think anyone will see me. Besides, Aunt Ella will be in the kitchen.

Walking up the stairs, I pull on the back door at the same time someone else forcefully pushes it open. It slams into me, unexpectedly knocking me backward. I miss the step below, and fall off the steps right on my tailbone. My hat and sunglasses fly off, and pain shoots up my back and down to my toes. I can't help but let out a low moan as I squeeze my eyes shut, grit my teeth, and roll onto my side. In the grass, I'm now lying in the fetal position, rubbing my backside.

Vaguely, I hear a deep male voice apologizing, but what does register is that his hands are all over me. He's crouched down next to me, touching my shoulders, back, and legs. His hands are warm—comforting surprisingly.

"Hey, are you alright? Do I need to call someone?" he asks, panicked.

"No, just give me a minute and I'll be fine," I say in a strained tone.

"I'm so sorry. I can't believe that I knocked you down. No one ever uses this door...my hands were full, so I didn't think anything of it and I just kicked it open," he rushes to explain himself.

I know that voice!

Peeking, I look over my shoulder and come face to face with the guy I assaulted with my mouth in front of the café. My body obviously recognizes him because, as soon as I hear his voice, it just slips into a welcomed awareness where everything about him feels familiar. Now I understand why I didn't mind his hands on me; it's like I already know them. His hair has fallen over his forehead, and the most beautiful gray eyes are staring at me, filled with concern.

Gray; now that is something I didn't expect. They are so striking and so clear, yet it's easy to see that they are filled with a mixture of passion, fear, and loneliness. The expression, "Not everything in life is black and white," comes to mind. There's that gray area, just like his stunning eyes.

Something passes between us, and my heart rate picks up. He must feel it, too, because he instantly leans back away from me, clearing his throat. He breaks eye contact and spots my hat and my sunglasses on the ground a few feet away. He grabs them to give them back to me, but pauses just for a second staring at the hat.

"You?" he says quietly.

Oh, of course he wouldn't recognize me, but he would remember the hat. A groan comes out of me and I roll over onto my back, closing my eyes. Self-consciously, I run my hand over my shorts and feel the dirt. I'm going to need to go home and change. These clothes must be filthy.

"Yep, me," I say to him, opening my eyes to stare at the blueness of the sky.

He doesn't say anything, so I look over. My hair has come loose from the braid, and some has fallen across my face. Through the strands our eyes meet again, and my breath catches in my throat.

I know I told myself that I never wanted to see what he looked like, for fear that it would alter my memory of that kiss but, seeing him now, I realize how wrong I was. His eyes, those full lips, the smoothness of his lightly-freckled skin above his cheekbones; he's stunning. I never did give much thought to what he might have thought of our kiss, but now that he's seen me, I can't help but wonder if he was happy or disappointed.

Without saying anything further, he reaches a hand out to me, and I break my gaze from his eyes to look at it. Slowly, I shift and place mine in his. It feels so good to be touched by him. He pulls me to my feet; we can't be standing but a few inches apart. The familiar smell of fresh laundry and something that is distinctly him swirls around me.

I watch as he lifts his hand and sweeps the hair back off of my face, tucking it behind my ear. His fingertips just barely brush my skin, but the nerve endings have exploded and are on fire. His fingers follow the hair down to the ends, where he rolls it between his fingertips. His eyes lock onto mine and I think that I could look at him forever. When he releases it, his hand squeezes into a fist. Neither one of us says anything.

His eyes move from mine to my mouth, pause, and then move down the length of me. He looks at my hat, shakes it out, and then places it on top of my head. His hands fall to my shoulders, gently holding them, and his eyes drop back to my mouth.

"I'm sorry I knocked you down," he says quietly. His voice is so hypnotic. Hearing him, seeing him, having his hands on me, I suddenly feel like I'm in a trance.

I attempt a half-shrug. "It's okay. Thank you for helping me up." My brain has shut off and I can't think of anything else to say. *What the hell is happening to me right now?*

His fingertips squeeze into me and I lean toward him slightly. I'm drawn to him in a way that I don't understand. I want to forget everything but this beautiful guy standing in front of me. I want him to kiss me again, too, so badly.

His breathing picks up just a little, and one hand slides around to the back of my neck. There's a storm in his eyes, behind that striking gray, instantly telling me even more about him than I think he would want seen. He's shy and uncertain. Trish was right; any other guy probably would have closed the distance between us by now, but this guy, Matt, as Aunt Ella called him, is filled with insecurity and it looks almost painful.

Deciding for him, because I need to feel his lips on mine almost as much as I need to breathe, I take a step toward him and lean into his large frame.

He sucks in a ragged breath, letting me know that he's as affected as I am. His other hand slips from my shoulder, down to my lower back, and presses into me.

His fingers dip into my hair and knock the hat off again as he tips my head back to gain better access. His tongue runs across his bottom lip as he lowers his head but, right before he finally connects us, he freezes.

"Ellie?" he whispers in confusion. His brows furrow and he pulls back just a little to look at me again, like, really look at me.

What!?

I jerk away from his hands and shoot him a wary look. How does he know my name? Does he know who I am? And why is he looking at me this way? He looks angry, and his entire body has gone tense.

"How do you know my name?" I ask him suspiciously.

He gives a brief laugh, looks up at the back door, and then at back at me while shaking his head.

"You know, now that I think about it, coming from you . . . I wouldn't expect anything less." He bends down to pick up my hat again and shoves it at me. He then grabs his things he had set down on the back steps, and turns to walk off.

"Wait a second!" I grab his arm. "You can't say something like that and then just leave."

"Why not?" He pins me with a look that says we are done. "You did," he mutters in a much lower tone before he turns back to head for the parking lot.

What is he talking about? And why did he call me Ellie? Aunt Ella is the only one who has ever called me that. I continue to watch him as he climbs into a large black Jeep and drives away. He glances back at me once more, and the irritation on his face only seems to have grown stronger. I can't understand why this person, this stranger, is so angry with me.

My stomach sinks and a wave of regret engulfs me. That hopeful feeling that was blooming inside of me is now squashed.

Brushing off my shorts, I head up the steps and into the kitchen. Aunt Ella sees me and frowns.

"What happened to you?" she asks, coming over to inspect me.

"That guy…Matt that you know, he kicked open the door a few minutes ago and I was on the other side of it."

She pinches her lips together to try to stop the smile, but it doesn't work. She lets out a laugh and I end up laughing with her. I don't know what else to do; it's either laugh or cry.

"That guy Matt that I know? You know him, too," she says, giving me a knowing look.

"No, I don't." I wouldn't forget someone as beautiful as him.

"Oh, really?" she says, challenging me. "I seem to remember you spending quite a bit of time in that shed with him during that last summer you were here."

All she had to say was the word 'shed' and I know exactly who she is talking about. My jaw and my stomach drop.

"I . . ." I'm speechless, and I feel disoriented. How could I forget the quiet neighborhood boy from the shed?

"Handsome nowadays, isn't he?" she says, giving me another sly smile.

My mouth snaps shut and my cheeks burn as I shake my head. It can't be him, but it is. I remember thinking that the boy who played in the shed was one of the cutest boys I had ever seen, even though he was a bit younger than me. Cute is nowhere near the word that I would use to describe him now.

"I'm surprised you didn't recognize him. He is kind of one of a kind." She's proud, thinking of him. I can't help but wonder what he means to her.

"Why would I? He was a thirteen-year-old kid. I haven't thought of him in almost eight years." I'm being defensive, and I wonder again if she is seeing through my layers. For two days, I have thought about that kiss and how it felt to be in his arms, over and over again. Now I just feel stupid.

My heart sinks with the realization that he was going to kiss me again, but the second he figured out who I was, he became completely repulsed by me. That kiss meant so much to me, but clearly the sentiment is not returned. I feel foolish and I haven't done anything wrong; at least, not that I know of.

"Huh. Well what do you think of him now?" She's fishing for something.

Looking away from her so she can't see the disappointment in my eyes, I spot an address book next to the kitchen phone; the reason I'm at the café in the first place.

"I don't think anything of him. I don't even know him." And apparently he doesn't want to know anything about me either. Remembering the way he frowned in disgust as he walked off, I'm stuck with a sadness that I shouldn't feel.

Whatever. He'd just be another complication; another person to disappoint when he learns how not-so-perfect I really am.

MATT

NEVER IN A million years would I have guessed that the girl from in front of the café is Aunt Ella's niece, Ellie. I haven't seen her in almost eight years and, even then, my memories of her aren't that great.

She used to visit during the summers, and the only reason I remember her last summer here was because it was right after I got back from helping Beau move to New York. He had let me stay for a couple of weeks, and I was devastated when I had to come home. I had asked him if I could stay there with him, but he said no. I understand now; after all, he was three years younger than I am now, but I felt like he didn't want me even though he said he did. He blamed it on Mom, and maybe she would have said no, but I wanted him to fight for me. Thinking back, I feel bad for the things that I wanted from him. He was still just a kid himself.

I spent a lot of time in the shed. It was where I was most comfortable. Mom was hardly ever home, and when she was, it was uncomfortable between us. Beau had been the buffer over the last year and, with him gone, she didn't know what to say. With Beau gone, I talked even less.

If I remember correctly, Ellie is two years older than I am. She would wander into the shed during the afternoon summer storms, sit on the floor, and watch me while I tinkered with whatever I was trying to build at the time. Every now and then, she would huff, express how bored she was, and complain about the heat. Maybe that's what all fifteen-year-old girls do, but she was a snob through and through.

When it was time for her to leave town, she came to the shed and asked me if I was going to come out and say good-bye. I looked at her funnily and said, "Good-bye." We weren't friends. I didn't have any, and we never even spoke. So why she thought I was going to see her off, I don't know.

Her face fell and then her eyes narrowed. "Whatever, freak," and then she stormed out.

Other than Aunt Ella and Uncle Ben, she was the only person to ever come and sit with me in the shed. Although she was miserable to be around, I was going to miss the company, and I was going to miss looking at her. She was beautiful then, nothing like now, but even then she was a walking dream to me: long hair, pretty face, legs that went on for days.

Freak. To be called a name like that at thirteen, by a pretty older girl, sticks with you. I just added this name to all of the others that I had been called over the years, and retreated even further into myself. I hadn't done anything wrong recently, that I could think of, so if she said it, it must've been true.

That one word shaped my teenage years. Already considered a loner, when girls started to stare at me, I thought that was why. The giggling, smiling, and attention that I received, I thought they were making fun of me and not once did I smile back.

Sure, Aunt Ella mentioned her every now and then, and I had kind of watched her success over the years. It's hard not to when it's splashed on the covers of various magazines. I would be lying if I said she wasn't drop-dead gorgeous, because she is. Seeing her now in person doesn't change that at all, except I think she is too thin.

Her hair is a dark golden blonde, and it was pulled back in a braid. Pieces had fallen out when she fell, and were hanging all around her face. It wasn't until she stood up and I wiped them away that I fully saw her face.

I kept thinking that she looked familiar, and I was trying to place her, but all that my body was doing was remembering how familiar the feeling of her mouth and body pressed against mine already was.

Her eyes are huge and chocolate brown; the exact shade of Aunt Ella's. She has high cheek bones and a mouth with perfectly pouty lips, and her skin is flawless except for the dark circles underneath her eyes. This girl looks run down and exactly like Aunt Ella. In fact, she could have passed for her daughter. That's when it hit me.

Uncle Ben did not like Aunt Ella's sister. I overheard them several times, arguing about how she was superficial, ungrateful, and a freeloader. I wasn't sure what all of those things meant, but if they didn't like her, then they probably didn't like her daughter either. After all, I'd seen firsthand how much of a brat she was.

I didn't mean to glance back at her as I drove away, but I couldn't help it. I left her standing there, stunned and confused, and I felt bad. I would never tell her that, though; not that it matters. I don't plan on seeing her or interacting with her any more. The thought of this makes my chest ache, and I reach up to rub the spot. The warmth that I had felt, the wholeness, was there again today and I don't understand it. Instead of feeling an electricity when I touched her, I felt shocked when I let go. It's like the hole in my chest would shrink, and then it would snap back open.

That isn't supposed to happen. Not with her. Not with anybody.

Frustrated, I pull up in front of my cottage, look over to number two, and that's when it dawns on me . . . she's the guest! She has to be. Aunt Ella put her in one of my cottages and didn't tell me. Now I understand why she was acting all weird about it.

Not wanting to be anywhere near where she might be, I throw the Jeep in reverse, and decide to head to the North Shore house instead. Even though it is less than a mile away, when I am there I feel like I am somewhere else, somewhere different. It's quiet and, because of the way it's been constructed, the breeze blows in differently. It's calming. I need calm right now. I need to wipe her away from my mind, past and present.

Stepping onto the back patio, I am met with intense heat from the afternoon sun. It's hotter today than it has been over the last couple of days, and sure enough there are the sun's rays; mocking, laughing, not letting me forget.

DAVE AND I had made plans to meet at the Sandbar. I lost track of time working on the North Shore house. The tile that I had ordered for the kitchen here and for cottage number two had come in in earlier today, so to work off my frustration I got down on my hands and knees and got to work. That's what I do; I shut everything out, and lose myself in focusing on only my hands and the work in front of me.

The sun set pretty quickly today, leaving it dark by seven-thirty. I glance up at the stars right before walking in, and think about Beau. Beau loves the stars, and it's kind of rubbed off on me over the years. He swears that if you wish on them long enough, your dreams will come true. They did for him. But I stopped wishing a long time ago. Now, I just admire them from afar and thank them for giving Beau his dream come true.

The restaurant isn't too crowded. I instantly spot Davy at the bar. He doesn't realize I'm here. He seems to be too busy watching someone else. His face is cloaked with amusement. I follow his gaze and my eyes land on Ellie. She's laughing with the bartender and instantly I see red. I'm furious that she is here. I spent all afternoon trying to work away the tension of the encounter with her this afternoon, and in less than one se-cond my progress is shattered. I'm suddenly not really in the mood to be out tonight.

As I approach Davy, he nods his head at me but his eyes flick back to her. "Hey, man, why don't we head outside? It's nice tonight." I say, without even looking her way. I'm hoping she won't notice me.

"Sure." He grabs his water and we both begin to head for the patio door.

Ever since I met Davy a year ago, I have never seen him drink a beer or anything else that would be considered an adult beverage. So, I was surprised when he asked if I wanted to go out tonight. Neither one of us is much of a night owl. I prefer mornings for running, and he prefers them for fishing.

Just as I am about to walk through the door, a hand lands on my arm before a very disheveled Ellie steps in front of me, stumbling and giggling.

"Maaatttty . . .," she drawls out my name.

My teeth clench in frustration and my eyes slide shut; so much for trying to sneak past her.

Davy turns around, and the amusement that I saw on him just a few seconds ago kicks up a notch. Scowling at him, I drop my eyes to her.

"That's not my name," I snap at her.

"Sure it is, and it suits you so well," she giggles again, and her hair swings around her face. My fingers tingle with the sudden urge to push it back, like earlier. She's a beautiful mess tonight.

My arm is burning where her hand is. Every nerve ending is on alert and pointing straight at her. My body is reacting as if it knows her, just like the other two times she's touched me, and the ache in my chest is getting stronger.

Frowning at her, I push her to the side and head for a table in front of the band. I don't know what she wants from me, and I am not interested in finding out either.

On the weekends, the Sandbar has a local band that plays and, for the most part, they are pretty good. They write their own music and play some classic covers, like Jimmy Buffet, that tourists enjoy.

"Sounds like you do know this one, huh, man?" Davy asks, smirking at me as he sits down on the stool next to mine.

I glance back and see that Ellie has made her way over to the outside bar, and the bartender is grinning widely at her. Anger streaks through me over looking at her, and then anger streaks through me again at myself. Why do I care who looks at her? She's a spoiled brat.

I shrug my shoulders, pissed off, and look over to Davy. "Not really. I know *of* her more than anything. Take a closer look; don't you recognize her?" I watch as his eyes travel over the length of her, stop on her legs, and that's when it clicks.

"She's the girl from in front of the café." He's so excited he figured it out, although that wasn't the answer I was expecting.

Leaning over to him, I say, "Yeah, but take a closer look."

We are both watching her now as she leans over and pats the bartender on the face. My heart rate increases a little and warmth floods my cheeks. I don't want her hands on anyone else. My lips pinch into a thin line. The bartender is loving every second that she is giving him, whereas I want to drag her out of here by her hair.

"She doesn't look familiar to me," Davy says.

"That's Elle Summers." Just saying her name makes me feel weird, and that spot in my chest starts to ache.

"The model?" Shock registers on his face and, as he looks over her again, so does the recognition. Ellie is beautiful. She could easily blend in everywhere she goes as the girl next door, but she can also class it up, making her stand out over everyone else.

"Yep, I'm surprised that wasn't your first guess."

"Honestly, I wouldn't know. I don't keep up with Hollywood stuff, dude." He looks away, ending the conversation.

The band strikes up a new song, *Sittin' on the Dock of the Bay* by Otis Redding, and she spins around to watch.

Given this moment, I know I shouldn't, but I drink in her every detail. She is so beautiful. Her hair is dark blonde and long. It looks messy, like she hasn't brushed it in days, but I can tell by the way it frames her face that she has. It looks good on her. She's wearing what looks like a large men's button-down dress shirt with the sleeves rolled up, but it's not, it is a dress. There's a belt around her waist, making her tiny frame look even tinier, and she has on flip flops. I let out a sigh and tear my eyes from her. She looks so damn perfect, as much as I hate to admit it.

"What do you think she is doing here on the island by herself?" Davy asks. He is still looking at her, too.

"I don't know. She's Aunt Ella's niece."

"Ella, Elle, I get it now." His gaze lingers on her just a beat longer and then he turns toward the band.

It's funny he says that, because I never picked up on the name resemblance before.

I spend most of the evening trying to ignore her, but every now and then, my eyes wander over back to her. She stays seated at the bar, drinks her drinks, and watches the band, looking lost in her thoughts. Thinking back to Davy's question, I start wondering, too; what is she doing here?

Two hours later, Davy and I decide to call it a night. He sees me eyeing her, and he pats me on the back before he walks out. As much as I don't want to have any interaction with her at all, should something happen to her tonight, I would feel responsible. Aunt Ella means a lot to me, and leaving her niece sitting here when she's very obviously been drinking wouldn't be right. I'm doing this for her.

"You should let me take you home." I move to stand right

in front of her so she can focus on me. Her knees brush my thighs, so I lean in a little closer, just to feel her for a second. There's that feeling again; the wholeness feeling.

Her glassy eyes shoot me an angry look. "Excuse me, but I am not that kind of girl."

I can't help but smirk back, and she narrows her eyes at me while her cheeks turn pink. Hearing her say this makes me so happy that something inside of me opens and relaxes.

I don't say anything back to her, and we just stare at each other, never breaking eye contact. Everyone around us slips away.

"I never wanted to come back to this place," she blurts out. Her eyes widen, like she didn't mean to tell me this.

"So, why did you?" I ask, tilting my head a little to the side.

"Because, I'm . . ." her chin begins to tremble, and she shakes her head to clear whatever thought has invaded her mind.

"You're what?" I push her to answer.

She straightens up and locks her eyes back on to mine. "I'm taking a break," she says confidently.

"Well, that's a vague answer. A break from what?" Not being able to resist anymore, I reach over and tuck a piece of her hair behind her ear. My fingers skim along her ear and down her neck. Her eyelids flutter slightly, but just for a second. I needed to make that contact with her, and I hate myself for it. Her reaction is not the one I expect, though; it's almost as if she needed it from me as well.

"Best I've got and a break from everything." She's not going to give me any more, I guess, and that's fine. I really don't want to know. I hand the bartender my credit card to close out her tab, and help her off the chair. She surprises me when she slips her hand into mine, never once looking at me. I tighten my hand around hers to let her know I've got her, and together we walk out of the bar.

She's quiet all the way to the Jeep. I open her door for her, and she climbs in and buckles her seat belt. I've never been more thankful that I'm a quiet person. I don't know what to say to her, so I don't say anything.

Pulling up to my cottage, she doesn't say anything about me not parking in front of her house. I wonder if she even realizes I live next door. Instead, she climbs out and hands me her keys. I unlock the door and she passes by me, blonde hair brushing me as she does. A large gray cat immediately starts circling her legs. She bends down, picks it up, gives it a hug, and hands it to me. I freeze instantly. *What the hell?* What am I supposed to do with this cat? Kicking the door shut, I follow her in and drop it onto the couch.

"My mother hates Aunt Ella," her voice echoes a little through the house, and I feel it everywhere. Even her voice is beautiful.

"Why?" How could anyone hate Aunt Ella?

"She wanted her house . . . her marriage . . . her niece . . . her life. She's never been happy with what she was given. She always wants what other people have." Her voice is withdrawn, sad, and now I'm wondering if I might have misjudged her. I mean, what do I really know about her? I'm judging her based on what I remember of a fifteen-year-old girl, some stuck-up socialite pictures found in a few tabloid magazines, and the fact that Uncle Ben didn't like her mom. Maybe she isn't like her mother at all. I'm not like mine, after all.

Looking around the house, it doesn't seem like she brought a lot of things. I had expected it to be cluttered and filled with shoes, bags, and other girly crap when, in fact, she's kept the place pretty neat. She doesn't appear to be overly high-maintenance, and the perception that I had of her being a brat begins to fade. The snobby teenager is gone, and in her place is a beautiful woman. One who is a complete mystery to me.

She briefly glances at me before wandering into her bedroom. Her eyes are sad.

"You know, I do know who you are. Aunt Ella told me," she says over her shoulder.

I don't say anything back to her, but now I'm wondering what she was told.

She kicks off her flip flops, pulls the belt free, and begins unbuttoning the dress. I can't tear my eyes away from her and she doesn't seem to mind. The dress drops to the floor and then she's standing there in the tiniest, laciest pale pink bra and underwear I have ever seen.

Holy shit.

I thought she was beautiful before, but seeing her like this . . . there isn't a word in the English language to describe her. I'm spellbound watching her, and I think my heart just stopped and skipped a few beats.

She turns around and climbs into her bed. I unfold an old blanket lying at her feet and drape it over her.

"I should have figured it out, or remembered at least. You were cute back then, but now..." She's staring up at me, a wide-eyed and innocent expression gracing her gorgeous face. She stares at me for a moment longer, neither of us saying a word, but I can tell she is fighting a losing battle with her heavy eyelids. She pulls the blanket up and wraps it around her shoulders. Her eyes close and, within seconds, her breathing evens out and she's asleep.

What does that mean? But now... What am I now to her?

Chapter Six

ELLE

THE POUNDING IN my head slowly begins to get louder and louder. Rolling over on to my side, that's when I realize it isn't my head but someone knocking on the door. Stumbling out of bed, I wrap my blanket around me and shuffle over. Peeking through the hole, I see Matt standing on the other side. His back is to me, and he is staring out toward the beach.

"What are you doing here?" I yell through the door. He jerks around and my breath catches in my throat. *Oh my . . .*

"Open the door," he says. I watch as he lifts the baseball cap, runs a hand through his hair, and then shoves it back on.

"No." I'm not opening the door for him. I don't care how handsome he is. He was rude to me yesterday at Aunt Ella's, and he can't just boss me around. Wait a second! *Oh, no . . .* I jump back from the peephole as flashes from last night come flooding in.

I didn't mean to drink as much as I did. I didn't expect for him to show up at the bar, and I didn't realize how much it would hurt when he showed no interest in me. He didn't want to talk to me or even be seen with me. He made me feel inadequate, which made me feel worse than I already did. Humiliated, I stayed at the bar and continued to drown my sorrows by myself.

It wasn't until the end of the night, after his friend left, that he made his way over to me. I'll never tell him this, but I spent most of the night watching him and his friend. In a distant way, I felt like I was out with them, even though I wasn't. And spending those ten minutes with him in the Jeep, from the bar to the house, I felt more whole and safe than I have in a long time. He may be rude, but he was still a gentleman. He brought me home and tucked me in.

"I have a key. Now, you have a choice." There's an edge to his voice.

Letting out a sigh, I twist the deadbolt and crack open the door. On the other side is Matt and, as much as I try not to think about it, he looks so good. His bright gray eyes find mine, and regard me warily.

"What are you doing here?" I tighten the blanket around me.

"I'm here to work on the floors." He says very matter-of-factly. It's then that his eyes leave mine and travel over the length of me. The heat of a blush burns on my cheeks. It occurs to me that I'm wearing hardly anything at all under the blanket, and that he probably saw me dressed like this last night.

"The floors?" I choke out, completely embarrassed.

His eyes snap back to mine. "Yeah, Ella told me she informed you that they are being replaced this week."

"Oh, so you're, like, her handyman?" I don't know what I

thought he did for a living, but side jobs and repairs wasn't it. Then again, maybe he likes it. Even at thirteen, he was building stuff in that shed.

He smirks at me and pulls open the screen door. "Something like that." Behind him is a large white truck, with the tailgate open. In the bed of the truck, there are boxes which I assume are the tiles.

Whatever. He doesn't need my help, and he's coming in regardless, apparently. Turning around, I head back to bed. I hear the door close behind me, and my heart rate picks up just knowing that he and I are in here alone. The little rental, which felt cozy and like home before, now feels small. He fills the space, and he carries around this tension that sucks the air out of the room. He doesn't say anything more to me; he just gets right to work.

Through the bedroom door, I watch him. He moves the furniture out of the way and, with an X-acto, knife he begins to cut away the carpet in the little living room.

Tossing back and forth under the covers, my eyes keep being drawn back to him. I'm sure he knows that I'm watching him. I don't know what is wrong with me. He hasn't even acknowledged me since he got here, but I'm hyper-aware of him. It's driving me crazy. Sure, I've had guys over to my condo before, but none of them left me feeling like this. Having him in my space is messing with my hormones. For hours, he's moved around the little room, completely ignoring me, which I am trying to convince myself is a redeeming quality.

He's wearing a pair of navy athletic shorts that hang perfectly on him, a light yellow island t-shirt that is sweat-soaked and clinging to him, and an old baseball hat that is flipped around backwards, probably to keep his espresso-colored hair off of his face. I can faintly hear music blaring from the earbuds in his ears, and every time he has to apply some type of strength to something, he pulls his bottom lip in between his teeth. He doesn't even realize how good he looks to me right now.

I could watch him all day, but what would be the point? I'm just torturing myself. He's made it perfectly clear that he has zero interest in me.

My eyes drift from Matt to my nightstand. My cell phone is sitting there, taunting me with the reminder of all the missed calls, voicemails, emails, texts, tweets and retweets awaiting me. The mere thought has me pulling the blanket around me even higher.

Yesterday, after I got back from Aunt Ella's, I knew I shouldn't have turned it on, but the responsible side of me wanted to see if I had any urgent messages, and I needed to review my calendar. If I planned on staying here for a while, I needed to make sure Livy knew which clients would need to be contacted and canceled.

Of course, immediately, ten missed calls from my mother and four from Connor flash on the screen. I knew that there would be some kind of ripple due to my disappearing, but I never expected my mother to use this as an opportunity to stir up drama within the media world. Without even opening the social media icons, the red bubble with the number of notifications alerted me to her dirty work.

I can just hear her. If she's said it one time, she's said it a thousand times: "There is no such thing as bad publicity."

She has always used every little thing she could think of to draw attention to me, and I should have known that she would use this, too. Just remembering her voicemails, the disapproving tone, then the yelling about how I am making her look, and finally how brilliant I am to gain some media face time . . . It's because of her that I ended up at the Sandbar last night.

I'm so tired of living my life for other people. Even in the privacy of my own home, I'm constantly being forced to consider others' expectations of me. *Watch what you eat. Watch what you say. Be mindful of what you wear. Be careful where you go. Watch who you associate with.* It's all an endless cycle of being watched and judged. Living in the spotlight and being somewhat well-known, everything about your life is open for discussion. And my mother is the worst. Thank God for Livy. I don't know what I would have done all these years without her.

Needing to get up and stretch, I step out of his line of sight through the door, and slip on a tank top and a pair of shorts. I need water and some Ibuprofen after last night. *What was I thinking?* I never drink like that.

Pretending Matt isn't here, I head into the kitchen. He's done such a great job pretending that I don't exist, I may as well return the favor.

"Nice sun tattoo," I hear him say. "What made you get it?" His voice is so unexpected, he startles me, and I jump around to face him. My eyes lock onto his. He looks . . . angry? His gray eyes are darker, and it's as if thunder clouds have filled them for an impending storm. I'm not sure why he would be, though. He has a sword tattoo on his arm. I spotted it yesterday when he was shoving my hat at me.

Running my hand across my lower back, I want to hide it.

"It's me. It's for my name," I answer him, looking away.

His brows are pulled down. His gray eyes have darkened, and he continues to stare at me. The silence between us, and his scrutiny, becomes uncomfortable, and I look away.

"Elle, short for Eleana. That's my actual birth name. At

the time, my mother was really into the zodiac, astrology, and Greek Mythology. Eleana in Greek means 'daughter of the sun'." I reach into the refrigerator and pull out a bottle of water that was already stocked when I arrived.

I turn back around, to see his jaw tense and his eyes narrow. He doesn't say anything else, but walks back over to where he was working. He was angry yesterday at the café, angry with me last night at the Sandbar, and it seems he's angry today, too. I want to ask him why. I want to know what I ever did to him. But I'm not sure if he would answer me, so I don't.

It was Livy's idea for us to get a tattoo. Right after our parents divorced, we were out one night and we decided right then and there that, no matter what happened with them, we were always going to be sisters. We needed a grand gesture to seal our pact. Little girls share lockets or bracelets, but we weren't little girls, and no one could tell us what to do.

After we agreed on getting a tattoo, I immediately knew what I wanted—the sun. Livy thought it was brilliant, and she decided to get the moon; each of us being two halves that made a whole. I loved it. Both of us went with the lower back, really lower back. Well, below the waistline. The fact that Matt just saw the tattoo means that these shorts are more loose than normal, and they slipped really low when I bent over. I'm used to people looking at my body, but for some reason when it's him, I'm nervous.

Letting out a sigh, I realize there's nothing I can do about it now.

I look down at the water bottle I pulled from the refrigerator. It's just a simple water bottle, and my heart sinks when I realize there is no way I'm going to be able to open it. My joints hurt, and gripping the lid will be impossible. This flare-up just seems to be getting worse, and now I have to ask for his help.

I can feel my face flush as heat rises in my cheeks. I don't know if it's more from the embarrassment that I have to ask, or if it's that I have to ask him. I am a grown woman and I have to have my bottles opened. I'm frustrated with myself and mortified and half-tempted to drink water straight out of the sink, only I hate the taste of tap water. Pushing my pride aside, I turn to face him, and mentally tell myself to suck it up and do it.

"Matty . . ."

He hears me call his name, pulls one earbud out, and he shoots me a look to remind me that he doesn't like to be called that. I want to smirk back at him, but I really need him to help me.

"I can't get this to open. Will you open it for me please? It's on really tight," I say in a rush.

He puts the tools down and walks back over to me. He looks confused. I can't say that I blame him. Even small children can open water bottles. He studies me just for a second, and then his gaze drops, looking me over from head to toe, and lands on the water bottle. Our fingers brush as he takes the bottle, and sparks shoot straight through me. His eyes return to mine as he easily twists off the cap and hands it back. Warmth is radiating off of him, and I want to grab on to him, feel his skin, and be wrapped in his arms. I want to go back to that moment on the sidewalk in front of the café and freeze time, but instead I stand here and do nothing.

"Thank you," I say quietly. "I mean, not only with this, but for last night, too."

His face is blank. *10,000 Summers* by No Devotion fills the air between us. He looks down at me through hooded eyes, and works his bottom lip in between his teeth. Oh, how I want to know what he is thinking, but then it occurs to me that I never looked in a mirror this morning.

Oh, my God. I probably look like a complete hot mess. I never let anyone see me without a full face. The thought that a photo of me this way could leak out has me taking a step back away from him. I move my eyes away from him and look at the Ibuprofen on the counter. I feel ashamed and I don't know why. My face flushes and I know he sees it.

His eyes follow mine and he sees the bottle. Reaching over he grabs it, opens it, and hands me two. Did he open the bottle just to be nice, or has he realized that I can't? Either way, I am grateful.

"Thank you," I say again.

He nods his head at me. He looks like he is about to ask me something, but then he turns around to go back to his work.

Walking straight into the bathroom, I close the door and lean back against it. My heart is racing. He's said all of six words to me over the last couple of hours, and I am completely affected by him; his beautiful face, his gorgeous tall physique. The way he smells like sweat and fresh laundry is intoxicating. And his hands . . . everything that his hands touch, I am jealous of. I know how they feel against my skin, and I want more. More of him. Too bad he doesn't feel the same.

Glancing in the mirror, I wince and quickly grab the foundation to even out my skin color.

MATT

ALL I CAN think is that life is laughing at me.

The one and only girl that I have ever remotely had any type of reaction to and she's named after the sun. How is that even possible? I'm destined to be punished, to be reminded constantly. This is just another reason in the long list of them that she is not meant to be mine, not that I'm entertaining the idea of pursuing her. I have to admit, she's gotten to me.

Letting out a sigh, I toss down the tools and pick up the carpet pile to take it outside. I need some space from her; I need to clear my head.

When she walked into the kitchen in that tight tank top and those tiny little shorts, I couldn't help but watch her. Her hair was all bed-messy, and I could only imagine how warm her skin was from laying under the covers. I wonder if she looks like that every morning because, right now, only one word comes to mind in describing her . . . perfect.

And then she bent over into the refrigerator. At first I thought my eyes were playing a trick on me but, nope, there permanently marked on her beautiful skin was a tattoo of the sun. I can never escape it; no matter what I do, it's there.

I do have to admit that the tattoo is really nice. Since she has it so low, it's a half-sun that is either coming or going on the horizon. It's not large and obnoxious like some are, and in a way it does look good on her. But a sun?

Throwing the old carpet into the back of the truck, I stop and look at the tattoo on my forearm. I wonder if she loves her tattoo as much as I love mine. Just thinking about the day I got it makes me smile.

"Wake-up, birthday boy!"

I open my eyes to see Drew lying next to me on my bed. I'm confused as to what he's doing here and wonder if I'm dreaming, when I hear Beau chuckle from behind him.

"Ah, are we disturbing you, Sleeping Beauty? Drew, you might want to be careful. Did you know that one out of fifty teenagers still wets the bed?"

Drew laughs, "Is that what they are calling it nowadays? And here I thought it was all about the teenage dreams."

"Dude," on that note, I push him off of the bed. "What are you both doing here? How did you get in?"

"We are here because it's your birthday and Aunt Ella gave us a key. The cottages are coming along nicely. Good job on them, by the way. We are both thoroughly impressed."

Hearing them give me the compliment makes me smile on the inside.

I look over to Bruno, who is standing on his hind legs, front paws on Beau's chest, and he is getting petted. "Some guard dog you are." He turns at my voice and I swear he smiles.

Drew hops off the bed, "Get up and get dressed; we've got plans today."

Both of them walk out of the room and Bruno follows. I can't believe that they are here. I had planned on Mom stopping by, and for Aunt Ella to make me a cake; she always does, but that was about it. It's crazy that they both flew here from the city to be with me. With me. Excitement fills me.

Quickly, I dress and walk into the living room, where Beau is watching Drew out the window. He's taken Bruno out so we can head out as soon as I'm ready.

"So, what are the plans today?" I ask Beau.

"Fishing!" He grins at me as he pulls a piece of salt water taffy out of his pocket. He raises it to offer it to me, but I decline. Him and that taffy.

I laugh because I should have known; the three of us fishing together has always been our thing. "I still can't believe you guys are here."

"Of course we're here. Today is the day you are officially legal." He smirks at me, shoves the candy into his mouth, and I grin back.

"But first, before we get to the boat, we are making a quick stop," he says.

"Oh yeah?"

"Yep! It's time to officially make you a ninja," he grins at me.

My breath catches in my throat and my stomach bottoms out. As silly as it sounds, these are words that I've dreamt about hearing and never thought I would, like, ever. He wants to make me a ninja? Why? It's not like I'm actually one of them. He knows this.

For years, I watched the two of them and their ritual of bumping their arms together as a sign of endearment. That was their thing. When they were kids, they loved the Teenage Mutant Ninja Turtles and they would fake fight, pretending their arms were swords. When I turned six, they gave me all of their turtles and told me to take care of them. I used to keep them in the shed along with the binoculars; now I have them here in a safe place in the cottage. When Beau turned eighteen, they got the tattoos and I was so jealous. I wanted one, too, although I never told them that.

"Does he know?" I turn and look at Beau.

"Does who know what?" he looks at me curiously, seeing

that the lightness of the moment is gone.

I can't say it out loud, so I just look at Beau and watch as the understanding of what I am asking spreads across his face.

"Wait, you know?" he breathes out, taking a step toward me.

I nod my head at him. He doesn't need to know that she never told me, that I overheard them talking. It's really irrelevant.

"It doesn't matter, Matt. You are every bit one of us and with us. We love you," he says while reaching over and squeezing my shoulder.

His words are like shock paddles straight to my heart. I've longed to hear those words—'one of us'—since the day I found out. I can see in his eyes that he means it.

"I know that, but I think we should tell him first." I had never planned on telling Drew, but before I do this, it now seems I have to.

"That's your decision, not mine. The blood that runs through you means nothing to me. All that matters is you, and you know that. You're my little dude, and nothing can change that, even if you aren't so little anymore." He chuckles, trying to lighten the mood, but there are unshed tears in my eyes.

When Dad was around, before he went to jail, I tried so hard to be everything that he wanted me to be. To be accepted and to feel like I belonged. After all those years of hearing, "You're no son of mine," after Mom's confession I heard, "You're no brother of ours." Drew and Beau never did anything to warrant me feeling like this; I just couldn't help it.

At that moment, the door flies open. Drew walks in and sees the emotions bouncing back and forth between the two of us.

"What's going on?" he asks.

Beau and I continue to stand there and stare at each other. Blinking, one tear rolls down my cheek. I feel like an idiot. In the span of ten minutes, I've gone from feeling accepted and loved by my two big brothers, to fear that it's now going to be ripped away.

Swallowing, I take a deep breath and turn to face Drew. Beau keeps his hand on my shoulder and I know it's his way of giving me support. "I'm not really your brother."

"What are you talking about?" his brows furrow and he takes another step closer to us.

"Apparently, our dear sweet mother had an affair," Beau chimes in for me. I'm so glad that he didn't make me say it.

"What?!" he looks back and forth between the two of us and runs his hand through his hair. "You knew about this?" he asks Beau.

"Yep," he says flatly.

"Huh." Drew's eyes turn and travel over the length of me. "I always wondered where your eye color came from. Just figured it was some recessive gene thing," he says like he's solved one of the world's greatest mysteries.

My heart is pounding in my chest and a cold sweat has broken out across my forehead.

"I'm sorry," Drew says as he places his hand on my other shoulder.

"What are you sorry for?" I peek back up at him.

He tilts his head to the side, "I'm sorry because our piece-of-shit father isn't even related to you by blood, but you still got stuck with him. Your life could have been so much different, so much better," he drawls.

I can't help but laugh, although it's a dry, humorless laugh. "Doubt it," I answer, frowning. I get to live with being rejected twice.

"Did you ever figure out who your real father is?" Beau asks, dropping his hand.

"Nope, turns out he didn't want me either." I shake out of Drew's grasp and go into the kitchen to feed Bruno. I didn't mean to say that out loud.

Drew follows me into the kitchen and props a hip against the counter, crossing his feet at the ankles. "Hey," he says, getting my attention. "Parents be damned. We've got you and you've got us. You know that, right?"

I just nod my head at him, afraid to say anything. Maybe he doesn't care after all. Now, I feel kind of stupid for worrying all this time. I should have trusted them a little more and had this conversation a long time ago. "We've got you and you've got us." I will never forget him saying this. All I have ever wanted was to keep them—my brothers—and that fear that they wouldn't want me releases its choking grip. It's been four years, and I feel like I can finally breathe. Taking a deep breath, I look at him, and he sees how much his saying that means to me.

He studies me for a few more seconds, then pushes off the counter and he breaks out into a huge grin. "Well, let's get going! Did Beau tell you about our first stop?"

"You still want me to get it?" He still wants me to be a ninja, and my heart just soars with a sense of belonging.

"Of course, why wouldn't I?" he runs his hand back and forth across my head to mess up my hair.

"Because . . ." my voice cracks and he hears it. I'm so happy and hopeful at the same time.

"Little dude, the fact that you just outed Mom for being a hussy changes nothing. I'm not sure why you thought it would." He winks at me and smiles.

Beau busts out laughing from the other room. "Man, I

cannot believe that you just called her that. That's gross and wrong on so many levels."

"Whatever. It doesn't matter now anyway. Our parents stopped defining who we are a long time ago. Let's go induct our boy here." He pushes me out of the kitchen and toward the front door.

I love how they never even asked me if I wanted it. I was getting it regardless.

Ellie's cat meowing by the front door snaps me out of the memory.

"No way, fur ball, back in the house." The girl already seems to have enough on her plate, telling her that her cat ran off because I didn't close the door all the way . . . not going to happen.

I walk back into the house at the same time Ellie comes out of the bathroom. She's fixed herself up the way that girls do, and this saddens me a little. I liked her all messy. She walks back into her bedroom and climbs back into the bed.

A couple more hours pass. I may not be blatantly watching her, but I am. She fell back asleep, and I couldn't help pulling her blanket up around her a little higher. I don't know why I did it; I just wanted to touch something that was hers.

On the nightstand is her bottle of water. I think back to earlier how she stared down at the bottle like she didn't know what to do with it. Her breathing picked up slightly and, as she held it in her left hand, I noticed that she tried flexing and fisting her fingers on the right. There's something going on with her, not that I would ask her, but not being able to open a bottle of water doesn't seem normal.

I walk back into the kitchen, open the refrigerator door, and loosen all of the water caps just in case she wants one and

I'm not here.

Chapter Seven

ELLE

SOME DAYS ARE hard. A lot harder than others. I've never given much thought to suffering from depression, but now I'm not so sure.

What is depression really, anyway? How is it defined? I've heard the term clinical depression, and I understand that some people really do suffer and battle everyday with this terrible illness, so I can't be compared to them, but are there different layers? Are there different kinds? Is this what is happening to me?

My everyday life is so busy that I am constantly moving, and there is never any time to think about things, to think about what my life has become. There's no pause, there's no slowing down; it's constant movement . . . but here, I've come to a screeching halt.

Staring out the window, I watch as the tree next to cottage number three sways in the wind. I can't see the beach from here. I'm facing away from it. I'm certain that it is sparkling and beautiful, but I don't want to see beautiful . . . I want to see nothing. I feel like nothing, which I know isn't true. I just can't help it. Tears leak out of my eyes, but I don't know why.

I try to remind myself of all of the good in my life. I should be proud that I have a job so many girls just dream of, I love where I live, and I have the most wonderful best friend anyone could ever have.

So why do I feel like this? Why can't I shake it? I feel like I am plummeting into a darkness face-first and there is no way to turn around and walk out. Sadly, though, today I don't know if I care.

Rolling out of bed, I stumble into the hallway. Otis slinks by me, and any other day I would be able to move around him, but not today. I hurt all over and I end up accidentally kicking him. He lets out a small cry and my heart frowns. It's finally time for me to see the doctor. It can't wait any longer.

I can feel Matt looking at me. The butterflies in my stomach have taken flight, but I just don't care. He's been here for at least two hours already, and I couldn't even bring myself to say good morning. He knocked on the door today, just like he did yesterday, only I didn't get up to answer it. He let himself in with his key and I couldn't have been more thankful. He doesn't say anything but, then again, I don't expect him to. I've grown used to the quiet.

I close the door to the bathroom and stand in front of the mirror. My reflection startles me. I don't even know the person looking back at me. I've been here five days and I'm shocked at how much my appearance has changed, especially over the last twenty-four hours.

My hair is matted and hangs limply down both sides of my face. The color seems duller and the shine is gone—just like me. Dark purple half-moon circles trace underneath my eyes, my cheeks are sunken in more than usual, and my lips are chapped. As for my skin color, it looks pale and homely. Nothing about this girl in the mirror says beautiful and perfect.

I glance down at my hands, and cringe. I should look at my feet, too, but I can't. Feeling and seeing are two different things and, if I see them, I know the sight will depress me even further. Getting away without people noticing my hands is hard enough, but the feet would give it away. I already know that there's no way I could slip on a pair of five-inch heels. Any jobs I had this week, if Livy hadn't already cancelled them, I would have had to.

No one can ever see me like this. Even I don't want to see me.

Letting out at sigh, I pick up my toothbrush and brush my teeth. Simple daily tasks feel so hard today. My hands ache trying to merely grip the brush, but I manage to suffer through it. Next, I look at my makeup, which is spread out efficiently on the counter. One by one, product by product, I start applying my face. I think about the other day and the freedom that I felt by not applying the bronzer. I decide that today I'm going to skip it once again. In fact, I'm also going to skip the eyeliner; that way I don't have to attempt holding the pencil to apply it. No one looked at me strangely and I am at the beach, after all. Lastly, I smooth down my hair, pulling it into a tight low bun. I can't be bothered with it today either.

Making the decision, I tell myself to just suck it up and do it. I look at the reflection and smile. I think it's the first time I have smiled in days. It's a crap, forced smile, but I have to know that I can leave the house and put on my career face. Who knows who I will run into, and it's always when I least expect it that a photo of me is taken and posted for the world to see.

Finishing in the bathroom, I wander back into my room and pull on a pair of jeans and a shirt that I had left on the floor. I grab a pair of sunglasses, and slowly walk into the living room, trying not to compensate for everything that aches.

I should probably call the doctor's office first, but I just don't want to turn on my phone. I mean, how busy could they actually be on this island? Surely they can squeeze me in.

Matt looks up as I walk into the room, and my heart catches in my throat. I swear this guy gets better-looking every time I see him. Does he even realize how gorgeous he is? He'd have to be blind not to.

"I'm headed out for a little bit. Do you need anything?" Although he continually frowns at me, he's been somewhat nice several times now, which is progress.

Matt looks at me questioningly, and then, as his gaze drops, so does my stomach. With his penetrating gaze, I feel a blush spread over me and I'm embarrassed. Clearly he can see that something's not right, but he doesn't say anything. He just shakes his head no. I appreciate his silence.

"HOW CAN WE help you?" an elderly woman behind the counter asks me as I walk in.

"I know I don't have an appointment, but I was wondering if there was any way that the doctor might be able to squeeze me in today."

"Is this urgent and have you been here before?" Her look changes to scrutiny.

"No, I haven't, and I suppose it could wait until tomorrow, but the sooner I refill my prescription, the better. I don't feel well." I shift my eyes to the others in the waiting room to see if they are listening to me. No one in my world knows about this little problem of mine, and it has to stay that way. Should word get out, the perfect image that I've created would be gone.

"Okay, we have a few patients who need to be seen ahead of you, but I'm sure he won't mind squeezing you in right before lunch. Fill out these new patient papers and bring them back to me," she says while handing me a clipboard over the reception counter.

My fingers wrap around the pen and my joints scream out in pain. I am cursing myself for having forgotten my medicine while I fill out her pages, and am so relieved when I get to the last one. She takes the clipboard and I sit back down.

Usually, I would scroll through my phone but, since I refuse to turn it on, I feel like I have nothing to do. Picking up the closest magazine to me, it's a copy of *In Style*. I've already gone through this issue once before, but seeing as how I have nothing to do, or anything to read, this is the next best thing.

Page after page, I analyze every detail. From the editorial work to the advertisements, I search out that one thing that is in each photo that made it the chosen one. The lines, the wardrobe, finding the light, when did this stop being fun for me? An image of my mother flashes in my mind and I know it's mostly because of her that it lost its magic.

"Elle Summers." My name is called. I'm thrilled that I didn't have to wait long as I am led to a nurse's station, where a nurse takes my vitals, and then directs me to a room.

As the door closes behind me, I look around the room and sigh. I've been in so many different types of doctor's offices over the last couple of years. For a small island town, this doctor seems very up to date, not only with the few pieces of medical equipment that I've seen on the way in, but also in décor. I'm not sure what I expected, maybe a little weathered and outdated, but the office is quite the opposite.

From outside the door, I hear the doctor grab the chart then flip it open. Some of the paperwork I didn't fill in like I was supposed to, but what does it matter? I'm sure I won't be staying here too much longer anyway. I just need enough time for that creep to lose interest, to figure out what I'm going to do next with my life, and to catch up on some much needed rest.

The door opens and the doctor walks in.

"Hi, I'm Doctor Overment," he says as he takes a seat on the stool to sit next to me and reads a little bit more of my paperwork before setting the chart down. He squirts some antibacterial gel onto his hands, rubs them together, and then reaches over for mine. Gently, I lay my hands in his.

"Tell me, when did all of this start?" He's looking at my fingers and softly squeezing the different joints.

"About two and a half years ago," I answer him.

"Okay, I was just wondering if you had it as a child." He looks up at me and his eyes are sympathetic.

"Nope."

"I don't see this too often in young adults your age."

"One out of seven hundred and fourteen get it age twenty and under. I was twenty," I say in a deadpan tone.

He gives me a small smile, understanding why I would know this. "You've done your research."

"Wouldn't you?" I ask him.

"Yes, yes I would. Are you hurting anywhere else?" He lets go of one hand and squeezes my knee. I hiss out in pain.

"I hurt all over." I want to beg him to not squeeze me anywhere else.

"I see." He lets go of my other hand and leans back to look at me. "So, you are here on vacation?"

I nod at him. He studies me briefly, and I know he can see that I'm tired and all around not feeling well.

"You know, they say these rheumatoid flare ups are very common after high periods of stress or fatigue. Based on the look of you, and that you are here, am I wrong to assume that both of these have happened?" He raises his eyebrows in question, but all I can do is swallow.

I don't say anything. I know he's right. I know about the stress, and figured that was the reason, but it never occurred to me that driving straight here would cause strain and may worsen my symptoms.

"Here's what we'll do. I'm going to write you a prescription for Methotrexate, since you forgot yours, and a steroid. The steroid should quickly bring down the inflammation of the flare. If you have any complications, or need anything else while you are here, don't be a stranger . . . okay?"

I suck in a deep breath and feel my heart rate slow down a little. I am so relieved that he isn't running a bunch of tests to make sure that I know what I am talking about. Every new doctor that I have ever been to has made such a big deal of starting at square one, only to get to the same conclusion—rheumatoid arthritis.

"Thank you, I really appreciate it and for squeezing me in today, too," I say with tears in my eyes. Damn tears. I'm not sure why I am crying over this and I'm reminded of the random crying this morning, too. Maybe I am just so happy to get the medication, or maybe it's because I really needed to talk to; someone kind and understanding. It's as if sharing the burden of this pain I am consumed with makes me feel a little better. I still feel overwhelmed with sadness, but I do feel slightly lighter.

He smiles at me again and tells me that the General Store down the road has a pharmacy and that they should be able to help me.

He pats me on the back, hands me the prescriptions, and guides me out the front door.

MATT

I HATED SEEING her the way she looked today.

When I arrived this morning and she didn't answer the door, my first thought was that she was just done with having me over at the cottage. I didn't say very much to her yesterday and, with how I'd treated her over the last couple of days, maybe she was returning the favor. Not that I could blame her. But when she got out of the bed to go to the bathroom, I could see just how much she was struggling physically. The way she moved, the look on her face, how she held her hands . . . my stomach damn near dropped into my toes and anxiety hit me out of nowhere. She was so much worse than yesterday and I hated seeing her like this.

About thirty minutes later, she came out, ready to leave. I should have manned up and asked her if she needed me to help her, but I chickened out and now I feel awful.

Since she isn't in her room, I take this as an opportunity to go in and rip out the old carpet. Moving the nightstand to the hallway, her cell phone falls, and I wonder if she meant to leave it behind. It's strange nowadays to go anywhere without one. I pick up and see it is turned off or dead. Hmm. Not my business.

It takes me about thirty minutes to get the carpet out and loaded in the truck. Finishing a little earlier than I had planned, I decide to take a quick shower and head over to the store to pick up some snacks for Quinn.

Checking my email to see if there are any tracking numbers for some material that I ordered for the North Shore house, I grab the handle of the store door and yank it open. Almost immediately a body crashes into me. I drop the phone and stumble back away from the door. Without even looking, I instantly know it's her.

Time doesn't quite stop, but it definitely plays out in slow motion. Her hands land on my chest, she winces in pain, and they fold in between the two of us while her face bounces off of my shoulder. Instinctually, my arms wrap around her to keep her from falling but, even after we settle, I still don't let go.

Neither one of us moves, and her tense body slowly seems to relax against mine with each breath.

My heart is pounding in my chest and I'm certain that she feels it. She lets out a sigh that drifts across my neck, sending goose bumps straight down my back. She shifts her head a little and lays it on my shoulder, while her lips brush against my neck. Instead of moving away from me, she has snuggled against me, and my arms tighten even more around her, bringing her closer. This feeling is incredibly foreign to me, but I like it—a lot.

I want to say that we should stop meeting like this, but that would mean I would have to stop touching her and, over this last week, I have been desperate to touch her again, to relieve the ache in my chest. I don't know why I keep trying to pretend there's nothing between us, when there most definitely is. I don't know what, but it's certainly there. She affects me more than any other person ever has, and I don't know why.

The smell of her shampoo hits my senses and, without thinking, I lay my head on top of hers. I'm hugging this girl, the one girl I shouldn't be hugging, and I never want to let go.

It's the few moments like these when I wish that I led a normal life, with a normal childhood; not one filled with shame and secrets that stand in the way of everything that I want. And, without a doubt, I want her. But I gave up on wishing for a different life a long time ago.

My heart frowns just thinking about it. If only . . .

The door opens and someone passes us, mumbling my name as a greeting. She flinches a little and slowly pulls away from me. I want to hold her tighter, but I don't.

"Thanks, I really needed that," she says shyly while looking at the ground. I don't know why she won't look at me, but there is no way I'm letting her go just yet. Ever since she left this morning, I have been worried about her. She doesn't need to know that I'm thinking about her, even though I am. I just have to see her and look into those beautiful brown eyes.

Cupping my hand around her face, I tilt it back and see the exhaustion that is all over her. I know she can't be that tired; after all, she's slept for days. But, then again, whatever is making her so ill must be making her look this way. I run my thumb across her cheekbone and the haunted shadow under her eyes. Her skin is so soft.

"You okay?" I say softer than I want.

"No, not yet, but I will be." Uncertainty blankets her face. She wants to believe this, but I can tell she's not so sure.

Without thinking, my thumb drops to rub over her bottom

lip. She sucks in a breath and her eyes widen just a little, and her hand finds its way onto my hip.

"Can I take you somewhere?" I ask her, trying to memorize every detail of her face.

"No, I drove…and it's not that far, but thanks." My eyes move to her mouth. The warmth of her breath and the way her lip moves across my finger is almost enough to make me cross-eyed.

I give her a small smile and drop my hands. Neither one of us moves. I think back to earlier this morning, and regret not having asked her then what was going on with her. The way she hugged me and how she just gave herself over to me lets me know that she's not okay; even if she won't admit it.

"Where do you live?" she asks me curiously.

A small smile forms, "Next door to you."

"What?" Those big brown eyes grow large in shock. "How did I not know that?"

"Yep, cottage number one."

"Oh, I didn't realize."

Running my hand through my hair, I take another step back from her. I can't describe the level of feeling that this girl inspires in me. It's surprising to feel when you hardly feel anything anymore. She takes her hand off of me and crosses her arms over her chest. I clear my throat, trying to maintain my composure. "Yeah, so if you need anything, anything at all while you are here, now you know where to find me."

"That's really nice of you. Thanks." She looks up at me and I forget to breathe.

"I do have my moments," I say with a smirk.

Her eyes brighten a little at my remark and her smile grows wider. She is so beautiful, smiling or not.

As she walks past me, she lays her hand on my arm, but

doesn't squeeze. It's such a simple move, but I feel like I have been branded. How will I ever forget this girl after she leaves? Maybe I'm not supposed to. Maybe these few moments are all I'm ever going to get, and I need to save them up and treasure them, because they are meant to be mine.

THE DOOR BEEPS twice as I walk in without knocking.

"Hey, I'm upstairs," Beau yells out to me.

Walking up the stairs, I stop and look at each photo Leila has perfectly hung. There are so many of them that span two decades, and for once I'm jealous of the love and time that they have had together.

There are pictures of them playing in the sand at eight, pictures of them at prom, pictures of them in New York, pictures of them at their wedding, and pictures of them holding Quinn at the hospital. Additionally, mixed in there are pictures of both families, hers and mine. They really have had a beautiful life together.

"Hey, in here."

I follow the sound of his voice and find him in Quinn's room. He is packing her overnight bag, and she is on the floor playing with some magnetic tiles. She hears me enter, looks up, and breaks into a huge infectious smile. My heart squeezes.

"Unca Matt, up please." She lifts her tiny hands to me. I can never tell her no. Bending over, I scoop her up.

"Hi, sweet girl." She wraps her arms around my neck and hugs me. That's two hugs now in one day, and something inside of me feels a little warm and fuzzy. I'm not used to all of this affection.

"Go see Bruno!" She bounces in my arms.

"Yes, as soon as your dad is finished, we'll get out of here."

She giggles and flings her head toward Beau.

"Hold your horses, little lady; I'm almost done. Why don't you carefully go down the stairs and see if Bambi is down there. You wouldn't want to forget him."

She lets out a little gasp, wiggles her way down, and leaves the room. Ali, Drew's wife, had bought the stuffed Bambi for her when she was born, and it was like love at first sight. She grabbed on to his leg, and for two and a half years they have been almost inseparable

"So, rumor has it that you were spotted in front of the café earlier in the week lip-locking with some unknown girl. Do you deny?" he's smiling at me and I want to deck him.

"Whatever, yeah. There was a girl. There was a kiss. So what?" I scowl back at him. It pisses me off how shocked he looks by my admission.

"Well, who is she?" he presses.

"No one, so don't worry about it," I answer him. The last thing I need is him questioning me about anything.

He tilts his head to the side and studies me. Slowly his mouth widens into a cocky smirk, and his hazel eyes flash as if he has just figured something out. I find myself gritting my teeth.

"Wish I could have met this girl," he says, chuckling and moving into Quinn's closet to grab some clothes for tomorrow.

"Why?"

"Because I've never seen you with a girl before. I'm kind of curious about what your type is like. Leila knows lots of eligible girls, so all you have to do is say the word."

"Davy said the same thing. Why is my love life so much of an interest to all of you? And, thanks, but I don't need your help finding a girl."

He comes out of the closet and his expression turns to one of seriousness. "Matt, relax. I just want to see you happy."

"What makes you think I'm not?" I counter.

He pins me with his 'no bullshit' look. "Because, you don't have what Drew and I have with Leila and Ali, and until you do, until you find that person, you'll never truly know happiness."

"I thought 'True happiness comes from within'."

"Well, that, too, smart ass . . . but add a good woman to the mix and life can be pretty perfect."

I can't really argue with him, because I saw firsthand how different both Drew and Beau became after they found 'the one'; the one for them, anyway. I'm happy for them, but it isn't anything I ever thought I could have for myself.

"Thanks for taking Quinn for the night. You know she loves to come sleepover at your house with Bruno." He reaches into a drawer and grabs her swimsuit.

"I know, and he lights up the minute he sees her. It's like they both forget all about me."

"We should be back sometime tomorrow night; she just needs to preview the completed new line and then we'll be home."

"Take your time. Quinn and I will be fine."

"I know, but you understand." He reaches up and rubs his chest.

And I do. Maybe it's because of the way we were raised, or maybe this is just the way it is supposed to be, but I understand that it's hard for him to be away from her because he loves her that much.

I give him a smile, he pats me on the shoulder, and hands me Quinn's bag.

Chapter Eight

ELLE

I LOVE BEING wrapped up in Matt's arms. It's a feeling I can get addicted to. Of course, it figures that the one guy who makes me feel the safest, the most comfortable, is also the same guy who has the expert ability to make me feel unwanted. He has these moments where he is so tender and attentive, but then, with the flip of a switch, he can also be cold and distant. I don't understand him.

I thought the highlight of my day was going to be getting my medicine, but it wasn't.

When the door flew out of my hand and I lost balance, his scent hit me before he did. He must've just showered, and he smelled so clean and so him. In a way, I wish my arms had wrapped around him. I would have loved to have run my hands across his broad back, pulled his body against mine, and had the opportunity to hold him. But, instead, the warmth of his skin, how his heart beat against mine, and when he laid his head on top of mine, I was in heaven and the pain from earlier suddenly didn't seem as bad. I could have stood there in his arms all day.

He makes me feel starved for affection. It's not anything I ever really thought about before, but with him I crave, starve, and steal any tidbits he'll throw my way. Really is pathetic.

Wandering around my kitchen, I take stock of how sparse my food supply is. Maybe I should take Matt up on his offer and send him out for groceries. Just seeing him frown at the request in my mind has me smiling.

I eat a nutrition bar, a banana, take my medicine, and finish off a bottle of water. Fuel—check. Medicine—check. I feed Otis and then climb into my bed.

Reaching for my cell phone, I debate whether I should turn it on or not, but being the type-A person that I am, I need to know if anything pertinent is dangling out there.

The Apple logo lights up and I wait. Almost immediately the phone starts vibrating, alerting me of missed communication. It's been two days since I last checked my email and there are 104 inbox notifications. Granted, most of them are spam, but there are still quite a few that aren't. I ignore the ones that are from my mother and quickly skim through the rest. One catches my eye and has my heart racing. It was sent yesterday.

Elle,

I'm not going to lie, I'm confused. I understand that you said you wanted to be friends, but I really did think that you just needed some down time. Maybe that's what this is—you hiding, or maybe it isn't, I'm not sure. I must have called you two hundred times since last Friday, and I guess I'm finally getting your message . . . you want to be left alone. So that's what I'm going to do, I'll leave you alone, but know that I will be here waiting for you when you get back.

Missing you like crazy,
Connor

An uneasy feeling sinks into my stomach. Why won't this guy go away? We weren't even that serious. He barely got to second base, and really I haven't been that nice to him. I told him we were over at least two weeks ago. I haven't spoken to him in over a week, since he invited me to his stupid party. He just can't take a hint.

Closing out the mail, I hit the text icon and pull up his name. There are so many from him that I immediately go to delete them all, but then freeze. If he is the one who is stalking me, then I'll need these for evidence. Instead, I open a new message.

Me – Connor, I can't be any clearer with you. I do not want to have any sort of relationship with you anymore. Do not wait for me. If and when I do decide to come back, it will not be to you. Please don't contact me . . . it's over.

With my heart racing, I hit send. Uneasiness runs through me, and I shake my arms out. Needing a drink of water, I slip out of bed and go grab another bottle. I thought he was such a nice guy, but really he's like a bad case of the flu where the coughing just won't go away.

Otis hops up onto the bed with me as I climb in. Reopening my email, there's a new one that just came in. The sender is illfindyou@gmail.com.

Oh, my God.

Without even opening the email, I already know it's from

him—from whoever this person is. It crossed my mind at one point that Connor could be the stalker, but in the end I really didn't think that he had it in him. But the timing just seems too coincidental to my sending him that text. I'm just so confused.

I feel like I'm going to be sick, and tears burn my throat. I don't want to open this email, but I know that I have to. My stomach has cramped and I suddenly feel cold all over. With shaking fingers, I hover over the name. I feel like it's a snake and, the second I open it, it's going to strike.

You stupid bitch,
How dumb can one girl be? Did you think running away and hiding would save you? Did you think "out of sight, out of mind"? Did you think that this little plan of yours was actually going to work? I guess the bottom line is, did you think at all?
Anytime, anywhere . . . and you are mine!
I'm coming for you.

Stunned and frozen, I stare at the email on my screen. I've stopped breathing and my lungs are screaming at me to remember how. A text notification flashes across the top of the screen. The message is briefly there before it slips away.

Connor – Crystal clear. Take care of yourself.

Turning the phone off, I get out of the bed and walk straight to the shower. My heart is fiercely racing, pounding through my chest.

Sitting on the floor, with my knees pulled up, I succumb to the onslaught of tears that is desperately trying to escape. Silent sobs convulse through my body as I try my hardest to wash away the fear. A fear that has settled into the deepest part of me.

I must have really needed the sleep, because I didn't wake up again until earlier this morning to use the bathroom, and then I went right back to sleep.

My stomach growls, so I go in search of something to eat. Taking a look out the window, I see that the sun has lowered a little in the sky, and I decide that today I am not going to be the victim. Whoever this person is, they are not going to have power over me, at least not today. The message said, *"I will find you,"* which means they have no idea where I am. *Yet.* For now, I am safe. I just need to keep taking deep breaths and put one foot in front of the other—starting with the beach. The beach just looks too inviting and, other than the walk I took on my first day here, I haven't spent any time on it.

Digging around in the storage closet on the porch, I find a beach chair. Smiling to myself, I feel almost giddy. I can't remember the last time that I sat out on a beach.

Slipping into a t-shirt and a pair of shorts, I put on my hat and sunglasses, grab the chair, a towel, and a book. The book is called *Whispers of Sand*, it was probably left behind by a past guest, but to me it feels freeing to pick up a book instead of a magazine.

Walking out the door, I pause in front of Matt's cottage and wonder what he's doing. I don't know why I am thinking about him. Wait, yes I do. Thinking back to yesterday, how unfortunate for him, and how fortunate for me. If I don't think too hard, I can still feel where he put his hands on me—my back, my face, my mouth. I could have melted on the spot. He's made it perfectly clear that he isn't interested in me in the slightest, but then he goes and does things like that. There's something about him, and deep down I hope he thinks that there's just something about me.

Up and over the dock footpath, I stop just as it meets the sand. There are a few people further down on both sides of me, but in general the beach is deserted. It occurs to me that I'm looking for something or someone suspicious. My heart frowns at the realization that this has now become my life. That I feel the need to analyze everything and constantly be alert.

My toes squish in the warm sand, and I make my way closer to the water before setting down the chair. There's a nice breeze coming off of the water and, sitting under the shade of my hat, I can almost pretend that I am lying in a hammock.

I stretch my legs out, just for an instant having regrets about not applying sunblock. I've never had a tan, I've never been allowed to have one. Deciding that I just don't care, I let out a sigh, soak in the sun, and close my eyes. I only intended to rest, but the sound of the water lapping on the shore put me right back to sleep.

Sometime later, the sweet sound of giggling wakes me. It reminds me of church bells, so pretty. I open my eyes and peek out underneath the brim of my hat to see that the sun has moved more toward the horizon, and the sky is filled with different shades of yellow and orange. I can't help but wonder how long I've been out here and glance down at my legs to see if they are tinged pink at all.

The giggling hits my ears again and my eyes move to find its source. A little girl is playing in the sand . . . and she's playing with Matt.

She's sitting on top of him and he is buried in the sand. The little girl giggles again, and Matt busts up out of the sand and starts chasing her. She runs away from him, squealing and laughing, and right this second I feel like I am a part of their life. He picks her up, swings her around, and then brings her in close for a hug. They twist toward me a little and that's when I see it . . . Matt is smiling. I suck in a breath and hold it. I don't think that I've ever seen him smile; in fact, I know I haven't, because it would have permanently etched its way into my memory, just like it is now.

Everything about his face has changed. He wears a mask. I should have realized this before, but I didn't know. Seeing him this way, free and openly loving this little girl, I'm drawn to him even more than I thought possible. I knew behind those gray eyes lived a secret storm. I just didn't realize how many thunder clouds there were.

He's breathtaking and, by far, the most beautiful and most haunted person I have ever seen.

MATT

"SO, WHO'S THIS little one?" I hear Ellie ask from behind me.

My head whips around to the sound of her voice, and I can't help but eye her warily. She's sitting in her chair, but I didn't realize she was awake. I've glanced at her quite a few times since we came out here, and not once did she move. Now, I'm wondering how long she has been watching us. Did she see me looking at her? My cheeks heat and I turn away.

"Quinn, come say hi to Ellie." Quinn had run down to the water's edge to fill her bucket. She drops it at my request and runs back to me. Just watching her makes my heart swell, and I smile.

"Ellie?" she shoots me a questioned look. "You know, the only person who calls me that is Aunt Ella."

"It's only fair, don't you think?" I smirk at her.

She starts laughing, and I hate how my body reacts to it. "I guess so, *Matty*."

Quinn comes to stand next to me and slips her hand into mine. She's looking at Ellie with her big blue eyes, and I know she is wondering who she is.

"Quinn, this is Ellie. Can you say hi?" She leans against my hand and gives Ellie one of her killer smiles.

"Hi," she says.

"Hi, it's very nice to meet you," Ellie says while pulling her sunglasses off and tipping her hat back, so Quinn can see her. They are smiling at each other and the hole in my chest shrinks drastically, taking that familiar ache away with it. These two girls together make me feel something I haven't ever felt . . . hope.

Ellie looks different today. In fact, I think she looks more beautiful than I have ever seen her, including in all of her magazine photos. The color has come back to her face. She isn't as pale. The purple rings under her eyes are not quite as prominent, her hair is down and untamed, and I don't think she is wearing any makeup. I've noticed she never leaves the house without putting a bunch of it on, but right now, seeing the natural her takes my breath away.

Quinn pulls on my hand and I let her go. She runs back to catch her bucket as it drifts along the water's edge.

"She's beautiful," Ellie says with a calm voice.

"Thanks, I think so, too," I say while keeping my eyes on Quinn.

"Is she yours?" A laugh escapes me and I look back at Ellie. She narrows her eyes.

"No, but I'd take her in less than a heartbeat. She's my niece." It makes me so proud to say that.

Silence falls between us and then, the next thing I know, brown fur is blowing past me and headed straight for Quinn. She squeals and Bruno comes to a screeching halt before he runs her over. He licks her face and she leans down to hug him.

"Is that your dog?" Ellie asks me.

"Yep."

"Cause, I've gotta say, I just about had a heart attack thinking that dog was about to run her over and eat her face."

I can't help but burst out laughing. I never laugh, and it feels good.

"No worries there. That's Bruno, and those two have the craziest love for each other. My guess is he'd rather eat off his own face before he ever harmed one hair on her head."

She doesn't say anything back, but I can feel her looking at me. Strangely, I like her looking at me. Usually, it makes me uncomfortable. I always feel like people will be able to somehow see the darkness inside of me, but with her it's kind of the opposite. She makes me feel lighter and, for a short time . . . free.

"We were about to head inside. Do you want to come in with us?" It's out of my mouth before I can even register what I am saying.

"Uh, sure." She looks surprised that I asked her, but then she looks up at me through her eyelashes and gives me a small smile. That smile gets me every time, and she doesn't even know it.

I help her out of the chair, and watch her wince as I squeeze her hand a little too tightly.

"I'm sorry," I say, softening my grip. "I didn't mean to hurt you." I reach for her chair and fold it up. She shakes out her hand, and then tucks the book under her arm.

"I know. It's not your fault," she says to me.

"Are you feeling better today?" I ask her hesitantly.

"I am, thanks. The steroids are working wonders."

Steroids? I look her over from head to toe. Coming back to her face, she blushes and I momentarily forget what we are talking about. She is affected, too. I did that, and I'm surprised at how good that makes me feel.

"It's not that I don't want to tell you things, or that I don't trust you . . . it's just . . .," she breaks eye contact and looks over at Quinn.

"You don't have to tell me; I understand." She looks so uncomfortable.

"No, you don't. I've learned that it's much easier to give as few details as necessary, simply for the fact that, should my name come up in conversation with someone else, you have less to talk about. Off the cuff remarks are always distorted and embellished. The gossip magazines are a business all on their own. Really, all they do is stir up drama."

I really do understand what she is saying. There was a period of time when people were always snooping around looking for some type of gossip or trouble to print about Drew, Beau, and Leila. Eventually, when we wouldn't give them anything they could use, they went away. I momentarily wonder if she knows that Drew and Beau are my brothers; that Leila is my sister-in-law. It's a small town, but she left a long time ago and has never been back.

"No, really; don't worry about it." I give her a reassuring smile. "Well, let's head in." I turn to face the beach and call for Bruno and Quinn.

Back inside my house, I watch as Ellie looks around, lightly fingering my things. I'm trying not to inadvertently stare at her, so I head into the kitchen to get Quinn a Popsicle. I always give her popsicles; it's kind of our thing, but she has to eat it on the patio.

My heart is beating faster than normal, I've never had a girl in my home before. I do find it ironic that it is her, though. She was the only girl to ever step foot into the shed, and she is the only one here. She stops at a picture and picks it up. So much for keeping that part of my life private.

"You know Drew and Beau Hale?" she looks at me curiously, and then back down at the photo.

"Yes." My brows furrow and I walk out onto the patio to give Quinn the treat and Bruno a bowl of ice. The picture that she is looking at is from my high school graduation. It is a couple of years old, but I love it. Drew, Ali, Beau, Leila, and I are all in it, and everyone looks happy. They surprised me by showing up, and that meant the world to me. I didn't really expect anyone to be there.

"Wait! Are Drew and Beau Hale are your brothers? You look just like them."

"Yes," I answer her and point over to Quinn, who's got purple juice running down her face. She sees the resemblance to Leila and her eyes grow larger.

"How did I not know this? When we were kids, Aunt Ella said that you were just a neighborhood boy who played in the shed. Wow, I know what they do . . . what do you do? Are you an athlete, too?"

I can't help but scowl at her at this question. Given that I am so much younger than the two of them, and that I already feel like an unwanted black sheep in this family, growing up hearing comments like that only made me feel like even more of an outsider. It was assumed that I would turn out like them and, in a way, I did. I just kept it quiet.

Am I an athlete? Yeah . . . I run. Not that she needs to know this. Running has always been my escape and a free form of therapy. The more exhausted I am, the less my brain wanders and thinks. It goes numb, and I welcome the silence.

During high school and, for a short time afterward, I competed. I knew that I never wanted to pursue it as a sport like my brothers did, so I pulled back. Yes, I won every race I entered and, yes, the financial gains were significant, but it just didn't seem fair to those who had made this path their dream. Sponsors and national coaches had found their way to me, but I've never wanted to be in the spotlight, and it just became too much.

I turn away from her and walk into the kitchen to grab a water for Quinn and a beer for me. "Can I get you anything?" I decide not to answer her question. It will just invite too many new ones.

She sets the picture down and turns back to face me. "No, I'm fine, thanks," and she sits down on the couch.

I walk out to the patio, hand Quinn her water, and wipe her face.

"So, what are you and Ms. Quinn doing tonight?"

I sit down on the chair next to the couch and look at Ellie. "Not much more. She spent the night here last night, and Leila is dropping by to pick her up later."

"Oh." Her face freezes and she draws her bottom lip in between her teeth. She looks instantly worried, but I don't know why.

"Matt," she looks at me warily, and I raise my eyebrows to let her know she has my attention. "Will you do me a favor? I get it now, you do understand what I was saying on the beach, so please don't mention to Leila that you saw me. Not that she would say anything to anyone, but in the industry we have quite a few mutual contacts, and it's just, I needed a break and I purposely didn't tell anyone where I was."

That explains why her phone is turned off, but now I'm starting to think there's more to her being here than just a vacation.

"Sure." I nod.

Her mood has shifted, and she gets up off of the couch and moves to the other side of the room to look out the sliding glass doors. Her carefree smile is gone and, in its place, something that looks like worry has replaced it. Quinn climbs up onto a kitchen chair to look with her. She slides her little hand into Ellie's, just like she does to mine, and for a second I am jealous. She's getting to touch her, and then, out of nowhere, I get a glimpse of what my future could look like. The idea, even just for a second, is nice.

Chapter Nine

ELLE

ALL THROUGHOUT THE day, guests arrived for the wedding. Aunt Ella had mentioned over dinner a few nights ago that there was one this weekend, but I had forgotten. Outside, people were laughing, talking, and unloading into the other cottages. Matt didn't stop by today to work on the floors. I'm not sure if it's because of the wedding, or if he just doesn't work on Saturdays.

Not wanting to be out and in the public eye too much, the only errand I ran this morning was a quick one back over to the General Store. I picked up enough food to last me a few more days.

The rest of the day, I read some of the book and played on the guitar. I had missed it and, as I strummed that first chord, my heart soared. I've been working on a new piece. The sound of the chorus came to me almost immediately, but the verses have been a little trickier. All of my songs have been about my life, but the more I think about this one, I'm not so sure. It's like it has a different calling or a different purpose. I just haven't been able to work out what that is yet. One by one, the lines have been coming to me, but they are out of order and all lying before me like pieces to a puzzle. I know eventually it will all come together, so I continue to work on the sound and wait patiently.

About an hour ago, I heard the sounds of people cheering. I smiled to myself, knowing that the ceremony must have just ended and they were officially husband and wife. That has to be such a magical moment for people. The music has shifted from a relaxing dinner sound to one of fun and dancing. I decide, why not? I'll just take a little peek at the reception.

Slipping on a simple dress, I apply foundation, mascara, and lip gloss. Other than my little trip down to the beach, I haven't left the house to go anywhere where I might see people with this minimal amount of makeup on, in years. But tonight, I feel like I don't need it. I have a bit of a glow from lying in the sun yesterday and I just don't want to 'put on my face'. I'm happy with the one I have.

Walking up and over the dunes on the dock footpath, my heart smiles as I stop and look down on the party. It's the perfect evening. The sun is setting and the sky is completely cloudless, stretching the dusk colors as far as the eye can see. There's a large white tent filled with glowing paper lanterns hanging from the ceiling, and twinkle lights. It has four beautifully decorated round tables that seat eight each and, next to the tent, a section of the sand has been squared off with tiki torches for dancing. Fabric is loosely tied to each one, connecting them. There's a bartender and a DJ. This little wedding looks perfect.

I've never given much thought to getting married. Most

little girls play wedding and dream about the details of that big special day. Nope, not me. It's not that I never thought I would get married, it's just for so many years it hasn't been a part of the plan.

I know the moment he steps up next to me. The heat from him slams into me, and my entire body starts tingling. After spending just a little bit of time with him last night, my heart starts smiling that he sought me out. Butterflies in my stomach take off.

"It really is the perfect night for a wedding. Don't you think?" I glance over to look at him, and my excitement from him joining me fades. His face isn't calm. His jaw is tight and he looks like he's focusing really hard on something.

"I do." His eyes move to watch the guests down below, silently.

I want to turn and look at him, but there's this tension radiating off of him. He's gone back to being his typical brooding self, and this causes me to frown. Maybe I shouldn't have come. I thought after yesterday we were moving past this, but I guess not. The butterflies settle down and, in their place, disappointment takes over.

I let out a sigh and take a few steps away from him, toward the party. I don't even know why he came over to me, and now my happy mood has just taken a nose dive. I hate that he has the ability to sway my emotions one way or the other.

"So how long do you think you'll be hanging around the island?" he asks me.

My eyes drop to look at the ground, and I squeeze the footpath handrail. No, "Hi, how was your day?" or "Did you do anything fun today?" or even any mention of last night. Instead it's, "When are you leaving?" Maybe I should find someplace else to stay. This merry-go-round that we are on—

round and round and round—I need off. It's been a week and other than Aunt Ella and the doctor, he is the only interaction I have had with someone, and he makes me sad. That disappointment I felt a few minutes ago slips to loneliness. Yes, I came here to isolate myself from others, but he evokes a heartache in me that feels much more like rejection than it does privacy.

He was not part of my plan but, after meeting him, I really wanted him to be. I don't understand the strong level of emotions that he brings out of me. He makes me feel on edge and confused. My heart aches at how cavalier he is of me, when all I want is for him to see me.

"I'm not sure, but don't worry, not too much longer till you're rid of me." I answer him, probably more sharply than necessary, but he hurt my feelings.

He lets out a long sigh. "Ellie, it's not like that," he says apologetically.

I turn to face him. "Oh, really? What's it like then?" I snap. "Yeah, we've had a few nice moments here and there over the last week, but you've made it perfectly clear that I'm this thorn in your foot that you can't wait to get rid of."

He sucks his bottom lip in between his teeth, and his nose flares as he watches me. I know I've probably overstepped my boundaries with him. After all, just because we've had flashes of normalcy here and there, it doesn't make us anything more. He rarely acknowledges me, barely speaks to me. He's made sure to keep his distance. It reminds me of the *not interested* message that I finally had to send Connor when he didn't get my more subtle signals. Am I the dumb girl who doesn't get it now?

Message received loud and clear, buddy. Friends.

Why do I even want to be friends with him? Other than

this unexplainable pull that I have to him, he's completely ignored me all week. He doesn't want it, any of it, and he's been very transparent about it.

I feel rejected, and that stings. My chest has tightened, and I'm trying so hard to pull in my emotions. I am a nice person and I am more than just a pretty package. I'm loyal, kind, loving, and I have so much to give someone. If we didn't have this off-the-charts chemistry, I would file this under the *he's just not interested in me* file, but that can't be it.

The breeze between us stops. There's a stillness hanging in the air, just waiting for one of us to break the silence. He's watching me and I'm watching him, and I feel the loss of what could have been.

Say you love me by Jessie Ware echoes off of the dunes and I decide this is the last chance I'm going to give him. Sucking up my pride, I lock my eyes onto his and ask, "Will you dance with me?"

His eyes never leave mine as he contemplates my question. I'm searching for anything that I might see filter through them, but there's nothing. They are unreadable.

"No," he says, almost painfully. His expression has slipped back to a scowl.

He doesn't say anything more, he just turns back to watch the guests while I continue to stare at him.

My heart drops and my soul folds in on itself. I feel stupid and thoroughly humiliated. A big part of me knew he would say no, but the hopeful part really wanted him to say yes. There's a lump in my throat and, as hard as I try to swallow down my emotions, they finally win. Tears burn at my eyes. My hands clench my dress and I start shaking.

How can he be so dismissive?

I'm so confused by him that my emotions finally get the

best of me.

"Why are you even standing here then?" He hears the exasperation in my voice, and he flinches. "I was having a perfectly pleasant time watching the party, minding my own business. I never asked you to come out here; in fact, I haven't asked for anything from you. I don't know when I'm leaving yet, okay? I promise you'll be the first to know when I do. I'm sorry if I'm in your way."

He looks over at me, and continues with his little silent treatment that he has so well perfected. Adrenaline is racing through me and my heart is pounding. I'm not a person who likes confrontation, but I just can't take it anymore. The sun dropped quickly tonight and now it's too dark to get a read on him. I have no idea what he is thinking. Tears of exasperation are rapidly spilling over on to my cheeks.

A breeze rolls over us and blows my hair into my face. Pushing it back and tucking it behind my ears. I see Matt's eyebrows pull down and his jaw tighten. His breathing is more forceful, but he makes no move to contradict what I've said. My heart is sinking with this realization. How did I ever get to the point where one guy has the ability to make me feel so bad?

"Why are you always so angry with me? I don't understand what I possibly could have done to you for you to be this way. You scowl at me, ignore me, and you've made me feel inconsequential. Is it so hard to be friends with me? Over and over this past week, you have hurt my feelings. Was that your plan? Do you feel good about yourself, knowing this is how you are making me feel?"

Letting out a long, exhausted sigh, I push past him to walk away. There's really no point in sticking around. Clutching my hands to my chest, my joints scream out in pain as I try to smooth out the ache that is pushing on the back of my rib-cage. It aches so much. My lips tremble, and I'm on the verge of completely sobbing now, but I will not allow him to see that. I will not allow him to see me mourn the loss of something that never was.

MATT

ALL AFTERNOON, I sat and listened to her play the guitar. There are so many things that I need to be doing, should be doing, but I couldn't leave. I'm confused after having her over last night. I always thought it would feel awkward to have someone else in my home, but it didn't. It felt right, almost like she belonged here. I feel like a total coward hiding in my house all day, but the way she makes me feel scares the hell out of me. I don't want it, any of it, but it won't go away. Instead, this foreign rush of feelings just gets stronger, and I don't know how to deal with it.

I don't let people in. Davy is the only friend I've ever really had, and that's because he doesn't ask any questions. It's our mutual understanding. As a kid, Beau was there, and once he left, there was Uncle Ben. But spending time like this with a girl is totally new to me. Just having her around makes me nervous, and she hasn't even done anything. My life was simple before she crashed into it, but very quickly she's made me feel out of control.

For hours, Bruno and I sat by the window. The melody to whatever song she is working on enthralled me, and I needed more. Every now and then I could pick up the faint sound of her voice singing. It sounded light and natural, and it was the most beautiful damn sound I had ever heard. That sound tormented me. I hate that I want her so much. I want her to be mine, but how could that ever be any kind of reality? I am the way I am for a reason, and I can't bring her in to all my crap. I can't burden her with the guilt that I live with. She deserves someone so much more than the recluse that I am.

I didn't mean to come outside and stand next to her. I had gone out onto the porch to see how the party was going, when I saw her standing at the head of the footpath. The sun was setting, and it had cast a glow on her that looked almost supernatural. Her hair and dress were both blowing in the breeze. She looked so gorgeous that, without even realizing it, my feet were moving toward her like a moth to a flame. I had no intention of bothering her. I just wanted to be near her.

My question about how long she was planning on staying was genuinely out of curiosity, not because I was trying to be an ass. I want her to stay forever, even if she isn't mine. She got so defensive, so fast, and then she totally caught me off guard when she asked me to dance.

I don't know why the hell I told her no. It's just a dance. Even though I've never done it, people do it all the time. The fact is, the invitation terrified me. But the look on her face crushed me. I disappointed her . . . no, I hurt her.

Her words replay themselves him my mind.

Why are you always so angry with me? I don't understand what I possibly could have done to you for you to be this way. You scowl at me, ignore me, and you've made me feel inconsequential. Is it so hard to be friends with me? Over and over this past week you have hurt my feelings. Was that your plan? Do you feel good about yourself, knowing this is how you are making me feel?

And the worst one—*you make me feel bad.*

After taking her home from the Sandbar, I knew that I had the wrong impression of her and, if given the opportunity, I knew she could demolish everything in my world and flip it upside down. I've always kept to myself for a reason. I have done everything in my power to avoid her, and it has taken so much out of me. I never thought I had the power to make her feel bad about anything. I was trying to leave her be. What's inside of me is ugly, broken, unwanted. I wasn't even supposed to exist. It would only be a matter of time before she realized this, and then where would that leave me?

I can't change the truth of my scarred existence. She doesn't realize it now, but I'm doing her a favor. That's what I've been telling myself. But then watching her walk away, something rips in half inside of me. All I can think of is what a royal mistake I just made. I finally managed to find a little bit of light, a little bit of hope, and I went and screwed it up. I can't pretend that this crazy connection we have isn't real. I know that I have the power to fix this.

Running up the boardwalk over the dunes to the cottages, I gently reach for her elbow as I catch up to her. "Ellie."

She stops, but doesn't turn around to face me.

Pulling her toward me, I could swear I hear her sniff, and I feel like an even bigger piece of crap. This beautiful girl who has come to mean so much to me is sad, and it's my fault. My insides are breaking, my heart is squeezing, and my soul is on fire. I push on her chin to get a better look at her face. There are wet streaks down both of her cheeks. Wrapping my hands around her face, I wipe them away with my thumbs and pull her closer.

"I'm sorry. Please don't cry," I choke out.

She doesn't say anything. Her glassy eyes roam over my

face. I know she is trying to understand.

"I'm not trying to hurt you . . . I'm just trying to stay away from you," I say, hoping she will understand. I need her to understand me.

Her bottom lip trembles. "Why?"

Why? And there it is. The unknown floats in the air around us, or rather, around me. She thinks she's done something wrong, but everything she does is so right. To me, she is perfect, and what do I have to give to the perfect girl? Not a damn thing.

"Because . . ." I close my eyes just for a brief second and allow that connection that we have to strengthen. The warmth from her skin seeps into my hands and spreads through me. I need to remain strong around her. "Because, I don't do relationships."

"I didn't ask you for one," she whispers.

"Relationships, friendships, they are all the same to me. I don't do them. Never have, never will." There's a conviction in my tone. I know she hears it.

The small sliver of hope that was in her eyes vanishes. She lets out sigh, and wiggles free from my hands. They drop to my sides, and instantly chill. I feel more lost than I have in a long time.

She takes a step back from me, and looks up at me through her eyelashes, "Well then, I guess we are done here."

Another tear drops and, with it, I am choking on the urge to take her back in my arms and hold her. I know I should say something, but I don't know what. Music from the party is still floating through the air around us, taunting me, daring me to hope for what could be found right over the dunes.

The air between us electrifies, just before she breaks it and turns around. Panic courses through me. My mind starts yelling at me.

Fight for her . . . let her go. Fight for her . . . let her go.

The fight wins.

I don't want her to go, *not yet*. But I also don't know how to make her stay.

"I've never danced before," I say in a rush, and she stops walking. This is something that she wanted, so I'll try my damnedest for her.

Turning back around, she tilts her head to look at me. Our eyes lock on to each other and there's that feeling again, the completeness.

Very slowly, I hold my hand out for hers. She eyes it suspiciously, and then walks back to me and places hers in mine. Her grip is soft and warm, and instantly I feel peace. It's crazy how complete I feel when I am near her.

The night sky is now filled with an endless number of twinkling stars and, with the moon shining down, I feel like I am in a dream. My left hand reaches around and firmly presses her lower back, causing her to take a step toward me. Somewhere in the back of my mind, sirens are going off that I shouldn't be doing this; at the same time, it feels too right to stop.

I had forgotten how tall she is, until she lays her head on my shoulder. The smell of peaches wraps around me, but even through the sweet fragrance I can still smell her. She smells and feels like home. A home I never knew I was missing, until now.

A breath shudders through her, and I pull her a little tighter. Holding her in my arms, having her so close, I feel like she is mine.

I'm not sure how long we dance under the stars. It could have been one song or ten, but with the feel of her up next to me, our hearts beating in sync, I could stand here forever.

A silent unexpected fullness fills my chest and, at the same time, my heart aches, knowing that I have to let go.

"I'm going to walk you back," I whisper in her ear.

She lets out a sigh and slowly pulls away from me. Before the dance she looked upset; now she just looks sad.

"Okay," she says this without looking at me.

Taking her hand, I thread my fingers with hers. This is also the second time I've ever held a girl's hand. Why the hell I'm thinking about that right now, I don't know.

As we reach her door, she stops and faces me. Her face is so beautiful. I want to permanently file away this moment.

"Hey, Matty?" her voice is determined, and her eyes flick up to mine. The tears have dried and I'm lost in them immediately. Under the moonlight, her face is luminous and so perfect. Biting my bottom lip, I feel my heart thumping in my chest. I'm slightly nervous about what she's going to say. My fingers lock over hers. I need to hold onto her just a second longer.

Chapter Ten

ELLE

WHEN WE WERE dancing, that same feeling of belonging and wholeness swept over me. It was so comforting to me that if I could have crawled inside him, I would have. I don't know what made him change his mind, but I needed that from him. I needed him to hold me, at least once. I needed to know what it felt like to be in his arms, and I needed to feel the warmth of his body wrapped around mine. Standing there under the stars, just for those few minutes, I felt like I was his and he was mine.

I'm even more baffled at his quiet demeanor now than I was before I went over to his house. It doesn't make sense to me after finally discovering who his brothers are. For years, pictures of both Drew and Beau have been splashed across magazines, tabloids, and the Internet. They are always smiling, and seem to be outgoing. But, as I well know, things aren't always what they seem. What could have happened to Matt to make him so different from them? This causes me to feel uneasy for him, but it shouldn't.

Thinking back to what Trish, Aunt Ella's waitress, said, I know it's not me, but that doesn't make me feel any better. From what she said, he's always been this way. He chooses this for some reason, and it makes me wonder what kind of life he must really have.

In rare moments, he can be so warm, tender almost. I know it's in there, he just won't let it out. Knowing that once tomorrow comes, this temporary openness that he has shared with me tonight will most likely be gone, I decide to take advantage of it. Pushing up on my tiptoes, I lean into him and place my lips on his.

He freezes, and neither one of us moves. My heart sinks as I think to myself that he must not want to kiss me, but I had to do it one more time.

Lowering to my heels, the connection breaks and my eyes burn.

"Thanks for the dance," I say, making eye contact with him and those mysterious gray eyes one last time.

I need to get inside. I need to get away from the humiliation that I am feeling. Just a little bit ago, I thought about moving out of the cottage and finding a new place to stay, when actually maybe it's just time to think about going back to New York.

I reach for the doorknob behind me and, just as I start to turn around, his hand that is still holding mine squeezes while his other settles on my hip. He gently pushes me backward into the door and closes the distance between us.

A small gasp escapes and I look into his beautiful face. His eyes are hooded, his lips are parted, and his breathing has picked up. Without another second of hesitation, his mouth crashes down on mine and the longing, connection, and desire that I have felt for him over this past week slams into me all at once.

The first kiss we had was foreign and tentative, but in the most intriguing way. This kiss is a little more demanding and full of passion. I didn't expect him to need this just as much as I did. I didn't expect to feel any of the different emotions that are pouring off of him right now.

Wrapping my arms around his back, I cling to him, holding him as tightly as I can. I can't get close enough.

Matt's hands move to cup my face, and his fingers tighten in my hair as I open my mouth to allow his tongue to tease mine. He groans. The vibration of the sound pushes through his chest and into mine. It shoots straight through me, causing every muscle to tighten.

His kiss gets a little harder, a little more demanding. The taste and smell of him, the heat radiating off of him, is overpowering, and I freely give myself over to him in this moment.

Giggling comes from behind us, and that's when it dawns on me that we aren't alone. A couple of girls from the wedding have wandered back up this way, and I remember we are outside where anyone can see us.

Reaching behind me, I turn the knob and the door flies open. Matt walks me backward into the house and kicks the door closed. His hands leave my face and fall to the back of my thighs. He picks me up and spins me around so I'm back against the door. My legs wrap around his waist, and he leans into me so that we are flush against each other.

"Just a little bit more," his voice is raspy and laced with desire. I can feel his eyes roaming my face, but I'm transfixed by his warm full lips that are just inches from mine. I can't seem to focus on anything else.

His warm breath fans across my face, and I want to breathe him and only him in.

One of my hands wraps around his neck, and the other sinks into the softness of his hair to pull him in for another kiss; a kiss he was already leaning in to claim.

"I've wanted you to kiss me again all week," I say as his lips leave mine and head for my neck. His tongue dips into the hollow above my collar bone, and my eyes close at the sensation.

He stills, but just for a second. "I know," he mumbles against my skin.

"Then why didn't you?"

He doesn't say anything, but moves his mouth back to mine and runs his tongue across my bottom lip, and stills. I can feel his heart pounding through his chest. He lays his face against mine, cheek to cheek, and I listen to him breathe.

He pulls back just a little and looks at me. Flashes of gray make my stomach drop. It's funny because, even though he doesn't say much verbally, I've begun hearing him in other ways. Right this second, his eyes are speaking volumes. They are telling me he's sorry, they are telling me that he, too, regrets not kissing me sooner, and they are telling me that he thinks he's not good enough for me. But, I don't understand.

"But, Matt . . .," he presses his lips to mine to keep me from asking him why he feels this way. His lips against mine feel better than anything I have ever felt before.

He kisses me again, only this time it is tender and sweet. He takes his time, making me feel cherished as he explores every crevice of my mouth. This is the longest kiss anyone has ever given me. It lasts a lifetime but, at the same time, it's over in no time at all.

Breaking the kiss, he places one hand on the wall next to

my head and leans in to rest his forehead against mine, each of us attempting to slow down our breathing.

"I should go." His eyes are closed. He seems like he's trying to control his emotions.

"What if I don't want you to go?" I barely squeak out. He leans into me a little further. I can feel exactly how much he wants to stay. The hand that is holding me up squeezes just a little, and my legs tighten around him.

Lifting his forehead from mine, he gives me a small smile, looking at me tenderly.

Those few moments over the last week where he has been himself, he's been thoughtful. A gentleman. He's opened doors for me, pulled out my chair for me, paid my bill at the Sandbar, brought me home, picked me up off the ground, didn't bother me when he was in my house, opened all my water for me, carried the chair for me last night, and just danced with me because I asked . . . I'm getting greedy. I'm hoping this is another one of those moments.

Watching him, one of the storm clouds surfaces in his eyes and, as quickly as it comes, it goes. He's battling something in his mind and I wish I knew what it was. He's emotionally pulling back from me. I can feel it. Our moment is over.

Letting out a sigh, I drop my legs from around his waist, and he lowers me to the floor. He takes a small step back and my hands fall to my sides. I miss him already even though he's standing right in front of me.

Dropping his gaze from mine, he licks his lips and draws them in between his teeth. He reaches for my fingers and tangles them with his. Electricity shoots through us, his body tenses a little, and then his eyes flash back to mine.

"Can I come over tomorrow?" he asks. There's no hesitancy in his question. He's determined, and my heart leaps.

His words echo through me. He wants to see me. He isn't going to pretend like this never happened. Maybe tonight is finally our turning point. I am so elated I want to throw my arms around him, squeeze, and jump up and down at the same time. I can't help the face-splitting smile that finds its way onto my face, and he smiles back.

"Yes."

MATT

I KNOW SHE isn't going to be thrilled with me showing up at her door while it's still dark outside, but I'm an early riser, so she'll just have to deal.

After last night, I know I should leave her alone, but I just can't. While she is still on the island, I want to see her . . . no, I need to see her, I need to hear her, and I just need to be with her. Years from now, I will remember this short time with her and how awesome she's made me feel.

Knocking on her door, it's dead silent. I have a brief moment of regret coming over so early, but then a loud clatter comes roaring from inside. I can't help but smile.

The door flies open and, my God, I have never seen anything as beautiful as the sight standing before me. She's got bed head, her hair messy and everywhere, sleepy eyes, and puffy lips. She's wearing a shirt that has slipped off one shoulder and little shorts that show off those gorgeous legs. Her eyebrows are scrunched into an adorable little crinkle that she seems to make whenever she's confused.

"What are you doing here? Is everything okay?" she asks. The fact that she's worried about me just confirms that I don't want to waste any more time not being with her.

"Yeah, I'm good. Rise and shine. I want to show you something," I say, smiling at her.

Her eyebrows pinch together again, but this time I'm pretty sure it's because she's not pleased. "Do you know what time it is?" she demands, exasperated.

"I do, yup. So let's go." I place both hands on top of the doorway and lean in toward her.

She looks me over from head to toe, and runs a hand through her hair as her eyes come back to meet mine. "I'm thinking you should come inside and we go back to bed."

I'm rendered speechless and contemplate her alternative suggestion; seriously. She has no idea how much I want to crawl in bed with her.

"Very tempting, but later." I grin at her.

"Fine." She rolls her eyes and turns around to walk back toward her bedroom. "But there better be coffee involved."

I walk in and close the door. Her cat, Otis, I think it's called, greets me by rubbing against my leg. *At least someone is happy to see me.* "We can stop by the café on the way."

"Where are we going?" she asks over her shoulder.

Through the bedroom door, I watch as she pulls off her t-shirt and her shorts. Her back is to me and, other than the sexy ass pair of white lacy boy shorts she is wearing, she is all smooth, bare ivory skin. She is, by far, the most mesmerizing girl I have ever seen.

"You'll see," I say in a raspy voice. Her gorgeous, slender figure and perfect skin have pierced my brain, as well as my ability to move or speak. I am trying like hell to rein in my desire for her.

She puts on a bra, slips a shirt on and turns back around, staring at me expectantly. "That's all you're going to give me?"

Shoving my hands into my pockets, I smirk back at her. "Yep."

She huffs at me, steps into what looks like a cotton skirt, and walks into the bathroom.

I actually thought it was going to be a whole hell of a lot harder to get her up and out, but once I decided that I wanted to show her the North Shore house, I was filled with an excitement that I rarely feel.

She comes out of the bathroom and walks straight to me. Unlike other times that I have seen her, she's chosen to skip all the makeup, and my heart skips a beat. Is there anything more perfect than her?

"Okay, I'm ready," she says, looking up at me.

Without thinking, I lean over and kiss her. It's just a small kiss, but I have to do it.

Her hand comes up and rests on my chest. Through her eyelashes, her eyes smile at me.

"Hi," I say quietly to her, bringing my hand up to cup the side of her face.

"Hi," she says almost shyly, leaning into my hand.

"You look beautiful this morning."

She stares at me just for a moment, blinks, and then leans in and wraps her arms around me. I give over to the sensation of being hugged, and tuck my head into her neck. Maybe we don't need to go anywhere.

"Matty," she whispers.

"Yeah?"

"I need coffee!" She smacks me on the ass and jumps away from me, laughing.

I can't believe she just did that, and it's crazy how happy it makes me. I'm having irrational thoughts about this being the best freaking day of my life all of a sudden. "Come on, gorgeous." I laugh while wrapping my arm around her shoulders and leading her out the door.

"GOOD MORNING, KIDS." Aunt Ella's eyes flash between the two of us. She looks surprised, but not, at the same time. In fact, she looks kind of thrilled. "Ellie, I'm surprised to see you up so early."

"He bribed me with coffee." She elbows me in the ribs, and I chuckle.

The look on Aunt Ella's face is a mixture of awe and curiosity. She looks at me, and our eyes lock. A grin splits across my face before I can even reel it in, and she just shakes her head. I guess to some, our coming in at six in the morning might look suspicious, but I really don't care.

"So, where are you off to?" Aunt Ella asks as she fixes us both some coffee to go.

"North Shore Drive," I answer her.

Her eyes flash to mine, and I can see the excitement in them. She knows that this is a big deal for me, to share something about myself with someone else. I feel proud that it's Ellie that I am taking.

"Well, alright then. You kids go have fun." She hands me my coffee and squeezes my arm. Her eyes are shining and I just shake my head at her, grinning.

Taking Ellie's hand, we walk out of the café and back to

the Jeep. I open her door and, as she slides by me to get in, she pinches my side.

"Ow! What was that for?"

"That was for your secret, silent conversation that you had with Aunt Ella. What were you two talking about?"

I laugh at her assessment, because she obviously doesn't miss anything. Closing her door, I walk around the back of the Jeep to collect my thoughts. I haven't stopped smiling since I showed up at her door. I feel like a different person today. It's both equally exhilarating and terrifying. I know it's because of her and, for now, I'm just going to go with it.

I climb into the Jeep, crank it on, and pull out of the parking lot. I can feel Ellie staring at me.

"Spill it, Hale!"

I smile again. "She's just happy for me; that's all."

"Why?"

"Because I've never done this before."

"Done what, take a girl for coffee?" she smirks at me.

Shrugging my shoulders, I glance over at her. "Yeah. Coffee . . . all of it. I told you, I don't do this kind of thing."

She sits quietly next to me, watching me. I wish I knew what she was thinking. Suddenly, I feel kind of vulnerable. Maybe I should have kept that to myself. My hand tightens on the steering wheel.

"Well, then, just so you know . . . this is the best cup of coffee I've ever had." Her voice is sweet and genuine.

Pulling into the driveway of the North Shore house, I kill the engine and turn to face her. She's smiling at me, and it occurs to me that the ache in my chest isn't there. It hasn't been there all morning.

Reaching over, I wrap my hand around her neck and bring her mouth to mine. I kiss her and she smiles against my lips.

I'm quickly beginning to get addicted to kissing her, stealing one whenever I can.

"Come on, let's go!" I'm so excited to show her my house. I hop out of the Jeep and walk around it to grab her hand. She giggles.

"Matty, are you sure we should be walking into this house?" she asks as we walk up the front steps. The house is set on stilts as a precaution against storm surges.

I smile at her as I unlock the front door. Together, we walk in, and I watch her eyes as they scan the open space. The house isn't super large. I never needed it to be. It's more square footage than I'll ever use.

"Whose house is this?" she asks, stepping away from me to get a better look. Her gaze takes in the bamboo wood floors, the living room where I custom-built the shelves around the fire place, the kitchen, and the back wall of the house, which is made of glass.

"Mine," I say proudly, walking over to the kitchen to sit down on a barstool that I had brought in.

Her head swings to me, but her body doesn't move. There's confusion in her eyes. "I don't understand."

"What don't you understand?" I place my elbows on the kitchen island and lean forward.

"It's just, this house, it must have cost a fortune." She looks around the house again and waves an arm as she says this.

"Yeah, it wasn't cheap, but I got a great deal on it. It was an older home. Been on the island for a long time. The bones of the house are strong, so I've gutted the inside to make it more current. More me, I guess."

"But, how can you afford this? Aren't you a handyman?" She walks into the kitchen, and drags her fingers across the granite countertop to stand across from me.

I can't help but laugh at her statement. "Uh, thanks for that; but, yes, I can afford it and, no, I am not just a handyman. Your assumption is wrong."

She drops her eyes and her cheeks turn pink. "I know. I'm sorry. That came out wrong. It's just, you're twenty-one and, with as much as you work, I know you aren't in college." Her eyes come back to mine.

"Nope, not in college. I inherited some money. That's how I bought this house."

She tilts her head. "So, why do you work for my aunt?"

"I don't," I say, laughing again.

Silence fills the space between us. There's confusion on her face again. She isn't following me.

"Ellie, I own the cottages, as well as a few other properties on the island. School was really never my thing, so I took the money and invested it. The rental properties do really well. Your aunt helps me manage them; the Oak Street cottages particularly."

Taking a step back away from the island, this time her neck flushes red along with her cheeks. "Wow," she says before she walks out of the kitchen and over to the windows that look down on the dunes and out to the beach. "I feel stupid," she mutters.

"Don't. I didn't tell you. It's not exactly common for someone my age. I get it." I get up off the stool, walk over to her, and take her hand in mine.

"Are you going to rent out this place, too?" Her fingers tighten around mine.

"No, this one's for me. I plan on moving in after the first of the year." I tuck some of her hair behind her ear so I can see her better. Her gaze lifts to mine and, as my fingers graze her neck, she leans into me.

"It's really beautiful. Thank you for showing it to me." She smiles at me, and I feel it shoot straight through my chest.

"You haven't seen the best part yet," I say, smiling back. With her hand in mine, I take her upstairs, through my bedroom and out the French doors on the north side of the house.

"Oh, wow," she says, looking around.

There's a tree line that separates my home from the one next to it, and it provides the perfect level of privacy. The sun deck here allows me to see the sunrise and the sunset. There is nothing obstructing the view, and it's one of my favorite places ever.

We've missed the sunrise by just a couple of minutes. It's already visible in the sky, but it doesn't matter. It's still glad I brought her here.

Sitting down on two chaise longue chairs, a comfortable silence floats around us. She's drinking her coffee, watching the sunrise, and I'm drinking mine, watching her.

"So, are you doing all of the renovations by yourself?"

"Yeah, the ones that I can, anyway. I do have a team of people that works with me on occasion. I like working with my hands, always have."

"I remember you in that shed in Aunt Ella's backyard. You were building a table then."

"If I could have lived in that shed, I would have."

"I think this is also a good time to apologize to you for what I said the other night at your house, too." She looks at me sheepishly.

"What do you mean?" I reach for her hand and lace our fingers together.

"Well, I didn't really think before I spoke. When I made that comment about your brothers and then asked you what did, if you were an athlete, it came out wrong. It's like they have these super-human talents and I was just wondering what yours was. I overstepped my bounds. So, I'm sorry."

"Super-human talents, huh?" I take a sip of my coffee.

She hangs her head a little and looks at me through her eyelashes. I rub my thumb across the back of her hand. I don't want her to think I'm upset with her, because I'm not.

"I can get used to that description; almost like super hero powers." I grin at her.

Her lips twitch and slowly lift into a smile.

"I actually do have one. I just never made a career out of it like they did. I run—really fast. It was always my thing"

Shaking her head at me, her smile turns into a smirk. "So, I shouldn't feel bad for asking, then?"

"Yes, you definitely should," I smile at her and try my best to look wounded. "With the age gap being so large between us, I have been asked that question pretty much my whole life. It got old real quick."

"So, if you can run, why didn't you pursue that?" She untucks her legs and stretches them out. I'm momentarily distracted.

"I don't know. If you haven't noticed yet, people aren't really my thing. I prefer the quiet. I like keeping to myself."

"Yeah, I've kind of noticed. Why is that? Why do you want to be so . . . alone?"

We are now moving into uncomfortable territory. I need to change the subject.

I clear my throat. "Let's not go there right now. The questions are now for you. Starting with, what are you doing here?" I want to learn more about her. No, not just more—everything.

"What do you mean? You brought me here," she says, narrowing her eyes at me with a devious little grin. I see that she can evade questions, too.

"I mean, on the island, but somehow I think you knew that. Don't you have a life to get back to?" I know that if I left the island for a week or more, tons of work would pile up. She has to be behind on something.

She's uncomfortable with this question, just like I was uncomfortable with mine. Apparently, we have more in common than I thought. I instantly regret asking it. If she wanted to tell me, then she would have. I hate that I just ruined the light-hearted mood we had a minute ago.

Letting out a sigh, she looks around the deck and out around the house before getting up, walking back down the stairs to the sliding glass doors in the great room. Her arms are folded across her chest. I know she's not trying to leave, so I stand back and give her the space that she seems to need, even though I desperately want to reach out to her. If I could, I would take whatever ugly demons she's fighting right now, and carry the burden for her.

"It's not that simple," she whispers, looking out over the water.

Yep. We have a hell of a lot more in common than I ever would've thought possible. "It never is, is it?"

Chapter Eleven

ELLE

I KNOW I need to tell him. I need to tell somebody, but by doing that I feel like I am losing even more control of my life. Every day, from the moment I wake up to the moment I go to bed, I feel so helpless and angry. No one understands the constant battle that I have going on in my head to try and gain some sort of normalcy, when all I feel is fear.

I'm not sure why I haven't told anyone yet. It's just taken over so many parts of my life that I don't want it to bleed into the little bit that's left.

However, if whoever it is finds me here, then having people know what is going on might be important.

Taking a deep breath, I close my eyes because, for whatever reason, this makes me feel like I am still avoiding the truth that this is really happening to me. "I'm here because I'm hiding. I'm being stalked."

He sharply sucks in a gasp of air. "What?!" I flinch at the

tone of his voice. I don't think he meant to shout at me, but he did.

My stomach starts to ache because I can't tell if he is mad at me or mad at the situation. What if he thinks I'm a coward for running away? Or what if he doesn't take me seriously, like my mother? I didn't realize until just now how important his opinion on this—on me—is to me. Opening my eyes, I rub my hands across my stomach to try to calm it. I know I need to see his face—his reaction—so I turn and face him. His jaw is locked tight, and anger is radiating off of him.

"Over the last couple of weeks, I started getting scary letters in the mail and at places I work. I discovered that this person had been in my condo, and two nights before I showed up here, someone grabbed me from behind. I didn't know what to do or where to go." Reliving these separate incidents causes my eyes to fill with tears. Each one of them was scary enough, but to talk about them all at once makes me start to sweat.

His expression immediately changes and becomes hard. He's pinned with an indecipherable look and I feel like the storm in his eyes is directed straight at me. "Did you call the police? Does Aunt Ella know?"

"No, I didn't call them. You don't understand, I can't have my name and all this drama splashed in the tabloids. Photographers will start following my every move, and that will lead whoever this is right to me. And, no, Aunt Ella doesn't know—no one does." He blinks at me in disbelief and then starts pacing.

"So, let me get this straight, the last time this person had any type of contact with you was the Saturday before you arrived, right?" He runs his hand through his hair.

"No, I got an email on Friday night," I say, watching him.

He stops and stands right in front of me. "What did it

say?" His cheeks are flushed. He's angry.

"That I was stupid for running and thinking that I couldn't be found." I drop my head. I can't stand his disappointment in me. All of this is hard enough without feeling like I'm doing something wrong.

"You should have told me," he says, very matter-of-fact, while lifting my chin so he can see my face.

"I'm sorry," I whisper. Maybe I should have told him but, up until last night, he didn't really make me feel like I could confide in him about something so delicate.

Gently, he grabs my arm and pulls me into him.

"Matt, I don't know what to do," my voice catches, and he hugs me tighter. "I've been living in this constant state of fear. Everything scares me. I'm afraid of the phone. Now I'm even afraid of my email. I'm afraid to leave the house. I'm afraid to be in the car. I'm afraid of the noises outside the cottage. I feel like I am afraid of everything, and I question everything. This person is out there, and I'm terrified. You asked me when I was going home. I don't know, because I don't want to live there anymore. This person was in my home." A sob breaks free, and Matt holds me as I start to cry.

"Why haven't you told anyone?" his voice is calm as he starts rubbing his hand up and down my back.

"I mentioned something to my mother when the first letter came in. She laughed it off and told me to feel flattered, that it was a perk of my job. But the letters haven't stopped."

His hand stalls. "Your mom sounds like a real piece of work," he spits out.

"She is. So many things about her over the last couple of months have become obvious. I don't know why I didn't stand up for myself sooner. I know she hates Aunt Ella. It's no secret." I turn my head on his chest and look back toward the beach. His hand has resumed the rubbing.

"Yeah, you told me when I took you home from the Sandbar."

"Oh," I mutter, pulling back to look at him, shock evident on my face. "That makes me wonder what else I told you."

He grins at me.

"You don't understand; time and time again I have had to listen to her complain about what she never got, but should have—starting with Aunt Ella's house. She pushed and pushed me into this career, because she felt that so many things were owed to her and she damn well was going to get them. It was never about me, always about her."

His hands cup my face as he studies me. His thumbs lightly swipe across my cheeks to remove the tears. "Tell me about the letters. What did they say?"

"Oh, just random things, but they always end with the same message, that's how I know they're from the same person. *Anytime, anywhere . . . and you are mine.*"

"What do you mean, 'from the same person'? Has this happened before?" Agitation crosses his face.

"Yeah, but it's never gone on this long." A shiver runs through me and he feels it. One hand leaves my face and resumes running up and down my back.

"I'm thinking I don't like your career choice anymore," he mumbles.

"Believe me, it wasn't much of a choice, and that makes two of us," I admit, letting out another sigh.

"So, what are you gonna do?" he asks me.

Thinking about his question, I give him the only answer I can come up with: "I don't know."

"You know, you can stay here as long as you like," he says quietly, and I burrow further into his chest. His words are exactly what I need to hear right now. I wish he would ask me to stay forever.

Taking a deep breath, I'm hit with relief. I thought that telling someone about this would make me more scared, but it's done quite the opposite. I don't feel as alone. *Alone*. My mind drifts back to Matt and, before I can stop it, the words are out of my mouth.

"No more about me. Now that you know my story, the question comes back to you. Are you ever going to tell me more? It seems to me that you have a few secrets of your own. Don't get me wrong, I like the way you are, but you are way too beautiful to be living a life of solitude."

He pulls back from me, the darkness from the storm clouds flickering in his eyes. He momentarily forgets about me standing in front of him, and I watch as some memory seems to move in and take over. He tenses and, suddenly, I regret bringing it up. Clearly, something big has happened to him and he isn't ready to share it with me, or maybe he doesn't want to, but I can't help wishing that he felt he could.

MATT

I HATE WHAT the memories do to me. Ellie shifts her weight and steps a little closer to me. I look down into her eyes and I am lost. No, I am found. I know that she wants to understand me better, but this is the best I can give her. And this is more than I have ever opened up to anyone. With this girl, I feel like I am finally finding some sense of purpose in this life and it scares me.

Lost in my own thoughts, she wraps her hands around my neck and brings her mouth to mine. This time I let her kiss me, unlike last night, where I completely took control and devoured her. She softly parts my lips with hers and, when our tongues meet, a moan escapes me. In less than a flash, I have her flipped around and pushed against the glass door.

"You taste so good, Ellie," I tell her, slipping my hands around her waist to pull her up just a little higher. She leans forward, up onto her toes. Her back arches and she opens up even more for me. Her perfect form is pushing into me, melding with me, and it's awakening every nerve ending in my body. Her heart is beating erratically and, by the way she is clenching the back of my shirt, I can tell she wants this kiss just as much as I do.

Needing to feel more of her, my hand slips down and under the edge of her skirt. I slide it up the back of her thigh and squeeze her backside, pushing her hips into mine. I want her, and she can feel the evidence of this as she shifts side to side to create a slight friction between the two of us.

Minutes pass, but it feels like time has stopped. Everything about her and about this feels like perfection, and there's that feeling again . . . home. Knowing that she isn't here to stay, though, that she will one day leave, I memorize what it feels like to have her in my arms and in my home. In so many ways, she doesn't have any idea what she is doing to me—she is saving me.

"Don't mind me," a voice comes from behind.

Ellie freezes, gasps, and hides her face. I quickly drop her skirt.

He laughs and I see red. I'm going to kill him.

"What are you doing here?" I ask him without turning around. Although hearing his voice was like a straight shot of ice water, I need a few more seconds before I turn around. As it is, I'm already going to be teased endlessly by this; no need to add details.

"I saw the Jeep outside and thought I'd come in and say hi to my baby brother. It never once occurred to me that you would have company." I can hear the humor in his voice. He is loving every minute of this.

Elle slowly lifts her head and peeks around my shoulder at him.

"Hi," he says to her, a little too enthusiastically for me.

"Hi," she answers back, stepping away from me, smoothing down her clothes.

I watch her reaction to him. All my life, people have gone all starry-eyed over Beau, especially since he's done so well on the courts. It's like people can't help themselves and, add in the fact that he is good-looking, immediately, they get tongue-tied. Watching Ellie, though, causes a surge of pride to gush through me. She's not fazed by him and, in general, looks indifferent. Seeing her reaction makes me feel even more like she's mine, and I have to fight down the big, stupid grin that's trying to make its way onto my face.

Turning around, I glare at him. "You know, you kind of saw that we were busy. You could have left and called me later."

"And ruin this opportunity to meet your friend? No chance," he deadpans directly at me.

He walks over to Elle and holds out his hand. "Hi, I'm Beau, the older, wiser, better- looking brother." He gives her one of his million-dollar smiles.

She laughs and returns his handshake. "Wow, arrogant much? You know what they say . . . those who like to talk have a very small . . ."

159

Beau's eyes get large, and he throws his head back and laughs. He glances my way and his eyes tell me that he cannot believe she just said that, but he approves of her. I raise an eyebrow at him and smirk.

Elle looks him over from head to toe, seemingly uninterested, and then she turns to me, "What do you think, Matty?"

"Yeah, what do you think, Maaaattty?" he drawls out the nickname, and I don't even give a crap right now. I'm too busy smiling at her.

Wrapping my arm around her shoulders, I pull her close to me and give Beau the same once-over. "As a matter of fact, now that you mention it . . ."

"Oh, you'd better stop right there!" Beau says animatedly while still laughing.

I smile back at him and squeeze her a little tighter.

"So, who are you?" he asks, his eyes still trained on her.

"Elle. It's nice to meet you." She turns into me a little, wraps one arm around my back, and places the other on my stomach. I love the feel of her hands on me.

The wheels in Beau's brain are turning. He's looking at her suspiciously, and then his face transforms like he's having some sort of revelation. "You've done some work with my wife, right?" he asks very excitedly.

"Yes, I have," she answers him, giggling. Beau is very infectious. When he laughs, everyone laughs. When he's moody, everyone's quiet.

"Well, that's awesome. Does she know you're here?" He runs his hand through his hair, and I look down at her to see what she's going to say.

"Nope, no one does, and on purpose." My eyes flip back to his, and his eyebrows shoot up as she gets her point across.

He studies her for minute and then smirks. "Gotcha. No

worries on our end. We know exactly how you feel. This little island has always been our secret sanctuary."

I let out a breath I didn't realize I was holding. Beau also likes to meddle in people's business, and I was worried for her. I wouldn't have put it past him to press her for more information.

"Yes, I can see that. This trip was much needed." She glances at me and smiles. That damn smile gets me every time, and a moment of silence passes between the three of us.

"Oooookaay, well, I won't stay," Beau says, forcing me to tear my eyes away from her. "I don't want to keep you two kids, but you both should stop by tomorrow night. I'm going to grill out and you should come for dinner."

He's pushing me, I can feel it. And suddenly, I want to bring her over to his house for dinner. I want to know what it feels like to have her as a part of my life, even if it is just for a short while.

"Okay. Ellie, what do you say?" I ask her, looking into her eyes.

"I'd love to," she smiles at me, and I realize I'm smiling right back at her.

"Awesome, settled then." Beau claps his hands together, gaining our attention. He smiles at me one more time, nods at Ellie, and walks to the door.

Watching Beau leave, I turn back to her and smile. It's like I can't stop doing it now that I've started. She's watching me closely, and I like it.

"So, is he always like that?" she asks.

"Like what, all in your face? Yeah," I say, laughing, while leaning down to kiss her again.

Chapter Twelve

ELLE

MY STOMACH HAS been hurting all day long. I don't know why I am so nervous to see her, but I am. Over the last week, for the first time in a long time, I feel like I've been able to just be me. Little by little, the makeup has come off, my hair isn't styled so perfectly, and I've felt relaxed and free. Now I'm torn, because I feel like I should be putting on my face, and stepping into the role I've been taught to play. Leila is a part of that world, a world that I feel has certain expectations, only I'm ready to set my own and not live by other people's standards. Insecurity is trying to prick its way into my psyche, but I refuse to acknowledge it.

Slipping on a long beach skirt, I pull on a tank top and cover it with a wrap sweater. The weather dropped just a bit in temperature, so it's a little cooler today.

Matt showed up earlier than planned, saying he couldn't wait any longer to see me. I'm still smiling.

I've left the bathroom door open as I finish getting ready, and he's standing behind me—leaning against the door frame, watching me. I used to feel self-conscious about people seeing what's underneath, but with him I don't. He's seen me at my worst this week, yet he still looks at me as if I am the most precious thing to him.

Screwing the lip gloss shut, I smack my lips together, and turn around to face him. His eyes sweep over me from head to toe, and the flecks of silver in his gray eyes darken. My cheeks blush under his perusal.

"What?" I ask him nervously.

"Just like what I see, and I'm wondering why you bothered with the gloss when I'm just going to take it off." He grins at me.

I shrug my shoulders. "I like it."

"I like you," he says, reaching for my hand to pull me closer.

Matt is wearing a black t-shirt, dark worn-in jeans that not only look super comfortable but totally hot on him, a wide gray canvas belt, and black flip flops. The jeans sit low on his hips and, without a doubt, I have never seen anyone look as good as he does right now. Just being near him affects me so much.

He leans down and kisses the corner of my mouth. It's such a sweet and tender move that another little piece of my heart breaks off for him.

"You ready?" his gaze is scanning my face. I nod my head and he smiles.

We don't talk much on our way to Beau's house. I have no idea where they live and, with each second that passes, my nerves get a little jumpier.

This entire situation is completely surreal for me. I know I am getting myself all worked up, but three days ago he barely acknowledged me, and now I am going to have dinner with his family.

Matt reaches over and lays his hand on my leg. My eyes shoot to his. He sees that I am silently freaking out, and that one touch from him comforts me immensely.

He pulls up to a gate and punches a code to get in. We drive forward and stop in front of a beautiful Mediterranean-style home.

Matt shifts to face me, "If this is too much for you, we can go home and do something else."

I regard him closely. My heart is racing, but I have to ask him, I have to know. "Why me, Matt?"

"What do you mean?" he looks at me curiously.

"I mean . . . have you ever brought anyone else over here for dinner?" I'm anxious to hear his answer, even though, based on what I know of him, I already know what it will be.

"No."

"Why not? And why me then?" I ask again. Why did he choose me?

He drops his eyes to my lap and reaches for my hand. Intertwining his fingers with mine, he bites on his bottom lip as he thinks about how to respond. I'm wiggling my toes because I can't keep still. Now, I'm worried I've changed his mind. I just should have kept my mouth shut.

"Because, you are the first girl I have ever wanted to bring here. I know what you are asking, but I don't really have an answer. You make me happy, and when I'm near you I feel more relaxed. It's hard to explain, but the way I feel about you I have never felt for anyone else." He brings his eyes back to mine. "Is that good enough?"

"But three days ago, you wanted nothing to do with me,"

I say quietly.

"That's because three days ago—no, eight days ago—I knew you were going to change me."

His answer is so honest, and I understand him, because he is changing me, too. My nerves settle and it hits me again how much I really do like him.

Leaning forward, I place my lips on his. His free hand dips under my hair and wraps around the back of my neck. He deepens the kiss, and I fall into the taste and feel of him.

Pounding on the hood of the Jeep causes us both to jump. Standing there, with his arms crossed over his chest, is Beau.

"Really?" Matt says to him, shaking his head.

"My wife cooked dinner, it smells freaking awesome, and I'm hungry. Let's go, kids!" He spins around, stomps back up the steps, and disappears into the house.

I reach for the door handle, but Matt has other plans as he pulls me back to him and kisses me one more time. Giggling, I wiggle free and hop out. He meets me at the steps, and he's grinning from ear to ear.

"I like it when you smile," I say to him.

"Well, that's what happens when I kiss you. Can't help it. Want more smiles? Keep the kisses coming."

"Deal," I lean in to kiss him again as we make our way up the steps.

"I told you you wouldn't need the lip gloss," he mutters as we walk in the front door.

BEAU WAS RIGHT, the house smelled amazing and dinner was delicious. Beau grilled some grouper, and Leila had fixed an asparagus salad, crab cakes, and an herb and vegetable risotto. I know it probably didn't seem like much to them, but I ate more than I have in a long time.

After dinner, Matt and Beau decided to make a quick trip over to Matt's house to look at something, no idea what, but it occurs to me that his house is only a few doors down. It will be nice for the two of them to live so close to each other.

Settling into a lounge chair on their back deck, I'm watching the sun set while Leila takes Quinn to bed. She is, by far, the cutest and sweetest little girl I have ever seen. I shouldn't be surprised, though; looking at her parents, there's no way she's going to be anything other than amazing. Less than ten minutes later, Leila hands me a glass of white wine.

"Wow, she goes down really easily." I look at Leila.

"Yeah, Beau and I are lucky. She really is perfect." Leila flops down in the chair next to mine. "I can't believe you've been here on the island and you haven't come to see me." She shakes her head, smiling at me.

All of my memories of Leila are of her smiling and laughing. She worked really hard to get where she is in the fashion industry, and people just love her.

"I'm sorry I haven't stopped by. I wasn't feeling well when I got here and, honestly, I was just trying to lay low."

"I understand. But now that I know you are here, we'll have to get together. How long are you staying?" she asks.

I don't mean to glance down at my glass, but the thought of leaving Matt so soon has everything inside of me screaming. I'm not ready to leave yet.

"I don't know. I need to figure a few things out and then I'll have a better idea."

"I see," she says with a knowing smile, but not pushing any further. "So, how has work been?"

"Busy. I know that time is not on my side, twenty-five will be here before I know it, but I'm tired and really needed this break."

"I don't think you need to worry about your age so much. I understand what you're saying, but you have built an amazing reputation and there are a lot of designers, including me, who prefer experience over youth. You'll be fine, don't you worry," she says reassuringly.

"Thanks, I appreciate that." Taking a sip of my wine, I look out at the water.

"You know, if and when you decide to slow things down a bit, I might have an opportunity for you," she says quietly, almost like she's uncertain, but also like she's trying to feel me out.

"Really? Such as?" I'm curious and desperate to know.

"Well, let me think over the fine details before we discuss it further, but you would come on board and be a part of my team. And as long as side jobs don't interfere or are a conflict of interest, you are welcome to continue the runway."

"Wow, I don't know what to say." Over the last couple of months, I have been so confused and uncertain about what I'm going to be able to do next. My eyes well up with tears. I'm looking at her, and right now she feels kind of like my savior. She started the first phase of my career, and it looks like she will be a part of the next, too. I am overwhelmed and feeling so grateful that I'm at a complete loss for words.

"Don't say anything; just say you'll think about it." She smiles at me.

"Oh, I already have and I'm in. I love what I do, but I need a change and I need to let my mother go." I didn't mean to say that last part out loud, but now that I have, I am relieved to tell someone.

"It's about freaking time!" she almost yells at me. "I'm not sure if you realize this or not, but she has directly hurt your career over the years. Don't get me wrong, the things you have done are beautiful and amazing, but no one wants her around."

Hearing Leila say this doesn't surprise me. I have picked up on the distasteful vibe that radiates off of different designers. I should have known; things have been slowing down a little, but I just thought it was because of my age.

"Leila, if I tell you something, will you keep it to yourself?" She hears the emotion in my voice and concern sweeps across her face. I don't want to cry in front of her, but being here, talking to her, I realize I really need someone.

"Of course," she says softly. "This isn't business. You are in my home as my friend and my brother-in-law's date." She grins from ear to ear.

"You may change your mind about the job offer." I look down at my hands as they are twirling the stem of the glass.

"I doubt it, but let's hear it," she says.

Taking a deep breath, I say the words that I haven't said to anyone. "I have arthritis."

"So?"

"Rheumatoid arthritis." A weight lifts off of my shoulders that I didn't know was there.

"How is that different?"

"It's an autoimmune disease that causes inflammation in the joints and surrounding tissues, but the body thinks that the healthy tissue is an invader and it attacks. Over time, the joints can become disfigured."

"What joints, where?" her eyebrows furrow and she frowns.

"Fingers, wrists, knees, ankles, feet—those are the most common." I bend my fingers. The mobility in them returned a few days ago, but they are still sore.

Her eyes move to my hands and my feet. "Does it hurt?"

"Yes, very much." More tears fill my eyes as I think about the pain from this past week's flare.

"Wow. I'm sorry to hear that." The wind blows, and silence falls between us as I pull myself together.

"You are the first person I've told." And I'm so glad I did. I glance at her out of the corner of my eye.

Her eyes widen in surprise. "Why?" She shifts in her seat, pulling her legs up under her to face me a little more.

"Because, people talk. There are no secrets in this industry and there are too many people trying to get ahead. Why would anyone want to risk hiring a model who may or may not be able to wear the shoes?"

"Oh, Elle, I think you underestimate people," she says sympathetically.

"Maybe, but this makes me not perfect, and I'm used to trying to be perfect all the time."

"I understand that." She tilts her head at me, still frowning, "You haven't told Matt?"

"No. He saw how sick I was all week, so he knows something's up, but he never asked and I never offered."

"Well, I think you should. Especially if he can help you."

"Maybe." I should tell him. I'm probably making this a bigger deal than it is but, then again, I'm the one who has this and has to live with it. It is a big deal to me.

The door beeps, alerting us that they are back. We can hear them laughing as they walk through the house, and I see Leila smile.

"By the way, I haven't changed my mind," she says quietly as the guys each grab a beer from the deck refrigerator.

My eyes lock on to hers. They are so blue and sparkly, and kind. She will never know what she did for me tonight. She listened to me and accepted me, even knowing I'm not perfect. I never thought she would make me feel bad about myself, but to feel this relief from telling someone is more than I could've ever dared to expect. I am so glad it was her.

Matt and Beau sit down in the chairs across from us. Matt's eyes find mine and he gives me one of his heart-stopping smiles.

"What's up, ladies?" Beau says as he leans back in his chair, glancing back and forth between the two of us.

I look at Leila, and she just shakes her head at him.

"What?" he grins at her and directs his attention back to me. "So, Elle, did you know that dolphins have sex for pleasure? Some even like to masturbate."

I blink at him, and then my eyes narrow. His grin is stretching into a smile, and he's obviously waiting for my response. I see Matt shaking his head and rolling his eyes in his brother's direction.

"That's interesting, but did you know that oysters can change from one gender to the other and back again, depending on which is best for mating? Seems to me they have the best of both worlds, don't you think?"

Matt chuckles next to me.

Beau shoots me a wide, approving grin, like I am speaking his language or something. "I think you're right; best of both worlds." He looks over to Matt and winks. "I approve."

"Whatever, dude," Matt says, smiling. An unspoken conversation passes between the two of them. It's clear that they love each other very much.

Matt and Beau together are something else. Most of the

night, I couldn't help but watch them. They look so similar, but their personalities are so different. Beau is funny. He likes to talk, crack jokes, and make people smile. Matt is reserved. He's quiet, thoughtful, observant, and never chooses to stand in the spotlight.

He's smiled more times tonight than I can count, and I *was* counting. Those smiles are so few and far between and, with each one, he's unknowingly stealing another piece of me.

MATT

"SO, HOW DID you meet her?" Beau asks me as we bring up the last of the tile from the garage at the North Shore house. I knew he was itching for details. I'm surprised he waited this long.

"Uh, I actually met her the first time when I was thirteen."

"What! You've had, like, a secret girlfriend all this time?" he says jokingly.

I can't help but laugh at him. "No, that was when I met her. I haven't seen her since, until I ran into her last Monday. She's staying in the cottage next to mine."

"Leila likes her, like, a lot. She was crazy excited when I told her I saw you both at the house. She thinks she is the perfect girl for you."

I scowl at his comment. "I still don't know that there is such a thing, Beau."

"Are you sure about that?" he raises his eyebrows in question.

I shake my head in response, lost in my own doubt. "She

doesn't even live here. She'll head back to New York soon enough, and that'll be it."

He studies me for a moment. "Is that what you want?"

No, it's not what I want. The mere thought of Elle leaving fills me with dread. It's like standing in the light and watching it dim until I am shrouded in darkness again. It's absolutely not what I want. But I can't ask her to stay.

"Does it matter?" My good mood just took a nose dive. Leila is right about one thing; she is the perfect girl . . . but probably the perfect girl for someone who is a little less imperfect.

Walking away from him, I wander out to the back deck. The sun has set, but the sky still has streaks of yellow and orange. He steps up next to me, eyes me, but keeps quiet and then looks out toward the horizon.

"What was that phrase Uncle Ben used to say all the time?"

"Follow the sun," I answer with no hesitation.

"That's the one. I like that phrase, makes sense."

My head whips around so I can face him. "What do you mean, *it makes sense*? Tell me." How does he know what that phrase means? Uncle Ben never told me what it meant to him, so I know he didn't tell Beau.

His eyes move back to me. "I'm not going to tell you. That's for you to figure out," he grins at me.

"What? You're an ass," I hiss out. "Who are you, Gandhi, now? I've been trying to figure out that damn statement for years."

I loved Uncle Ben and I'd like to think that, over the years, I came to know him very well. I'm sure he had his secrets; after all, he was the adult and I was the kid, but in general he wore his heart on his sleeve—what you saw was what you got. I want to know what that phrase means, because it feels like a missing puzzle piece to him. I don't think it's going to change my outlook on life, but I always wanted to know more about his. He lived by this motto. I just wish I understood it.

"Speaking of ass, did you know that it is impossible to pass gas silently if you remove all of the hairs around your anus?" he smiles real big at me. Beau is obviously completely unaffected by my frustration with him for refusing to share more of his enlightened, philosophical crap with me.

"Dude, that's gross and I'm not even going to ask how you know that."

He laughs at my response and I walk away from him, back into the house. I'm appreciative of his help, because I recognize that this is exactly what this was, but I'm ready to get back to Ellie.

"Yep, just think about all those girls out there who go full wax and are uneducated." He follows behind me, and is still grinning as I lock the doors.

"MATT, I'M SURPRISED you didn't bring Bruno." Leila says as she hands me another beer.

"I thought about it, but changed my mind. He's fine at home. What we should have brought is Ellie's guitar." I look at her and grin.

"You play the guitar? That's awesome! I always wanted to learn how to play," Beau chimes in.

"Yeah, I can play, but I don't play for people. That's *way* out of my comfort zone." She pins me with a look that says, "Thanks a lot."

"She should. She's really good," I say encouragingly.

Her eyes narrow. "How would you know?"

"Because I've heard you almost every day since you've been here."

"Oh." Her cheeks redden and it's damn adorable.

"I bet Quinn would like it," Beau says, and my eyes drift to him and Leila.

I'm not sure what she and Ellie talked about while we were gone, but since Beau and I got back, Leila has watched her a little more intensely. Not in a negative way, but more, I don't know, almost protectively. She seems to be very attuned to Ellie's comments and reactions.

"I'll think about it," she says with a small shrug.

Noticing she's out of wine, I reach over, take her glass, and stand. "I'll go get you some more."

"Thanks." She smiles up at me and I feel it reach into every hidden part of me.

"I'll show you where it is," Leila says, climbing to her feet, too. I follow her inside, wishing it was Ellie instead.

Ellie.

I never thought I would be with anyone. I always thought that I would be alone. I wanted it this way, but now I'm not so sure. Being here tonight and having her with me is confusing me. It's all frighteningly normal, and I am afraid to bask in how damn awesome it feels. It's causing me to think about the prospect of wanting more, a more that I've never dared to consider before. Both Drew and Beau found their *more* in two amazing girls who love them for who they are, faults and all. Would Ellie do the same for me?

Sitting down at the kitchen island, my eyes are drawn to a

light that is flickering against my skin. Varying colors of yellow and orange, just like the sun. There's a big jar candle sitting next to the sink. I wonder how I never noticed it before.

"You're burning a candle?" I look at Leila. Sweat breaks out across my forehead, and I'm hoping she doesn't notice.

"Yeah." She tilts her head as she looks at me curiously. "I like the way they smell. Why?"

"But . . ."

Her look softens and she smiles. "It's okay, Matt. We aren't afraid of fire anymore; we haven't been for a while."

I tense at her words. *But I am!* I don't like it and don't want to see it, certainly not in the house. Without thinking, I lean over and blow it out. Smoke from the wick floats through the air and hits my nose. I'm repulsed by a smell that I haven't had to smell in years, and I jump out of the chair.

Leila's watching me, and her eyebrows pull together as concern washes over her face. Needing to get away from the smell, I turn and walk straight up the stairs and into Quinn's room. I don't know why I went to her room, maybe it's because I have this insane need to protect her always—even though, at the moment, the flame is out and nothing is wrong—or, it's because I need to fill myself with her sweetness, her innocence.

"Unca Matt?" I woke her coming into the room and instantly feel bad.

"Hi, sweet girl. Want me to rock you for a few minutes?"

She sits up in the bed and nods.

I pick her up, she cuddles into me, and my heart slowly begins to calm down. She smells like baby soap and lavender. Holding her tight, I sit in the rocker and rock. Looking around her room, my eyes fill with tears. I would do anything to protect this, protect her. Why didn't anyone do the same for me?

Closing my eyes, I see the candle sitting next to the sink, and it reminds me of the first time my 'father' showed me how to make a fire.

"Matt, come in here," my father says as I pass by the garage.

I don't say anything. I just walk into the garage as he commanded.

"Come over here. I want to show you something."

Weaving past the bikes, I find him in the back where his work bench is. His eyes are dark as he regards me, and filled with an unknown excitement. I'm confused as to why he is talking to me. He never talks to me.

"Do you like science?" he asks.

I nod my head. I know better than to speak.

"I want to show you an experiment that I just learned. It's all about chemical reactions."

I step closer to see what he has in the sink. The bottom of it is lined with newspapers.

"Most houses around here have a pool, so there is never a shortage of pool cleaner or 'shock'." He takes a large white industrial bottle of the pool cleaner and pours some into an empty plastic water bottle. He sets the bottle down, puts the cap on the cleaner and pushes it to the side.

"Next, we have brake fluid. This fluid can probably be found at any home where the owner likes to work on cars in their garage." He picks up the water bottle and pours this fluid in with the pool cleaner and quickly sets it back in the sink. He puts the lid back on the brake fluid and sets it on the shelf, away from the pool cleaner.

Leaning over to look in the sink, he puts his hand on my chest, and backs us away. We can still see the bottle and to-

gether we watch and wait. About fifteen seconds later, the mix-
ture becomes cloudy and starts to bubble. Slowly, it rises in the
bottle and smoke starts to come out the top of it. I watch in
awe as the bottle begins to melt and then all of a sudden it
bursts into flames. The newspaper catches and the sink is on
fire.

"Isn't that amazing how these two liquids can make
fire?"

I nod my head, my eyes huge at what he just made.

The fire burns down a little, and he walks over to turn the
faucet on. Instantly, the flames go out.

Movement from the doorway catches my eye, and I blink
away the memory. Leila is leaning against the door frame,
watching me.

"You okay?" she asks.

"Sorry, I don't like fire," I whisper to her.

"I'm sorry, Matt. I didn't think about how the candle
would make you feel. I won't burn any more of them when
you are here."

I nod my head at her.

"I made a key lime pie. You should come down in a few
and get some before Beau eats it all." She grins at me and disappears.

Taking a few more deep breaths, I stand and place Quinn
back into her bed. Looking down at her, I think again about
how much I love her and will always protect her. My mind
drifts to Ellie; if I could, I'd protect her always, too. I suddenly
remember Ellie's wine, the reason I came inside in the first
place. Hopefully, Leila refilled it for her.

WALKING OUTSIDE, I spot Ellie standing at the edge of the deck, looking out at the water. Her hair is blowing in the breeze, and I can't help but feel possessive of her, like she's *mine*. She must sense my approach because she turns in my direction and gives me a warm, beautiful smile. Even if it is just for a little bit, right here, right now, she *is* mine and I think it's time we leave. I need to be alone with her.

Chapter Thirteen

ELLE

"SO, HOW DO you feel about walking back? I can run down tomorrow morning to pick up the Jeep." Matt asks as he steps up behind me and wraps his arms around my waist.

Twisting, I turn around to look at him and my heart instantly starts beating harder. He leans forward, pushing me into the deck railing and pulling on my lower back at the same time to close the distance between us. With the warmth and leanness of his body against mine, I forget whatever it is that he just asked me. My hands slide up under his arms to his mid-back.

He knows he's affected me, and one side of his mouth lifts in a small smile. He licks his lips and bends down, placing feather-light kisses across my neck and up to my jaw. It doesn't matter how many times we have kissed before, all I can think right now is that his mouth is on me, *on me*.

The night air cools the moisture left behind, and chills

rush down my arm. My body shivers and I feel him smile against my skin at the same time his scent hits me. He always smells so good, and this time it's a mixture of sandalwood, something sweet, almost like vanilla, and him. I want to bottle this smell. It is so delicious.

"About that walk?" he asks, mumbling the words against the corner of my mouth.

"Oh . . . yeah, a walk sounds nice," I whisper.

He pulls back and gives me the most genuine smile. That's the thing about Matt's eyes. Since the night of the wedding, I haven't once worried about whether or not he wants to be with me. In his eyes, I can find the truth. It shines out of them and leaves me feeling humbled.

"I haven't been out that much over the last week, even though I've wanted to be."

He nods at me knowingly, while lacing his fingers with mine.

"Alright, then. Hey, Beau . . .," Matt says as we turn around, and he and Leila are watching us from the sliding glass doors. Beau has his arm wrapped around her, and they are both smiling at us like proud parents. I can't help but blush and he chuckles. "We're going to take off. Thanks a lot for having us over for dinner." He steps away from me at the same time Beau lets go of Leila.

"Anytime, little dude!" He claps Matt on the back, and then gives him a quick hug.

Leila skips over to me and throws her arms around me. "I am so happy that you are here. You'll never know what seeing him like this means to us," she whispers. Pulling away from me, she keeps her hands on my waist and smiles real big, "Promise me you'll come back over before you leave."

"I will, I promise," I say, smiling and squeezing her arms.

Matt and I trade places. He's attacked by Leila and Beau scoops me up in his arms. "Thank you, Elle," and I know that his sentiment matches Leila's. I grin back at him knowingly.

"Let's go, gorgeous." Matt grabs my hand and drags me down the steps and into the sand. I can't help but laugh.

Slipping off our flip flops, Matt takes mine in one hand and wraps his other around mine.

The sand is cold, but nothing about my insides are. I glance at Matt as the moon light shines down on him, and I'm awestruck by how handsome he is. He is definitely what most would call tall, dark, and handsome. But, he's so much more than that. Studying the intricate and fine details of his face, I realize I could stare at him indefinitely.

He feels me gazing at him, smiles one of his adorable shy smiles, and then looks down at me. "You have a good time tonight?" He squeezes my hand.

"I did. I was nervous and I didn't need to be." I'm not sure why I just told him this, but I don't want to keep things from him. I know that he has his own secrets that he's not ready to share, but if I open up to him with all of mine, maybe one day he'll feel like he can do the same with me.

"Why were you nervous?" His thumb begins to brush back and forth across my hand. It's soothing and I know that he is trying to relax me.

"Because of Leila." She is his family, and I expect his re-action when his head whips my way, so he can look at me.

"Really? Why?" His thumb stops moving and I give him a small smile to try to ease some of the tension that just sur-rounded him.

"She's industry, and there are specific standards that are non-negotiable. Just my own insecurities . . . that's all. It's nothing that she has done."

He relaxes and this thumb starts moving again. "What standards? I've never known Leila really to stick to many standards. She's always done whatever she wanted to."

"The standard to be perfect." I hate saying this, but it's true.

"There's nothing wrong with you. No one is expected to be one-hundred-percent perfect all the time."

"Yes, *I* am expected to be perfect all the time. That's my job."

He studies me as we walk in silence. "You felt like she was going to be watching you tonight? Holding you to some impossible standard, just because she's *industry?*" he asks, frowning.

"Well, when you say it like that it sounds silly...and pretty shallow of me. But, I didn't know, and yes, she is your sister-in-law, but she is an extremely well-known and respected designer, too."

"She would never think anything bad about you." He's defending her, and that makes me adore him even more.

"I'm not saying that she would. It's just, over the years, I've learned to be aware of my words and my actions at all times. For example, one time I was out to lunch with Livy— my best friend—and as we were leaving, I made the comment "I'm stuffed and now I have a food baby," while rubbing my bloated stomach. Of course, someone heard that, snapped a cell phone photo, and the next thing I knew, that photo was everywhere, claiming I was pregnant and out to lunch to feed the baby."

Matt chuckles, and I can see him fighting a smile. "Sorry, but that sounds awful."

"It was awful. Clients that I had booked out over the next couple of months all called just to make sure it wasn't true."

"Is that why you didn't eat much tonight?" he pinches his lips into a thin line.

I look away from his penetrating gaze. "I don't know; didn't realize you'd notice."

He nods his head. "I notice everything about you."

His comment makes me blush on the outside and beam on the inside. "It wasn't that I wasn't hungry. I ate as much as I could, but my stomach is probably only the size of a kiwi."

"What? A kiwi?" he laughs.

"Don't make fun of me," I bump his hip with mine. "Yes, a kiwi. I really don't eat much, so my stomach is small. I watch every single calorie that goes into my mouth. It's part of the job. I've had to live this way for so long, I don't know how to live any differently. I've been better since I've been here," I say, glancing in his direction. Suddenly this moment feels like it's become way too serious. "Come on, Matt, you know models don't eat. Day in, day out, it's a trapped cycle."

"You shouldn't feel trapped," his voice is soft and his hand tightens around mine.

"I know I shouldn't, and I'm trying, but it's hard because I don't know if it's the job I don't like anymore, or me."

Matt stops walking and stares down at me. There are a few little wrinkles between his eyes that let me know he's thinking hard; I just wish I knew about what. His free hand moves to tuck some of my hair behind my ear, and then he cups the side of my neck. Using his thumb, he pushes up on my chin to tilt my head back.

"Well, I like you," he says, and I know he truly means it.

"I like you, too."

Standing there in silence, with the only sound being that of the water breaking on the shore, I want him to kiss me. I want him to kiss me so badly, but he doesn't.

Giving me a soft smile, he wraps his arm around me, pulls me flush against his side, and we start walking again. My arm slides around the back of him, and I grip on to his waist.

A comfortable silence envelops us as we continue walking. Eventually, we reach the turnoff to Oak Street.

"I knew you were nervous about tonight, but I thought it was because you were going to be around my family, not because of an employer."

My heart breaks a little bit at his words. Now I feel like I've made this whole night all about me and my issues. "Trust me, it was both. But once Leila and I sat down to talk, I calmed down. She really is just wonderful."

"She is. Did you tell her why you are here? About the stalker? She might know what to do."

The thought crossed my mind, but just briefly. I didn't want to ruin the night by burdening her with this, too. I was having such a good time. I didn't want the mood to change, and it would have. "No, but I did tell her about the arthritis."

"Arthritis?" he looks down at me.

I just nod my head. I look down and try to examine my toes in the darkness of the sand.

"So, that's what's been going on with you?"

"Yep." Now he knows. I thought I would feel more relief telling him, but I don't. I feel self-conscious, even though I know I shouldn't. Old habits—like the obsession to be seen as a portrait of perfection— are definitely hard to break.

We reach the wooden footpath and he drops our flip flops. Brushing the sand off the bottoms of our feet, we slip them on, and he wraps his arm back around me.

"Why were you so sick then? I was really worried about you the other morning." He rubs his hand up and down my arm as we walk up to the street.

"It happens when I have a flare up; at least it does with this type of arthritis, but mostly it's under control."

"What causes the flare up?" He looks down at me.

"Stress."

"I see," he nods to himself. "How's your stress level now?"

"I'm not sure. At this point, I think it's fear more than stress."

We've reached my door and Matt peers down at me. "You've got me. I'm here for you, so don't be afraid."

His words are soft and his eyes are on our joined hands. They run through my mind and melt my heart. I would be lying if I said that our situation didn't make me nervous, because it does. I don't know what is going to happen between us tomorrow, the next day, or even next week. But hearing him say that he's here for me, right now, makes me forget about the doubts. It makes me feel not so alone.

"Thank you. I appreciate that." I squeeze his hand gently.

His eyes meet mine again and one side of his mouth lifts slightly into a grin. "I may have ulterior motives." I can hear the smile in his voice.

I release a long breath. "Is that so?" I step closer to him.

"Mmm hmmm." His other hand comes up, and his fingers trace down the side of my neck.

"Maybe you should tell me about these motives."

"Maybe I will some time." His hand cups my face and his thumb runs over my bottom lip.

"How about now? Do you want to come inside?" I ask him. There's no tremor and no hesitation to my voice.

His eyes are locked onto my mouth and slowly they lift to mine. His expression changes to one of ardor and incredulity. He's thinking the same thing I am; should he come inside tonight? Will he be here the whole night? He's searching, searching for anything that might make him say no, when I know for certain he wants to say yes.

MATT

UP UNTIL THIS point, the most physical contact that I've had with her was yesterday at my house when I ran my hand up her leg. But standing here now in front of her door, she is asking me if I want more—no, she is offering me more.

I don't answer her when she asks me if I want to come in. Not because I'm unsure, but because I need to know that she really wants this.

She gives me a small smile, turns around, and unlocks her door. Together we walk into the cottage, and stand facing each other in the dark. Her eyes are big and brown, and she stares up at me expectantly. I'm so excited and suddenly nervous that I can hear myself breathing. I want her more than I have ever wanted anything in my life.

"Do you feel it?" She holds up her hand next to mine and, without even touching me, the electricity sparks between us.

"I do," I reply without even thinking, because I don't understand it. How does this girl complete me and undo me at the same time? Just knowing that she is so close and that any second now, her hands will be on mine, has me trembling. I'm craving her touch, craving the emotions she stirs within me, and craving that sense of calm that only she has ever been able to give me.

Gently, her fingers brush mine and static shock ricochets

between each nerve ending.

She steps closer to me and I'm just paralyzed. There's a good possibility that if I move, I will snap, and take her without any restraint.

"Don't move," she whispers.

My eyes have adjusted to the darkness and, with the moonlight coming in through the window, I can see her almost perfectly. She licks her bottom lip and then draws it in between her teeth. I'm lost, thinking how I want it to be my teeth that sink into her lip, when her fingers find their way up under the hem of my shirt and brush against the skin just above my waist. All of the muscles in my stomach tighten, and I suck in a quick rush of air.

Her hands flatten and all ten of her fingertips press into me, leaving me wondering which spot I should focus on. I feel as if I am being touched in ten different places at once.

Needing to hold on to some type of balance, I reach for her hips.

"Uh-uh, hands off, Mr. Hale." She smiles up at me and begins to slide her hands up my chest, bringing my t-shirt with her. I lift my arms as she tugs the shirt off and drops it on the floor. It lands on my foot, warmth still lingering in the fabric.

Not breaking eye contact until the last second, Ellie walks around behind me. The anticipation of not knowing what she's going to do, in combination with knowing she's about to touch me, makes me tremble.

"I want to feel every part of you," she whispers.

I've just died and gone to Heaven.

Her fingertips flank my sides and run along the edge of my waistband to the center of my lower back. If her touch wasn't so erotic, it might have tickled. Instead, heat trails in its wake.

Lazily, she flattens her hands against my skin and they travel up my back and to my shoulders.

My eyes drift shut and my head drops back. It feels so good to be touched by her. I can feel my skin break out in goose bumps.

Her hands run across the width of my shoulders and down my arms, only to repeat the path all over again. What she is doing to me feels hypnotic and I love it.

After the fourth time, her hands slide under my arms, and across my lower stomach. Her pinky fingers slip below the edge of my jeans and linger there. She has to feel the tensing and relaxing of the muscles underneath her fingers.

Her lips lightly graze my back and I jerk slightly. I can't help it. I'm so focused on her fingers, and where they are, that I forgot she was behind me. She steps in close, heat from her body covering mine, and her hands drift up to my chest. Her left hand is covering my heart, and I know for certain that she can feel it thundering in my chest. My breathing has escalated to the point that I am damn near panting. The heavy sounds are the only noise around us.

Her hair brushes against me, and then her cheek settles in the spot between my shoulder blades. Her warm breath fans across my skin, and I can feel each blink she takes as her eyelashes sweep back and forth.

I reach up and cover her hands with my own, and she hugs me a little tighter, pushing her body against mine.

"You're so warm," she whispers.

"That's your fault," I say back to her.

I can feel her smile, and then she giggles. That giggle moves through me faster than a bolt of lightning. Needing more of her, I step forward. She easily releases me, and I turn around. She is cloaked in vulnerability and desire, and I want it all, right now.

Wrapping my hands around her face, my thumbs brush across her cheekbones one time before I take her mouth with mine. Hungrily. Possessively. The teasing touches have gotten me worked up to my limit, and I am a man starved. She tastes so good. I can't pinpoint what it is, but it's exquisite and over-powering. I feel drunk.

Moving my lips across her cheek, I reach her ear and whisper, "You know, it's only fair." I lean down so I can nuzzle my nose against hers.

"What's fair?" her voice is husky and I love knowing that I am making her feel this way.

"That I get to touch all of you, too," I say before pressing a light kiss to the tip of her nose. She sucks in a breath and I continue, kissing the spot under her ear just over her pulse.

Pulling away from me, she holds her arms up over her head and smiles.

I don't waste a second. In one swift move, her shirt is up and off. I grin down at her and delight in the ability to run my fingertips over her shoulders and across the top of her breasts.

I love touching her. Her skin is soft and warm and so damn inviting, that place inside my chest squeezes.

Her fingers hook into the waist of her skirt, she shimmies, and it drops to the floor. I'm awestruck over this gorgeous girl. She's standing in front of me in only a few little scraps of black lace, and my mind has gone blank. Her body is absolute perfection to me. All soft curves and flawless skin. Her long blond hair reminds me of spun gold as it spills over her shoulders to the tops of her breasts, keeping that part of herself just slightly hidden from me.

She reaches out and grabs the buckle of my belt, pulling a little. I sway toward her. She leans up on her tiptoes and rubs her nose across my jaw. My eyes close at the sensation while she continues to unbuckle my belt. The button on my jeans pops, the zipper slides down. Her hands slip under the edge and push out over my hip bones. Just like my shirt, the jeans take instruction from her hands and drop with ease. Stepping out of them, I haul her up against me to revel in the feel of her skin against mine.

She wraps her arms around my neck and lays her head on my shoulder. My hands, which together are wide enough to cover the width of her back, are all over her and end up on her toned ass. Gripping her, I realize that I need to keep moving. Keep feeling. If I don't, I know my nerves will catch up to me over the magnitude of this moment. I pull her harder into me. I want her to feel what she is doing to me, and I want her to feel what I'm about to do to her.

Her fingers thread through my hair and her lips find their way back to mine. This kiss is deep, so deep. I swirl my tongue inside her mouth, feeling her everywhere there, too. I can't get enough. I'm certain her lips will be slightly bruised.

Somehow we make it into her room. The back of her legs hit the bed and I pull back to break the connection between us. She lets out a small whimper at the loss. Anxiety races through me, and for a split second I wonder if I will be enough for her.

"You are so beautiful, Ellie," I whisper through the dark-ness, reaching behind to unhook her bra. The elastic around her body gives and the shoulder straps go slack. I push them off and the bra falls to the floor. Needing to taste her skin, my mouth drops to her collarbone and begins to work its way down. My hands wrap around her ribcage and my thumbs brush back and forth across the bottom of her breasts. She lets out a small moan.

"When you say it, I actually feel like I am." Her voice is

breathy and that sexy tone, combined with the weight of her words, make me feel like the happiest guy on the planet. I love that I can do this for her. And I want to. I want to show her how beautiful I think she is. Her fingers slide down my stomach to the edge of my boxers. Again, she slides her hands underneath and over my hip bones. But this time, my boxers drop.

"I love your skin," I say, running my hands up her thighs to her underwear. "You are the most beautiful thing I have ever laid eyes on, inside and out." She lifts her hips and I pull her underwear down and off. Staring at her naked body, I start to shake. I wonder if it's always supposed to feel like this.

Words are forgotten as my mouth begins to explore every inch of her. The little noises and moans she makes fuel me even more and, by the time I've reached her breasts, I can't wait any longer.

"Um...should we—I mean...do you have any condoms?" I rush out.

She nods quickly. "Drawer," she tilts her head to the nightstand.

"You brought those?" I don't know why this surprises me. I look up and lock my eyes on to hers.

"No," she looks momentarily embarrassed. "They were already there." Her lashes brush against her cheeks as she blinks.

"Hmm." I lean over to grab one and she reaches down, wraps her hand around me, and slowly begins to move it up and down. *Oh, my God.* Laying my forehead against hers, I pause. I want to commit this moment to memory.

"That feels so good, Ellie." I groan against her lips.

Her other hand takes a hold of the back of my head and she runs her tongue across my bottom lip.

Needing no further encouragement, I take over. Ripping the foil package open, I roll on the condom and shut my mind off. I've thought about this moment for so long that I don't want to think anymore. I just want to feel. I want to feel her on the outside and on the inside. I want to feel her gasping for breath as she arches her chest into mine, and I want to feel her tremble beneath me. I want her to feel with me.

I slide into her, and both of us let out a sigh, mine shakier than hers. I haven't even moved yet. I can't. The sensations are overwhelming. I kiss her again, more tenderly this time, reverently. I know she doesn't see this kiss for what it really is, but it's a thank you for so many things. It's a thank you for accepting me, wanting me, and for sharing herself with me.

I try like hell to force my overexcited body to calm. I don't want this to be over before it even starts. I want this moment to last. If I could stay forever, just like this, with her . . . I would. I rock back slowly before pushing fully this time. Her eyes drift shut for a second before fluttering back open. "Matt…" It's my name, but it's spoken like a sigh, like a prayer as it brushes past her lips. She's looking up at me right now with a look that I've never seen, like I'm her everything. It's intoxicating. I lean down and press my forehead against hers again, wanting to feel as close to her as I possibly can. I don't trust my voice, so I commit to speaking with my body instead. As I continue to move inside her, I press a kiss to her forehead, to her eyelids, and to the tip of her nose, before moving down to her neck. I continue worshipping her body, and it's total ecstasy. I'm crazy with lust, with warmth, and with something else. Our language becomes one of gasps of pleasure, answering kisses, and moans of passion. She owns me, and she doesn't even know it. She's changed me; imprinted herself on me. And I know now, with utmost certainty, even after she is long gone, that I will always be hers.

Chapter Fourteen

ELLE

WAKING UP THIS morning, I knew he would be gone, but that didn't diminish how much I instantly missed him. At some point during the night, he mentioned that he would need to head home early to let Bruno out. I had forgotten about him last night, or we could have gone to Matt's place instead.

Rolling over, I look at the night stand to see that it's already ten. I'm shocked that I slept in so late and that's when I see the note.

A smile stretches across my face and I grab it.

Morning Gorgeous,

Just wanted to say thank you for last night. It meant more to me than you know. Hope you have a great day, I'll be thinking of you...

Matt

Laying the note on my chest, I close my eyes and take a deep breath. The room still smells like him or, should I say, us.

My heart starts to pick up pace as I think about how wonderful last night was.

Awareness sinks in that I'm sore all over. As I move around in the bed, there are muscles sore in places I didn't even realize could be. Matt wasn't rough with me, but he didn't handle me like a china doll either.

Visions of him flash through my mind. The way his dark hair fell over his forehead as he looked down at me, his lips swollen and moist from kissing me and the sheen of sweat on his shoulders as he moved with me to give us what we both needed. A blush spreads over me.

I have never experienced anything remotely like last night. I knew the feelings that I have for him are intense, and maybe that's what the difference was, but being with him felt more right than everything in my life combined. He makes me feel like I am enough, just the way I am.

Needing to take a shower, I climb out of bed and walk into the bathroom. Glancing in the mirror, I stop to look at myself. There's a glow to my skin and my eyes are brighter than normal. Knowing what the cause of this is, my cheeks shade pink. I like this look, and the girl in the mirror smiles back at me.

Turning on the water, steam quickly fills the bathroom.

Stepping under the water, I tilt my head back and let it blanket me in warmth.

Out of nowhere, words come flooding in, the missing pieces of the song that I've been working on hitting me from every direction. Jumping out of the shower, I wrap a towel around myself and head straight for my music journal. I don't want to miss or forget anything and, as the words lay out before me, I can't help but smile. They are perfect.

HOURS LATER, THIS is how Matt finds me when he walks right in.

I startle, having been so lost in the song lyrics, but recover as soon as I see his gorgeous face in front of me. "What, you don't knock anymore?" I tease him.

My statement is returned with an assessing look as he raises one of his eyebrows at me. "Kind of figured we were past that, and technically this is *my* house." He grins and his gray eyes dazzle me before they drop and run over the length of me. I got so caught up that I forgot to put clothes on, and I'm still in the towel. A blush heats my skin.

I'm nervous. It never crossed my mind that I would be after our intense connection last night, but butterflies have taken flight at the sight of him. He's wearing linen pants, a light blue t-shirt, and his dark hair is sticking up like he's just run his hands through it.

"What are you doing?" he sits down next to me on the couch and looks at the scraps of paper, my notebook, and in general the mess I've made.

"Inspiration struck."

"Yeah? Can I see?" His eyes are bright today. He's happy.

"Uh, no!" I giggle. "Not yet at least. It's not ready, but when it is I promise I'll play it for you."

He smiles at me, the nerves dissipate, and those feelings of completeness settle back into me.

"I'm gonna hold you to that," he says before placing a soft kiss on my lips. "Are you hungry?"

"Yes," giving him a light scowl at the fact that he took those delicious lips away from mine so quickly. "But not for food." *Holy vixen!* I cannot believe I just said that out loud.

His eyes widen in surprise and then darken. "Well, there's goes my plan to wine and dine you tonight," he says around a chuckle.

"You wanted to take me out?" I'm surprised, and I don't know why.

"Yes," he says and nods his head. He almost seems nervous, but I have no idea why.

"Like on a date?"

A look of anxiety sweeps across him and he leans back into the couch. "Umm, yeah. I want to take you out on one of those. I've never been on one."

I'm kind of shocked, and I turn to face him a little more. "You've never been on a date?"

He shakes his head and stares at me. I guess I shouldn't be so surprised; from what I've seen and heard, he chooses not to have very many friends. He runs his hand through his hair and looks away from me. My unintended silence just made him uncomfortable.

"Well, then, I would love to go on a date with you," I say, placing my hand over his reassuringly.

His eyes come back to mine and a heart-stopping smile splits his face. "Okay, I'm gonna knock on your door in five minutes to pick you up. Wear shorts."

I can't help but giggle. "Okay."

Fisting the towel, he pulls me toward him and kisses me sweetly, gently biting my lower lip. A soft moan escapes me, and he chuckles. "Five minutes," he says before popping a kiss on my nose, and then he's out the door.

Jumping up off the couch, I scramble into my bedroom

and throw on a pair of white shorts and a white button-down. I dart into the bathroom, pull my hair back, and look at my makeup spread across the counter. Feeling a surge of self-confidence, I decide to skip it, and only apply some mascara and lip gloss. Looking in the mirror, I realize that I like the way I look tonight.

Slipping on my flip flops at the front door, I hear a knock at my door and I throw it open. There's Matt, leaning against the door frame. He gives me a quick once-over before meeting my eyes with a warm smile. It's a smile that almost communicates pride. "You look beautiful."

He wraps his hand around my ponytail, tugging gently to tilt my head back, and kisses me long and hard. *Wow, I really like this side to Matt . . . a lot.*

He breaks away and gazes down at my mouth. His eyes are darker and locked onto my mouth. "I thought we talked about the lip gloss."

I smile up at him and he smiles back with an all-American boy smile. It leaves me breathless.

"I love your smile." It slips out without my thinking first.

He blinks and then smiles again. "I told you, kisses for smiles." And then he releases me. "Come on, gorgeous, let's go." There are two bikes in front of me. He walks over, climbs onto one, and then looks back and forth from me to the bike.

"You want me to get on that?" I ask, shocked.

"Yes." He bites his lip in attempt not to laugh at me. "Don't you know how to ride a bike?" He raises his eyebrows at me.

"Yeah, but I haven't ridden one in years." I walk over and stand next to the bike.

He's looking at me like, "So?"

"Get on the bike." His voice is insistent, but his gray eyes are still laughing at me. He's enjoying this.

"When did you become Mr. Bossy? And what if I fall?" I snap at him.

He grins at me and shakes his head. "Elle, just get on the damn bike."

"Fine!" I climb on to the bike and scowl at him.

"Just pedal; it'll come back to you," he says over his shoulder as he pushes off, grinning at me.

Crap! He's leaving me. Nervously, I push up and down on the pedal, and the handle bars twist from side to side. Gaining control of the bike, I pedal a few more times to catch up to him.

"Where are we going?" I ask.

"To the other side of the island. That okay with you?" he glances my way.

"Yep."

"You look good on a bike," he says to me, grinning.

I let out a huff and look him in the eyes. "You don't look so bad yourself, I guess."

He throws his head back and laughs. "Uh, thanks for the compliment?"

The novelty of hearing Matt laugh is a song that is being sung straight to my soul. It makes me want to learn a thousand jokes so I can hear that sound indefinitely. It's beautiful.

Riding bikes with Matt is fun. He's carefree today, not so serious. He zigzags back and forth across the road, going in circles around me, and fakes like he's going to ram into me at least fifty times. Each time I squeal at him, and he laughs.

Reaching the other side of the island, we prop the bikes against the fence next to the pier.

"How hungry are you?" He turns to face me and he's windblown. *Oh my.* His hair is sticking up everywhere, his cheeks are red from the exertion, and my mind automatically drifts to the possibilities of later. My mouth goes dry, and he sees the effect he is having on me. His eyebrows shoot up and he blushes. It is, by far, one of the sexiest things I have ever seen.

"Just a little hungry," I answer him.

He grins at me knowingly, takes my hand, and he shakes his head. "Come on."

Together, we walk across the street. There are a few clothing stores, a restaurant, and an ice cream shop.

He stops in front of the ice cream shop, called Scoops, and opens the door.

"You wanna to eat here?" I ask him.

"Nope, we're getting it to go." He places his hand on my lower back as we walk inside.

The ice cream shop is quaint; what you would expect to see in a beach-side town. Behind the counter is an older man. He sees Matt and smiles, and then his eyes drift to me and shock registers on his face.

"Evening, Matthew," he says with a kind familiarity.

"Hey, Mr. Dan."

"Who's your friend?" he asks.

Matt looks at me and winks. "This is Elle. She's Ella's niece." He wraps his arm around my shoulder and pulls me in tight. I pinch him on the side and he laughs.

"Oh," Mr. Dan drawls out. His eyes seem to widen with approval. "What can I get you kids?"

"Two Sunset Boats, please, to go." Matt grins.

"Alright! Coming right up." Mr. Dan grins back at him, and then walks off to start making the dessert.

I step away from him and cross my arms over my chest. "What if I had wanted to order for myself?"

"Nope, not tonight." He's happy. I love seeing him like this.

"You don't even know what I like," I challenge him.

His eyes smolder as he looks down at me. That one look hits the bottom of my stomach and all of my muscles tighten. "Yes, I do," he says in a much lower tone than a minute ago, dripping with innuendo. I fight to keep a blush off my cheeks as I pinch him just below the ribs. Hard. He grabs my hand and yelps before glaring at me.

"Here you go, you two, and it's on the house." Mr. Dan breaks us from our stare down, and hands us each a large plastic bowl. He smiles at Matt and then at me. In the bowl, there's a brownie boat filled with coconut ice cream, peach ice cream, strawberry ice cream, sliced banana, blackberries, whipped cream, and a pirate flag toothpick.

"Thanks," Matt says. Mr. Dan nods at him.

Matt grabs my shoulder and guides me out the door.

"Do you expect me to eat all of this?" I look at him, astonished.

"Eat as much as you want," he shrugs his shoulders, and then scoops up a big bite.

"I don't think I've eaten ice cream in over ten years." I hold the bowl out in front of me as if it might bite.

"Really?" Matt looks at me in surprise, and then starts walking. "That's sad. Ice cream is, like, the best food ever invented."

"I thought you were going to wine and dine me," I say sarcastically as I follow behind him.

"I just did." He glances at me and chuckles, "I knew you were going to whine about the bike and I've just bought you dinner." He takes another bite, grinning.

"Oh, my God, you think you're so funny, huh?" I bump

him with my hip and take my first bite of the ice cream. He's right . . . it is *sooo* good. I do my best not to moan in pleasure.

"Mmm hmm." His eyes sparkle at me knowingly as he continues to eat the ice cream. "Told you so."

Together we walk down the pier to a bench at the end. There are several people up and down the length of the pier fishing, but I barely notice them. Sitting next to each other in silence, we eat the ice cream, and watch the sun as it slowly approaches the horizon.

"Thank you for dinner," I glance at him.

He gives me a lopsided smile. "Best dinner I've ever had," he says to me quietly. He's referencing my coffee comment from the other morning, and I find that so endearing.

"Speaking of the best, I didn't get a chance yet to thank you for last night." I angle my body to face him slightly. "It was amazing. *You* were amazing, and I just wanted you to know that."

His cheeks tinge pink and he looks back out to the sun. "Ellie, you're the amazing one," he says quietly.

Standing up, he takes the plastic bowls and throws them away. He runs his hand through his hair and then sits back down next to me. He angles his body toward mine, throws one arm across the back of the bench, and picks up my hand.

"So . . . about last night . . ." He starts playing with my fingers, and instantly I'm nervous that he's going to say it was a mistake and can't happen again. He's not looking at me. *Why won't he look at me?* "That was a first for me," he says, letting out a deep breath.

"What was a first for you?" I'm confused.

He looks at my face, and I watch his gaze take in every detail until it lands on mine. He's nervous. There's tightness in the muscles around his eyes and he's tense, like really tense.

"Everything," he whispers, and shrugs his shoulders once.

Everything?

Slowly, his words sink in and I understand what he is saying to me. I'm completely shocked. How is that even remotely possible? Yes, there were moments when I felt him tremble or his breathing was shaky, but I thought it was because of the intensity, not because it was his first time. Shaking my head, my thoughts turn to the way he handled me . . . a blush spreads up my neck and across my cheeks.

"Are you sure?"

"I'm sure." He lets out a small, awkward laugh, and relaxes.

"But . . . well, you were so good at it. How'd you learn to do all that?" A tiny smile graces his beautiful lips, and immediately I feel his ego swell. Such a guy. The hand that is behind me begins to play with my pony tail.

"Lot of time alone with my thoughts, I guess." His smile falters. "Listen, please don't make a big deal out of this. I never have." He lets out a sigh and thunderclouds move across his eyes. "I bought the cottages five years ago, and threw myself into making them rentable. I went to school, I went to work, and I collapsed into bed every night. Once I graduated, I just went to work. My circle of people is small. I've liked it that way for a while now."

"But why? Why do you choose not to have many friends? It makes me sad to think that you're lonely."

The thunderclouds turn dark, and something passes over his face. He pulls his arm out from behind me and leans forward, placing his elbows on his thighs. My heart clenches because whatever that something is must be bad.

"I'm fine. I just prefer it this way." He glances at me and then shakes his head, trying to clear his thoughts. "But just because I'd never . . ." He sits back up and gazes at me with his trademark grin, "doesn't mean I haven't thought about it *every day* since I turned fifteen. I may keep to myself, but I'm still a guy, and guys think about sex, a lot—whether they are having it or not."

Reaching up, he runs his finger down my cheek, across my lips, over my throat, stopping at the spot between my collar bones. My skin is tingling where he's touched me, and my breathing picks up.

"Also, since the day you ran into me," he pushes on my chin to tilt my head up towards his, and his dark eyes lock on to mine. "I have imagined so many different ways to touch you, taste you, and feel you. I already knew all the things I was going to do to you, given the chance." His lips brush against mine.

This pier is suddenly way too small and way too crowded for the thoughts I'm having. The importance of what Matt and I shared last night resonates with me, and has me bursting with feeling. I want nothing more than to have him to myself right now. Jumping to my feet, I blurt out, "I think we should go." I can think of nothing better to say.

Matt stands. "Do you?" he murmurs.

"Yes, right now." I turn to leave, and suddenly I'm turned and pulled flush against his body.

"One more. You—me—sunset," he says softly. I melt into him, and he covers my mouth with his. His kiss is so tender and so loving, that thoughts of forever flash through my mind.

He lays his forehead against mine and his eyes are closed. Does he even realize how breathtakingly handsome he is?

"Thank you for my date," I whisper.

Gray eyes flash at me and blink. "I'm hoping it's not over."

I pull away from him and push my teeth down into my bottom lip, fighting a ridiculously huge smile. "Race you back to the house!" I jump in the opposite direction and start running down the pier. I hear him laughing as he catches up to me.

"Are you serious? You know you'll never beat me." He teases, grinning from ear to ear.

"I know; I was going to let you pick your prize," I say suggestively.

His eyebrows shoot up and his grin slips a little. Desire washes over his face. "The only prize I want is you." He's closing the distance between us again, his arm snaking its way around my waist. This boy…this boy is going to ruin me.

I can't help but giggle. *Giggle.* I now know how hard it is for him to put himself out there for me with every sweet line he is giving me. I want to kiss him for hours on end to thank him for making me smile, and I want to stomp on his feet for making me feel so much. But instead, I look up into his hopeful grey eyes and run my hands up his strong chest. "Deal!"

I follow behind Matt all the way back to the house. With each pedal, the anticipation of our night stirs stronger in my stomach. Never have I met someone who lights me up like he does.

We park the bikes and, in an instant, Matt's hands and mouth are on me. Stumbling into the house, he closes the door and his arms embrace me, pulling me to him. One hand slips behind my neck, holding my mouth to his, while the other travels lower to push me into him.

When Matt kisses me, the world tilts. He's forceful and gentle. He's possessive and giving. He's consuming me, and I love every second of it.

His lips leave mine and travel down to my neck. His

tongue is tasting me, his teeth scraping against my skin, giving me chills. "I want you again, Ellie," he breathes out.

"Then what are you waiting for?"

He pulls back and looks down at me. "I didn't realize it was possible to want someone as much as I want you."

The feelings that I have for him expand in my chest. He has to know what he means to me. Can't he see it? Can't he feel it?

"I'm yours," I whisper, picking up his hand.

His expression darkens as he watches me lightly kiss each one of his fingertips. His breathing picks up. Flipping his hand, I kiss the middle of his palm and then the inside of his wrists. His pulse is thundering under my lips, and he lets out a moan that I feel it in every part of me.

Knowing what I know about him, I'm still shocked that he's let me touch him so much over the last two days. After his admission on the pier, I realize that he's giving me a part of himself, and I love it. I love the idea that it will always tie me to him in some special way, that he will never forget me now.

With his free hand, he starts unbuttoning my shirt. One at a time, they come undone and, after the last one, he dips his hand under the fabric and clasps my side.

"There's something about sliding under your clothes that really turns me on." His lips quirk up on one side.

"Oh, there's a lot about you that turns me on," I reply.

He sharply inhales, and his fingers press into me.

Piece by piece, our clothes hit the floor as we make our way to my room.

Reaching into the nightstand, I pull out a condom and turn back to face him. With the light shining in the window, I'm stunned again by his incredible male beauty. The muscles in his arms and across his chest are so well-defined that my hand has a mind of its own. It runs slowly from one side to the other, and then down his flat stomach.

With the sudden urge to taste him, I bend over and place my mouth on him. He startles, but freezes. Wrapping my hand around him, he groans at the sensation, and his fingers find my head. I begin moving in a way that I know will make him shake when he whispers my name.

"Ellie . . .," he sounds pained, but I know he's not. My insides smile.

His fingers are running through my hair slowly, tenderly. "Ellie, you feel so good." I chance a peek up at him, and see that his head is dropped back and his eyes are closed. His whole body is tensed and on display for me, and I've never felt more triumphant at giving someone pleasure. I want him to feel every good thing and no more bad.

"Okay," he grunts, "no more." He pulls me to my feet and snatches the condom out of my hand. I climb on the bed, and he follows me seconds later after putting it on, allowing his tongue to explore on his way up.

Lying down half on me half off, his fingers trail up the inside of my thigh and then dip inside me. His head hits my chest and he moans.

"Matty," He looks up at me, "More," I whisper.

He smiles at me, and it's one of his sweet half-smiles. I'm overcome with emotion as he moves to settle between my legs, pushing into me. The fullness of him is so exquisite that blood pulses throughout my entire body.

Looking down at me, he gently cups my face in his hands. His mouth lowers to mine and his tongue moves in sync with his body. I soak up every breath and every sound that he makes. It's a heady feeling knowing that I am doing this to him, and it sends chills down my spine. I wrap my legs around his waist, and he tightens his fingers in my hair and tilts my head a little more, bringing us closer together. His kisses are deep, meaningful, and they speak volumes about who he is and what this means to him without him having to say one word.

He moves his face so it rests against mine, and I hear the change in his breathing. One of his hands slips under my hips and tilts me, bringing us closer and letting him go deeper. The feel of the stubble on his cheek, his sounds, the angle, my racing heart; it's all it takes and my world fills with bursts of bright colors that remind me of looking at the sun. It's so bright and so beautiful and, just as his skin feels like it's about to overheat, his entire body tightens around mine and he falls over the edge.

Nothing in the world is more perfect than that.

Matt sighs and then pulls back to look at me. There's so much I could say to him right now, so much that I see reflected in his eyes as well, but I know it's not the right time. He's flushed, his eyes are clear, and he looks so beautiful. A small smile pulls at the corner of his mouth, he kisses his way across my face to my lips, and then climbs out of the bed to go clean up.

Watching him walk in and out of the bathroom, I know I'm permanently changed. My chemical makeup has been altered, and it begins and ends with him now.

Climbing back onto the bed, he pulls up the blanket and kisses me softly. I sigh into him as he moves his hands lower and winds his arms around me. Laying my head on his chest, I soak up the feeling of being pulled into warmth that is uniquely his. His heart is beating and I can't tell if I am hearing it or feeling it, but it has lulled me into the same sense of security that I felt that first day in front of the café. His breathing has slowed, and I turn my head toward him just a little more to soak up the fresh and clean smell of him. I close my eyes, wanting this moment to last forever; wanting him to want me forever.

MATT

THE EARLY MORNING light slowly filters in through El- lie's window, just as the sun starts to make its appearance in the sky. Seeing the sun, a frown creeps on to my face. Not only is it my daily reminder, but it also means our night is over and I'll need to get going soon. I wish I could stay in bed with her all day, but I can't.

Two nights ago, I had the best sleep I've ever had. Last night, I didn't get any at all. Yes, we were up for quite a while but, once she drifted off, I couldn't tear my eyes away from her.

When I'm with her I feel so good and happy, but I shouldn't. I don't deserve this or her. I deserve the life that I was born to live—one of solitude, alone with my secrets. The wholeness that I feel when I'm with her is so heavy that the ache in my chest feels almost unbearable.

For hours, tears have been swimming in my eyes; not be- cause they can't fall, but because they are trapped—in me— just like everything else. In the end, it doesn't matter. She'll never be mine, these days of bliss that we have shared will never be our reality and, soon enough, she's going to leave.

"I had a crush on you when we were kids," she says, star- tling me. Her voice is filled with sleep, but sexy as hell. I didn't even realize she was awake.

Looking across the pillows at her, her eyes are open and they look luminous in the dawn light. "What? You didn't even know me." I reach over and smooth her hair back off her face—just needing to touch her.

"I know. I tried to be friends with you, but it was like talking to a wall; you never talked back." She wiggles under the covers to get closer to me, and the smell of her shampoo drifts over me.

"You were two years older than me and, honestly, really annoying. You complained about everything." I give her a small smile.

She glares at me with a look of mock insult. "That's only because I was trying to get your attention. Still, the favorite part of my day that summer was watching you build in that shed. There was something about it, about you, which was magnetic. Even now, I want to sit and watch you all day."

My cheeks blush. I don't know what to say to that. A huge part of me is thrilled, but the other part of me feels hopeless.

"You still have that crush?" I ask her, teasing her.

Her playful eyes get serious and her teasing smile slips. "No, now it is so much more," she whispers, never taking her eyes off of me.

I stop breathing. "What do you mean?" I whisper back. I'm afraid to hear her answer, but I'm desperate for it at the same time.

"Now I'm falling in love with you."

Happy . . . sad. Ecstatic . . . disappointed. Overjoyed . . . pained. Yes . . . no.

No!

I pull back from her, and I feel the distance looming between us. Closing my eyes, I sink into an immediate melancholy. I already know this isn't going to be good, and now I have to hurt her. "Ellie—"

"Well, actually I think I've always loved you, but it wasn't until that first moment outside the cafe that I felt like I found you. It's like part of me was lost and for the first time ever, I felt whole."

Silence stretches between us as my blood thunders in my ears. She's telling me she loves me. No one ever tells me that, and I can't process it right now. This is wrong.

Self-consciousness washes over her face. She's just opened herself up to me, and I've left her hanging in a vulnerable state. But I can't control the panic that is coursing through me to answer. How do I answer her?

Whatever expression is all over my face, she sees it, and frowns.

"Elle, you don't love me," I choke out. "You can't love me. You're wrong."

Her eyes grow wide, confusion etched all over her gorgeous face. Her chin quivers and, with it, so does my heart.

She sits up and pulls the covers tight around her. "I'm not *wrong*, Matt. I know what love is, and there is only one way to be loved, truly loved, and that's unconditionally. It's not something that I just woke up one day and decided. It just was. It was never as choice, not that I want it to be one, because I don't. You are under my skin, in every breath that I take, and permanently branded on my heart. Everything I feel for you is so soul-deep that I ache when we are apart and I find myself desperate to be close to you all the time. I want to be near you. I burn for you. I want you to tell me you feel this, too, because I know you do."

No. Please don't say these things. I can't. The walls are closing in. I'm suffocating. I can't breathe.

"I don't feel the same, Ellie," I lie and she gasps. That gasp may as well have been a cheese grater, as it just scraped across my heart.

She's silent for what feels like an eternity. Only the sound of her harsh, labored breathing filling the air. "I don't believe you. I've seen the way you look at me. I've felt the way you touch me, kiss me, make love to me. Why are you doing this?" Her beautiful brown eyes turn glassy and, one by one, tears start to drop.

Please don't argue with me. Please don't fight for me.

"I've told you. You don't understand my life!" I don't want to lie to her. I want to be honest with her, but she can never know.

"So, tell me!" She stares at me and I can't find the words. "Fine, then, what's not to understand? I get it! It hasn't been perfect, but whose has?"

"No one can ever love me!" I say sharply. Anger is starting to creep in; I can barely control it. .

"Says who? That piece of shit man sitting in prison? Well, I hate to break it to you, but there are a good number of people who love you, including me." She crosses her arms over her chest, and glares at me.

"I'm not having this conversation with you." Heat is starting to pour off of me as my anger gets more intense. I scramble to get out of bed. I don't have to explain myself to her.

"Then who are you going to have it with?" She watches me as I move into the living room to put on my clothes.

I've turned on her, I can feel it. That calmness that she usually brings me has suddenly vanished, and in its place is anger. I don't want to be angry with her, but she doesn't know what she is talking about. I don't know why she had to go and change things between us, when she's headed back to New

York soon anyway. She's hurt us both by crossing an invisible emotional line, and now we can't go back.

Standing here, staring at her, I feel like if I'm touched just the wrong way, I'll go off and take everything out around me, like a cannon.

"Matt . . ." I angle my head a little in her direction. Her voice is small now, nothing like the tiger from a second ago. I refuse to look at her as I pull on my pants. "I know you love me, too, and I know you don't understand it, but I'm giving back to you what you give to me. Every emotion between us is mirrored. That's what love is. Don't you see and feel these things in me?"

I do and I want to tell you . . . but I just can't. Stop pushing me!

Slipping my shirt over my head, I walk back into her bedroom and look down at her. I never should have caved in to the feelings that I have for her, but I have to end this here and now. "I do see things and feel things, but it's not love, Elle. It's been an opportunity, a mutual need. But we both knew the whole time that it had an expiration date. I don't love you."

She flinches, a pained expression covers her face, and a deafening silence fills the room. Her hands clench the sheets around her. She starts breathing harder and faster, and I know I have to walk away from her now. It's for the best. Every part of me inside is shattered. My soul is crying. My heart is bleeding. I was already a shell of a man before. I can't fathom what will remain of me after this.

I turn around to leave, and start walking to the door.

"Matt, wait! Please don't go," she says. I hear her trying to get off the bed, and then a loud thud. Glancing back, she's on the floor, tangled in the sheet and she's trying to get free. I should help her up, but I can't. I can't go back to her. If I do,

I'm certain I won't have it in me to leave again.

Walking out the front door, I am immediately slammed by the light of the sun. Every tiny little thought I had about giving in and confessing my feelings for her just evaporated. Feeling the heat, it's the wakeup call that I needed. I close her door. I have to let her go.

Bruno greets me as I barge in and grab my keys. He follows me out to the Jeep, hopping in as I crank it on. I can't be here next to her. I don't trust myself not to go back to her.

We drive to the North Shore house, a place where I find solace, a place where I can be myself . . . by myself.

It's windy today. Walking up the stairs into my bedroom, I open the sliding glass doors and all the windows. Cool air swirls around me and fills the room. Spotting the lounge chairs, I go grab one and drag it inside to the middle of room.

Lying down, I'm wishing, hoping, and praying that the sound of the Gulf and the wind will drown out her voice, but it doesn't. I run one hand through my hair and the other over my chest. It aches so much.

"I'm falling in love with you and I know you love me, too. It's in the way you look at me. It's in the way you touch me. It's in the way you kiss and make love to me. I know you don't understand it, but I'm giving back to you what you give to me. Every emotion between us is mirrored. Don't you see and feel these things in me?"

Love.

I do see it, and it is a feeling that I so desperately want to allow myself to feel. I want to feel it pouring out of me, and I want to feel it being poured into me. I know it's real. I see it in the way Drew looks at Ali, the way Beau looks at Leila, and the way Ellie looks at me.

She brings me healing in a way I didn't think possible,

but what do I bring her? I bring her hurt. She bravely just told me how she felt about me, and I did the cowardly thing of lying and running away. She deserves so much better.

Why can't I just let the guilt go? Why can't I free myself long enough to believe that I deserve this girl—this beautiful girl standing in front of me—who, for some unknown reason, has decided she wants me?

Everything hurts and everything aches. My eyes burn and the trapped tears clog my throat. I once tried to remember when the ache in my chest started and, after much deliberation, I decided that it's always been there. But next to this, the worst it's ever been was when I was nine.

It was a day just like every other day. School had let out, and I watched the other kids laugh and play as they all gathered their backpacks to leave. I remember thinking that everyone here has someone but me. Mostly, I tried to block out what others were doing, but that day I felt the loss of something that I had never had even more—a friend.

Racing to the shed, I burst through the door and dropped my bag. Things went sliding out, and I got down on my hands and knees to find them. A tear dropped and hit the floor, leaving a wet spot on the wood, and I froze. Breathing started to get harder, so I hit the floor and rolled over onto my back. There, with arms and legs out wide, I stared at the ceiling as tears leaked out of the corners of my eyes and dripped down the sides of my face.

On one half of the ceiling, I had painted a sun for Uncle Ben and, on the other, stars for Beau.

My heart was breaking because no one ever chose me. My life was and is a ground hog's day of loneliness.

It was this day that I truly understood the word unwanted.

I wasn't important to anyone. For hours I lay on the floor and cried.

The sound of Bruno trudging up the steps causes the sun and the stars to fade and the ceiling to revert back to white. He sits down next to me and lays his head on my leg.

I feel broken, more so than I have at any other point in my life.

I lied to her.

I do love her.

Chapter Fifteen

ELLE

HE LEFT.

I'm sitting on the floor next to the bed, tangled in the sheets, and my heart broken. I couldn't get to him in time before he reached the door. I needed him to stay and talk to me. I know down in the deepest places of me that he doesn't think I am just some passing fling to him. He's clearly lying to me and to himself, but why? He's been so honest about everything else . . . as far as I know, at least.

Staring at the door, I'm willing it to open, but I know it won't. My heart feels buried in anguish and, as time passes, all I can do is sit here and think about all the different moments that we've had together in such a short time; moments where we smiled, laughed, talked, and touched. If I don't focus on the moments, then all I'm left with is this inevitable pain in my chest, trying to crush me. I have to have hope that these moments meant something to him, too, because the way I'm feeling can't be one-sided.

No one can ever love me! I think back to the vulnerable look in his eyes when he said this; almost pained, almost scared. He had looked like that quiet, lost kid from the shed for a moment. He's not dark and untouchable, he's inexperienced—he said it himself. Knowing what I know of him now, I think the real problem is that he doesn't know how to give and receive love. He thinks he doesn't deserve it, but I don't know why. I do have the very strong suspicion that something about this has to be connected to the reason he doesn't have many friends, why he chooses to isolate himself. I've seen him with Beau, Leila, and Quinn, and the love and affection in his eyes is as clear and as crisp as a blue winter sky. I just wish I understood.

Gripping the sheet, slow and steady tears roll down my face. I never meant to upset him. I'm kicking myself for pushing too far, too fast. But, shouldn't being loved by someone be a good thing? I know I just changed everything between us. All I can hope is that, after the dust settles from my admission, he'll let me be the one to pick him up and brush him off.

After some time, I get up off the floor and walk straight into the bathroom. For years, I've spent more time in front of a mirror than anywhere else. I've perfected the art of giving different emotions on command, and right this second I need to see what heartbreak looks like. That's one I've never seen before.

Gazing at my reflection, the first thing I notice is that the glow is gone. Swiping my hair away from my face and into a ponytail, my skin is blotchy and my eyes are red. Suddenly, I realize I don't want to look like this. Heartbreak looks miserable and terrible, and it consumes me with grief. I want to look like me again.

Turning the water on, I scoop some up with my hands and rinse off my face. I grab a towel to dry it off, but instead I keep it covered and sink to the floor. All of these feelings and emotions from the last couple of weeks are overwhelming me, and I can no longer hold back the grief. Huge gut-wrenching sobs break free, and I let the tears flow.

He has to be lying . . . he has to be.

Otis meows from the doorway, and then walks over to me. Running my fingers through his fur, I pick him up and hug him to me.

How did I get to this point; in love with a guy who doesn't want to be loved, and crying on the bathroom floor?

Taking a deep breath, I get up and walk back to my bedroom. Immediately, I pick up my phone, turn it on, and call Livy. I need to talk to her, need to hear her voice. She answers on the second ring and I let out a huge sigh.

"Oh, my God, I am so excited that you called!" she squeals. Just hearing her voice calms my rapidly-beating heart.

"Well, I figured you were up and on your way to that barre class you like."

"I am. You know me well. When are you coming home?" she demands.

"Miss me that much?" I can't help the small smile that forms. After the morning I just endured with Matt, it's nice to know that someone wants me around.

"You have no idea," she replies dryly.

"Ha! Come one, you can't be that bored," I answer her. "Probably in a couple of days." I reach up to rub my chest. The thought of leaving forces my short-lived smile to drop and my heart to ache.

"You don't sound too thrilled about coming home. Where are you, by the way?"

"At the beach, where my aunt lives." That thought gets me thinking I should go and see her one more time before I leave.

"You went to the beach and didn't take me with you? Seriously, Elle, we could have had so much fun. It's forty degrees here this morning, by the way, and now I know why you aren't excited about coming back."

"Actually, I met someone." I squeeze my eyes closed as if I am hiding from her response.

She gasps. "You went on vacation and hooked up with someone? I am soooo jealous."

The smile comes back at her reaction. "He's a little bit more than a hook-up." I really do want to tell her all about him, but right now I don't know if my sore heart can handle it.

"Wait! Did you fall for the guy, or something?" Of course, she gets straight to the point.

"Yes," I say, defeated, my face falling into my hands. It feels so good to admit this to someone other than him, though.

"Whoa! I'm kind of shocked right now. This hasn't happened for you in . . . well ever, right?"

"I know," I whisper.

"Oh, please *please* tell me I'm allowed to fly down so I can meet this guy. Does he have a brother?" she gasps, as if this is the solution to all of her problems.

I can't help but chuckle. "He has two, but they are both married." Thoughts of Leila make the ache a little worse. She is so awesome. I would have loved to spend more time with her.

"Bummer. Best friend?" she asks hopefully.

"He does have one of those, but I don't know anything about him. Doesn't matter anyway; Matt doesn't feel the same way I do. Like I said, I'm gonna head back in a couple of days."

"So, you're telling me that you fell for this Matt guy, and he doesn't love you back? What's wrong with him?"

"There's nothing wrong with him," I say a little defensively.

There's a knock on the door, which immediately sets my heart racing. It was too forceful to be Matt, so I'm not sure who it is.

"Hey, there's someone at the door. I gotta go." I get up off the bed and look around on the floor for some clothes.

"Okay, but we aren't done talking about this guy. Can't wait to see you in a few days."

"You, too. I'll call you when I know I'm leaving." The knock comes again and I grab a pair of shorts.

"Sounds good. Talk soon…"

"Bye, Liv," and I hang up.

I would dodge the door altogether if I could, but I'm sure whoever it is heard me talking on the phone and knows I'm here. Slipping on the pair of shorts, I creep over to the door and peek through the eyehole. It's the mailman. A rush of air leaves me, and I blink long and hard to calm myself.

Opening the door, he hands me a package and walks off. It's a small, yellow padded envelope, and I instantly feel uneasy. There's no return address on it, but the post mark says New York. I glance over toward Matt's house before I close the door. His Jeep is gone. I wonder if he headed out because he couldn't stand being this close to me.

Closing the door, I head into the kitchen to grab a pair of scissors, and then wander into the bedroom to sit down on the bed. Gently cutting off the end, I spread apart the sides and peek inside.

My heart stops. It can't be, but it is . . . my medicine; the medicine that I forgot at home. There's a single sheet of paper folded in half and shoved inside. I reach in with trembling fingers and pull it out.

Just thought you might need these . . .
Like I said,
Anytime, anywhere . . . and you are mine.
I told you I would find you.

Terror grips me. Frantically, I look around the bedroom and out into the cottage, but I don't know what I'm looking for.

How did they find me? I didn't tell anyone where I was. I haven't called anyone in over a week, nor have I logged into any of my accounts. So many thoughts and emotions are firing through me. Tears blur my vision. Whoever it is, they were in my condo, going through my stuff. Just this thought alone makes me feel violated and sick. It's an invasion of privacy, and between the flowers and this, nothing feels sacred just to me. They've snooped through my drawers, fingered my belongings, and who knows what else. My stomach clenches as insecurity takes over along with the fear.

My home doesn't feel like a home anymore. Even the beach doesn't feel safe. I think maybe I should leave, but where would I go? I don't feel like I have a place where I can escape that's mine. I feel lost knowing that, no matter where I go, they'll find me.

Looking down in the package at the bottle, a sob rushes out. They know about my illness. Other than Leila and Matt, no one knows. I glance at my hands and make two fists, bending my fingers. I shove the now-crinkled note back into the envelope. Today my fingers are better, but soon the whole world will know. Stress causes sudden flare ups, and the thought makes me cry even more.

Uncontrollable shaking racks through my body. More knocking comes from the front door, only this time it isn't as hard. I jump back, startled, and instantly panic. I'm so afraid to go and open the door that I'm frozen. No one should have to live like this.

Another knock and silence. The silence is so loud that my ears feel like they are ringing.

"Hey Elle, its Leila. Are you home?"

Leila? Leila! Letting out a breath I didn't know I was holding, I jump off the bed, run to the door, and peek through the eyehole. Relief floods through me and I throw open the door.

Her eyes grow large as she looks at me, and I realize I probably look like a complete disaster, but I don't care.

"Oh, no. What did he do?" she whispers in a concerned voice. If only this was just about Matt.

My eyes shift right, left, and all around behind her. Is someone watching us? I feel like they are, but I don't know if that's the fear and uncertainty talking.

"Elle?" Leila reaches out and places her hand on my arm. My chin starts trembling, and I just can't hold it in anymore. I walk straight to her and start sobbing.

"Hey . . . what's going on?" She wraps her arms around me and lets me cry. "Come on, let's go inside." She pushes me through the doorway and closes the door.

I move past her, peek into the hole again and flip both locks—the door handle and the deadbolt.

Leila has paused to watch me, and then shakes off my behavior and heads to the kitchen.

"I brought brunch. I was hoping we could spend some

time together before you leave, but now I'm thinking the food can wait." She slides a bag off her arm and sets the whole thing in the refrigerator. I know she is going to want answers, so I go grab the package and head for the couch.

She sits down next to me and, without saying anything, I hand her the package. She pulls out the medicine and then the note. Confusion and anger wash over her face.

"This is why you're really here?" she asks, lifting her eyes to look at me.

More tears drop and I nod my head.

"How long has this been going on?" Her hands tighten around the envelope, squeezing it.

"About six weeks," I answer her.

Her eyes grow wide and she sucks in a breath. "Have you told anyone?" she asks in an exasperated tone.

"My mother and Matt," I whisper. My throat hurts from the crying and the fear.

"What did your mom say?" Her tone has quieted. She's trying to remain calm for me.

"That I should feel flattered; it's a perk of the job."

Her eyes narrow and her jaw drops open. "Okay, it's official, I hate your mother," she snaps.

A small smile breaks through and I let out a deep sigh. "Yeah, I think I do, too."

"What did Matt say?" she looks at me curiously.

Hearing his name makes my heart ache. "Not much. He doesn't understand why I didn't go to the police, but I just got this right before you got here, so he doesn't know." Just thinking of Matt, more tears fill my eyes.

"When is he getting home? You need to tell him," she says enthusiastically.

I look down at my hands.

"What happened?" she asks.My eyes flick back up to hers. "I told him I was falling in love with him."

"And?"

I shrug my shoulders. "He said that I was wrong and that he didn't love me." My throat closes a little telling her this, and my mind sticks on *he didn't love me*. I feel jilted and, in many ways, cast aside.

"He said that?" She gets up off the couch, paces the room, and then walks over to the window to peek through the blinds toward his house. "I'm gonna ring his neck! You know that's not true, right?" she says as she turns back around to face me.

"I don't know anything anymore. Everything is so messed up." The tears that have been hovering near the edge drift over and hit my cheeks.

Her lips press into a thin line and her blue eyes stare down at me. I don't think she knows what to say, so she doesn't anything. She just watches me.

"Leila . . . why me?" I ask, and she moves to come and sit back down next to me. "Why does my mother use me like this? Why am I being stalked? Why doesn't he love me? I feel so railroaded."

"I can understand that, but you are not alone. You have me, and we'll figure all this out." She reaches over and wraps her hands around mine.

"What am I going to do?" I whisper to her and drop my head.

"For starters, I wish you had told me sooner. Beau has had several incidents like this over the years, and we've learned a few things. I need you to write down every detail you can remember. All of the when's, where's, and how's. We have a few deputy friends here who we've worked with before, and they should be notified."

"But the press? If they catch wind of this, it'll be a nightmare." There's panic in my voice.

"The press won't hear about this, at least not right away; after the fact, maybe, but not before."

"After the fact?" I know where she is headed with this, and in many ways I don't want to hear it.

"Elle, stalkers gain their strength by living off your fear. Whoever it is, they are coming for you. They may already even be here. It takes three to four days for mail to arrive. You can't hide from this, but the more you do to prepare, the better."

No! I don't want them to be here. I don't want to have to deal with this. I want it all to just go away. The thought of someone watching me makes me shiver, and I have the sudden urge to hide.

"But why are they doing this?" I ask her.

"Who knows? For Beau, it was obsession, but it can be anything from rejection to revenge."

I try to think of someone who I might have upset over the last six months, and no one comes to mind. I just don't know.

"I feel so helpless."

"I know but, judging by this package, it's all about to be over soon." She pats my hands.

"That's what I'm afraid of." I let out another sigh and she gives me a small smile.

"I still think you should tell Matt. He needs to know to be on the lookout for anything strange or suspicious."

"Maybe." Telling Matt would mean talking to him, and he doesn't want to talk to me . . . he left me. What I wouldn't give to just rewind this entire day. He'd still be here, and I would be oblivious to the danger that's headed my way.

"No *maybe* . . . tell him! And I'm starving. Time for us to eat."

"Thank you, Leila." She'll never understand the relief that I feel just having her here and having her know.

"Of course! That's what friends are for." She smiles at me again and skips into the kitchen.

MATT

IT'S BEEN THREE days since I last saw her. Three of the longest days I've ever had. Granted, I've been spending most of my time at the North Shore house—leaving the cottage early and getting home late—but I still thought maybe she would come after me. But, then again, after the way I left her and what I said, I wouldn't come after me either.

A couple of hours after I left Ellie, Leila texted me to call her ASAP. Leila hardly ever texts me, so this made me think that they must have talked. I ignored her text. She then sent another one, telling me it was an emergency. A slight wave of panic hit me, so I texted Beau to see how everyone was. He said fine, and that's when I knew my original assumptions were right; she must have talked to her and, honestly, I just wasn't in the mood to be lectured. Turning off my cell phone, if someone really needed to reach me . . . they knew where to find me.

Each morning before the sun rose, I hit the beach running, running harder and faster than I have in a long time. And each evening, I sat outside on my porch, and watched the sun set while listening to her play the guitar.

The hole in my chest is the biggest it has ever been. Nothing seems to dull the ache except the melody from her guitar. It soothes me in a way I can't describe. I haven't even seen her, but hearing the music and the faint sound of her voice makes me feel like she's near. I don't know what I'm going to do to feel close to her once she's gone.

Like a broken record, I've kept replaying her telling me that she's falling in love with me. I so desperately want to believe that she could love me. I try not to torture myself with the notion for too long each time, because I know I don't deserve it . . . no one with my past would. Davy dropped by the North Shore house earlier, and told me I was meeting him at the Sandbar tonight for a little live music. As much as I don't want to go out, it'll probably be for the better. I need to get my pre-Elle routine back and just continue to push on with my life. That's what I'm used to doing; that's what I know how to do.

Glancing at the clock, I've got about an hour before I'm supposed to meet him, so I decide to drop by the café for one of Aunt Ella's sandwiches.

She eyes me as I come in the back door and wander into the kitchen. She doesn't say anything; no greeting, no smile, no nothing. She clearly has something on her mind. I know to stand here and wait for it, because she'll speak when she's ready.

"You're an idiot. You know this, right?" she says to me in a low tone, while stirring some sauce on the stove.

My eyes widen at her comment. I can't think of another time when she has been angry or upset with me.

"What?" I cross my arms over my chest and scowl across the room at her.

Setting down the spoon, she turns down the heat and turns to face me. "She's going to leave here, leave you, and it'll be your fault."

What the hell?

"You need her and she needs you," she continues.

I'm not going to argue her point, because I know I do, but at this point it's irrelevant.

"I'm the last thing she needs."

She huffs. "You know, for someone who sees so much, you are completely blind when it comes to her." She puts her hands on her hips and frowns at me.

"I'm assuming you've talked to her, because I don't know where this is coming from."

"No, I haven't talked to her, but I did see her yesterday and I'm seeing you right now. Whatever happened between the two of you . . . it's written all over your faces." She waves her hand in the air at me.

Aunt Ella saw her yesterday? I feel a pang of crazy jealousy at this information. Does she look as bad as I do? If she does, then it's my fault. Uneasiness settles in.

"Look, I don't know what you're talking about." I want to turn around and leave, but that would be disrespectful—and that's not me.

"Yes, you do! She looks terrible and, quite frankly, so do you. Open your eyes, Matt! Take a step back and really look at her. She needs you. Not someone else, which is what I know you're thinking. She needs *you* to show her how to be strong, independent, and to stand up for herself. Her whole life has been dictated. She's got strings attached to every part of her. Where she goes, who she talks to, what she wears, how much she can eat . . . She's trapped, just like you think you are."

I don't think I'm trapped. I know I am! No one is a prisoner in their miserable life like I am. Anger surges through me and every muscle tenses.

With my eyes trained on her, I watch every step she takes

as she comes to stand next to me. She places her hand on my arm and my eyes flick down to it. For years, whenever she touched me, I felt special. Now I just want to jerk away.

"She needs you. Let her in. Let her show you what unconditional love can be like."

Picking my head up, I look at her. The pleading look she is giving me is filled with love and certainty. She wouldn't think these things if she knew the truth, though, and that thought makes my stomach turn over with anxiety.

"I don't want to talk about her with you."

I hear her sigh loudly and she is quiet for a minute. "I know what you are thinking right now, and, Matt," she tilts her head to the side, "I do know the truth that you are so worried about," she says calmly and slowly.

I work to keep my face emotionless; the only change in my expression is in my eyes. They've grown wider in disbelief while, underneath, my heart rate has picked up substantially. What is she talking about? Surely, we aren't thinking of the same thing. It's not possible.

"You are the strongest person I have ever known. The things you've seen, experienced, and kept buried all these years . . . no one should have to deal with alone. I had hoped that you would come to me or Uncle Ben, but you didn't. You've persevered all on your own, and I am proud of you . . . both of us are." Her hand squeezes my arm.

I should probably say something back to her, but I don't know what. The intense stare she is giving me isn't wavering, and I start shaking. She does know . . . and she sees the moment I realize this by nodding her head. How did she find out? How long has she known? And, if she knew, then why didn't she say something sooner? My chest has gone tight, and I feel like I can't breathe.

"There's nothing to be proud of!" I jerk my arm away from her and take a step back, needing some distance. "I ruined people's lives," I blurt out. "And how did you find out?"

The thought that there are people out there who know my secrets and I didn't know it causes a cold sweat to break out. Suddenly, I don't just feel trapped; I feel like I am at the mercy of others and I don't even know who they are.

"Nobody's lived were ruined, Matt. They were just changed. You're looking at it all wrong." Is there pity in her eyes? I don't want her pity; I don't want anything except for this conversation to end!

"Well, I don't know where you got your information, but it must be incorrect." My hand trembles and I run it through my hair. Recalling the memories causes fear and self-loathing to seep into my pores.

"Matt, you were just a child. It's not your fault. That's why we've always been there; to make sure nothing happened to you."

"*Who* was there?" The hairs on the back of my neck stand up.

"Not important," she says, calmly taking a step toward me.

What!

"It *is* important! You should have told me that you knew. For years, I've been living with this, and dying just a little bit each day. I've had so many sleepless nights, worrying over people finding out, especially you and Uncle Ben, and now here you are telling me you knew all along—and that other people did, too! I don't know what you expect me to say here."

I need to get out of here.

"Fine, don't say anything, just . . . listen." She places her hand back on my arm and looks at me so genuinely . . . so

231

motherly. "I'm sorry you worried over Uncle Ben and me. That never should have happened, because there is nothing that you could do or say that would make us love you any less. You mean the world to me. You always have and you always will. You can't change your childhood. It is what it is. But it's time to stop worrying about your past and start thinking about your future. You could have a beautiful future ahead of you. It's yours for the taking. I know you have feelings for her. I've known you your whole life, and not only have I seen a change in you, but in her as well. Love doesn't come around every day. When it does, you grab it and hold on to it as tightly as you can, because you never know how long you're going to have it. There are no do-overs in life. You get one chance and that's it. Sweetheart, it's time to bury the ghosts and follow the sun."

That damn line is the last thing I need to be reminded of right now.

"I have to go." Feeling frantic, I turn my back to her, push through the back door and gasp for air at the same moment the brightness from the sun hits me. Squinting, I stand there and wait for the reminder and the wave of regret that always comes; only this time it doesn't. Nothing happens, nothing inside me changes, and it's confusing.

Needing to move, I put one foot in front of the other, walk down to the beach and turn in the direction of the Sandbar. I know there are other people out this evening, but I don't see any of them. All I see is the sand as I trudge through it.

I'm appalled that Aunt Ella knows the truth about me. Of all the people in the world, she and Uncle Ben were the two that I never *ever* wanted to find out. How could she possibly feel anything but hate towards me, knowing what she does? And it doesn't matter that I was a child; what I remember is a reality. I was there. No one will ever understand how it all shaped me. And love . . . how is it that everyone seems to be so sure about my own feelings, when I don't even know what the hell I am feeling? For three days, I have thought about nothing but my feelings for Ellie. I'm trying to understand them, but none of it is clear to me. Ellie said she knows I love her. Aunt Ella says she knows I love her. Although I've just recently figured it out myself, I can't help but wonder, if it would ever be enough. What I feel for her . . . will I be enough?

The only real examples that I have are Drew and Beau, and I've analyzed their relationships nonstop. Can I give Ellie what they give to Ali and Leila? Love was never in the cards for me, and I don't know if I will ever be able to love someone like they do.

Drew and Ali are inseparable. From the moment he realized she loved him, he hasn't left her side. He literally packed his bags, moved into her house, and never looked back. But, then again, neither did she. Through unfortunate life circumstances, together they chose their path, and decided that it was up to them to make their own destiny. I admire them for that. They don't let anyone or anything stop them from their dreams. Their love not only runs deep, but it runs long as well.

Beau and Leila aren't much different. Whereas Drew can't keep his eyes off of Ali, Beau can't keep his hands off of Leila. I used to think it was because he was afraid she would disappear again, but now I know it's because of the way she makes him feel. I don't even know their entire story, but what I do know is that Beau has loved her for his whole life. Forgiveness and trust has made them who they are, and they've built this whole other level of communication that is just for them. I would make fun of him if he wasn't so crazy in love with her. I mean, how can anyone make fun of a love like that?

A love like that.

Do I have a love like that with Ellie and I'm totally blind to it? I know I need to talk to her, but I have no idea what to say. This entire week has been shit, and now I'm more confused than ever.

Walking up the wooden ramp to the outside bar, I spot Davy off to the side. He sees me, nods his head, and then his forehead wrinkles with concern.

"Dude, what's up?" he asks me as I sit down.

"Nothing," I answer sharply. I need a beer, I want to listen to the music, and I want to forget . . . at least for a little while.

Chapter Sixteen

ELLE

"HEY, ELLLLLE!" I hear coming from outside. It's Leila's voice, and I can't help but giggle. Throwing open the door, I find her on my porch, grinning from ear to ear.

"What are you doing?" I beam at her.

"I didn't want to knock and scare you, and your phone wasn't on, so I thought yelling your name was the best solution." She rocks up on her toes with excited energy.

"Well, come in."

She breezes past me and into the living room. I shut the door and make sure to lock it.

"So, I just left the Sandbar. Beau wanted this fish sandwich that they have, and who do I see but Matt and Davy, just sitting down at a table outside." She's smiling at me with a conspiratorial look.

My face falls, and I narrow my eyes at her. I don't understand why she is so happy about this.

"What does that have to do with me?" I haven't heard from him in days and, truth be told, my spirit feels bruised.

"Because, it's neutral territory! You have to get dressed right now, and I'll take you there so you guys can talk." She's bouncing on her toes again, and this makes me need to move.

"What? I don't want to go there!" I say, pacing the room.

"Yes, you do. Are you just going to keep sitting here and pretending like he never happened?"

Actually, yes, that is exactly what I planned on doing at this point. He said he didn't love me, and he's done his very best to avoid me ever since.

"That seems to be what he's doing," I deadpan.

She shrugs this off, like the small shred of dignity that I would like to preserve is inconsequential. "Doesn't matter; you are older and wiser, so get dressed!" She points to my bedroom with rushed actions.

"I'm only two years older than he is, and no."

"Really?" Her arms drop and she stops moving. Her playfulness is gone and seriousness takes over. "Think about this for a second. It's not a private location. He isn't going to cause a scene, and he isn't going to run away from you. You must have a few things you want to get off your chest and say to him. Now's the time!"

Maybe she's right. Staring at each other in a face-off, the tension I felt at the mention of his name starts to dissipate slightly, and nervous anxiety sets in. I can do this . . . I know I can.

"Okay, fine. I need five minutes." I turn and head into my bedroom and slip on a pair of shorts and a long-sleeved shirt that drops over one shoulder. In the bathroom, I put on some mascara and some lip gloss, and then freeze as I look at myself in the mirror. For just a split second, I feel the need to 'put on my face', but it passes, and what I see looking back at me is someone who is beautiful just the way she is. I run my hands through my hair, smile at myself, and realize this is who I am; take it or leave it. I'm ready to be me.

Shoving my feet into a pair of flip-flops, I grab my guitar off the couch and move to stand in front of Leila.

"I'm ready. Let's go." I motion to the door, and she looks at me strangely.

"You want to take your guitar to the Sandbar?" her eyebrows lift in curiosity.

"Yep." I smile at her.

"Umm, okay; whatever you say." She follows me out the door and I kick it shut.

AFTER LEILA DROPS me off, the hostess goes to find the manager for me. I explain what I want to do; he smiles at me, and sets off to talk to the band. Looking over the crowd on the deck, there aren't a whole lot of people, but there are enough to make my nerves want to jump up and run and hide.

I spot Matt and his friend easily enough. They aren't saying much to each other, more like sitting there in silent companionship.

Matt looks distracted, but still insanely handsome as he sits there with that brooding look that he does so well. He's leaning forward in his chair with his elbows on the table, running both of his hands through his hair. He has on a navy blue t-shirt, and it stretches perfectly across the muscles of his back. It pains me to see how tensed up he is but, at the same time, it gives me hope that whatever is going through his mind is about me.

"Ms. Summers?" a voice breaks me away from my thoughts of him. I look over and see the manager standing next to me. I didn't even realize he had returned. I smile at him.

"The band has two more songs to play before they take a quick break; if you don't mind hanging out just a few minutes, the stage is all yours."

"That sounds great. Thank you." I let out a deep sigh.

"Good luck." He pats me on the arm and walks off.

This is it, just two songs away from pouring out my heart. I realize the importance of what I'm about to do; either he's going to hear me . . . or not.

The opening arrangement to *Sittin' on the Dock of the Bay* drifts across the deck and quickly sets me at ease. I can't believe it, but it has to be a sign that one of my favorite songs in the world is being played right now, right here, at this moment. I love Otis Redding's version of this, but I love Sara Bareilles's even more. This was also played the first night I came here, and Matt ended up taking me home. I know it's a commonly played song, but tonight I feel like it's being played just for me.

I find myself getting lost in the melody as I stare at Matt. It makes me think of when he took me down to the end of the pier to eat ice cream and watch the sun set. I loved that date.

His eyes are cast down, and he's peeling the label off of his bottle. My heart aches as I think of this beautiful lonely guy. I don't want for us to be held down by the past, by fears, or by other people anymore. I want us both to have the best life, because we only get one. As the song ends, he glances up at the band and then sits back in his chair.

"Alright folks, one more and then we are going to take a

quick break," the lead singer announces. He turns, nods to the guy with the electric guitar, who begins to play *No shoes, No shirt, No Problems* by Kenny Chesney. It really is the perfect song for this place, and instead of saying Mexico, he subs in Anna Maria Island. I can't help but smile.

All too quickly the song ends and the drummer points his stick at me, letting me know that I'm up.

Instantly, I break out in a cold sweat. Panic slices through me at what I'm about to do. Doubt fills me, but I've come too far to turn back now.

Step by step, I make my way to the stage. The drummer holds his hand out to me and helps me up the step, even though I could have done it myself. Out of the corner of my peripheral vision, I see movement among the tables. Well, that's fine by me. The more who run off to use the bathroom, the fewer people will hear me.

"Thank you," I say to the guy.

Leaving one foot on the ground, I take a seat on the stool that has been placed in front of the microphone. I prop my other foot on the wooden rung and balance the guitar across my lap. Taking a deep breath, I look out across the crowd. *Here goes nothing.*

"Good evening, ladies and gentlemen. I appreciate the band and you all allowing me to interrupt your night, but I have a song that I wrote . . . and it needs to be sung. I've never done this before, sung in front of a crowd, that is, so my apologies in advance." My voice is shaky and my smile wobbly.

My ears pick up murmurings throughout the crowd, and I can't help but glance down and focus on the sand that's made its way on to the stage. I don't know if it's because people are curious about my sudden and impromptu performance, or if I am being recognized. I'm praying it's not the latter. But even if it is, I don't care. This is my life, and I'm taking it over.

"When I originally started writing the lyrics to this song, they were about me, but I never could get it to work—something was missing. Now, after being here for almost two weeks, I see I was wrong. They are meant to be about *us*." My eyes finally flick across the crowd and land on him, the one person who I need to hear me the most.

Matt looks shocked and, even from this distance, I can recognize the storm in those gorgeous gray eyes of his. I watch as his eyebrows pull down, and his lips are pinched into a thin line. Instead of curiosity at my sudden appearance, he now looks angry. Insecurity sweeps through me that maybe this wasn't such a good idea, but there's no going back now. I need to do this—for both of us.

Breaking eye contact with him, I look around crowd and at nothing in particular. I can't focus on him or I will never get this out.

"My name is Elle, by the way, and my song is called *Standing Free*. I hope you like it, and thank you for listening." Am I talking to the audience or him? I don't even know.

Angling my body to face more toward the beach, I gaze out across the sand and over the water as it sparkles under the setting sun. The burnt oranges and deep golden yellows cause me to pause. The sky is cloudless and this is the perfect sunset, the perfect backdrop to what I have to say.

Keeping my eyes on the sky, I know as I finish my song that the sun will dip below the horizon, but that's okay. My fingers shake as I move them into place and strum the opening chords. Quieting my mind to the onslaught of varying emotions, I close my eyes and begin to play from my heart.

Mmmm…

I'm standing on the edge of the water, looking at the horizons light.

It's so close, so far, reminding me of my life.
I look left, I look right, which way do I go?
I just wanna move to a place that's free,
and that's when I see you standing next to me.

As the rays stretch out and the heat hits my skin,
I'm reminded of all the places that we've never been.
How do we get there, I wanna know.
We can't change where we come from,
but it's up to us to choose where we go.

I wanna live, I wanna laugh, I wanna love that's for me.
I wanna shout, I wanna scream, I wanna fight somebody.
I wanna stand, I wanna choose, I wanna be strong,
Because it's … My choice. Your choice. Ours to be free…
Nothing to stop us, just you and me…

What does it take to feel alive?
What does it take to feel free?
I wanna break these chains, smash these walls, and have the light find me.
I wanna run down the beach, breathe in the air,
I wanna hold your hand and tell the world we just don't care.

I wanna soak up the sun and dance in the rain.
Run through the fire and forget the pain.
Let's shed all the tears and then laugh till we cry,
Hand and hand we'll walk through the night,

And with a million smiles we'll light up the sky.
I wanna live, I wanna laugh, I wanna love that's for me.
I wanna shout, I wanna scream, I wanna fight somebody.
I wanna stand, I wanna choose, I wanna be strong,
Because it's . . . My choice. Your choice. Ours to be free...
Nothing to stop us, just you and me...

In another place, in another time
I was lost until you became mine.
I want us to be free, free to stand on our own.
I'll be by your side, I'll never let you fall
Everything's better together, rather than not at all.

I see you and you see me, just imagine how amazing our life could be.
Don't you get it? What you are to me?
A love of a lifetime that I'll cherish for all eternity.
Our time is now, let's grab it and go.
To feel alive, to be free, standing strong just you and me.

I wanna live, I wanna laugh, I wanna love that's for me.
I wanna shout, I wanna scream, I wanna fight somebody.
I wanna stand, I wanna choose, I wanna be strong,
Because it's ... My choice. Your choice. Ours to be free...
Nothing to stop us, just you and me...
Living the life we choose it to be.

Tell me, what sets you free...
Make that choice for you and me...

Faintly, I register that people are clapping for me, but my

242

ears are still ringing from the last note and the adrenaline coursing through me.

I did it.

Taking a deep breath, I smile to myself. I hope it was enough.

I open my eyes and risk a peek at Matt's table, a table that only has one person sitting at it . . . his friend.

MATT

I HEAR HER voice before I see her, and I'm pretty certain my breath catches in my throat and my heart skips a few beats. Every muscle freezes except in my neck. My head whips up so fast I could have given myself whiplash. *Holy shit.*

I feel Davy's gaze land on me, and out of the corner of my eye I see his head swivel back and forth between the two of us. Ellie leans forward to look at her feet and she adjusts her foot that's placed on the stool rung. Her hair has fallen forward, partially covering her face, and I can't drink the sight of her in fast enough.

She starts talking, but my heart is pounding so hard I barely register what she is saying. She's here, in front of me, and on the little stage.

Us? She wrote a song about us? Oh, my God. I think my heart just stopped. Before she even runs her fingers across the guitar's strings, I already know the song she's going to play. It's the one she's been working on since she got here, but I've never heard the words.

Time suspends and everything around me fades away. I'm

rooted to this chair because I know whatever she says is going to be a turning point in my life. Meeting her, listening to Beau, having these feelings, being yelled at by Aunt Ella, being discovered by Aunt Ella—all of it has been leading me to this moment where it's time for me to make a decision.

Ellie looks out to the sunset, closes her eyes, and starts to sing. The combination of the melody that I've heard over and over again, along with her voice tightens my chest. I was selfish enough to want her to fight for me, and now here she is, only she's not fighting for me, she's fighting for us. The words she's written are crashing into my soul, and she's healing me in a way I didn't know could be.

How did I get so incredibly lucky to find this girl?

I wanna live, I wanna laugh, I wanna love that's for me.
I wanna shout, I wanna scream, I wanna fight somebody.
I wanna stand, I wanna choose, I wanna be strong,
Because it's ... My choice. Your choice. Ours to be free...
Nothing to stop us, just you and me...
Living the life we choose it to be.

Tell me, what sets you free...
Make that choice for you and me...

Nothing in life is a coincidence. I'm convinced of this, because there is no other way to explain *her*. She's got me second-guessing everything that I have known about myself since I was eight years old. Listening to the words of her song, I'm spellbound by what the light of the sun means to her, what it can mean for us.

She finishes her song. The chords from the guitar echo and linger in the air. Her eyes are closed and I feel like I can't breathe. People around us are clapping. They're clapping for her, and I'm so damn proud. Every word that left her beautiful lips resonated with me, and I know she's right. I can't keep hiding. Only I have the power to free myself from the hell that I have been living.

I don't want to fight for her. I, too, want to fight for us. I don't want to feel the sun anymore and remember those horrible moments that I've never been able to forget. I want to feel the sun and feel alive. I know I should stay and talk to her. She's just put herself out there, in front of everyone, for me, for us—but I can't. I need to leave. There's something that I have to do. It's time.

Pushing out of the chair, Davy reaches up and grabs my arm.

"Where are you going?" he asks, shock and concern on his face.

I don't say anything back. He sees the desperation in my face and releases me. He nods his head, and I turn to walk off of the deck and onto the beach.

I glance back at her one more time, and see that her eyes are following me. There's heartbreak in them, and this crushes me because I am making her feel this way. I never want to hurt her, or make her feel pain, and hopefully after all this is over, she'll understand. But right now . . . I have to. I can't move forward with her until I get the closure I need from my past.

The sun has dropped below the horizon, and a sharp chuckle escapes me as I think how perfect this conversation is going to be, taking place at night.

Sand slips in between my toes, and I welcome the discomfort of the grittiness. With my hands shoved into my pockets and my head down, I push forward to the one and only place I need to go.

By the time I finally walk up the back steps to Beau's house, my heart feels like it's going to burst out of my chest. Anxiety is rippling through me in waves, but I just don't care. Ellie's words are on repeat in my head, and over and over again I hear her singing, *"Standing strong just you and me, living the life that we choose it to be."*

I want to be free to choose my own life . . . so desperately.

The motion lights on the porch kick on. Through the sliding glass doors, I watch Beau's head as it turns, and his eyes lock on to me. He smiles and my heart clenches. Knowing what I have to say to him, I don't have it in me to smile back. Time stalls between us and his happy, welcoming expression drops. Concern replaces it, and he tilts his head toward the sliding glass door for me to come inside. I shake my head no, and my gaze shifts to Quinn. She's sitting on the counter in her purple footed pajamas and he's holding a sippy cup out to her. She takes it from him, and he picks her up, never breaking eye contact with me.

The longer he looks at me, the more I feel weighed down by the guilt. I drop my eyes from his and move to sit down on one of the porch chairs. I'm trying to hold my composure together, but I'm sick with apprehension. Leaning forward, I place my elbows on my knees and run my hand through my hair. I'm such an emotional mess after hearing Aunt Ella and then Ellie, there's no way I can go inside. He'll come out once Quinn is in bed. I just have to wait.

Most of the sky has darkened, but there is still the faint glow where the sun disappeared. The beach is empty, and the only sounds are the swaying of the sea oats and the water as it gently laps the shore.

I hear the door open behind me and I close my eyes. I

246

stop breathing and, with each foot-step he takes toward me, my heart starts pounding harder. A cold sweat breaks out across my skin and chills in the night air. My insides are shaking and I'm being slammed by one emotion after another: worry, fear, stress, panic, dread. I need the onslaught to stop, but for four-teen years I've kept this all to myself. I don't even know where or how to begin this conversation.

Beau sits down next to me and I look over at him. His eyebrows furrow and concern etches across his face. Without saying anything, he hands me a cold beer, and we both sit back and stare out over the water.

When I think back over my life, yes, I have my mother, Drew, and Aunt Ella, but truly the only person who has ever really mattered to me was Beau. It's his love that I so desper-ately craved and needed; no one else's. My throat closes with anxiety. I have never wanted to disappoint him, and I know what I'm about to tell him is going to be so much worse.

"Little dude," his voice startles me and I turn to look at him. He pauses to study me before continuing. "I'll sit here with you—as long as you need—but I need you to tell me what's going on."

My eyes fill with tears, and slowly one slips over the edge and drips down my cheek. He sees it and his breathing speeds up. He's never pushed me to talk. He's always just let me be, but he knows this is why I am here tonight. I need to let him in . . . he needs to know the truth.

I drop my head, not wanting to see the genuine love and care he has for me. Beau's devotion to me as a brother, some-one he loves, has always been unwavering, and I'm so afraid I'm going to lose it. He has always been my hero. I've idolized him since the day I was born.

Silent sobs start wracking through me. As hard as I try, I

can't contain them. What if he hates me after he knows the truth? What if he tells me to leave and never come back? What if he thinks I'm just as horrible as *him*, my so-called father?

I set the beer down as the tears drop. Rubbing my chest over my heart, I feel like it's splintering into a thousand pieces. Years and years of fear of being discovered, and I'm terrified to utter the words. I'm about to tell him something that I've never dared to tell anyone else before. I've not so much as even uttered the words to myself, because I never wanted it to be real.

Staring at the boards of the porch, the tears that have blurred my eyes suddenly clear and all I see is the fire. I've somehow been sucked back in time to the one night I so desperately try not to think about; the house glowing with fire, the heat from the flames, and Beau's screams are coming from the front porch. The red flashing lights, my dad shoving me, and the smell; that pungent smell of smoke as it seeps into every pore. I know that this is an irrational flashback, but I'm on sensory overload.

I'm panicking and I feel frantic. The world is spinning, and I don't know how to make it stop. I can't breathe. I can't escape it.

And then I feel Beau's hand on me. The vision clears.

His hand gently grabs my shoulder and I look over at him. He's scooted closer, and I see unshed tears swimming in his eyes as well. I'm upsetting him and I know it's only going to get worse.

It's now or never.

Swallowing, I take a deep breath and look him right in the eye. "I started the fires," I whisper.

He sharply sucks in some air. His face pales and confusion replaces concern. "What fires?" he asks, even though we both know what I'm talking about.

"All of them." I drop my gaze to the ground. I can't bear to see his disappointment in me, or the anger, both of which he is certain to have.

Out of the corner of my eye, I see him sit back in his chair. He lets out a deep sigh and silence wraps its way around us. He takes another pull on his beer and stares out at the beach.

I've carried this secret with me for over two-thirds of my life, and now that it's out there, I'm blanketed in fear and gripped in pain. Every muscle is tense; they have been for years, carrying around all this shit around, and suddenly they've decided to unwind, and pain is radiating throughout me. Getting up out of the chair, I go to walk to the edge of the deck to stretch them out when Beau's voice interrupts the quietness.

"Sit. Down," he commands. His voice echoes across the porch, only to be absorbed by the dunes.

Without looking at him, I ease back into my chair and nervously rub my hands back and forth across my shorts.

He leans forward again, "You better start talking, and don't leave one single detail out." His tone is a no-nonsense one. It's what I need in order to start talking. Looking over at him, his eyes are pinning me to my chair and his cheeks are flushed red.

"Dad first came to me when I was seven and told me that my time was coming. I wasn't sure what he was talking about, but then right after Christmas he started setting his plans into motion. I was going to help him start the fires. He told me if I didn't, that he would kill you, and after seeing how much he hurt you all the time, I believed him."

His body tenses and his eyes are now glaring at me.

"You were right that day in the kitchen, when you flew home from New York to confront Mom about Leila. You said that it was just too coincidental what happened to Leila's family. That it all seems premeditated. How interesting it was that, when he went to jail, all the fires stopped. But how could I tell you after everything that had happened? All those years, I was so afraid of him and so afraid for you."

I'm frozen, watching him, and I feel like I'm going to throw up. My chin trembles and I take a deep breath. Breathing in and out of my nose, I'm trying to pull myself together, but my emotions feel out of control. He continues glaring at me, saying nothing. I want to wither under his unspoken scrutiny.

"How? How did you start the fires?" His voice is monotone, and his expression is now blank. It unsettles me even more. I'd rather see a reaction from him than nothing.

I pick up the bottle and take a swig of the beer. My mouth is dry and I need to wash down the uneasiness I feel explaining how I committed these crimes.

"That part was actually pretty simple." Looking at the bottle, I begin to fidget and peel the label. "One of the easiest is to leave a pizza box on the gas stove. Another, pour brake fluid into a water bottle and then add pool shock. It melts the bottle and then combusts. At Christmas time, you can't just light the tree on fire, it goes up quickly and, unless it catches on something, it will burn out. If you cut a hole in the ceiling above the tree the flames will fly up into the attic and catch the house on fire. Crayons, they make great candles. There are so many different ways." I pause to look at him, "For Leila's house, I used a bag of potato chips. You crush some up, sprinkle them on the carpet, light the bag on fire and toss it over the crushed chips. The grease from the chips catches on fire, and

250

the whole thing burns. It's non-traceable."

His jaw drops open in shock and horror. "He taught you all of this?" he says, sounding completely appalled.

"Yes," I say on a long sigh. I have always wondered if and when the time came, and I confessed to what I had done, if I would feel liberated. Now I know, and the answer is no. I've now burdened him with the knowledge of all the horrible things I did, and the depth of my guilt grows deeper. I feel more regret and remorse than I ever imagined. I wish I could take it all back.

"I always wondered what started that fire," he mumbles. He leans back in his chair and runs his hand over his face. I know that, by talking about that night, I'm not the only one reliving it. He looks like he is too. "How did you never get caught?" he looks at me with contemplative eyes.

"I don't know. We were careful, I guess, but I can't even begin to tell you how many sleepless nights I've had, wondering when they were going to figure it all out and come for me. I wish they would have. It's what I deserved." I can't take the way he is looking at me, so I look away. "Arson investigations take a really long time and are really hard to prove. Unless there is actual physical evidence that can be tied back to the person involved with intent of a criminal act, charges can't take place. Just like those examples I gave, unless someone saw me and collected proof, there was no way to prove that I did it."

He's watching me in astonished horror, and it suddenly occurs to me that he could turn me in. All of this time I have been so worried about what he would think of me. I never once thought that he just might be so disgusted he would tell my secrets. Shame washes through me.

Closing my eyes, I stutter out, "Do you want me to turn

myself in?"

"Hell no, Matt!" he yells.

He pauses for a beat, and I can see that he has so many questions for me in his mind that he's trying to filter through.

"I always thought it was him, but I couldn't prove it. The pattern was there, with the repetitive fires and the bank-seized properties; him buying, clearing, building, and selling. He was making money hand over fist. I never, in a million years, thought it was you. Does anyone else know about this?"

"I don't know. I never thought so. I thought I was living with this all by myself, but then Aunt Ella, yesterday she told me she knew and that *others* were watching out for me. It's all so confusing and so overwhelming," I whisper. My nose burns as the tears again flood my eyes.

"Why didn't you tell me sooner?" his tone is laced with irritation, but I can't tell if it's at the situation or at me.

"Would you have told me?" my voice is a little louder as I gape at him. "I stood there and watched you almost burn to death. You have no idea how that permanently changed me. You became scarred on the outside, and I became scarred on the inside. Shit inside of me is so ugly." Tears roll down my face. I'm taking deep breaths but I don't feel like I can catch my breath. "Besides, I had been trained to not say a word. He very explicitly detailed what would happen if I did. I didn't stop talking all those years for reasons people think; it was all because of him. Beau, I can't tell you how sorry I am. What happened to you, and to Leila, it's my fault, all of it."

Leaning over, my head drops again and falls to my hands. Fisting my hair and squeezing my eyes closed, large sobs start wracking through me. To love someone as much as I love him, and to know that I ruined part of his life and his life became harder because of me, is almost too much to bear.

"Hey," he says softly, putting his hand back on my shoulder. "Listen to me; you may have struck the match, but I don't, for one second, believe that you did this. You know that each of us had a role in his miserable life. He used us all for different things, and this just happened to be yours. And what happened between Leila and me all those years ago had nothing to do with you or the fire. That was poor communication on our parts—we caused our own problems, not you. I am just so sorry he did this to you. God, I wish I had known."

What?

This is not what I expected him to say. I expected him to yell at me and tell me that I'm nothing more than the crap stuck to the bottom of his shoe, that I'm an indecent, horrible person, and I deserve to continue living my life alone.

Blinking at him, I see that his expression is filled with empathy. "You're not angry with me?"

"Oh, I'm pissed . . . but I don't know at whom at the moment." Under the porch lights, I see his face flush. "I'm pissed that you've lived with this for so long. I'm pissed because I'm your big brother and I'm supposed to protect you from shit like this. I'm pissed that we all were stuck with that ass. I'm pissed for Leila's family. And I'm pissed for me, because aside from everything, these scars are because of him. Yeah, I'm plenty pissed."

He lets out a sigh and runs his hand over his face again. We stare at each other and then he takes a swig of his beer.

"Beau, I don't want to live with this anymore. I don't want to live in fear that someone is going to find out. I just don't know what to do."

"We'll figure this out together, okay? How many?"

I know what he was asking, and my stomach clenches. "Eleven."

"That's it, eleven? Seemed like so many more," he says, sounding surprised.

"You're kidding, right?" I sniff and wipe my face on my shirt sleeves.

"What happened to make you want to tell me?" he tilts his head to the side to study me.

"Elle happened." Just thinking of her, a cool calmness falls over me and my heart rate slows.

"I see," he says giving me a small smile. "I like her."

"Me, too," I chuckle lightly. "Are you going to tell Leila? I'll understand if you need to." The thought of her being disappointed in me is equally nerve-wracking, but if it's part of what I need to deal with in order to get through, this then I will gladly do it.

"Do you think I should?" He's asking me because he's my brother, but knowing the two of them, keeping this from her would be detrimental to the trust they've worked so hard to build.

"Yes."

"Okay, then." He tilts the bottle up and finishes off the beer.

"It's something I'll regret for the rest of my life. It's the reason I don't let myself get close to anybody. I don't feel like I deserve it. He made me into something terrible and detestable, just like him. I . . . I really am sorry." My eyes flood with tears again.

"Matt, it was a long time ago. It's in the past and, even though we want to, we can't change it. Am I angry? Yes. I need a little time to process all this, and we'll talk about it more another time. One conversation isn't going to cut it. I can't think straight right now." He pauses, looks out over the water and then back at me. Sighing, he looks at me sadly. "I am so glad you finally talked to me. I've been waiting for this for a long time. I didn't know it was going to be about this, but I knew that one day, when you were ready, you would come to me. You can always come and talk to me. I really want you to know that."

I sniff again and give him a small smile.

"Come here." He stands and pulls me into a hug. "Love you, little dude, no matter what."

At his words, something inside of me dissolves. The anxious wariness that I had built up over the years at him finding out the truth is suddenly gone. The walls are down, and in its place is solidarity with him that I never truly felt until now. This secret has kept me so isolated and trapped. Elle was right; making this choice to finally tell him has set me free.

The sliding glass door opens behind us and Leila tentatively walks out. There are tear tracks down her face, and although I know she didn't hear our conversation, the guilt is still there. I know it is going to take some time to work through all of this with them, but I am beginning to see the light.

"What's wrong?" Beau is instantly on alert.

Leila walks over to him, she lays a hand on his chest, and he wraps his arm around her while kissing the side of her head. She looks at him and then looks at me, frowning.

"Nothing, it's just . . . my heart hurts for you," she says, her gaze softening, "And I love you. I just want you to be happy."

"I'm trying," I whisper.

"How's Elle doing today? Did you see her tonight?" she tilts her head, and I see worry written all over her. Alarm bells start to go off in my head.

"I did, I need to go look for her now. I just needed to talk to Beau first."

"Ok, well that's good to hear. I hope you two are working things out. I *really* like her. Not to mention, she shouldn't be alone at night, now that we know that psycho has tracked her down."

My jaw drops open. "What! What do you mean tracked her down?"

"She got a package in the mail after you left on Wednesday morning. I left you a message. Didn't you get it?" she asks me incredulously.

"No, I didn't. I turned my phone off and forgot about it." My hands ball into fists. I'm about to become unhinged and I need to pull it together. "Why didn't she come and tell me?"

"Gee, I don't know. Maybe it had something to do with you being a complete ass to her earlier that morning," Leila snaps.

Oh no. Closing my eyes, I let out a sigh and run my hand through my hair. What if Ellie left me a message, too?

Leila's right. She's absolutely right, and I suddenly feel like a gigantic ass.

"I've got to go." My head snaps over to Beau and his eyes lock with mine. A silent conversation passes between us. He sees the fear in me and he's telling me to go, but he's also telling me that this isn't over. I nod to him and he gives me a small smile.

Leaning forward, I kiss Leila on the cheek, and then bolt for the porch stairs. As soon as my feet hit the sand, I start running. I'm trying not to panic, but what if something happens to her? It would be my fault for not being there for her, and I don't know if I could live with that. Forcing one foot in front of the other, I push hard. For what feels like all of my life, I've been running away from people, and now I'm running toward the one person that I truly believe is the cure for the pain.

Chapter Seventeen

ELLE

HE WALKED OUT.

I watch as he glances back at me once from the beach. He's too far away for me to see what the expression is on his face. I can faintly hear people clapping, but the pounding of my heart overrides it.

My heart constricts in my chest and humility washes over me. Why did I ever think this was going to work? He already knows that I love him, and I thought maybe, just maybe, if he heard me sing this song, *our* song, he might see this as my big, grand gesture. I put myself out there and now I just feel so stupid.

"Elle?"

My head snaps back and I see his friend standing in front of me, looking concerned.

"Yeah?" There are tears swimming in my eyes and I need to get off this stage. I scramble off the stool, clumsily holding my guitar.

"Come on, I'll walk you out." He takes the guitar from me and holds his other hand out to me. I take it. I am so grateful for him at this moment. There's a good possibility that, once I regained my composure, I was going to run out of here with tears streaming down my face.

"What's your name again?" I ask as I climb down off the stage.

"Davy." He smiles at me, but it's a sympathetic smile.

Once we reach the door, he drops my hand and holds out the guitar.

"You did really good up there," he says quietly.

"Thanks," I mutter, taking the guitar, not wanting to look at him. There's something about standing here with his friend and not him that makes me feel worse.

"For whatever it's worth, he did hear you." He places his hand on my arm and squeezes it slightly. Silence slips between us, he gives me a small smile, and then walks away.

I'm assuming he means that Matt heard the words, and not just in the literal sense, but a lot of good it did. He's not here, and I am. Alone.

Slinging the guitar over my back, under the dark night sky I set off to walk back to the cottage. Tears slowly begin to roll down my cheeks from the all-consuming heartache that I feel. At least I put it all out there. I'll never wonder what if, and I won't leave here with regrets.

OPENING THE DOOR to the cottage, I inwardly scold myself for running out earlier and not locking it. Leaning back against it, I slide down to the ground and the sobs that I had been holding in start to silently slip out. Otis comes over to me and rubs his head against my leg. Picking him up, I just want to go to bed and forget this whole night ever happened.

Without turning on any lights, I pick myself up off the floor, lock the door, and start walking toward the bedroom when, to the right of me, I hear the unmistakable sound of the hammer on a gun being pulled back and locked into place. It echoes in the silence and I freeze.

Terror engulfs me. My breath catches in my throat, adrenaline instantly blinds me, and my heart starts thundering so hard it's causing pain in my chest. Panic slices through me, over and over again. I'm instantly freezing and start to shake. This must be what it feels like to experience "fight or flight".

The stalker is *here*. They've finally come for me, and the anticipation of discovering who it is, after all this time has me terrified and relieved that this is about to be over, one way or another.

Suspense lingers in the air and I can't breathe. My chin starts trembling, and a cold sweat breaks out across my chilled skin. I've never been so afraid of anything in my life. I feel surrounded by a black haze, and slowly it begins to smother and suffocate me.

"Don't turn around," I hear through the ringing of my ears.

NO. . . I recognize the voice, and it paralyzes me. My aching heart cracks in half and my eyes slide shut. This can't be happening . . . No. NO. NO!

A gun is being pointed at my head, but all my emotions flip instantly. Through the haze, disbelief, disappointment, betrayal, and anger begin to prick through and that darkness turns to red. I'm so furious and stunned, that it's then I realize this is the calm before the storm. I don't want this to be my reality. I want to be dreaming and then wake up and everything is as it should be. This can't be happening.

At the thought of a bullet entering me, the pain associated with it, and possible death, my eyes snap open and begin to look for a way out of this. I take a deep breath to try to slow down my raging blood. My hands stop shaking and I tightly ball them into fists, not even feeling my fingernails breaking through the skin.

"How did you find me?" I ask in a low tone. My eyes have adjusted to the darkness of the room, and I look around frantically for anything; a weapon, something to defend myself, and an escape. It would take too long to get the door unlocked and open, and I'm too far from the bathroom and bedroom to make a run for it.

"It was pretty easy, actually. A while ago, I downloaded the Find My iPhone app, connected our iCloud accounts, and then hid the app in one of your many utility folders that you never use. I just opened the app and it gave me a nice little map, telling me right where my missing device was. It was brilliantly easy, actually, and incredibly *stupid* of you to not turn your phone off sooner."

"Why?" I ask quietly. I'm certain she can hear the heartbreak.

"What do you mean, why?" she snaps at me. Her tone is sarcastic, and dripping with hatred.

Disbelief and confusion consumes me.

"So, all this time it's been you?" I ask, needing to know the truth.

"Of course!" Her laughter echoes, and my heart clenches

at the sound. "It was so fun to watch you stress out over it, too. I just wish I could have seen your face at the gallery when you found the flowers."

"Who approached me at the gallery?"

"Jase."

I should have known. The familiar smell. How many times over the last couple of months, when we'd all been out together, has he wrapped his arm around me?

"Has he been in on this the whole time, too?" Just the thought of them conspiring against me together, there being two people, causes an uncontrollable shiver to run through me.

She lets out an evil laugh. "No, he thinks that you and I just like to play pranks on each other, and the poor fool will do anything to make me happy."

She used a guy to throw me off track, and it worked. All this time, I never *ever* would have thought it was her. A silence falls between us and I think that, up until now, I would have done anything to make her happy. I loved her like I have never loved another person. How could she do this to me?

"I don't understand." And I really don't. For the past five years, she and I have been inseparable. She is my best friend . . . or was.

"Everything was always about you," her words slither out, and I hear her moving out of the corner behind me. The hair on my scalp prickles.

I pause to think about what she's just said, and an unexplainable loathing for her takes over. I've never done anything to make her think that her life was any less important than mine. Every decision she has ever made was her own and, with sudden clarity, I realize my mother was right. She never trusted Olivia and thought she was shady but, then again, it takes one to know one. No wonder my mother disliked her so much;

they were cut from the same cloth.

"Yes, I can see how you would think that. You spent most of your time at my apartment, working for me, spending my money, enjoying my life. You and Mother, I'm surprised the two of you weren't collaborating against me. It seems you two just stuck around to ride my coattails. I've never forced you to be my friend, or stay. If you hated it so much, you could have left whenever you wanted. You knew where the door was."

"Say whatever you want, but know this, the expression *keep your friends close and your enemies closer* never meant to anyone what it means to me."

Well that stung. "Why am I your enemy? I've never been anything but loyal and kind to you."

"Don't you get it? Since the day my father met you, all he has ever said to me is, "Why can't you be more like Elle?" Do you have any idea what it's like to hear that from your one and only parent just about every day for years? Well, now, it's my turn!"

"Your turn for what?"

"It's my turn to be loved and admired. Everyone has always loved you more, but they won't anymore."

So that's what this is about? Getting attention?

It hurts me to hear her talk like this. I have noticed over the years that her father was hard on her, and it used to make me so angry. Livy isn't built like me, which isn't her fault, but he had these unattainable expectations that she should have a career just like mine.

"No, they love the idea of me . . . just like you, apparently." I'm so angry that she's put me in this situation.

"Shut up!" she screams at me.

I can't stand here with my back to her anymore. I need her to look me in the eyes as she says these things.

Silence falls between us, and the only sound I hear is Bruno barking in the background. Does he know that I'm in trouble? That means Matt's not home. Where is he? Not that I want him here. He could get hurt, and I wouldn't survive that.

With my arms held slightly out away from my body, showing my intentions, slowly I shift my weight and begin to turn around.

Her image drifts through the darkness, and I spot her standing next to the couch in the living room. I quickly do a scan to make sure she is the only one here. She's the only one that I see here. My heart skips a beat at the thought of someone else being in the cottage.

Everything about this moment just became so real. Staring at Livy, as she points the gun at my chest, I search my brain, wondering how I missed the fact that Livy was this unhinged. She still looks like my best friend, but her image, for me, has morphed, and I barely recognize her. The warmth and easy carefree aura that I used to feel radiating off of her is gone, and in its place are dark, flat eyes, pale skin, and coldness. I suddenly doubt myself. I always thought I was a great judge of character, but apparently not. Her friendship was fake. She's been lying to me, and I have no idea for how long. Nothing makes me angrier than someone lying to me.

She shifts her weight at my perusal of her, and she raises the gun higher.

"So, that's it? Shooting me is the big solution to fixing your pathetic life?" I hiss out at her.

She snorts. "Yes. You don't get it, do you?" She tilts her head at me and squints her eyes. "You were always a stupid bitch. Your life will become mine. In fact, I've already contacted clients telling them about your *little problem,* and they happily gave me the job in your place."

I know she's talking about the arthritis, but she's wrong. She doesn't have what it takes to do what I do, and no one, I mean no one, would give her my job. Seriously, she's the stupid one to think that I would buy that lie. Deception isn't very attractive on her, and I've officially had enough. I think through all of the things that I've ever been taught, and I know the most important thing is to stay calm, but my blood is boiling, and I am livid.

Minutes pass. She's had every opportunity to shoot me, but she hasn't. This tells me that maybe she really isn't after my life; she's after something else. *Money? Her father's acceptance? What?* Maybe she doesn't even know. But what I've figured out is that, even though she's not who I thought she was, she is just as spineless and weak as before. She's never been anything more than a pushover. She's doesn't have what it takes.

The darkness has completely washed away, and now I can see her clearly. I lock my gaze onto hers, narrow my eyes at her, and lift my head higher. Confusion sweeps quickly over her features. I hear her suck in a gasp, and I know her confidence just wavered.

Was she expecting me to panic, plead, and beg for my life? No chance. I am stronger than that, and she has just underestimated me. She will never have the upper hand on me. I understand that some part of her has cracked, bringing her to this point, but she needs to see and know that although I may not have a firearm, I will never succumb to her, and that gives me a psychological advantage over her.

I keep calm and maintain my gaze. Every second that passes, is an advantage to me. Discomfort has crept into her crazed glare.

I take a step toward her and her eyes widen.

That's right; I am not afraid of you.

She miscalculated my inner strength, though. I may have fled to the island to escape the reality of this situation, but being forced to come face to face with it, I am prepared. Did she actually think I would sit around while creepy, disturbing letters came in, and do nothing? She has no idea the number of self-defense classes I have taken, while she's at her fancy barre class.

Thinking of those self-defense classes, the only weapon that I have at the moment is deflection, and that's what I am going to do. I need to get her mind off of whatever is upsetting her, and I need to get her thinking about some of the good times we had together; make her doubt this decision so I can get close enough to disarm her.

Without breaking eye contact with her, I use my peripheral vision to become completely aware of my surroundings. With sure feet, I shift just a little again.

"All those years, Olivia. We've had so many good times together. I think one of my favorite memories of us is when we went to Disney World. I was eighteen, you were seventeen, and our parents had just gotten married. Do you remember?" I smile at her and her eyes widen again.

"Of course I remember, and you need to shut up!" she yells at me. She's starting to shake.

"That night we went over to Pleasure Island at Downtown Disney, and snuck into that dueling piano bar. That was so much fun. Look," I flip my hand over to show her the scar that I still have from when I tripped and fell and landed on a piece of glass from a beer bottle, "it's still there."

Her eyes drop to my hand, and her lips twitch like they want to smile. Maybe this plan will actually work. She doesn't realize this, but I chose that memory because it made me look not so invincible. She helped me up, she took care of me, and I needed her.

Bruno's barking suddenly gets much louder and we both flinch as he slams himself against my front door. I'm not sure if he escaped from Matt's cottage, or if Matt is actually on his way, but it doesn't matter.

Livy is looking at the door, and this is the opening that I need.

Without hesitating, I step to the left and out of the line of fire. Livy is right-handed, and I need to be on the side that the gun is being held. A person is slower to twist, aim, and fire from the shooting side of their body, rather than the support side.

Adrenaline rages through me, my heart is pounding and, even though I know this is going to be fast, everything comes into perfect focus and moves in slow motion.

With all the strength that I have in me, I punch her wrist and kick her knee backward.

The gun fires.

MATT

RUNNING BACK TO the cottages as I leave the beach and hit the dock pathway, I hear Bruno barking like crazy. He never barks, so when he does, I know something is wrong. More panic than I was already feeling rushes through me, and I start sprinting toward my house.

Throwing open my door, Bruno lunges out as fast as he can, and heads straight for Ellie's cottage. I'm trying to keep up with him, but I can't. He bolts around the side of my house and slams himself into her door. Not even two seconds later, a gun shot from behind it goes off. Past the echoing of the blast, a girl's screams reach my ears.

No!

I trip over the gravel as my world stops, and I skid to the ground. My hands are scraped, my eyes burn in shock, and my heart starts to bleed with the fear of the unknown. Bruno is jumping, scratching, and howling at the door as I push up off the ground to reach it.

"Ellie!" I yell her name as I grab the knob, but it's locked. All I hear are the screams and cries from behind the door. With shaking hands, I pull my keys out of my pocket, but I drop them somewhere in the sand.

Shit!

I reach down to feel around for them, but it's dark, and I can't take it anymore. I'm frantic and need to get in this door, so I rear back and kick it repeatedly until it gives. Bruno busts in and charges toward the screaming girl on the floor, wrapping his jaws around her neck. She instantly quiets and freezes, while holding on to one of her legs.

My eyes skim across the floor and I see the gun lying almost under the couch. Deciding to leave it where it is, I find Ellie lying on the floor and my eyes prick with tears.

No . . .

Reaching into my pocket, I pull my phone out to call for help.

I rush over to her, drop to my knees, and look over her from one end to the other.

Is she bleeding? Is she hurt? I can't tell. She's curled up into a ball, shaking, with her hands over her ears, and she's crying. The reality that I almost lost her hits me square in the chest. I reach over and lay my hands on her. She's warm, but her skin is cold at the same time.

Just seeing her and feeling her, I know, without a doubt, I am so in love with this girl.

From a distance, I can hear the sound of sirens, and relief washes over me. I glance over to the girl on the floor and she is whimpering. Bruno is still locked on to her neck and he's growling at her in warning. It's then that I see her shirt has risen, and there is a tattoo of the moon on her lower back. Immediately, I know who she is, and my heart breaks for Ellie.

"Ellie." She doesn't respond and I wonder if she can hear me. I don't want to scare her, but she needs to know I'm here with her. She's not alone.

"Ellie," I say a little louder, and I gently pull on her wrist to move her hand away from her ear.

She jerks backward while, at the same time, taking a swing, her fist connecting with my arm. *Shit!* That hurt.

Her eyes are large and full of fear. It takes a second for it to register who I am, but it does, and she launches herself at me.

One sob at a time rips through her, and even though I haven't asked her anything, the tears sound more due to sadness than due to pain.

"Hey, I'm here . . . it's all over. It's gonna be okay," I say, trying to soothe her while running my hand up and down her back.

She doesn't say anything; she just squeezes me harder while her tears soak through my shirt.

"Matty, please don't leave me," she stutters out.

Just hearing how broken and lost she is right now makes me see red, and I want to pick up that gun and shoot her so-called friend's other leg. How could someone who called herself a friend do this to her? My heart aches so badly for her but, instead of giving into the severity of this moment, I have to remain strong. That's what she needs from me.

"Ellie, I am never going to leave you . . . ever. Do you hear me?" And I really hope she does. As long as she wants me, I am hers.

She nods her head and scrambles into my lap to get even closer to me. I wrap my arms around her even tighter and just hold her.

The police are the first to enter the cottage and do a sweep-through. They flip the lights on, momentarily blinding me. Their guns are drawn, and Ellie hides her face even further into my chest. She's still shaking, and I'm so angry that she's had to go through this. Two of the officers immediately take over the other girl, relieving Bruno, who moves to sit next to us. Another one drops a marker near the gun, and one comes to stand near us.

"Are you the one who called in the B&E?" he asks me.

"Yes," I answer them.

"Sir, we are going to need you to step outside." The officer says in a semi-calm voice as the paramedics enter the cottage at the same time.

I don't want to step outside. I told her I wouldn't leave her. My breathing starts to get more labored. I want to yell at them that I almost lost her and that they can't take her.

"Matt, we are going to need you to let go of her," says one of the paramedics. I look over at him and recognize him as someone I went to school with.

Eye to eye, he stares at me and I stare at him, almost in a challenge, but Ellie pulls back and releases me.

Gently cupping her face in both of my hands, I wipe her tears with my thumbs and look deep into her beautiful watery eyes. "I'm going to be right outside, okay? If you need me, just call for me, and I'll be right here."

She shivers, but nods her head and moves off of my lap and back on to the floor.

I thought walking away from her earlier today, after she sang to me, was hard, but that doesn't even come close to this. My heart aches for her and I have no idea what even happened.

Standing outside under the moonlight, I watch through the window as the paramedics assess her.

Knowing that Aunt Ella needs to know about this, I grab my phone and text her and Beau, and tell them to be here as soon as possible.

Seeing all of the people, the chaos, the flashing lights, I'm instantly taken back to seeing Beau on the front porch. Memories of him, the screaming, the fire, it all flips through my mind. I've spent so many years trying to not think about or remember any of those details, and now twice in one night I'm assaulted with the smell of smoke.

Time passes, I'm not sure how much, but I can't pull myself back to the present. My eyes have glassed over and I'm reliving that night, minute by minute. Somewhere in the background, I hear my name being called and register that my arm is being pulled on.

"Matt, can you hear me?" says a man's voice to the left of me.

Blinking, I look over and see the fire chief. He's concerned but in control at the same time. His words are muffled through the thundering sound of blood pumping through my ears. He asks me a question, but I have no idea what it is.

I look back over to Ellie and he tugs on my arm again.

"Son . . ."

What did he just call me?

271

My head whips back to him and I'm met with slate gray eyes. For the last seven years, I have analyzed every single man I have come in contact with to see if there was any type of resemblance, recognition, anything to clue me in that I might have found my father. I have thought about who he might be, and what this moment might be like more times that I can remember . . . and now here it is. How did I miss it? How many times over the years have I looked at this man, spoken to this man, and have never seen what I am seeing now? His eyes, his hair color, his skin color, the different shapes of his features. He looks like me. Everything around me tilts, straightens, and then sharpens with complete certainty. *This man is my father.*

He sees the minute that I understand what he is saying, and he takes a step back. The look on his face is one of sadness and regret.

Shaking my head at him, he doesn't react; he just watches me. "I can't deal with this now. Can I go back in?" There's attitude and irritation behind my voice, and I just don't care.

"Yes," he says, shoving his hands into his pockets.

I walk away from him—and the reality that he's thrown at me—and into the cottage. A blanket has been wrapped around Ellie, her hair is hanging all around her face, and her lips are blue and quivering. An ice pack is covering her hand.

"What's wrong with her?" I ask the familiar-looking paramedic sitting on the couch next to her.

"She's in shock. It can happen when someone suffers from a severe emotional disturbance. When our bodies endure any kind of emotional or physical trauma, it can go into fight or flight mode. She fought when she needed to, and right now her mind is in flight.

Knowing what she needs, I walk into her bedroom, grab her quilt off of the bed, and sit down on the couch next to her.

She watches me warily as big fat tears form in her eyes and drip over.

"Come here, gorgeous." I reach out to her, and she willingly lets me pull her onto my lap. She tucks her face into my neck, and I wrap the quilt around us and block out as much of the chaos surrounding us as I can.

CLOSING THE DOOR to my house, I watch through the window as the last police car and Aunt Ella drive away. It's been several hours, and the adrenaline from the evening has finally worn off. Knowing how *I* feel, I wouldn't be surprised if I walked into the bedroom and found Ellie sound asleep.

After Aunt Ella showed up, she suggested that Ellie and I move over to my house. She was right. The minute I scooped her up and walked out the front door, an involuntary shudder passed through her and she relaxed in my arms.

Quietly, I move through the little living room and toward my bedroom. The need to be near her is so strong, I feel the pull and the ache at the same time.

As I reach the doorway, I can't help but stop and soak her in. Bruno is curled up at her feet, and the reality that I came so close to losing her tonight is almost more than I can bear. A lump forms in the back of my throat, and I force myself to swallow it down.

This has been, by far, the craziest and most emotionally disturbing day I've ever had. The confessions, revelations, whatever you want to call them . . . have just left me mentally and physically exhausted. Aunt Ella's words, Ellie's song, the decisions I made for myself, telling Beau, discovering who the stalker is, and then finding out who my dad is, I don't think there are any more secrets left untold. That freedom that I've always wanted is finally here, and I'm at a loss as to what to do with it. Maybe that's the point; I don't have to do anything anymore, I can just be . . . me.

Ellie is lying on her back, hugging a pillow to her chest, and she's staring at the ceiling fan as it spins around. If the situation wasn't so surreal, I might have laughed at this. That ceiling fan comforts me, too.

Not wanting to frighten her, I move slowly through the room, slip off my shoes, take off my clothes, and put on a clean t-shirt and a pair of gym shorts.

I slide into the bed next to her and, even though she's come out of the shock, she's still shaking. I desperately want to reach out and hold her, but I'm not sure if she wants to be touched.

"I can't believe that she did this to me. She was my best friend," she says without turning my way. Tears roll down the side of her face and drip into her ears. Her chin trembles and my gaze falls to her mouth. Her beautiful mouth has the ability to make or break me, and it just broke me. She's frowning, and it's easy to see the grief all over her face.

"Matty," she turns her head and her big brown eyes lock onto mine. "What do you think is going to happen to her?" Even after everything that's happened, she's scared for her friend, and I think that speaks volumes for her character and the forgiving person that she is.

I brush some hair off of her face and her eyes briefly flutter shut. "I don't know. She was arrested, so she's in jail, at least for tonight. As for longer, I'm not sure how these things go."

Hugging the pillow, she rolls over to face me. "Do you think jail is as awful as they make it out to be in the movies?"

"Not sure. I hope so, though." Her eyes widen in surprise and I let out a sigh. Needing to touch her, I run my hand down her arm and let it settle on her hip. "My dad, well he's not really my dad, but he's in prison."

"He's not your dad? Who is?" she says, shocked.

I just shake my head at her. I don't want to go into this with her right now, and she puts her hand on the side of my face in understanding.

"I did go see him once. It was actually an eye-opening experience for me." I can still see him from that day perfectly in my mind.

"Will you tell me?" she asks softly and curiously.

"Soon, I promise." I look her in the eyes, and she sees that my promise is real, not just spoken.

"I want to know you . . . all of you," she whispers.

"And I you. I told you, I'm not going anywhere." I lean forward and lightly brush her lips with mine.

She gives me a small smile, and then moves to snuggle up closer to me. One of my arms slides under her and the other wraps over her. She yawns, closes her eyes, and I kiss her forehead. As I much as I want to tell her all the details, and I will soon; tonight is not the night.

Thinking about the prison, I was sixteen years old the last time I saw him. That was five years ago, and I wish it was longer.

It wasn't my mother who came to me, but the local bank manager I ran into outside the café, who said my dad had been requesting meetings with me. Apparently, my mother had denied every one of them, not even bothering to tell me, but this guy made it sound like what he had to say was important. Curiosity got the best of me.

I remember thinking that it was hot in the room as I sat down in the chair across from him, the only divider being a two-sided desk with a piece of reinforced glass in between.

I couldn't take my eyes off of him. He always seemed so large and put together. But here in front of me was a man who had aged so much so quickly that he looked almost unrecognizable. I found this ironic since appearances meant so much to him, we all knew this. Yet, here he was with stringy thinning hair, stubble on his face, and really bushy eyebrows.

The one thing that hadn't changed was the hatred in his eyes.

As I watched him glare at me, I realized in this moment that within the silence there is power.

I wanted to tell him that he had nothing on me anymore. He couldn't touch me or my family. I wanted to tell him what a pathetic excuse for a human being he was, but what would be the point?

Just this one glare from him, and I could see that he was still wanting, craving that need to manipulate me. He wanted to see if he could have me help him continue his deceitful ways—even from jail, and I knew that's why I was here.

"Well, say something!" he barked at me.

The tone of his voice slipped under my skin. Although many days had passed, they were not enough to not be affected by his venom. The thing was, though, I'd never let it show. 'Don't say a word,' drifts through my mind and I respond by giving him the look I've perfected over the years. The look of innocent indifference. He should know this better than anyone, but he's too caught up in himself to ever notice.

Time passes as we watch each other. I continue with a

blank, indifferent stare, while he fidgets, growing more agitated.

Slowly, I rise from the table and think to myself, "This is the last time I am ever going to see this man."

His face is red with anger, and I look him right in those beady, evil eyes of his and say the only thing to him that ever needs to be said, "I am not your son."

He sucks in a breath of air and, as my words register, his eyes narrow and then widen. He knows that I know, and I am officially cut free of his strings. There is nothing he can say or do to me anymore.

Leaving the chair in the middle of the aisle, I walk away from him and don't look back.

Ellie's moans coming from next to me pull me from my thoughts. I feel her scrunch her face up against my skin. She's sleeping, and it crushes me to know that she is dreaming about all of this. Running my hand over her head, I smooth down her hair and continue down her back. She lets out a sigh next to me and relaxes further into my arms. My fingers slip under the edge of her shirt; her warm skin feels so soft and so mine. I'm never going to let her go, and tomorrow I'm going to tell her.

Chapter Eighteen

ELLE

THE CEILING FAN above me spins around and around. I've never given much thought to one before, but it's almost hypnotic.

The sun is beaming into the room, and Bruno has shifted so his head is under my hand. He wants to be petted and I think it's cute. Matt is gone. Like before, he left a note on the nightstand and it said that he went out for a run. I know now that running is what he needs to do to process things. I can't say I blame him. The last twenty-four hours have been a bit overwhelming.

It's interesting how life can change in a flash. I'm confused by the events that transpired yesterday; from him leaving me at the restaurant, to Olivia destroying years of what I thought was the best friendship. Climbing out of bed, I need to go brush my teeth and shower. Matt's bathroom is a little bigger than mine and, at this moment, it looks so inviting.

Standing under the warm water, I hear the front door close and I jump. My heart instantly starts racing and I frown to myself, wondering how long I will feel the after-effects of what she did.

"Hey," I hear when Matt walks into the bathroom.

I peek out around the curtain, and he's leaning against the doorway in just a pair of running shorts. His hair is damp, his is skin flushed and sweaty, and those shorts are hanging on him in the most alluring way.

"You okay?" he asks me, still breathing a little hard and running his hand through his hair.

I shrug my shoulders.

"Can I join you?" He gives me a small lopsided smile.

I feel my cheeks heat and I know that I'm blushing. "It's your shower."

His smile grows larger, he drops the shorts—*oh my*—and climbs into the shower.

"Have a nice run?" I watch as he steps under the water and then pushes it off his face so he can see me.

"Yeah, I needed it."

Steam surrounds us and my heart rate speeds up a little.

Reaching down, he gently picks up my hands and runs his fingertips over the joints. "Did you take your medicine today? I'm worried after last night that the flare might come back," he says, frowning.

"I haven't yet, but I will in a few minutes. Thank you for thinking of it, though." I give him a small smile. I'm so touched that he thought of that.

His beautiful gray eyes on me make the butterflies in my stomach take off. Neither of us says anything, and the only sound is that of the water spraying down around us. Needing to move, I grab the washcloth and pour some soap on it. Holding it up so he can see that I'm about to run it over him, he smiles that adorable half-smile that I love so much while watching every move I make.

Wiping the cloth across his skin, I wash him from head to toe. Some sand falls off of him, letting me know he ran on the beach and not on the road. When I'm done, he takes the cloth and drops it on to the floor. His hands wrap around my face and his fingers tangle in my hair.

Tilting my head back, his gaze closely scans over my face, and then locks on to mine. "I'm sorry you are so sad right now. . ." he whispers, and his forehead wrinkles.

Knowing he can see how sad I am makes my swollen eyes prick with tears. I feel so exposed, like there's nothing I can hide from him.

"Don't be; it's my fault for trusting her. I should have known." Shaking my head, I break eye contact with him and look at a spot over his shoulder. "I just can't believe I never saw the signs." His thumbs brush across my cheeks and I let out a sigh. "They always say it's the people you love who end up hurting you the most. I think they're right."

"Those are always the ones who leave you, too." My eyes dart back to his, and I'm met with wide eyes. Judging from his expression, I don't think he meant to say that out loud.

"What do you mean?" I ask him, running my hands down his sides and settling them on his hips.

"I don't know," he says, trying to down play his reaction. "People always seem to move on and away with their life, that's all."

My chest aches that he feels this way. The expression 'speak it, think it' comes to mind, and obviously it's something that he's thought about a lot. He must be talking about his brothers, maybe his father, I don't know. But whoever it is . . .

this has greatly affected him.

"Is that what you thought about me? That I was just going to tell you that I loved you and then leave you?" I ask softly.

He shrugs his shoulders and looks away. This topic makes him feel raw, and he's trying to mask the vulnerable sides of him.

"Well, I would have figured something out." And I would have, if he had asked me to stay.

His shoulders slump a little and his eyes come back to mine. "Would have?" he whispers, looking completely defeated.

Letting go of me, he steps past me and out of the shower. *What did I say?*

Running my hair under the water one more time, I turn it off, get out, and dry off. Wrapped in a towel, I walk into the bedroom and find him sitting on the edge of the bed, dressed in a heather-gray t-shirt and another pair of athletic shorts. He's leaning over so his elbows are on his thighs. He looks so sad. I move to stand between his legs, right in front of him.

My fingers find their way into his hair, and he reaches out to run one hand down the back of my leg.

"Ellie, I loved the song. More than you'll ever know. Thank you for singing it," he says, breaking the silence, but not looking at me. I can hear his sincerity, but he sounds resigned, too.

My breath catches. *He loved the song?* It's kind of felt like the white elephant in the room to me for the last twelve hours. But to hear him say he loved it, I'm kind of shocked—in a good way, and angry at the same time.

"Then why did you leave?" my voice breaks. He has to know how much that destroyed me.

He looks up, and there are shadows moving back and

forth across his eyes. His mind is troubled. "There was some-thing that I needed to do. I, uh . . .," He's struggling with how much he wants to tell me, and I hate that this is making him uncomfortable. His fingers tighten on my leg. "I needed to talk to Beau about something before I could talk to you. I'm sorry if I hurt you, but I had to do it."

"Well, it did hurt. What was so important that you left me sitting there on the stage? What did you have to talk about that couldn't wait?" He sees Beau all the time. He couldn't have waited to talk to me first?

"I'm sorry . . ." He doesn't offer me anything more.

"It's okay, don't worry about. I just want to move on from yesterday."

His eyes narrow a little, his nostrils flare, and his breath-ing picks up. He looks slightly panicked, and I don't know why.

"Move on," he clears his throat. "When do you think that will be?" He pinches his lips shut.

Oh, he thinks I'm going to leave here, leave him.

"That depends," I run my hand through his hair to calm him. The muscles in his face loosen, and he visibly relaxes at my touch.

"On?" he raises his eyebrows at me.

"On whether or not you've changed your mind," I say to him. My heart starts racing in anticipation of his answer. I feel like I keep opening myself up, and here I go again. My stom-ach turns uncomfortably with anxiety.

He tilts his head as he thinks about my question. "I ha-ven't," he mutters, shaking his head.

"Oh." I close my eyes to hide the incredible pain that just sliced through me. I put it all out there for him, but it wasn't enough. He hasn't changed his mind. He doesn't feel the same way I do.

"Ellie . . .," he pulls on my leg to bring me closer, and his other hand tugs on my arm to bring me down. "I haven't changed my mind because I loved you then, just like I do now."

Wait! What? He loved me then? And he loves me now?

My eyes fly open, and I gasp, "But you said I was wrong."

"I know. I was the one who was wrong." Shaking his head at me, he's imploring me, with his eyes, to understand. "I wasn't ready. I wasn't free. I had to deal with my shit, and talking to Beau was the first step in doing that." His voice fades as he tries to explain himself.

"And now?" I need to know what he thinks.

"Now, I'm falling in love with you, too." His words are so clear and they speak straight to my soul. I'm so elated and over joyed that I can't move. I just stare at him and remind myself to breathe.

He reaches for the back of my neck and pulls my mouth to his. My hand tightens in his hair and the other grasps his shoulder so I don't fall. His lips are warm and so familiar, even though it's really been such a short time. Falling onto his lap, I give over to the sensation of him and his taste. This kiss is passionate, apologetic, and filled with so much love.

Breaking us apart, he turns a little and pushes me down onto the bed. Both of us are panting slightly as he hovers over me and blinks those gorgeous eyes at me. "I don't want you to leave." His face is so serious and so determined, how could I ever tell him differently?

"Okay, then I won't," I smile at him.

He jerks his head back a little in surprise. "But . . . how?" He's confused and I can see the insecurity sneaking into his features. He's still expecting me to go, even after all that he just confessed to me.

"Because . . ." I can't help but grin and cup his cheek in my hand, "standing strong just you and me, living the life we choose it to be," I say quietly.

Recognizing my lyrics, he smiles and he drops his forehead to mine. "What if we don't work out? It hasn't been that long . . ." he whispers, not really wanting to ask the question, but needing to vocalize his concerns at the same time.

"Then we don't. But you're worth it to stay and find out." I wrap my arms around him to give him reassurance.

He sucks in air, holds it and, with his eyes locked on mine, he lets it out as his lips slowly return to mine.

SEVERAL HOURS LATER, Beau and Leila drop by with a late lunch. I'd like to say that lunch between the four of us was pleasant, but it wasn't. Beau was quiet and glared at Matt, frequently. Matt matched his look, but gave nothing away. A few times, Leila and I looked at each other like we should probably escape the tension that was rapidly escalating between the two of them.

Together, Leila and I clean up lunch and retreat to Matt's room. We sit on the bed with Bruno, and wait for one of them to break. Leila hasn't said much to me about last night, but she doesn't need to. Just the fact that she was there then and is here now is all I can ask for.

"Where's Quinn?" I ask her.

She turns and looks at me as if it's an obvious answer.

"She's with Beau's mom."

"Oh, I didn't realize that they talked to her. Matt doesn't say much about her."

"Yeah, they each have their own issues with her, but they're trying."

"Huh." There's so much to Matt that I still don't know. I can't help but wonder when he'll feel more comfortable to tell me more.

Scooting down on the bed, Leila starts running her fingers through my hair. I'd noticed before that she fidgets with her fingers, well she can do this anytime she wants. It's so soothing, I'm just about asleep when I hear Beau's voice pick up.

"You still should have told me!" he snaps, from the living room. Leila flinches, but keeps moving her fingers.

Most of their conversation is hushed. We can hear them talking, but I don't know what it's about. It sounds heated, and I think it must have to do with whatever he told him last night. My eyes open at the tail end of an insult hurled at Matt.

"Don't worry about him. I know it sounds awful, but it's long overdue," she lets out a sigh.

"What do you mean?" I roll over so I can get a better look at her.

"You know how people say that you have to let go of your past before you can move on with your future? Well, love, that's what Matt is doing. I know he's hard to understand, but he has his reasons for being the way he is. I just hope you won't give up on him. He's trying."

I know he is and that's all I can really ask for him to choose to do.

I SPENT MOST of the morning on cloud nine; a place my dark soul has definitely never graced the perimeter of. Ellie's words replayed themselves over and over in my mind. Hearing her say that she thinks I'm worth it to stay and find out has healed a part of me that has been damaged for years. The hole in my chest feels full, not so empty, and for the first time in what feels like forever, I feel complete—and daringly close to happy.

Beau texted me late morning that he and Leila were going to swing by with lunch. I honestly didn't know what to expect from him after my confession the night before, but the minute they walked in, I knew. His face said it all. He'd spent the night thinking about it, and now came his anger.

"You should have told me," Beau snaps at me after the girls left to go in the other room.

"What difference would it have made? What do you think you would have done?" I glare at him. "I'll tell you what . . . nothing! You had enough of the after-effects of him to deal with yourself." I glance toward the bedroom door and then walk over to stand near him. I really don't want Ellie hearing this conversation. I want her to hear it from me. "We could have figured something out," he snarls at me, pacing back and forth in front of the couch.

"When? When you were at the rehab facility and he was already planning the next one? Or when you got home, were a completely different person, and I felt like I didn't have anyone? Or maybe when I would lie in bed at night, and cry because I was so worried that he would think I told someone and he would kill you." I ball my hands into fists as he comes to stop in front of me.

"Is that why you slept with me so much?" He tilts his head to the side.

I turn my head so he can't see how remembering all this shit makes me feel.

"Why didn't you tell Drew or Mom?" he asks.

I look back at him and shake my head incredulously.

"First of all, Mom? Is that a joke? Beau . . . I was seven," I hiss through my teeth. "There is nothing you can say that will change the way he made me feel. He put the fear of God in me that I had to remain quiet. For years! I'm not sorry I told you, but I'm also not sorry that I kept it to myself for all those years."

"If you seriously thought one conversation was gonna cut it, you are sadly mistaken, little dude."

"That's fine. We can talk about it. But that doesn't negate the fact that it was my secret that I had to live with. I still do."

"No, you don't!"

I know what he's trying to do. He's trying to understand and take some of the burden away from me, but that'll never happen. I lived it, I did it, I saw it, and now I want to move on from it.

A knock on the door stops our conversation. Beau narrows his eyes me to let me know that this conversation isn't done. He walks to the door, peeks through the eye hole, and then opens it.

"Oh my, God, is she here? Is my baby here?" a woman croons from outside.

Moving to stand next to Beau, there's Elle's mother, standing with some guy who is way too young to have his arm around her. I remember Elle's mother perfectly. Aunt Ella used to shake her head and say, "drama, drama, drama." Looking her over, not much has changed, except maybe her clothes. Either she is heavier or they are just tighter. No matter, they don't look very flattering, which is ironic since Ellie tells me how much this woman stresses the importance of outward appearances.

What the hell is she doing here?

She eyes Beau in an appreciative way that makes me feel uncomfortable. Out of the corner of my eye, I see Beau cringe with a look of disgust. He takes a step back.

"No, she's not," I say, firmly and rudely. Beau's head whips over to me in amazement. I never raise my voice or show much emotion so, although he doesn't know who she is, his reaction to her is now just as palpable as mine.

Disbelief registers on her face, and she eyes me, knowing I've lied. Her upper lip twitches as she sneers at me and then storms into the house. "Yes, she is. The reporters outside told me she was here and she hasn't left." She looks around my house and then yells, "ELLE!"

"Lady, if you don't get out of my house this instant, I will have you arrested for trespassing. Get out!" I shout at her, pointing to the door. Beau's fingertips sink into my shoulder as a warning to calm down.

Her boy toy steps in front of her, and he glares at me.

"Really?" I cock my head at him and cross my arms over my chest. "What do you think you are going to do here? I'll be happy to send you to jail along with her. Is that what you want? You think this old woman here is going to bail you out? Hell, no, she won't spend a dime on you. She's selfish and manipulative."

Beau immediately releases me, and begins snapping his fingers in the guy's face.

"Time to wake up!" I roar at him.

Elle's mother gasps in horror from behind the guy, and she steps aside to stand next to him.

"You little shit. I don't know who you are, but don't think I haven't already talked to the press to tell them how you are keeping my daughter here against her will. I can just see the headlines now." She waves her hand in the air as if she is looking at something invisible.

Anger starts to radiate off of me. The audacity of this woman astounds me.

"You better come at us with something better than a press threat. The question that you really should be asking yourself is, do you think we care?" I say to her, reaching into my pocket to pull out my cell phone.

"Mother?" Ellie's voice comes from behind me.

"Oh, there you are." She rushes toward her with her arms wide, but Ellie averts her and moves to stand next to me. I wrap my arm around her and I feel her hand slide across my lower back.

"Hey, man, what the hell?" comes an unfamiliar voice in the room.

The three of us turn toward boy toy and Beau, who has crushed the guy's phone under his shoe.

Beau looks at us and his face is cloaked in anger. "He was recording their little reunion."

"What!" Ellie turns to face her mother.

"People love a happy ending, darling. I was doing it for you," she says in a tone that is meant to sound sweet, but only sounds conniving. "But now that I am looking at you, it's best if we do it again after you have fixed yourself up. You need to go put on your face. God, you look terrible. No one wants to see you looking like this."

Ellie cringes next to me and her fingers squeeze my side.

Is this bitch for real? I'm so livid, I could spit nails.

"Alright! That's it . . . get out!" Beau yells at her, pointing again toward the door.

We all flinch at the volume, but Ellie's mother just smirks at him.

"Mother," Elle says.

She glances back to Elle with a condescending look that says she's won.

"You're fired," Elle says quietly, but deadly enough that all four of us turn to her at the announcement.

"What?" she says, laughing it off. "You can't fire me!" She marches over to stand directly in front of us.

"I just did," Elle says calmly and triumphantly. I'm so proud of her in this moment. "I have a new attorney. He will be contacting you with your severance package. You *will* go quietly. And if you don't, I'll have my new accounting firm go through every expense and withdrawal over the last eight years to see where my money has gone. My guess is that it will be a very educational report, don't you think?" Her eyebrows raise in question.

She sucks in air at Elle's allegation. Scrambling with a comeback, she starts shaking her hands in exasperation. "I made you who you are," she spits out through her teeth.

"No, you didn't. I made myself." I don't know how it's possible, but I think Ellie just got taller.

Leaning over, she regards Ellie with smug contempt. "It's going to be a real shame when the world finds out about your little problem. Did you think I didn't know? I've made it my business to find out what was going on with you. The jobs will stop coming in. No one wants a model who has disfigured hands and feet. What are you going to do then?" she smirks.

"It's a good thing she doesn't have to worry about that,"

Leila says, as she goes to stand next to Ellie.

"Leila Starling . . ." Elle's mother whispers as she throws her hand over her mouth and her eyes grow large in shock.

Beau saunters over to her with a crooked grin. He wraps his arm around her and kisses the side her head.

Ellie's mother gasps, and her gaze darts back and forth between Leila, Beau, and then Ellie. The wheels are turning in her head, and it's obvious to all of us that she's angry with herself for not figuring out who he was sooner.

Her eyes land on me and widen as she sees the resemblance between Beau and me.

Leila breaks the silence forcing the attention back on her. "Two days ago, I offered her a job to work with me, and she said yes. Your services are no longer needed."

"But . . . but . . ." she stutters, paling.

"Elle has agreed to be my partner, and the face of my new line."

All of this is news to me. I have no idea what she is talking about but, watching Elle smile at her mother in victory, it doesn't matter. This must have gone down over the last couple of days. Regret for walking away from her on Wednesday hits me.

"I get twenty percent of whatever she is paying you!" her mother stomps her foot and glares at Elle.

"No, you don't," says Leila. "See, your resolution papers, which were effective immediately, were drawn up before my employment offer. And as it turns out, the contract that you had Elle sign years ago to make you her agent is very basic. I mean, where did you find that, the Internet? Legally, there is nothing you can do. However, there is a lot she can do to you. Starting with the finances and then on to slander, which is considered a civil wrong and a basis for a lawsuit. If you want to keep that severance she has so generously offered you, you will go quietly."

The room goes quiet, and all eyes watch as Elle's mother stares at Leila with a mixture of fear and anger.

Beau waves in the air over Leila's head to get my attention. I glance at him, and he's grinning from ear to ear.

"I love it when she gets like this, all business like—it's hot, don't you think?"

A laugh busts out of me at his comment. Leave it to Beau to diffuse a situation in three seconds with humor.

He looks back at Elle's mother. "Did you know that there's a prison in Alabama where over one third of the employees have admitted to having sex with the inmates as bargaining for things like toiletries. I mean, wow, just think about it. Sex for shampoo . . . tsk tsk tsk."

Her faces wrinkles up in an appalled look, and I can't help but chuckle.

"Oh, you stop it." Leila elbows him in the side, grinning at him. He smiles down at her affectionately and, for once, I'm not jealous of them.

Elle looks at them, looks at me, and then smiles. God, I love her smiles.

"Alrighty, then!" Beau says, clapping his hands together as he looks back and forth between Elle's mother and the boy toy. "Thanks for stopping by. This little conversation has been most enlightening and informative, but now it's time for you to go." He walks to the door and opens it wide.

No one moves as Ellie's mother has locked her eyes onto Ellie with a hateful scowl. "You won't get away with this," she says between her teeth.

"Get away with what? I took a new job and it doesn't include you. It's time to get your own life, Mother, and to stay out of mine." Elle pins her with one last warning look, and then turns around to head back into my bedroom.

Smirking at her mother, I glance over at Beau, and he nods his head, telling me to go on. I turn and follow Ellie. I am so damn proud of her.

Ellie's eyes are on me as I enter the room. She's sitting on the edge of the bed, and I sit down next to her, wrapping my arm around her shoulders. She lets out a sigh, leans her head against me, and then starts shaking.

"Hey," I turn so I can face her. Her eyes are clear and untroubled and, for the first time since she's been here, she looks at peace.

"I'm okay . . . really." Her hands move to lay on my thighs, and the warmth of them seeps through the shorts. "I just think that the adrenaline of the moment is trying to wear off." Looking up at me through her eyelashes, she's so beautiful that I lean over and gently kiss her lips.

"If you need to work off some adrenaline, gorgeous, I'm your man!" I say, grinning at her, trying to lighten the mood.

We hear the front door close, and she smiles at me from ear to ear.

Chapter Nineteen

ELLE

OH, MY GOD! I cannot believe that just happened. I've dreamed of that moment for years, and honestly, it couldn't have gone any better.

Matt is sitting next to me looking like he's worried, and I can't help but smile.

Leila peeks her head into the room. "You okay?"

"I am more than okay," I grin at her as I get up off of the bed and walk straight into her. "Thank you so much." I hug her tightly.

Releasing me, she guides me back to the bed. Matt scoots over so we can both sit down, and Beau comes to stand in the doorway. His eyes are trained on Leila, always on Leila.

"I can't believe she flew all the way down here for that," I say as I look at all three of them. "How she ever thought that was going to go well . . . I have no idea." I shake my head in disbelief.

Matt smiles, "Well, it's over now."

I almost sigh. Yes, I think to myself, it *is* all over now. I'm momentarily lost in his smile . . . he's so handsome.

Leila's voice pulls me out of my head and I shift closer to her. "So, do you remember three years ago, we were at the studio in New York? I was pregnant with Quinn, and your mother went on and on about how beautiful I was and how I was just glowing?"

"I do remember, but for a different reason." I look away from her feeling ashamed. My mother had belittled me in front of her entire executive team and made me feel two inches tall.

She squeezes my arm; it's gentle, but it forces me to look back at her. "No, I remember for the same reason. She turned, looked you over from head to toe, and said that you could take a few lessons from me in the art of looking exquisite. That, even being pregnant, I had more beauty and grace in my little finger than you did. I was stunned and, believe me, I was so mad." Matt's arm wraps around me protectively. It's nice to know that, even though they're just old words, he doesn't like it.

"It was that moment, with your face in mind, that I began planning this new campaign, 'Free and Perfect'. I know I jumped ahead a little out there, but you said at my house that you wanted to work for me, and I really do want you to be the face of this. It was made for you," Leila says, watching me. She looks so excited and hopeful.

"But, why me?" I need to know.

"Well, it started with you, so you're the one I always envisioned. But, really, it's about encouraging young women, and older women, too, that it's okay to be free, to be exactly who you are, because that is more beautiful than anything else. Will you do it?"

"Free to be me, and perfect just the way I am." I roll the idea around in my head while looking at Matt. I know he's thinking the same thing I am . . . free.

"Yes," I answer her, with a smile that comes from so deep within me that tears spring to my eyes.

"I'm so excited!" Leila squeals as she jumps off the bed. She skips over to Beau and hugs him, too. He just chuckles as he looks down at her. "Okay, we're going to go, but if you feel up to it, we'd love for you both to stop by tomorrow." Her eyes are so bright, blue, and happy, how anyone could not be enamored with her instantly is beyond me.

"Okay. And thank you, again, for everything," I whisper.

A huge smile stretches across her face. It's infectious; I can't help but smile back.

Beau looks at Matt, tilts his head and says, "Come by tomorrow." There's no question in his voice; it's more a command.

I can feel as Matt tenses next to me and then nods his head. Their conversation from earlier was disrupted, and it's too bad. Leila's words play back in my mind, *"You know how people say that you have to let go of your past, before you can move on with your future? Well, love, that's what Matt is doing."* Hopefully, he'll tell me about his mysterious past when he's ready.

With one last look at both of us, Beau and Leila turn and disappear from the doorway. We hear the front door close, and silence takes over.

Matt shifts next to me, his eyes scanning my face. The worry he's harbored for me since last night seems to be gone. He's not as tense, and it lets me relax. His hand lifts, tucking some of my hair behind my ear. The warmth of his fingertips gives me goose bumps. He watches as I shiver, and his eyes darken. I could stare at him all day.

"Do you want a beer? I could really go for one right now," he asks, giving me a one-sided smile.

"A beer sounds great."

He grabs my hand and pulls me off the bed. We walk into the kitchen, and I lean back against the counter as he takes two out of the refrigerator and opens them. Stepping in front of me, he hands me one but doesn't move. He's in my personal space, and it's affecting me immensely.

His eyes never leave mine as we both take a long pull on the cold drink. In typical Matt form, he doesn't say anything; he just watches me.

"How should I be feeling right now?" I ask him. A thousand emotions and thoughts are flying through my mind, ranging from being happy and free of my mother, to the awkwardness between him and Beau. I'm so happy I feel like I could bounce off the walls, but if he's troubled, I want to feel some of that, too. I hate that he keeps things from me; I can't wait until he feels comfortable enough to share these things. I don't care what, or how long it takes. I'm here for him.

"I don't know. Tell me what you're feeling and we'll sort through it."

His tongue runs over his lips, wet from the drink and, despite everything I just thought, they're all I can focus on. My mind is blank. It's not lost on him that I'm staring at his mouth. He sets his beer down, lifts me up onto the counter, and steps between my legs, even closer to me. Eyeing me mischievously, he picks the bottle back up, takes another drink, and then pops his lips together.

"Umm," my mind is still blank.

Matt has a way of doing things that are so exceptionally sexy, that he doesn't even realize the effect he has on people—

on me. Even though we've already shared several intimate
moments, he still stirs up butterflies in my stomach. They seem
to be permanently alert whenever he's around. Right now, I'm
lost in the feeling of him being so close to me; all other coher-
ent thoughts melt away.

My feet unconsciously wrap around the back of his legs
and I pull him closer. "Maybe we'll sort through those feelings
later," I say, looking up at his handsome face. His dark hair is
sticking up from running his hands through it; there's light
stubble across his chin, and he smells so good—like sunshine,
fresh laundry, and him.

He gives me a small, shy smile, and cups one side of my
face. His eyes are trained on my mouth and his thumb runs
across my bottom lip. My skin is on fire where he's touching
me. Setting the bottle back down, he moves his other hand to
my thigh. It's cool from the bottle and chills my skin, making
me shiver. Fire and ice; it is such a contrast from one to the
other.

"Cold?"

"No," I whisper, watching him closely.

His thumb pulls down on my bottom lip. The blood in my
body starts to pulse through me. Darkened gray eyes flicker to
mine once more, before he leans down and claims my mouth.
His lips brush back and forth across mine, searing me with
heat and a flavor that is so uniquely him. I could never tire of
the way he tastes. In fact, I'm pretty certain I'm just going to
crave it more and more.

Kissing Matt is like being swept up by the tide; there's no
fighting it. You need to accept it and just enjoy the ride.

He groans, and both of his hands move through my hair to
my back. He pulls me flush against him as his tongue tangles
with mine. Being in his arms, giving myself over to him, is

exactly what I need. I don't want to think, I just want to feel. Matt makes me feel like no one else ever has . . . cherished.

There's no urgency in the way he's kissing me. Kiss after kiss, he explores my lips and my mouth. There's a roughness to his cheeks and around his lips from not shaving. I welcome it because it's him. He's mine and I am his.

His lips leave mine and travel over my cheek to under my ear. I tilt my head a little as his tongue finds and tastes my skin. "I think we're gonna stay in and order pizza for dinner," he murmurs against my neck.

Pizza! A rebellious smile splits my face and Matt stills, feeling the change.

"Sounds good to me; I haven't eaten pizza in years."

He pulls back with a shocked expression and studies me. "Oh, Ms. Summers, it's going to be so good to reintroduce you to so many things."

"I can think of one thing in particular, right this moment, that I'd like to be reintroduced to," I say brazenly.

His eyes light up as he smirks at me, "As you wish, Ms. Summers." He jerks me up off the counter and I squeal. My legs wrap around his waist as he laughs and turns for the bedroom.

MATT

THERE'S A SOFT knocking on the front door and Bruno lets out a small bark that fully awakens me. Sliding out of the bed without disturbing Ellie, I throw on some clothes to see who's knocking on the door. Peeking through the eyehole, I see the fire chief on the other side. There is any number of reasons he could be here this early in the morning, but only one instantly comes to mind. Concern for Ellie spikes through me as my heart races.

Has Olivia been set free?

I throw open the door. The look on my face must startle him because he takes a step back. I don't say anything . . . He needs to tell me why he's here.

Bruno is standing right next to me, and the chief smiles down at him. A few of Ellie's things are on the floor; he must realize she's here, since he looks behind me. The house is dark and quiet.

His eyes come back to mine and, again, I'm face to face with gray. My breath catches in my throat and neither one of us says anything. An uncomfortable silence surrounds us as we stare at one another.

"I know the last couple of days have been crazy for you, and I know it's early, but I was wondering if you might take a walk with me down to the beach," he says, shoving his hands into his pockets.

I eye him cautiously; I know this has to do with what he said to me the other night. So far, with everything that has happened, I've blocked that moment and not given any thought to it. I need time to process, and I haven't had any, but how do I tell him no? I've dreamt about this conversation with a faceless man, over and over. Now, here he is. Isn't this the moment that I've wanted for so long? Maybe it's the anticipation, or maybe it's finally knowing the truth but, either way, my stomach starts to ache.

"Sure," I say, letting out a sigh and running my hand through my hair. I move to walk out the front door and look down at Bruno. He takes a step away from me and looks back toward the bedroom. The love that I already feel for my dog just multiplied. I reach down to pet his head, "Alright, big guy, go on." Bruno turns and heads back to the bedroom to be with Ellie.

The door clicks as I close it behind me. The air is cooler this morning than it has been. It feels brisk and clean, free of humidity. As we head for the dock footpath, I glance to the left. The sun has just started to rise, and the orange glow is slowly expanding in the eastern sky. It's my favorite moment of the day, that moment when I set off for a morning run and chase the sun. I can't help but wonder if this little conversation with him is forever going to taint this moment.

We reach the water's edge, and turn to walk north toward Bean Point when he takes a big breath of air. "I know about the fires," he says.

"What do you mean?" I try to sound curious, but my voice cracks. My nervous stomach suddenly turns and fills with dread.

"I know that you were the one who set them for all those years." He turns to glance at me.

My heart slams into my chest, my throat feels like it's closing, and my hands start shaking. Quickly, I shove them into my pockets to hide the evidence of my nerves.

He does know.

I feel like I'm going to be sick. Aunt Ella and Uncle Ben knew, he says he knows, and Beau, too. They all know the darkness that I carry with me. They know what I've done. In two days, I've gone from feeling like I have control over my life to feeling like I have none. Even more so than Aunt Ella or Beau, this guy has the ability to ruin me, and I haven't said anything to contradict him or make him think otherwise. My secrets are finally being exposed, and now he's going to tell me that I'm going to jail. Maybe this conversation isn't what I thought it was going to be; maybe it's so much worse. I've finally given in to loving someone else, and now I'm going to have to tell her good-bye. How do I even have that conversation?

"I can see you panicking, Matt. Stop," his voice has risen and sounds authoritative. I've picked up my pace, and I can see him struggling to keep up with me. "No one will ever know anything. The way I filed those reports, time and time again, there is nothing that can lead any of it back to you."

What? The force of hearing these words cause me to stumble and slow down.

"Why?" I ask, not looking at him. There's no point in trying to argue; it is what it is, and now I just need to know why. Why would he do this for me?

"Because you're my son."

Four words that are so clear, any slight reservation that I might have had just vanished.

I stop walking, and he stops alongside me. I look him in the eye for a long moment, my gray eyes boring into his. I see it. He's telling the truth; instantly my mind begins to race with a million thoughts running rampant.

I take a step back and look him over from head to toe. Same size. Same build. Same eyes. Same hair. Same ears. So many things that are the same, why is it I'm only noticing this now?

"I know you have a lot of questions so, if you don't mind walking with me a little more, I'll start at the beginning."

The moment of truth. Fourteen years of wondering—now I'm finally going to find out.

Turning, I put one foot in front of the other and continue walking. He falls in step with me. I can't look at him. I need to keep looking ahead. It feels like I am walking next to him rather than with him.

"Your mother was my high school sweetheart. When she went away to college, I joined the academy. I was young, stupid, and one night I lost a bet to my friends and let them pressure me into spending time with a local girl we'd gone to school with. The drinking age for a beer back then was eighteen and, needless to say, I had too many. I should have stopped it, but I didn't. Biggest regret of my life . . . until you, that is." His head drops as he stops talking to collect himself. "Your mother found out, we broke up and, not too longer after, she met Hale. He swept her off her feet with everything that a girl wants to hear, and married her as quickly as he could. I'm sure you know more of their story than I do."

He's right; I do know more of their story than anyone, and it's the worst kind of story. The hatred, the fear, and the abuse that was constant, day in and day out . . . No one should have to live like that.

"Years went by. I ended up marrying my wife who, by far, was the kindest, most loving person I have ever known. We tried to have kids but, for whatever reason, she never could get pregnant. We fought a lot, were frustrated with each other, and that's when I reconnected with your mother. She was miserable and so was I. Not long after the affair started, my wife got pneumonia and ended up going into the hospital. Very quickly, it turned to sepsis and, within three days, she died. I've never gotten over the loss of her and, even though I know it wasn't my fault, at the time I felt like it was. God was punishing me for the affair. I cut off all contact with your mother—everyone really—and lost myself for a while. I didn't know she was pregnant. I didn't know she had another baby until months after you were born. She never told me about you." He glances at me, and there's pleading in his eyes, pleading for me to understand.

Wait! What? So he didn't know about me? All these years, I thought my father had just walked away.

"You were seven when the first fire happened. It was the Starling house. I'll never forget it. The fire never reached the back part of the house; it was mainly contained in the front. Your fingerprints were found all over the back doorknob that entered the kitchen, both inside and out. It wasn't until Beau's statement about the fire that I began to question your involvement. He said that you were standing in front of the house, watching it burn, when he got there." His tone is hesitant and sympathetic; dredging up these memories isn't pleasant for him either.

I thought I'd been so careful, and now he's telling me that he's known since the very first one? My face shifts into a scowl and internally I'm shaking my head. I was a seven-year-old setting fires, what did I expect? It wasn't a foolproof plan—none of them were—that's why I always worried someone would find out. Someone was bound to, and he did, only he didn't do what I expected him to.

"We wanted to question you, too, do you remember? But you'd stopped talking. Mr. Hale had ordered you to run along, and that's when he told me."

"Told you what?" I stare at him expectantly.

"He said, "Now, would you really send your own son to jail? Your own flesh and blood?" He didn't confirm or deny that you were behind the fire, and that's when I realized you had been set up. His words sink in, and my world shifts. Over and over, images of you growing up flashed through my mind; after all, the island is small, and I can't even begin to tell you about the pain that would strike my heart. You were part of

Diane, and when you were born I wished more than anything you were mine. You were the cutest kid. I even laughed to myself once, at how similar our eyes were; that we could be a family and no one would look out of place. I never once put it together. How I missed it, I'll never know."

I hear him talking; his voice is so sad and filled with regret, but I'm having a hard time comprehending what he's saying. So many times over the years I have seen him at the café, around the island, at the Sandbar. Never once did I get the impression that he knew who I was, or that he knew more about me than he let on—from before the fires or after. Yes, he would smile at me in passing, but that was it.

"I wanted kids. I wanted you, so I tampered with the evidence and changed the findings. Case closed. A few months later, I went to confront your mother, and he was there. He threatened to expose us both. Her having the affair resulting in the bastard child of the fire chief, and me falsifying files to keep you out of trouble. Two days later, there was another fire. Once again, he set you up to do it and planted more evidence. He thought he was planting evidence at every fire to keep me away, but I caught on quickly and did the same. Interestingly, over that last year there was always a partial unknown print that went into every file, but was not part of the report. After he was sent to jail, I pulled that last file and matched the print. He went on and on to anyone who would listen, about me altering it, and how it was really you, but the damage he'd already caused to his family was done. No one believed him. The judge looked back over the last few fire files, matched the fingerprints, and added arson to his list of charges."

I'm shocked to hear that he did all this for me. My dad— Mr. Hale— was always working against me. I never knew I had someone working for me, because of me. He was protecting me, he risked his career for me, and he did it because he cared for me. That ache in my chest—the hole in my heart—the one that only Ellie has been able to mend, feels different, not as severe. He's making me feel different.

"I didn't know that," I mumble, looking at him.

"I know you didn't; we kept it quiet. The less attention that was on you and your family, the better off you were."

I would agree with that. We all needed quiet and we all needed time to heal, especially Drew. It's one thing to be repeatedly on the receiving end but, that last day, the day Mr. Hale was finally arrested, it was Drew, who put an end to him. Drew, who never wanted to be like him, but had to use his fist to stop him.

"Diane told me what life was like with him." He pulls on my arm to stop me, but doesn't release me. "I'm sorry." His eyes fill with tears, and I watch this man who I've only known in passing take a deep breath to keep from crying.

"Nobody wanted me. Daily, I lived with him telling me I was no son of his. You will never understand how he made me feel. I was the mistake." My words come out cold, but my heart is burning.

He squeezes my arm and looks me straight in the eyes, "You are not a mistake to me, and I've wanted you for so long; long before you were ever even born. Hell, I still want you now." There's no reluctance in his voice, only a devotion that's intended just for me.

I shake my head at him and pull my arm from his grasp. This is all too much . . . I just can't handle it.

Needing to run, I turn and take off down the beach. Dad—Mr. Hale—set us up, he set me up, even after I did everything that he wanted me to do. I feel so many emotions; pain and anger because I tried so hard to be what he wanted me to be, and pain and anger because someone out there did love me and he wanted me.

His voice from the memories infiltrates my mind. I shake my head to try and clear them away, but one by one I hear them.

"You're no son of mine."

"You're nothing but a worthless piece of shit."

"Don't say a word. Don't say a word."

"I'll kill Beau, and it will be all your fault."

NO! I scream out loud, squeezing my eyes closed. The sound is lost as I run past it, and it sinks into the sand.

My heart is bleeding from the inside out, and then I hear a new voice, one that silences the darkness and makes me feel the light.

"You are not a mistake, and I've wanted you for so long."

Reaching my house, I run inside, slam the door, and sink to my knees on the floor behind it. The grains of sand cut into my skin, but I don't even feel it. I'm gasping for breath, trying to breathe, and sobs that come from so deep within begin to rip through me.

The last two days have sucked. I feel like hell and I've cried more than I have in my whole life. I can't pinpoint all the single reasons why, but now it seems the tears are mostly for a little boy who felt he had no one in this world and that he had to hide all alone in a shed.

Hands touch my back and I jerk away, startled.

"Ellie . . ." I gasp. I forgot she was here. I thought I was alone. *Shit!* She can't see me like this.

"What happened?" her voice cracks at the sight of me and, instantly, tears begin streaming down her face. I can see the love she has for me pouring out of her beautiful big brown eyes.

"You need to leave." I need her gone. I need to finish this breakdown on my own. I need to be alone. That's how I've always been, and that's how I need to deal with this.

"No," she pleads, shaking her head at me as if I'm crazy. "I'm not going anywhere," she says definitively.

No? It hurts my chest even more, and I squeeze my eyes shut. If I can't see her, then she's not here. Bending over, my forehead hits the floor, and I wrap my arms around my head.

I don't want to cry in front of her, but I can't stop.

Her hands gently slide up my back. Her heat seeps through my shirt. It's soothing in a way I wasn't expecting. Slowly, she wraps her arms around me and lays her head on my back to hug me.

She's comforting me. Aunt Ella is the only other one who has ever done that for me, but with Ellie it just feels like so much more.

Sitting up, I look at her beautiful face and realize I'm not alone anymore. I have her. I need her. Grabbing her face, I slam my mouth down on hers, twisting her, and lowering her onto the floor.

The desperation and need I have to consume her right now pounds through me at a velocity so fierce I feel like I could break her. She responds to me unquestioningly, and I love her even more.

This girl . . . What she does for me, how she makes me feel, is unparalleled to anything I've ever felt before—good or bad.

Her hands find their way to my back as she pulls me closer. Her heart is pounding through her chest for me, and it makes me feel alive. I have so much to tell her, so much to express to her.

Tearing my mouth away from her swollen lips, I look

down at her beautiful, flushed face. I'm looking at my forever.

"I'm so sorry," I tell her.

Her forehead wrinkles with concern, and her brown eyes search my face. "For what?"

"For everything; for the way I made you feel that first week here, and for my reaction after you told me you were falling in love with me. I just . . ." Shaking my head, I drop it and lay my forehead against hers. "For walking away from you after you sang to me, for not opening up to you, and for not being the person you needed me to be."

"Whoa . . . hold up there," she pushes on my shoulders to move my head away from hers. Brown eyes find mine and implore me to stop. "I don't know what happened to you this morning to make you act this way, and I don't care if you ever tell me, but you need to know that you are exactly the person I need you to be."

Her hands reach up to cup the sides of my head. A tear drips off of my nose and splashes her face. I still can't control my breathing as she moves one hand, placing it on my chest and over my heart. Everything slows.

She calms me. She steadies me. She saves me.

Chapter Twenty

ELLE

MATT'S BREATHING CALMS the longer we stare at each other. Eventually, he blinks and his eyes drift back to my mouth. He's laying half on top of me, staring at my lips, and every muscle in me tightens with anticipation. He's going to kiss me again, and I can't wait.

I pull his head closer, his lips settle against mine, and his eyes drift shut. He is so intoxicating. My mouth parts and I latch onto his full bottom lip. I can feel his smile as he shifts to take over. I revel in the sensation of his hands as they push into my hair. He tilts my head for more access, and I let out a small, appreciative moan.

Our kisses become deeper, and Matt moans and shudders as his tongue moves over mine. His emotions are tangible and I can almost taste them. I want to swallow them, just to allow him the freedom to sort through his battered heart.

I want to know what happened to him, and who did this.

Gently, his teeth pull on my bottom lip, and then he licks away the pleasurable little sting it caused. It's so incredibly hot, vibrations of desire shoot straight down deep into my stomach and tingles spread throughout my body.

Matt shifts and abruptly pulls back from me. Creases are lining his forehead.

"What's wrong?" My eyes scan his face, searching for an answer.

"There's sand on the floor," he says, very matter-of-fact.

"So?"

"I don't want you lying on the dirty floor in the sand."

I can't help but smile up at him. I'm getting lost in the taste and feel of him, and he's thinking about me getting dirty on the sandy floor.

"Come on, up you go." He moves to his knees, grabs my hand, and together we stand. Releasing me, he starts brushing me down. His hands are moving methodically over me as I stand here in just his t-shirt and a pair of underwear. It's probably not his intention, but I feel like I'm being gently caressed, and I'm certain that I'm enjoying this a little too much.

I let out something between a giggle and a moan.

"What?" he cocks an eyebrow at me.

"I like your hands on me," I say suggestively, leaning toward him just a little more.

His cheeks redden and, although he looks completely drained, he gives me a shy smile. Running his hand over his face, he lets out a deep sigh, and then looks me over from head to toe. "I like you in my shirts."

"And here I thought you'd want to take me out of it."

"Oh, I want to do that, too, but right now, just seeing you here . . . it makes me happy." He pinches his lips together in a straight smile.

I hate that he seems to carry so much around with him, and I hate that he internalizes everything even more. Soon enough, when he's ready, my quiet guy will talk. Hopefully, once he does, he'll never shut up. I want to hear him forever.

I begin to return the favor and, from head to toe, I wipe away the sand from him. After what I just witnessed, I know he needs a little extra TLC, and I plan to give him as much as it takes.

"Are you okay?" I ask.

He looks down at me with those beautiful gray eyes. "I'm getting there."

I nod and walk into him. His arms snake around me as he envelops me with the biggest hug and tucks his head into my neck.

"Thank you for not leaving," he mumbles.

"I'm never leaving you."

He tenses, so I tighten my arms around him even more until he slowly begins to believe me and relaxes.

His lips find their way to my skin as he brushes them down the side of my throat. Goose bumps race down my arms as his breath fans through my hair.

"I like the way you smell," he whispers. His hands begin to wander under the edge of the t-shirt and up my back. "You smell like . . . mine."

"I am yours." I pull back so he can see how serious I am.

He blinks and his eyelashes brush against his cheeks. Wrapping my hands around the sides of his face, I watch as his eyes darken and his lips fall apart. There's only a matter of inches that separate us, but suddenly it's too far.

His hand, which is resting between my shoulder blades, pushes me and I fall into him. His mouth lands on mine, and I'm lost in an instant. The magnetism between us peaks, electric currents are swirling around us, and I can't get close enough to him.

Over and over, his tongue dips into my mouth, tasting, exploring, and taking. His free hand runs over my waist and down to my hip as he pushes us flush. His fingers grasp and pull on the cotton of my underwear, and I'm suddenly wishing I was wearing a daintier pair that he could tear off.

He's everywhere, and all at once.

He pulls my shirt up, breaking our connection, and I whimper at the loss. He removes my shirt and grabs his from behind his neck and drags it off. I reach for him as he reaches for me.

The skin-to-skin contact, the warmth of his body pressing into me, has me trembling with need. Sliding my hands up his arms and over his shoulders, I marvel at how hard and yet soft he is to touch. Smooth. Manly. The lines of the muscles that shape him are well-defined, and I trail my fingers along them, getting lost in his perfection.

Matt's arm tightens around my waist and we start moving. He's walking us toward the bedroom and a thrill of excitement shoots through me, knowing where this is headed.

The back of my legs hit the bed and we stop. Matt's mouth moves down over my jaw to my neck, and he places open-mouthed, moist, hot kisses in a trail down to my collarbone. I arch my back in response. His tongue moves across my chest, tasting and savoring all the different parts of me. My fingers find their way into his hair and twist as he pushes my need for him higher.

"Matty . . ." He must hear the longing in my voice and, without missing a beat, his hands slide down to my hips and under the waistband of my underwear. Slowly, he pushes it down and it drops to the floor. I sit on the bed and drag my eyes up the length of him.

His eyes land on mine, and my insides squeeze at the un-bridled desire I can see in them. They're crystal clear.

I reach for his shorts, and he doesn't move as I pull them down, freeing him. I lick my lips in anticipation and then scoot back so he can join me on the bed—only, he doesn't.

Silence surrounds us as we stare at each other.

"You're beautiful," he says with a seriousness that I've never seen before.

A blush creeps up my neck and heats my cheeks. Instead of answering him, I give him a small smile.

The air around us shifts and his fingers flex. What I thought was going to be a 'caught in the moment' experience, now seems to be settling into a far more intimate one. His eyes leave my face and slowly run over the length of me. Instead of feeling uncomfortable as his gaze slides across me, I feel bold. I bend one knee, and pull my leg up to give him a better view. His eyebrows rise to meet his hairline, and then his eyes fall back to mine. I smile seductively at him; he grins back and shakes his head in disbelief.

"You continually surprise me," he says.

"Why?" I tilt my head at him

He shrugs his shoulders. "Not sure . . . but, damn, please don't stop."

"Not planning on it."

"Good." His shy smile makes another appearance.

With that, Matt grabs my ankles and drags me down the bed to him. Bending over, his lips grace the inside of my knee as his fingertips run up my thighs. My skin ignites, and it makes me squirm.

Kiss by kiss, he explores every inch of my body, taking his sweet time and leaving me just about to burst at the seams.

I've never felt the need for anything or anyone like I do for him right now. He's driving me crazy, and how this isn't doing the same to him I'll never know.

By the time he's crawled up the length of me, my eyes are squeezed shut, and I'm panting. If I could speak, I would, but I can't.

He chuckles, and the sound vibrates against my chest. His familiar scent envelops me and has me breathing in, searching for more. He's had his fun, and now I want mine. I want to feel him inside of me, moving with me, and feeling exactly what I do. No, I don't want this—I need this.

Grabbing the back of his neck, I pull his mouth to mine. His taste completely consumes me, and the intense ache that I have for him grows even more. His weight pushes me down into the mattress, and I never want to forget this.

"Matty, please make love to me," I beg him.

Reaching over, he fumbles around with the drawer in the nightstand. Hearing the rip of foil, he pulls back to roll on the condom, and then positions himself over me.

Nuzzling his face into my neck, his hand travels down to my leg and he wraps it around his waist. My other leg follows, allowing him perfect access to slide in. His heart is pounding through his chest, and I love that I'm the one doing this to him.

Lifting up, his eyes meet mine as he pushes inside of me and makes me his. His breathing stutters and his eyes drift down to my mouth. I lick my bottom lip, and then he moves to do the same. His tongue moves across my lips and into my mouth as his hips move with mine. The heat and friction between the two of us is exquisite. I'm in complete sensory overload.

Back and forth he rocks, slowly, causing the world around us to fade away. He's taken his time to learn and explore what makes my body sing, and it hums with awareness and pleasure for him. We're lost in the feel of each other, giving and taking exactly what the other needs. I can feel myself climbing, and my fingers glide down across his damp skin to grab ahold of his hips.

His arms wrap around me even tighter, and his head falls against my neck. My heels dig into the backs of his legs, and I squeeze my eyes closed before letting myself go. Euphoric tingles hit my bloodstream and race from one end of my body to the other. Matt feels the change in my body and instantly he responds.

"Ellie," he breathes into me, my name sounding more like a benediction than anything else.

My skin is warm from the flush, and I feel the sting of tears beginning to fill my eyes at the perfectness of this moment. My heart is beating fiercely with the love that I have for him. If I could stay like this with him forever, I would.

"Matty?" I whisper.

"Yeah?" he mumbles against my skin.

"I love you." My words are quiet. I'd be lying if I said I wasn't still a little nervous telling him this, but my heart is bursting and I want him to know.

He relaxes even more into my arms, and his lips kiss their way over my face to find mine.

"And I love you," he says against my lips. Gray eyes shine into mine. Raw emotions are pouring out of them and I soak up as much as I can. His face slips down and rests against mine. Cheek to cheek, we lie in the silence as our heartbeats slow down, and our eyes begin to drift shut.

"If only I could stay here forever," he chuckles.

"Fine by me." I squeeze him tighter.

MATT

IT'S SOMETIME IN the early afternoon when I wake. I'm hot, and I'm not sure if it is from the sun or because Ellie is wrapped around me. Images from earlier flash through my mind, and warmth spreads up my neck to my cheeks.

Wow, what this girl does to me.

Looking down, I see her head on my chest, her arm draped across my stomach, and her leg is wedged in between mine. The sun is streaming in through the window and it's illuminating her perfection. She looks and smells sun-kissed.

Without waking her, I gently stroke her hair and think back to this morning's conversation.

I'm glad that he came over when he did. I'm also glad that we went for a walk, since he told me the details about his past and mine. I'm not sure that I could have sat still in a confined space. Part of me wants to be angry with him for waiting so long to tell me, but the other part understands. I did the same thing to Beau. And, just like with Beau, I know that there will be more conversations than just that one, but I'm ready for them.

So, he's my dad. No, he's my father. Well, that doesn't sound right either. Now that I know who he is, what am I supposed to call him? I'll have to ask him. Everyone has always called him 'Chief', so tossing around 'Mr. McFarland' sounds kind of strange.

Mr. Laurence McFarland.

Matthew McFarland.

Although it does have a nice ring to it, I know that I will

always be a Hale. Not so much because of that pathetic sorry existence rotting in prison, but because of my brothers. Even knowing this, Beau's right; I am and will always be one of them. I think to myself, *I have the tattoo to prove it.*

Ellie stirs, and her leg rubs against mine. Big, sleepy brown eyes open and blink at me.

"Hi," she murmurs and smiles.

"Hi." I love waking up to that smile.

Her hand slides up my chest and she nuzzles a little closer, her hair tickling my face. All thoughts cease and my mind goes numb.

My arm tightens around her and pulls her on top of me. Her head moves to lie over my heart, and my fingers trail up and down her back.

All of my life, I've never felt truly wanted, but in a matter of days I feel like that's changed. Hearing him tell me this morning that he always wanted me, I believe him. It's not from his words or the things he did to protect me. It's just a feeling that's taken over, and Ellie, well, she's changed my world.

The hole that existed in my chest feels significantly smaller. I don't know if it will ever be completely filled; after all, I'll never forget. But most of the ache is gone, and I have her to thank for it.

"Are you going to tell me what happened this morning?" she asks quietly.

I tense underneath her. I knew she'd want an explanation for my behavior this morning. Hell, I would, too; I can't blame her.

"My dad wanted to talk to me," I answer hoarsely. Combining the word dad with an image of him feels weird and right at the same time.

"What?! He's not in jail?" she jerks up to a sitting posi-

318

tion, straddling me. The sheet falls and so do my eyes.

Damn, she's gorgeous.

I swallow and bring my eyes back to hers, and she grins, feeling the reaction that I'm having to her nakedness. "Not him; my biological one."

Her jaw drops open a little and her eyes grow large. "Oh, I didn't realize that you knew him."

"I didn't until two days ago." Needing to touch her, I run my hands up her thighs. Her skin is so soft.

"What?" she lets out a giggle, and we stare at each other.

I shrug my shoulders at her, and she starts to laugh so hard that one of her hands lands on my chest for support as the other wraps across her stomach. She sounds beautiful. I can't help but join in. We both laugh, until she's doubled over and tears are leaking out of our eyes. It feels so good to laugh, even though I don't know why we are. Maybe it's just an emotional release, but I needed that.

"So, let me get this straight. Over the last couple of days, between the two of us, there's been a live performance, a broken heart, a fight with your brother, I was held at gunpoint by my best friend, declarations of love, a verbal assault by my mother, a new job, and you found out who your long lost father is? That's crazy intense."

I let out a chuckle, "Well, when you put it like that!" We both start to laugh again, and I'm mesmerized by her beautiful face, swollen pink lips, and so much blonde hair. Pulling her down to me, I kiss her addictive mouth, getting lost in the taste of her.

"Is there anything left?" she mumbles against my lips.

Her words instantly sober me. I know she feels me tense under her. She pulls back to look at me, and I regard her carefully because I know now is finally the time.

"Yes. Confessions," I whisper.

"Confessions about what?" she asks, tilting her head.

"I need to tell you a story." Breaking eye contact, I look past her and at the streams of sunlight coming in through the window. Dust motes swirl around in the air and momentarily distract me.

"I like stories," she says, sitting up again.

"You won't like this one." I look back at her, and the expression on her face is one of concern; not for what I'm going to tell her, but for me. She knows that talking about things is a big deal for me, and this girl amazes me.

"Does it have colored pictures, too? Most of my stories revolve around magazine articles with nice glossy photos." She gives me a small smile.

I know she's trying to be funny, but this story does have photos, lots of them.

"Actually, it does," I answer.

"Really?" her eyebrows shoot up in surprise.

"Yep." I think about the newspapers that are stacked in a box in my closet. I've saved every one of them. Starting with Beau's fire and ending with a feature that was done on his wedding. If there was ever an article printed about my family, I saved it, including the one from yesterday that mentioned the attack on Ellie.

A lot of them follow Drew and Beau's sports careers. Thinking about it now, I wonder if either one of them would like to see them. Our island is small, so when someone local makes the news, it's a big deal.

I don't know why I started collecting them. Maybe it was because, after each fire, I wanted to see if there were any suspects. I never threw them away and, in a way, they've become the story of my life—our life.

Ellie wiggles on me, bringing her back into focus. "Okay, before we get started I need to run to the bathroom and make some coffee." She moves to get off the bed, but I grab her hips, sit up, and kiss her first.

She wraps her arms around me and gives me a huge hug. It's crazy to me how I went from never wanting to be touched, to not being able to get enough of it . . . enough of her.

"I'll start the coffee," I offer.

She leans back, gives me a big smile and then I hop up, grabbing my t-shirt off the floor.

Walking into the kitchen, I notice both Bruno and Otis following me. I've never given much thought to having a cat before, but when I look at the fur ball, all I see is Ellie.

Ellie.

Just her name makes me smile.

As I go about a making the coffee, I remind myself to keep taking deep breaths. I need to tell her, she needs to know. That expression, "And the truth shall set you free", is pretty fitting for my life, and the life I want with her.

Flipping the switch on the pot, I walk back into the bedroom to retrieve the box. I always kept it on the floor, since I seemed to be always putting articles in it. Picking it up, I stall. I remember this box being heavier than this.

Ellie walks out of the bathroom wearing only my t-shirt, and sees me holding it. She raises her eyebrows at me and I stare at her, feeling completely exposed. I'm not gonna lie, her seeing the evidence of my life is terrifying.

"Lots of pictures," I murmur to her.

She nods her head and gives me a small, reassuring smile. I follow her into the kitchen, setting the box on the table as she pours us two cups of coffee and then turns to face me.

My biggest fear has always been that someone would discover my secrets, especially someone I loved. But it turns out that people already knew. I can't help but wonder if my life would have been different if I had known this at a younger age, but then again I probably wouldn't be here with Ellie if I had.

I don't want to live in fear anymore. I need to man up and end this; I need to face it. James Baldwin once said, "Not everything that is faced can be changed, but nothing can be changed until it is faced." I can't change the past, but I can change my future. Ellie's song comes to mind, and I make a choice . . . freedom. I need to be free; free from the fear, free from discovery, free to live my life and finally just be me.

Taking a deep breath, I lock my gaze on to her beautiful face and lift the box lid.

Epilogue

ELLE

VERY QUICKLY, THINGS began to settle down. After my mother left the cottage, she tried to barge into Aunt Ella's house, playing the sister card. The minute she started complaining about how ungrateful I was, she was thrown out; her boy toy, too.

Aunt Ella's been amazing to me. I always knew she was kind, but I never realized the depth of that until recently. I'm thankful for her and the support she has given me. Even though all these changes have been my choice, it's still change, and sometimes that can be a little daunting.

Leila did put me in touch with her attorney and, within no time at all, the formal separation papers were drawn up, with the severance. We overnighted them to New York, my mother signed them, and I haven't heard from her one time in the last six weeks. She's toxic, and being free of her is like a breath of fresh air.

Matt did take me back to New York, but we only stayed for three days. He helped me clean up the condo to get it ready for renters, pack what I wanted to take, and had movers load up the rest. Currently, most of my belongings are sitting in the garage at the North Shore house. He and his crew have been working around the clock to get it livable, and once it is, we'll move into our new home.

Our new home.

In a way, I can see how some people might think that we're moving too fast, but when you know . . . you know! He's all that I want. Nothing in life is really guaranteed. But if I try my best, stay honest and kind, and love with my whole heart, there won't be regrets. I refuse to live with what-ifs and regrets.

I think about Olivia often. She was a part of my life for so many years, but I'm finally realizing that what I miss about her was never real. Our friendship, on her part at least, was completely fake. Just like my mother, she used me; only, she told me what I wanted to hear versus trying to control me.

After the first of the year, Leila and I will start our new venture together. She has a press release scheduled for February first, so most of January will be taken up with shooting mock ads and getting ready for the launch of "Free and Perfect". I finally feel free, and that is the most perfect feeling in the whole world.

I still have days where it's hard to get out of bed. I get so sad and confused, that sometimes it's hard to breathe. Matt doesn't ever ask me what's wrong. He understands that talking can be difficult when different emotions are weighing down your voice. I don't know how long this will go on, if it's circumstantial or for forever, but what I do know, is that he'll always find me and he knows exactly what to say to make me feel better.

Matt's changed. He's no longer the dark and brooding guy I found on the island. He's lighter, happier, and he smiles more. Don't get me wrong, he's still quiet, shy, and likes to keep to himself, but that's just who he is and I don't think it's possible to love him any more than I do.

Twice a week, he meets his biological father at Aunt El-la's café, and they talk for hours and about anything and everything. We can all see that he really does want to know Matt, to be a part of his life, and that makes me so happy for him. He was alone for so long.

The most recent development is that the Chief and Diane have begun dating, again. They tell us that the third time's the charm, but none of us is holding our breath. Diane still sees a therapist, even though it's been years. Matt's never asked her why; those are her demons that she has to deal with and, honestly, I don't care. All that matters to me is him.

"Hey, babe, what are you doing?" Matt's come up from behind me as I slip on my hat and sunglasses.

I turn to face him and, behind the glasses, run my eyes over the length of him. He's only wearing a pair of white athletic shorts, and they hang deliciously low off his hips. I don't think that I will ever tire of looking at him.

"You've been busy, so I thought I'd take Bruno out for a quick walk before I hop in the shower to get ready." He's been in the second bedroom, which serves as Quinn's room and an office, working on some paperwork for the rental properties.

"Can I join you?" he grabs my elbow and pulls me flush up against him.

"Of course; you know he loves to be outside with you," I grin at him, knowing it's not what he was asking.

"I meant the shower."

I grin at him again. He shakes his head at me and then bends down for a kiss. His lips brush against mine, and I let out a sigh at the sweetness of it.

"I love you like this," he says, lifting up my sunglasses.

"What do you mean?" My eyes lock onto his.

"Just that . . . you . . . like this, you're so beautiful." And I know he means it. He prefers me all natural, just the way I am.

I still dabble with my make-up. I've been working on trying to find a nice balance where I accentuate my features without covering them up with layers of foundation and color. But even still, I'm addicted to my mascara and lip gloss. I even switched to the flavored ones for Matt. He argues with me about why I continue to wear it, but at the first chance he gets, he licks it off.

A blush spreads over my cheeks, and I hold my hand out to him. He knows he doesn't even need to ask about the shower; I would never tell him no.

"Come on, let's go for a walk," I tilt my head toward the door.

"Okay," he smiles at me, dropping the glasses. Lacing his fingers with mine, together we step out the front door and into the sunlight.

MATT

STANDING IN THE kitchen, we all hear the beep beep of the front door alarm, letting us know that Drew and Ali have arrived.

Trying to get together for the holidays never seemed to

work out so, years ago, after Beau and Leila settled into their life in New York City, Drew and Beau both made a pact that they would be here on the island with me for New Year's Eve, no matter what.

"Quinn," says Leila. "Who's here?"

We all look down at Quinn. She's sitting at her little kiddie table in the kitchen, coloring. She raises her shoulders and shrugs at Leila.

"Go find out!" Leila says enthusiastically.

Quinn's eyes brighten and she jumps up. We all watch as she races down hallway, and then we hear Ali squeal.

I turn toward Ellie, and she is grinning from ear to ear. I know Beau mentioned something to Drew about Ellie and me, but I don't know if he told Ali. Pride fills me as I think about introducing her to them.

The giggling coming our way gets louder, and I take a hold of Ellie's hands to link my fingers with hers.

The three of them round the corner and Ali stops, stunned. Her eyes grow large and start jumping back and forth between Ellie, me, our joined hands, and then back to me. She looks over to Leila for confirmation. My eyes follow, and Leila is grinning at all of us.

The room is quiet; no one says anything. Ellie's grip on my hand suddenly gets tighter; she just got nervous.

Ali's eyes shoot back to us and then up to Drew. He, too, is smiling.

"You knew about this and didn't tell me?" she asks, him narrowing her eyes at him.

"Yep," he grins down at her.

Ali passes Quinn off to Drew, and takes a step toward us. Her eyes connect with mine, and I see tears of happiness shimmering in them. Ali has always loved me so uniquely differently than everyone else. It's hard to explain. Maybe it's because she wasn't always present in my life—like Leila was—or maybe it's because she filled our family with hope during a time that I so desperately needed. Or maybe it's that she's always made me feel wanted when I felt like so many didn't. The love she always had for me was just for me and, at thirteen, she made me feel special.

Standing right in front of us, she looks at Ellie and smiles from ear to ear.

"Hi, I'm Ali Hale. I belong to that one," she points over her shoulder to Drew.

"Hi, I'm Elle Summers. I belong to this one," she points to me. I think if my heart could have burst, it would have. I smile affectionately at Ellie and squeeze her hand.

Ali looks at me and then back at Ellie, starts squealing, and launches herself into Ellie's arms, taking her by surprise. Everyone starts laughing. I forgot how small Ali is until she stands next to Elle.

Stepping back, she squeezes Ellie's arms and then pins me with an angry look.

"Thanks so much for giving me a heads up, Matthew! This is huge news and deserved to be shared." She turns to look at Drew, narrowing her eyes, "I'll deal with you later." He chuckles and she turns back to me, shaking her head. "You know, you were always *way* too handsome for your own good. I shouldn't have expected anything less than for you to finally find a girl *and* one who's a supermodel."

Light laughter fills the room.

Grinning, she throws her arms around me and squeezes. I can feel the love pouring out of her.

"Forgive me for the sudden shock," she pulls back and looks at Ellie, who is watching and smiling at us. "If you're with him," she punches me in the stomach and I flinch, "then you know him, and being here is a really big deal."

Ellie looks at me and our eyes connect. I can see so many emotions swim across her face. She understands what Ali is saying, and I know that there is nowhere else she would rather be.

"Yeah, I do know him." There is so much meaning behind those words. "And I can assure you, I am not going anywhere."

That's good to hear, because I'm pretty certain if she tried to leave I would chase after her.

I wrap my arm around Ellie, pull her close, and kiss her forehead. The smell of her shampoo invades my senses and I breathe it in. It's familiar, comforting, and reminds me of her in the shower.

Ali's eyes get huge again and, at the closeness of Ellie and me, I see her trying to swallow down her emotions.

"Sorry, don't mind me. I'm just having a moment here," she says. We all laugh.

"Tiny! Enough already. My ego's being bruised over here. You've so quickly forgotten me for the new girl."

We laugh again and Drew mumbles 'new girl', shaking his head and smirking.

"Bruised ego, fat chance," Ali says as she jumps and wraps her body around Beau's, giving him the biggest hug. We all bust out laughing.

Setting her down, he guides her over to the kitchen island where he has laid out all of the ingredients that she will need to make him a homemade pizza.

"Seriously, Beau! I've been here all of five minutes and you already have me cooking you food?" she looks from Beau to Leila.

Leila throws her hands up in the air, "Don't look at me, he did this all on his own."

Ellie is watching them, slightly confused. "Beau has a sick obsession for Ali's pizzas," I whisper to her.

Beau hears me and his head snaps up. "Little dude, I am not obsessed with her pizzas. That would be implying that I am constantly preoccupied thinking about them, which I am not."

I smirk at him, "Whatever, you've been talking about today and her pizzas for like the last month!"

"Hey, now! Bro-code! Besides, they're not just hers anymore. Did you know that pizza comes from the Latin root word *Picea,* which means the blackening of crust by fire. I'm gonna turn the grill on for Drew," he says, as if we all should have known this.

"Ellie," he turns to face her, "be prepared to be amazed." Beau looks at her and winks.

She responds with one of her award-winning smiles. "Actually, did you know that a single serving of almost all varieties of pizza can deliver more fat than a cheeseburger?" Beau's mouth falls open as if she's speaking blasphemy. "Yep, it's all in the cheese. You should think about as you're getting older," and then Ellie nods her head, as if he knows she's right, and rubs her stomach, as if it was extended and large.

"Are you saying that I'm getting fat?" he demands very animatedly of her.

Ali busts out laughing and Drew chuckles. "I like this girl . . . very much," says Ali.

"Me, too," I grin down at her.

"Yeah, well, I don't. Not anymore. You've officially made my list," he points at her.

I wrap my arm around her shoulders and grin down at her.

"Well, in that case, we should talk about all that salt water taffy you eat, too," Ellie says. Beau's jaw drops again and I grin. Leave it to my professional model/nutrition-crazy girlfriend to get him all worked up. We all know how much he loves that candy.

He looks over to Leila in shock, "Are you just gonna let her stand there and talk to me like this?"

Leila blinks her big blue eyes at him and then giggles, "Yep."

"That's it, you're all on my list and I'm out!" he throws his hands up in the air and storms out toward the back patio. "Come on, Quinn, you'll be nice to Daddy."

Quinn squirms out of Drew's arms and runs over to Beau. We laugh watching them go.

"SO, ALI AND I have some news." Drew says, taking her hand in his.

We've just finished dinner. I had forgotten how much I loved Ali's pizza. Even Ellie said it was delicious, and ate three pieces. I was so proud of her.

"You're moving back to the island!" Leila squeals with excitement. Everyone laughs.

"Nope, not yet . . . but we are having a baby," he says.

A collective gasp comes from the four of us as we stare at them. Drew and Ali were not on the baby path, at least I didn't think they were. Ali has spent so much time being focused on and dedicated to her career.

And then Leila jumps to her feet.

"Us, too!" she yells.

"What!" Ali jumps up and grasps Leila's arms. The two girls gape at each other, and then start squealing and hugging.

I glance over to Drew and then to Beau. The two of them are smiling affectionately at each other and sharing a silent conversation. My heart hears most of what they are saying, but I turn away to give them their private moment.

Suddenly, in unison, the girls turn and face Ellie. They are grinning from ear to ear when Ellie shouts, "Don't look at me! No baby!"

What!

I choke on the beer I'm drinking, and start coughing. All five of them bust out laughing and Ellie pats me on the back.

"No baby!" I say, looking at each of them and loving them more than I ever have.

RIGHT AFTER DINNER, Ellie and I snuck away, saying we were going for a walk on the beach. What we actually had planned was to run over to the North Shore house and watch the sunset. The timing worked out well, because Leila needed to put Quinn to bed, and Drew and Ali wanted a quick trip to their house to clean up after traveling. We all agreed to meet back at Beau's at nine, to light fireworks and ring in the New Year together.

The North Shore house is coming along great. I decided at the last minute to re-plumb it before we moved in. It was something that I was already considering, but had planned on holding off. Since Ellie will be moving in with me, it just made sense to take care of it now. She doesn't know it, but we're almost done and, by the end of the week, we'll be all moved in.

The night Ellie was attacked, I brought her back to my cottage, and she never left. As much as I hate the circumstances that forced it, I love that she feels safe with me; we never needed to discuss her being here. It was a mutual decision. We've talked a lot over the last couple of weeks about our choices in life. I've never considered her one. She's always been a gift, and one I plan on treasuring for as long as I live.

Closing the beach access gate behind me, Ellie winks as she drops my hand, and sprints off toward the back door.

"What are you doing?" I call after her.

She spins back around and is grinning from ear to ear. "Oh, you'll see. I brought a surprise!" Her blonde hair is blowing all around her. *Damn, she's beautiful.*

Our favorite spot in the house has become the deck off of our room. Maybe it's because there's no other furniture here, just the two lounge chairs, or maybe it's because it's slowly become our place. By no means is the deck completely hidden from passersby but, with the surrounding trees and its elevated location, most wouldn't even glance our way. Even if they did, we're pretty hard to see.

Flopping down in my chair, I look out toward the horizon at the yellow and orange glow illuminating the sky. It's funny, because I've always loved to watch the sunrise but, now, with her, it's all about the sunset. Night after night, we find ourselves sitting out on the cottage porch, watching that large ball of fire dip into the water, and we talk. I've learned more about her through those conversations than I have at any other time, and I'm sure she could say the same about me.

Dusk has become our time, and watching sunsets has become our thing. No matter where we are or what we are doing, we always stop to watch.

I often think back to that day in the kitchen, when I asked Uncle Ben to explain his favorite expression. He said, "Well, now, I can't tell you all the sun's secrets; you'll have to figure them out on your own. But as long as the sun keeps rising, you just remember to follow it and you'll be alright." I finally get it. I finally understand what he was saying all those years ago.

Follow the sun.

The sun is the light and, each morning when it rises, it chases away the dark.

It chases away the dark.

Each of us has a sun, a light that lives within us. If we allow the light to rise and shine, it will always chase away the darkness . . . in and around us.

For so long, I've let the sun be the reminder of the bad things that have happened to me, but no more. I no longer feel burned by it. I'm no longer afraid of losing Beau. I'm not worried about people discovering my past or uncovering my secrets. Those who need to know, do, and that's all that matters.

Maybe I wasn't ready to see the truth behind the sun, but now that I have . . . everything inside, about, and around me feels brighter.

I never thought I would say this, but I'm thankful for my life and for the battles I've had to overcome because, without it, I wouldn't have stumbled across my strength. I know, after everything that's happened, that I am a good man. I've accepted the life I was born into, and I'm better now because of it.

I no longer hate November first. That's the thing about finally being free, I've found a new perspective on life. Instead of dwelling on things from the past, I'd rather embrace them and move on with the future. November first now marks the end of my past life, and the beginning with Ellie. That was the first day that I saw her unloading her car, and stumbling into cottage number two. If someone were to ask me when the turning point for me was, I'd tell them then.

For twenty-one years, I've felt broken. Each day that passed, I felt that vacant hole in my chest grow a little bit larger, and the edges around it become a little bit harder. I honestly thought that no one would ever want me, and my life was nothing more than an empty shell occupying time and space until my time was up. Then, in a blinding flash of light, there she was, and the heat from the sun's rays that usually skimmed my skin soaked through, and began to soften my edges. Instantly, a change began to take place inside of me, and now I welcome its warmth.

"Okay, I got it!" Ellie yells. I tear my eyes from the sky, just as she runs through the bedroom and out on to the balcony, grinning.

I smile, she makes me so happy. I freaking love this girl so much.

She plops down in her chair and waves a bottle of Champagne, two glasses, and a Tupperware of strawberries at me. She always thinks of everything.

People often talk about role models, how children need them and, yes, I had Uncle Ben, but it isn't the same. Boys supposedly need a father to show them how to love and treat women, to give them confidence and direction, and to show them how to be a man. Maybe that's true for those who have had it, but it's not true for those of us who didn't. It was the lack of all of these things that will give me the strength to be the best that I can be. The one thing I have learned through all of this is that, no matter what, it's our own responsibility to make ourselves happy; no one else's.

Look at Drew and Beau, they are shining examples.

I watch as she sets the glasses and berries down. "The Champagne is really cold, I'm so glad I was able to sneak over here earlier and put it in the refrigerator."

"When did you do that?"

"When you were out for your run," she grins, then holds out the bottle. "You have to open it."

"Why me?" I ask, taking the bottle from her.

"The cork pop scares me."

"You're kidding, right?" I smile.

"Nope," she pops the 'p', and her eyes sparkle.

"Okay," I begin to untwist the wire cage that covers the cork and Ellie squeals, then scoots away from me, covering her ears.

"Really?"

She nods her head and squeezes her eyes closed.

She's a little nuts sometimes but, oh, what this girl does to my heart.

I pop the cork slowly, keeping the Champagne from over-flowing. She opens her eyes and smiles.

"Yay! I love Champagne, we should drink it more often," she says, leaning over. She grabs the two flutes that she placed on the ground, and her shirt lifts up a little. I spot the sun tattoo that's across her lower back, and I can't help but laugh as I run my fingers over it.

"Watch it, Mister!" she slaps my hand away and narrows her eyes at me. Her skin's warm and she knows what that does to me.

I throw my hands up in surrender and she smiles.

"I'll hold the glasses, you pour the champagne." She holds one in each hand, in front of me.

"Deal." Carefully, I fill each one and set the bottle down.

"So, what should we toast to?" she asks.

I glance back out over the water and immediately I know. "To following the sun."

She pauses for a beat, searching my eyes as they come back to hers, and then she holds her glass up a little higher. "To following the sun."

We clink them together and take a sip of the cold bubbles. Silence falls over us as we watch the sun lower in the sky, and I'm pretty certain that I have never been happier in my entire life. It's crazy how things have changed in just a short amount of time. But, as Ellie leans forward to grab the strawberries, my eyes drift down once again to that tattoo, and I think to myself, *"Yeah, I'd follow that sun just about anywhere."*

The End

From the Author

Thank you for reading *Unforgettable Sun*, book three in the Hale Brothers Series. If you enjoyed this book, please consider leaving a spoiler free review.

OTHER BOOKS IN
The Hale Brothers Series

Drops of Rain
(Book 1)

Starless Nights
(Book 2)

Unforgettable Sun
(Book 3)

Acknowledgments

TO MY HUSBAND, I think my favorite line from you over the last couple of months is, "Today the day?" I adore you and am so thankful for the strength you continually give me. This book definitely wouldn't be possible without you. I love you.

To my sweet boys. You make the world such a brighter place and you fill me with a happiness that I didn't know was possible. I love you both so much and know that I will always meet you in our dreams.

Author Elle Brooks, my book bestie, we did it! Number three! It's still crazy to think that just a year ago, all of this was a dream. I am so proud of us. Thank you! Thank you! Thank you! For everything. Your friendship means more than you will ever know and I can't wait to spend lots of time with you this year. This book isn't complete without a toast, so cheers to us with our pink Moet Champagne!
http://ellebrooksauthor.wix.com/blog

To my dear friend Megan C., my book soulmate, I think it's pretty safe to say that this book would not be what it is without you. Line by line, we have discussed the ins and outs

340

of these characters, the overall plot, and any holes or feels that needed to be filled in or added. You have pushed my boundaries and in the end made me a better writer. Thank you for understanding the story I was trying to tell and for helping me nurture my craft to make it the best imaginable. Your special touch has made these pages heartfelt and beautiful, and in many ways this book is as much yours as it is mine. I can't wait to do it all over again... Love you!

Vanessa, from PREMA, thank you so much for the time you spent digging into *Unforgettable Sun* to make it the best story possible. I enjoyed so many of our conversations and appreciate all of the advice and suggestions that you made; not only for the book but about the industry as well. I look forward to meeting you one day soon... xoxo

Debbie B., thank you for stepping in and offering your time, support, and expertise. Daily, you shower us with some kind of love and you'll never know how much that means. Thank you, and I'll meet you on the bricks with some wine to celebrate.

Sejal A., Jenn H, Cindy T., thank you so much ladies for your willingness to BETA read *Unforgettable Sun* in its roughest form to offer me ideas, suggestions, and improvements. Your continued support, which came to me at different times throughout this process means more to me than you will ever know. I love each of you. Thank you again.

Elexis D., Irma J., Rachel N., Jennifer S, and Heather Y. You ladies are awesome. Thank you so much for continually sharing my teasers and links to the book community. Every time a notification pops up, and one of you has mentioned me as a favorite author or listed one of my books as a best recommended read, I am so touched. You'll never know what that means to me. Thank you for your friendship and thank you for continuing to share me with the world.

Kim H., thank you so much for being my final set of eyes, and the best proofreader ever, on *Unforgettable Sun*. As you know, putting this book together has been an adventure and I love the role that you've played in it. I appreciate your time, sense of urgency, and professionalism. I am excited to get to work with you more in the future... Thank you again... xoxo

Ari, from Cover it Designs, I love the cover for Unforgettable Sun and I love how you have spent so much time making this series all look like they belong together. The three books and the boxset cover are beautiful. Thank you. I look forward to working with you more in the future and I can't wait to see what you come up with next!

Julie, from JT Formatting, thank you for being my formatter and for creating the inside look for all of the Hale Brothers Books. Every time I open one of the paperbacks, I think of you and smile. I love knowing that each manuscript I hand over will come back looking perfect and professional. Thank you for what you do . . .

To the book bloggers . . . Thank you! The book community on a daily basis still humbles me. Thank you from the bottom of my heart for the endless amount of support and enthusiasm you have shown for my stories. It's crazy how so quickly life changes and you meet the most amazing people. As I start make book signing appearances this year, I hope to get to meet many of you in person. So make sure you drop by my table, I'd love to squeeze your necks! Oh, and I can't wait to hear what each of you think of *Unforgettable Sun*. Don't be shy . . . I'll be looking and waiting for your messages.

And finally . . . to the readers: Wow, each day I wake up and think, "I love my job." It's because of all of you that this has been possible and I am truly humbled. Can you believe that I've finished my first series? I'm still in awe. A year ago, it was just a dream and now it's my reality. I am so excited about what's to come and I hope you are too. I can't wait to share with you more of my stories. Always remember to *Follow the Sun* . . . Take care . . . Kathryn xoxo

About the Author

OVER TEN YEARS ago my husband and I were driving from Chicago to Tampa and somewhere in Kentucky I remember seeing a billboard that was all black with five white words, "I do, therefore I am!" I'm certain that it was a Nike ad, but for me I found this to be completely profound.

Take running for example. Most will say that a runner is someone who runs five days a week and runs under a ten minute mile pace. Well, I can tell you that I never run five days a week and on my best days my pace is an eleven minute mile. I have run quite a few half marathons and one full marathon. No matter what anyone says . . . I run, therefore I am a runner.

I've taken this same thought and applied it to so many areas of my life: cooking, gardening, quilting, and yes . . . writing.

I may not be culinary trained, but I love to cook and my family and friends loves to eat my food. I cook, therefore I am a chef!

My thumb is not black. I love to grow herbs, tomatoes, roses, and lavender. I garden, therefore I am a gardener!

I love beautiful fabrics and I can follow a pattern. My triangles may not line up perfectly . . . but who cares, my quilts are still beautiful when they are finished. I quilt, therefore I am a quilter.

I have been writing my entire life. It is my husband who finally said, "Who cares if people like your books or not? If you enjoy writing them and you love your stories…then write them." He has always been my biggest fan and he was right. Being a writer has always been my dream and what I said I wanted to be when I grew up.

So, I've told you who I am and what I love to do . . . now I'm going to tell you the why.

I have two boys that are three years a part. My husband and I want to instill in them adventure, courage, and passion. We don't expect them to be perfect at things, we just want them to try and do. It's not about winning the race; it's about showing up in the first place. We don't want them to be discouraged by society stereotypes, we want them to embrace who they are and what they love. After all, we only get one life.

In the end, they won't care how many books I actually sell . . . all that matters to them is that I said I was going to do it, I did it, and I have loved every minute of it.

Find something that you love and tell yourself, "I do, therefore I am."

Ways to Connect

www.kandrewsauthor.com

https://www.facebook.com/kathryn.andrews.1428

https://twitter.com/kandrewsauthor

Monthly Newsletter http://eepurl.com/9qAqr

Made in the USA
San Bernardino, CA
08 October 2018